FURY TURNS TO PASSION . . .

Luke slid his hands around her waist, tortured by the feel of her in his arms. She felt even better close, her body squirming against his, her skin like satin beneath his rough fingers.

He was kissing her, his fingers tangled in her hair, his other arm wrapped around her waist, holding her still. The passion of the argument they just had was transformed into a heat between them that had nothing to do with logic. Luke eased his mouth from hers, then buried his face in her neck, tasting her, touching her, unable to get enough of the feel of her soft skin and her innocent, mindless response.

Amanda gasped, allowing him to caress her, liking the surprising contrast of his gentle manner with the sandpaper roughness of his fingers. No man had ever touched her like this before, like she'd read about, written about, and imagined. It was better than she had thought; confusing and exciting at the same time . . .

Wild Is The Night

Colleen Quinn

DIAMOND BOOKS, NEW YORK

WILD IS THE NIGHT

A Diamond Book/published by arrangement with
the author

PRINTING HISTORY
Diamond edition/June 1991

ISBN: 1-55773-521-2

Diamond Books are published by The Berkley Publishing
Group, 200 Madison Avenue, New York, New York 10016.
The name "DIAMOND" and its logo are trademarks
belonging to Charter Communications, Inc.

PRINTED IN THE UNITED STATES OF AMERICA

10 9 8 7 6 5 4 3 2 1

*For my brother Jack,
who made me laugh
when I needed it most.*

Acknowledgments

Special thanks to Gary and Lisa Rainey, who shared their cattle ranching experiences with me.

To my daughter Erin, who knew that owls ate mice.

And to Leslie Gelbman and Gail Fortune, for their talent and enthusiasm.

Chapter

∞ 1 ∞

The air was thick with tension as Logan Benteen stepped from the porch of the Silver Spur Saloon, his gun hand resting lightly on his holster. He was dressed in black, from his weather-stained trousers to his dyed cotton shirt and his Stetson. Sand blew down the street, glittering like gold dust in the hot Nevada sun. The windows remained shut, the curtains drawn; except for one window, which was open, high above the bar. A young woman stood there, motionless, frozen with fear. She tried to scream, but the sound died in her throat as the outlaw walked down the empty road kicking up small puffs of dust with his spurs.

"You coming out, Haines? You're gonna be sorry if I have to come in after you."

A man emerged from the shadows, his face hidden by his hat. "What the hell—"

"Draw, Haines." The black-garbed man spoke softly, continuing to advance. The woman at the window choked as the distance closed between the two men. The one stalked the other like a cat playing with a sparrow—knowing, inevitably, what the final result would bring.

"I ain't got my gun. You can't do this, Logan. I'm unarmed. See?" Haines displayed an empty holster.

Logan grinned. The woman at the window could see the flash of yellowed teeth beneath the black Stetson. He paused for a moment, as if considering his options, then his hand swept downward so quickly that the woman saw only the blur of motion. Suddenly, she heard a gunshot, saw Logan's knees bend, smelled smoke in the late afternoon breeze. Haines crumbled, his mouth sagging. His gun hand grappled uselessly for a weapon that wasn't there.

The woman at the window cried out, no longer able to restrain herself as the stench of gunpowder and death stung her nostrils. She had witnessed a killing, a cold-blooded murder. Pressing her hands to her mouth, she froze in horror as the outlaw's eyes drifted upward, then locked with hers. For a split second, she couldn't move as his black eyes wandered over her, memorizing every detail of her face, her smooth brown hair, her blue cotton dress. Logan cursed, his gun still smoking, then started for the building where the woman watched him.

She had less than a minute. Forcing her body into motion, she plunged beneath the bed, her heart pounding. She could hear the killer's boots as the man slowly climbed the stairs, then paused at the door. Her breath stopped as the door creaked open, taking a lifetime, throwing a sinister triangle of light on the wooden floorboards.

The boots were black also, smooth from horse hides and covered with a light film of dust. The silver spurs jingled as he stepped into the room and stood just inches away from her. She dared not move, dared not breathe. Her blood seemed to dry up in her veins as she sensed him searching the room, looking for his quarry. Any minute now he would stoop down, peer under the bed with those deadly black eyes, and then kill her, just as mercilessly as he had killed the man outside. She would be dead, would never see the sun again, smell a flower, love a man or a child . . .

The bed creaked as he leaned on it, pressing his weight against the mattress with his hand. His body lowered. In a moment, it would be over. . . .

"Logan!" A masculine voice cried out. "Damn you, Logan! It's the law! Let's ride!"

Logan hesitated, then cursed as the voice cried again: "Logan!" Unbelievably, his body straightened, then he crossed the room, the spurs clinking against the floor. Whatever he saw outside must have convinced him, for he climbed through the window, stepping easily through the frame, his lean, dangerous presence vanishing from the room. Only the scars on the floorboards evidenced that he had been there at all, that her life could have ended. . . .

KANSAS, 1870

Amanda Edison closed the book, wincing in self-criticism and the terrible consciousness of seeing her own words in print. Stuffing the cheap novel inside her ink-stained pocket, she gazed out the window of the moving train. Papers, scribbled one-liners and painstakingly researched notecards, tumbled onto the floor from her overstuffed carpetbag, and with a sigh, she bent to pick them up, almost losing her glasses in the process. Her light brown hair tumbled out of its prim knot, falling all over her neck like spun brown sugar. She shoved it back in exasperation, oblivious to her unkempt appearance. Something rustled in the covered bird cage beside her, and she lifted the canvas hood and spoke quietly to the indignant barn owl. When the bird was comfortably settled, she glanced around the interior of the coach. It was a small train without a caboose and was nearly empty. Only two passengers, a businessman and his female companion, talked quietly in the seat across from her. Amanda dipped into the fold of her navy stockings, withdrew a letter and read it again, her blue-green eyes scanning the document while her brow puckered in thought.

". . . while it is good, it is simply not realistic enough to be literature. Perhaps you are working too hard, Amanda. Or maybe you should be content with your success as Fess Tyson. Your westerns certainly sell well enough, within the limitations of the audience.

"Should you still desire to pursue a career as a literary writer, I do have a suggestion. You need to see what you are writing about, to research beyond the confines of your library, which I understand is excellent. I'm not suggesting that you endanger yourself in any way. I know that since your father's death, you are living quite alone. However, a trip may be the answer. I know that one of your fans deeded a piece of property to you, in Texas, I believe. Perhaps you should visit the place. It is only a suggestion, Amanda. I know that you don't get around much, and such an idea may not be within your boundaries. However, most of my better writers stick to what they know . . . "

The rest was too painful to read. Amanda once again experienced a sharp stab of disappointment, then folded the tear-stained letter and placed it back in her stocking.

She had no choice. All of her education, all of her research, all of her years of careful work, writing and rewriting, editing, checking places, dates, locations, then double checking them . . . all of it amounted to nothing. She had spent her life bent over her Remington typewriter, the gaslights burning well into the morning, trying to perfect her work, yet she still couldn't achieve the recognition that had become so important to her.

Her brother Jeff would have laughed, ruffled her hair, and informed her that it didn't matter in the least. Even when they were children, he would teasingly call her a bluestocking and try his best to entice her into what he deemed more appropriate activities for a young girl, such as ice skating on a frozen New England pond, snowball fights, dances at the local town hall. Amanda, unaccustomed to any such frivolity, felt awkward and out of place. She didn't know how to skate, couldn't dance to save her life, and none of the young men wanted her for a partner anyway. None thought her pretty, or even passable. She did not fit the beauty ideal of the time, the blond-haired feminine woman, "head no higher than my heart." She was a brunette, and her eyes were blue-green, a bewildering shade. They stared too directly from her tortoiseshell glasses, showing an intelligence that wasn't fashionable. Her nose was fine and straight, sprinkled with freckles like a plover's egg, and her mouth was too tight and too tense. Yes, Amanda was no beauty, and it was only because she was Jeff's sister that the boys treated her kindly at all.

Her cheeks burned as she remembered. It was only in school that she felt wanted and appreciated. There she could compete and win, for she had discovered early on that she had a brain, if not beauty. She devoured Shakespeare, Milton and Dickens. She read everything, from mathematical treatises to romantic poetry. And it was there she discovered a way to make a living, writing penny dreadfuls under the male pseudonym, Fess Tyson.

Her study of newspapers became invaluable. She could pick up any of her subscriptions to the western dailies and find a wealth of story ideas, complete with details. It was there she'd read about the murder of a man called Haines, though his killer had not been identified. From that mere scrap of an article she had developed a story of a ruthless gunman. It was just the kind of western that satisfied her readers, gave them plenty of action and a villain they could hate. In the end, justice was done, and Fess Tyson had another success. For a while, her life felt complete. She had money coming in, satisfaction with what she was doing, and protection from the rest of the world where she never belonged. And especially now, with Jeff lying in a southern grave and her parents gone, she often congratulated herself on her choice.

But lately, she wanted more. Her father would have never been content with her silent success; he would have encouraged her to go on, to become a real writer. Hadn't he told her as much on his deathbed?

Mrs. Pincus, her landlady, thought her insane. But when she realized Amanda was determined to go west, she'd packed her a parcel of food, three extra handkerchiefs, a flask of coffee, and a tiny derringer. The gun rested in her pocket, a heavy, foreign weight. Amanda could feel the derringer against her thigh as she shifted in her seat.

The train whistle blew, and Amanda glanced up, startled out of her thoughts. The wheels screeched, the engines choked furiously, and grey-black smoke blew in the windows. They were slowing down, almost to a stop. Strange, they weren't due to arrive at the next station for nearly an hour. . . .

Gunfire broke out like a distant thunder. The few passengers remaining in the car scrambled for cover. A woman shrieked; a man cursed as he fumbled for his gun. Amanda stared out the window in disbelief. This couldn't be happening, not to her, not now. The train slowed even more, and the door flew open, the sound angry and metallic in the noonday sun. A man stepped through the passageway between the two cars, framed by the blazing sunlight, his gun drawn, his body lean and dangerous. He took one surveying glance around the car, then seized Amanda roughly around the waist and pulled her to the floor.

"Stay down, it's Sam Haskwell's gang."

Amanda struggled for breath, her belly aching from the pressure of the man's leg holding her down. For a moment, she thought she would pass out, so intense were the emotions that numbed her. Gradually, she became aware of little things, like the dark stubble of the man's beard, the blackness of his hair, and the intense blueness of his eyes. His brows curved over those eyes, lending him a sinister appearance, while pitch-black lashes softened them, an almost incongruous contrast to the stark contours of his lean face. A southerner—his drawl told her that—and a gunman. No one else could aim with such deadly precision, and squint in relief when his bullet struck home.

"How many are there?" An eastern businessman asked, peering up from behind the seat.

"At least six." The gunman answered, pausing to reload. It was the last question the businessman asked. His feminine companion cried out in horror as an outlaw's bullet found its mark and the man slumped to the floor in a pool of blood.

"Stay down!" The blue-eyed gunman shouted.

"He's dead! He can't be . . . " Within minutes, the slender, red-haired woman joined the man as another bullet from outside the train struck home. Amanda grew sick with horror as a red stream of blood snaked its way across the floor, ending in a still, wet pool just above her face.

"You got a gun?" The man released her, his body poised at the window, his gun still firing steadily.

Amanda nodded, thinking of the ivory-handled pistol in her pocket. She withdrew the tiny derringer, trembling with fear, then heard the southerner's derisive chuckle.

"You call that a gun? Well, it should do for laughs. Stay beneath the window and see if you can hit anything. Except me."

At that moment, Amanda hated him. Hated his filthy southern accent, his cocky manner, his obvious disregard for the deaths of the two people lying behind them. Brushing her loose hair out of her face, she crept determinately up to the window. Her hands shook as she aimed the gun, and she clamped her eyes shut and attempted to squeeze the trigger. Perspiration dripped from her palms and the barrel trembled miserably, then the weapon slipped from her fingers through the window and onto the ground below.

"Jesus Christ." He cursed as the gleaming ivory derringer disappeared into the grass. "You have a goddamned pop gun and you're afraid to shoot it. Stay the hell down."

Amanda opened her mouth to retort, but a bullet whined by, the sound softer than she would have thought and far more sickening. She'd written dozens of gunfights, all of them wrong. The irony of that would have made her laugh except this was real. She stared in horrified fascination out the window as another barrage of gunfire exploded.

"Get down, or you'll wind up like them!" He gestured to the corpses behind them.

Humiliated, frightened and ill, Amanda ducked. The birdcage toppled over and she scrambled for it, ignoring the disgusted look the gunman gave her.

"What the hell is that?" He lowered himself beneath the window and gazed curiously at the covered cage. The owl rustled inside.

"Aesop." Amanda answered, hugging the cage. "He's an owl."

The gunman shook his head, then leaned against the wall. "Owl. She's got an owl. We could be killed, and she's worried about the damned owl."

"But Aesop . . . "

The gunman put his finger to his lips, silencing her. The gunfire slowly died as the train surrendered to the outlaw band, and Amanda choked as she heard the sounds of screams, of men cursing and women crying out in protest. She could hear the coarse laughter of the Haskwell gang as they made their way through the cars, taking their reward from the passenger's wealth.

"He could have a gun." The southerner gestured to the dead body of the businessman, while Amanda froze in revulsion, knowing what his next words would be. "See if he does."

"I can't . . . "

"See if he does." The southerner repeated in that same, bored drawl. Appalled, Amanda put the owl's cage aside and crept across the floor fighting the nausea that threatened to overwhelm her. Throwing up would certainly complete her misery, yet as she fumbled through the dead man's pockets, trying not to look at his open eyes and pale, white skin, she came remarkably close. It was only the thought of further embarrassment and the gunman's caustic reaction that made her retain her lunch.

"He doesn't." Amanda scuttled quickly away from the corpse, taking deep breaths and fighting her natural queasiness. "His pockets are empty."

"Great. They're still three cars ahead." The southerner said, almost to himself. "Ferriman gave orders not to stop under any circumstances. Shame this train doesn't have air brakes."

Amanda barely heard him. The engines whined but did not stop. Terrified, she gazed up at the southerner, her fingers clutching the bird cage, her blue-green eyes wide and unblinking.

"Won't they kill them? Us?"

The southerner shrugged. "Won't they anyway?"

Horrified, Amanda closed her eyes, refusing to let the thought complete itself. *Think, you have a mind, for God's sake, think!* she scolded herself. The owl squawked. The southerner reloaded, his gun smoking, burning his fingers, while the sounds from the other cars continued to terrify her . . .

"The coupler." She glanced up, her eyes bright and intense. "Can't you uncouple the car? This train should have a simple pin coupling. When the train pulls out, we'll be safe."

He looked at her in amazement, then he broke into a chuckle. His sides shook as he shoved the gun inside its holster, then he stood up and glanced through the soot-covered window.

"You just may have something there. There is some risk involved. We could get killed, you know. This train, uncoupled, could derail . . . "

"They'll kill us anyway, you said so!" Amanda protested.

"You're right." He agreed. "And worth a shot. For a woman, you may have a good idea."

He was gone, his body crouched between the cars. He struggled with the iron bolt that linked the last car to the rest of the train, twisting and yanking the pin while trying to maintain his balance between the two moving cars. The train lurched around a corner and Amanda gasped as the gunman disappeared, the two coaches colliding on the far side, the metallic crash harsh and sickening. Her breath returned as the car straightened and she saw him, plastered against the train, his face white as death. Yet, as soon as it was safe, he knelt down again and resumed tugging at the pin. Amanda was almost tempted to call to him, to tell him it was too dangerous, when the bolt slipped out with a rusty squeak. The gunman stood erect, still clutching the useless pin, then the two cars slid apart. Slowly, inexorably, the train slipped away from them to the west, and the caboose started its own eastern migration to nowhere.

He turned back and stepped inside, his triumphant smile vanishing as he saw the tracks behind them. "We're on a hill! This damned thing isn't going to stop!"

"The incline isn't too dramatic." Amanda shouted back. "Just for the last few miles. We should be all right . . . "

The train lurched, the car careening out of control. The gunman fell into Amanda, then the two of them toppled across the floor, rolling like acorns in a jostled barrel.

"Wonderful idea, lady." The southerner growled. "We escape outlaws, only to be killed in a goddamned train wreck!"

"How was I to know?" Amanda blushed hotly, terrified at the rusty scrape of the wheels against the iron rails. "You couldn't think of anything better."

"Bet me. I could have kept out of this damned mess to begin with. I should have stayed in my own car, but no, I had to be a hero and see if anyone needed help. Then somehow, I'm on a runaway train with a school marm. Did you wake up and decide to ruin my life today?"

"I am not a school marm!" Amanda shoved him indignantly, losing her fear at his insults. "Would you get off me?"

"Sure." He tried to rise, but the train lurched and he tumbled unwillingly against Amanda once more. This time his long lean body nearly covered hers entirely, and when he could finally move, bracing himself on his elbows, he looked down and found her blushing hotly. His legs were between hers, his chest pressed to her breasts. He couldn't help but noticing that they seemed much more impressive in this position than they did when she sat up with that prim, spinsterish posture. She had lost her glasses and her blue-green eyes, ocean eyes, he thought, were fringed with soft gold lashes. They stared at him, wide and alarmed. Without premeditation, he started to laugh.

"Are you all right?" he asked, between chuckles.

Amanda choked, more embarrassed than anything else. To have a man lying on top of her, in a position that even intimate people never talked about, was more than she could handle. She nodded her head, too shaken and mortified to speak.

The train slowed, the wheels gradually ceasing their frantic revolutions. The gunman remained on top of her, hushing her when she would have spoken, his head turned sideways, listening. Amanda strained to hear what had caught his attention and became aware of the cessation of noise, of the decrease in velocity, of the sharp grinding as the wheels decreased in speed. Finally, the train ground to a halt.

Amanda tried to draw a deep breath. The gunman grinned down at her, his expression boyishly inappropriate, obviously enjoying her discomfort.

"What's your name?" He asked with a grin.

His teeth were very white, his smile charming and infectious. Numb, Amanda found herself answering.

"Amanda. Edison. My last name is Edison." She managed, still unable to believe that they were alive.

"Luke Parker." He chuckled, the vibration warm against her body. "This train must have been going fifty miles an hour! I haven't experienced anything like that since I was thrown from a wild horse back in Charleston."

"Would you please let me up?" Amanda asked, growing more awkward and embarrassed by the moment.

"Sure," he shrugged. Rising from the floor, he extended a hand, silently offering to help her up. She ignored his gesture, pretending to be absorbed in brushing her dress and smoothing back the tumble of chestnut-colored hair that spilled forth. She felt around the floor, and when he handed her the pair of tortoiseshell-rimmed glasses, she blushed again, but immediately put them on and glanced around the interior of the runaway car. He saw her flinch as her gaze settled on the two bodies that were crumpled against the wall. She shuddered and tried to stand, her legs shaky and unsteady.

"Looking for this?"

Amanda nodded in relief as he handed her the bird cage, the cover tumbling to the floor. Aesop stared at her indignantly, then gazed at the surrounding carnage, as if thoroughly disgusted. Seeing the gunman's sarcastic glance, Amanda reached for the cover, spoke soothingly to the bird, then hooded the cage and placed it beside her.

"Thank you," she managed.

Luke nodded, then peered out the window. "Looks like we've got less than an hour till nightfall. Way I see it, we're a half-day's ride to Abilene. Right in the midst of Arapahoe country. I couldn't have planned this better myself."

Amanda stared up at him, only gradually realizing what he was saying. They had escaped outlaws, but by no means were they safe. Her eyes went back to the southern gunman.

"We have to get out of here," he said decisively. "In this train car, we're a sitting duck for any goddamned Indian who takes it into his head to investigate. There was a deserted Harvey house a few miles back. We could make for that, spend the night, then get to Abilene come morning."

Amanda looked at him doubtfully. He could see the thoughts racing through her mind, and the strange, uncanny wisdom in her eyes. She appeared to be dissecting his logic and testing his argument.

Luke shrugged. "We could try for Abilene tonight, if you want. If we stay on the western trail, we might be able . . . "

"There's still an hour until nightfall." Amanda said, mentally assessing the risk. "The Arapahoes won't care that we don't mean to trespass." She glanced down at the dead businessman and the redheaded woman, and couldn't repress a shudder. "You'll bury them, first, of course."

"Like hell." The gunman answered, already heading toward the door. "You coming or not?"

Amanda stared at him, stunned by his cruelty, but already Luke was walking away from her. She had no choice, and he wouldn't wait. Amanda picked up Aesop's cage and her carpetbag, then followed the gunman out into the waning daylight.

Chapter

2

Walking through the charming city of Boston, properly dressed, was very different from trudging along the railroad tracks of Kansas in tight, high-heeled, thick-laced boots, a dark muslin dress with a bustle and a corset beneath, carrying a bird cage with an unhappy owl. Amanda's glasses fogged as the temperature changed with the approaching nightfall. She removed them, then struggled to clean them on her skirt while clutching the bird cage and carpetbag stuffed with wads of notes and pencils.

The gunman strode far ahead of her, his manner cocky and unconcerned. His hat was pulled low over his face, his boots were scuffed and obviously well broken in, his clothes comfortable and adapted to the outdoors. He even whistled a show tune that was vaguely familiar to Amanda and had a risque connotation that she couldn't immediately place. She hated him now even more than she did when they were on the train. A pebble lodged in her boot, stabbing mercilessly into the arch of her foot, and she gasped in outrage and pain.

He stopped, turned slowly, and gave her an annoyed, penetrating look. "What's the hold up? We don't have that long until night, and I'd like to make it to shelter in one piece."

Amanda Edison never glared at anyone in her entire life, but she glared at Luke. "I have a stone in my shoe."

The gunman was about to make a scathing comment, but something in her voice stopped him. He nodded, studying her as she plunked the bird cage down, followed by the rumpled carpetbag that looked as bumpy as a badly stuffed mattress. She adjusted her glasses, seated herself on top of the carpetbag, then began to painstakingly unlace her shoe and remove her stocking.

The foot that emerged was surprisingly well-shaped and pretty. Luke noticed the flash of her calf, the delicate bone structure of her ankle, and the smooth, high curve of her arch. The skin was pierced with a nasty gash, and he winced for her as she shook out a sharp stone from her boot. She started to replace the stocking when he approached and stopped her, then boldly reached for her foot and examined the cut.

"What do you think you're doing . . . " Amanda gasped as Luke ran his rough hand along her foot, then he examined the soft underflesh where the stone had cut her. Strange sensations tingled where he touched her, surprising her, then she winced with pain as he gently probed the cut. He withdrew a red bandana from his pocket and tied the cloth around her foot, creating a makeshift bandage. When he finished, he took the stocking from her hand and slipped it back on, ignoring her outraged look. When he slid her boot on over the stocking and the bandage, caressing her skin in the process, it was too much. Amanda snatched her foot back, blushing at the intimacy of the gesture and her own reaction to him.

"I can finish it," she insisted hotly, lacing the boot herself.

"I was trying to help," Luke snapped.

"Well, don't," Amanda replied. "Just leave me alone. I can take care of myself."

"Right," Luke agreed. "That's why we're out in the middle of nowhere, with no food or water, in Indian country, you're injured and dressed for a garden party, carting a damned owl. Yeah, I'd say you're doing a great job of taking care of yourself."

Amanda couldn't say a word in her own defense. Picking up her cage with as much dignity as she could muster, she stalked ahead of him, then looked back. "Are you coming? 'The morning steals upon the night, melting the darkness.' Shakespeare." She gave him a smug glance, delighted to see his scowl.

Luke picked up her carpetbag, fighting to keep from caging her. Thank God they would part come morning.

The Harvey house was deserted, and bore all the signs of having been so for a long time. Luke tried the door, but the hinge had long since rusted and the handle refused to budge. Shrugging, he stepped back and gave the rotted panel a swift kick. The door swung open, revealing an interior decorated with cobwebs, suspicious nests in every corner, and broken chairs and tables.

"At least the roof's intact, and there's water." Luke tried to sound optimistic as he gestured to the trickling stream that ran beside the lonely restaurant. "And there's plenty of wood. We'd best get inside; night's falling."

Amanda said nothing, but followed him into the room. It was true that nightfall was imminent; already the western sky was suffused with orange and pink, and a ragged black edge of darkness smothered the east. Lowering herself stiffly on a chair with the bird cage placed carefully on a table out of the way, Amanda could have smiled at the irony of it all. She was alone in a deserted road house with a southern gunman who had absolutely no gentlemanly qualities, no education, and no civility. He had killed this afternoon with no more compunction than he would have sipped a whiskey. He could kill again.

Her eyes didn't leave him. The tension increased as he bent to pick up a broken chair, then smashed it on the edge of a table with a methodical violence that made her jump. Giving her a derisive glance, he put the wood in the potbellied stove and lit a fire. Accomplishing that, he turned to the cupboard above the counter and smiled in satisfaction as he discovered several tins of food. His smile changed to a grin as he withdrew a full bottle of 90 proof whiskey.

"Those Harvey waitresses sure know how to take care of a man." Luke uncorked the bottle, then drank down a huge swallow of the fiery liquor. He wiped his lips with his shirt sleeve, then turned to Amanda. "Want some?"

"Liquor is detrimental to the physical well-being," Amanda recited. "Alcohol is a direct cause of liver disease, mental illness and depravity. It is also linked to many accidents and killings, including shootings."

"Really?" Watching her expression carefully, Luke picked up the bottle, drank another swig, then placed it beside her.

"In case you change your mind."

Amanda fumed, then jumped to catch the metal pot he tossed to her. "Can you cook?" he indicated tins of stew, brown bread, and peaches.

Amanda bit her lip. Her writing had paid for a few luxuries, and one of them had been meals at the boardinghouse. She knew nothing about preparing ordinary food, other than what she'd seen. She was too embarrassed to admit it, however. She picked up the tin and attempted to read the label for directions.

Heat gently, stirring often, until done. Amanda frowned, wondering how she was going to know when the food was done, but the can gave no other clues. Fumbling with the can opener that Luke had supplied, she tried to pry open the lid, but succeeded only in denting the tin. She fought to keep from crying, especially when he came to stand behind her, lifted the can from her awkward hands without a word, and opened it immediately. He handed it back to her, a grin still plastered on his face, and Amanda toyed with the idea of reaching for his gun and blasting him. It was only the thought of the Indians and the remembrance of what had happened when she'd tried to fire the derringer that made her swallow her pride and dump the stew into the pot.

"What does this thing eat?" He peered beneath the cover and poked his finger into Aesop's cage. Amanda wished she'd trained the bird to bite.

"Mice," she replied acidly. "There's some in my bag." Ignoring his stare of disbelief, Amanda opened her carpetbag, fished through a wad of papers, and pulled out a cookie tin. She dipped her hand inside, withdrew a mouse, and without the slightest hesitation, fed it to the wide awake, blinking owl. The bird scooped up the half-starved and confused rodent, then placidly swallowed his dinner. The owl's amber eyes gazed suspiciously at the southern gunman while the mouse vanished inside his curved beak. Luke swallowed hard, then stared curiously at the odd woman across from him.

"Who the hell are you?"

"I've already told you my name," Amanda said, primly washing her hands. "I'm a writer—of western novels." She checked the stew and found it barely bubbling on the woodstove, then took the seat he offered at one of the intact tables.

Luke's mouth dropped. "You write books?"

Amanda nodded. "Penny dreadfuls, they call them. They don't pay much, but enough for the bills and a little extra. It's nothing special. I'd rather not talk about it."

Luke nodded, then lit a candle, aware of the shadows that now threatened to swallow the room. He turned to look back at her. She was trying so hard to distance him. The firelight fell on her, illuminating her chestnut hair, her ink-stained dress, her dowdy hairstyle. She stared at him, her eyes unnaturally large behind her glasses, gleaming with intensity. Without those glasses, with her hair taken down, she might even be pretty, he decided. It was amazing that she wrote books, and even more amazing that she shrugged it off as if she washed dishes for a living. Everything about her piqued his curiosity.

"Look." He gave her a charming smile. "We have nothing to do for the next few hours. We could at least be civil."

"There really isn't any need to talk. You and I are obviously two very different people, with different values and morals. I see no reason to make this any harder than it is."

Luke leaned back in his chair, taking another swig of whiskey before placing the bottle on the table before her. "How do you know what my morals are?"

Amanda stared at him in amazement. "You kill without remorse, curse like a sailor, order people around without any regard for their feelings. Although I agree with Carlyle, that it is essential to see a man's good qualities before pronouncing on his bad, I can't ignore the obvious. Therefore, it is clear—"

Amanda's words broke off in a scream as Luke pulled out his gun and fired a shot. The bullet whined so close to her face that she could feel the disturbance of the air. Gritting her teeth, she whirled toward him, intending to berate him, when she spied a dead rat on the floor.

"Sorry," he smiled. "You were saying?"

Amanda's mouth went dry. The rat lay beside her, its body jerking from nervous reaction, just inches from her feet. "Why, I . . . "

"Yeah, it was ready to bite." Luke nodded. "They're full of diseases out here. Oh, Jesus." A sputtering sound caught his attention and with an oath, he rushed to the stove where the stew spattered merrily. Gripping the pot, he gasped as the metal burned his hand, then he pulled out his shirt and used the tail as a potholder. Amanda watched in mortification as he pulled the smoking pot from the stove and slammed it down on the table.

"Great, this is just great. The stew's burned. Dammit, what kind of a woman are you? Can't you do anything?"

Amanda stammered as he poured out two bowls of burned, awful smelling stew. "I can do a lot of things," she answered furiously.

"Yeah, so I see." Luke flopped down in his chair and pushed the burned stew at her in disgust. "You'd better eat this; it's all we're liable to get. Christ." He forced down a mouthful of food, then drank some whiskey to eradicate the taste.

Amanda, still shaking from the rat, took a bite of stew. Trying to act as if everything was fine, she swallowed the stuff, then choked on the pungent taste. She grabbed the whiskey bottle, heedless of his grin, and took a long pull. Hot liquor tore its way to her belly, making her gasp in surprise, then the sensation died, leaving her feeling warm and fortified.

"I thought you were against alcohol," Luke said.

Amanda shrugged and replied absently, " 'A man lives by believing something; not by debating and arguing about many things—' "

"Stop it," he interrupted angrily.

"What?" Amanda peered at him from behind her thick glasses.

"That. I don't care what someone else says, I want to know what you think."

"I . . . don't know." For the first time in her life, Amanda was at a loss. She couldn't think, couldn't reason, couldn't take her eyes from the southerner who was sitting across from her, staring at her with those captivating blue eyes, challenging her instead of running away.

"I'll tell you what I think, and it isn't some damned quote. I think the political system is a sham, that Shakespeare wrote all his own works, and that Carlyle was the worst excuse for a coward that this century has produced. I think Dickens overrated, Twain under-acknowledged, the South should have won the war, and that Tocqueville was a prejudiced French bastard. I think the frontier theory a farce, and that one man killed Lincoln."

"Is that all?" Amanda choked, stunned by the force of his statement.

"No." He came to stand beside her, his hand slipping through the knot of her hair, releasing it to fall around her shoulders. "I think a man should make love to a woman by starting at her toes, and ending up at her neck about three days later."

The color drained from Amanda's face. She stared at him in disbelief, even as he continued to play with her hair. She had been wrong about him, dead wrong. He had at least as much education as she did. Yet somehow, it was exciting and stimulating, to be challenged by this man. Taking another sip of the whiskey, she stared at him thoughtfully.

"I think you're wrong about Dickens. His work has a lot to say about our values, but it is often overlooked because he has popular appeal. I think Carlyle is brilliant, and I agree with you about Twain. But how can you say that about the democratic system? And the frontier theory?" She flushed with passion as she leaned forward, her strange eyes glittering with emotion. "Don't you agree that American democracy was shaped by man's struggle with the wilderness? And that the contest eliminates class distinction and ensures equality?"

"No, I don't agree." Luke shrugged, fascinated by the flush of hot color that came to her face, and the sparkle of her eyes as she distractedly removed her glasses. "I think other factors are overlooked."

"Such as?" Amanda taunted.

Luke smiled, releasing a lock of hair he had been caressing. Without her glasses, she really was pretty. And the fervor he heard in her voice made him wonder just how much passion she reserved for anything else. His hand fell to her shoulder and began to rub it, loosening the tension in her upper arms.

"I think the change in the work force will have more of an impact." Luke noticed her color deepen as he continued to caress her, but she didn't stop him. "I also think the frontier community is not as classless as it's assumed. Take the railroad."

"The railroad!" Amanda laughed shortly, barely aware that his hands had moved lower, and that he was massaging all of the tightness from her back. "But that's the classic example of man conquering the environment. East unified with West. Man working with man, equal and the same, triumphing over nature."

"Equal?" Luke snorted. "Who do you think actually did all the work? Those fancy investors back east, who made a mint selling railroad stocks? Or the poor, the unemployed, the immigrant Irish and Chinese, who sweated their brains out laying tracks through deserts and mountain passes for a lousy two dollars a day? Some equality."

"They had a choice!" Amanda protested, appalled by his reasoning. She felt his hands move to her neck, stroking the tight muscles there and forcing her to relax. "They didn't have to take those jobs!"

"Really?" Luke asked in amusement. "And where else would they work? They couldn't find anything out east, or they wouldn't have left. I'm sure you're familiar with the gate theory. Three immigrants for every job. As long as they're lined up, waiting at the gate, they'll never get ahead. Never get a raise. Never be equal."

"You're advocating socialism?"

"No, I'm pushing reality. Let's call it what it is, and not sugar coat life with dead theories and romanticism. Naivete never benefitted anyone."

"Who are you calling naive?" Furious, Amanda stood up, finding herself in the gunslinger's embrace. She was so angry, she hardly noticed. "I graduated with honors. I'd hardly consider myself uninformed."

"Well-read, maybe. But you've got to look past the books, sweetheart, and make up your own mind. Dead philosophers and political ideologists are also not out working on the train tracks."

"That's totally illogical," Amanda said, stunned that he'd attacked her precious philosophers. "How can you say such things?"

"It's easy." Luke slid his hands around her waist, tortured by the feel of her in his arms. She felt even better close, her body squirming against his, her skin like satin beneath his rough fingers. "You've got to judge for yourself. Like this."

Somehow, he was kissing her, his fingers tangled in her hair, his other arm wrapped around her waist, holding her still. The passion of their argument was transformed into a heat between them that had nothing to do with logic and

everything to do with feelings. Luke eased his mouth from
hers, then buried his face in her neck, tasting her, touching
her, unable to get enough of the feel of her soft skin and
her innocent, mindless response.

Amanda gasped, allowing him to caress her, liking the
surprising contrast of his gentle manner with the sandpaper
roughness of his fingers. No man had ever touched her like
this before, like she'd read about, written about, and imagined. It was better than she had thought; confusing and exciting at the same time. When his hand moved from her
throat down to her breast, lightly cupping the round fullness
in one hand, she could feel her heart flutter against his fingers. Her face flushed hotter, and she struggled to regain
control, to stop all this before things got out of hand.

"The frontier theory . . . " Amanda whispered breathlessly.

"Right. The frontier theory." Leaning closer, Luke kissed
her into silence, then let his mouth trail along her cheekbone
and throat. He had expected a fight, and instead tasted a
desire on her lips that equaled his own. Her pulse throbbed
against his tongue and he heard her unmistakable gasp of
passion as his mouth brushed enticingly against the intri-
cacy of her ear. Physical pleasure, heightened by intellectual
fencing, was an intoxicant that apparently neither one of
them wanted to resist. Luke wondered if all college women
were like this, and decided it wasn't a bad idea to educate
a woman after all.

Amanda sighed, reveling in the warm feeling of his body
close to hers. For the first time in her life, her mind deserted
her, and she didn't care. The room grew hotter, the candle
flickered, and Amanda could only think of the incredible
sensations that raced through her, the feeling of this man's
lips against her. His hand returned to her breast, his thumb
lightly grazing the sensitive nipple, arousing her, introduc-
ing her to an entirely new level of feeling. Amanda fought
with the logic that told her this was ridiculous, then with
the feelings that urged her young body to take what he was
offering. Having denied herself all the normal experiences

that most girls took for granted, she had no defense against his seduction, and absolutely no desire for any. She wanted to live, to touch, to be held, loved. She wanted him. It was as simple as that.

Yet her mind rebelled, even as she urged his mouth back to hers, answering him in an instinctive, ageless way, without words. She couldn't do this. God, but she wanted to. His hand reached up behind her, effortlessly undoing her buttons and releasing her from the prison of her clothes, the dress, the tightly laced corset, then finally, her shift. Conflict gripped her as he pressed his mouth to her soft flesh, making her breath stop short and her knees weaken. She was standing within his arms, holding onto him for balance as his tongue teased her, drawing sensual patterns against her breast. His mouth closed upon a nipple, sucking powerfully, making her gasp in surprise and pleasure. Shock tingled through her as his mouth moved lower, his fingers artfully exploring her body, sweeping down past her slender waist and thighs, then touching her there, where she was throbbing and aching, wanting him . . .

"It's all right," he whispered soothingly, lowering her to the floor. But it wasn't all right. The whiskey churned in her stomach, the burned food rose like bile in her throat, and her nervous reaction, fostered by indecision, made her body tense. When he tried to enter her with his fingers, she pulled away from him, her face reddening in embarrassment, her eyes wide and stricken.

"What is it?" He attempted to draw her back into his embrace once more, but she pulled away, resisting the intoxication of his kiss.

"I can't." She fought to explain, for once completely incapable of speech. She saw the confusion in his eyes as he raised his hand to touch her, but she flinched as if afraid, then struggled for words, mortified beyond reason. "I . . . I'm going to be sick."

Luke stared at her in disbelief as she choked, clapped a hand over her mouth, then rushed to the waiting bowl on the counter. She was definitely sick.

Chapter

3

Luke couldn't believe it. No woman had ever done this to him, not even when he was much younger—fourteen to be exact, and learning about love from the giggling Hamilton twins who'd lived on the outskirts of Charleston. But Amanda wasn't teasing him or playing coy. Her face lost much of its color, and even as he watched, her eyes became as glassy as glazed china. Luke stood behind her, helpless as Amanda violently retched.

"You all right?" He moistened his handkerchief and pressed the cool cotton to her face, then to the back of her neck. Amanda nodded, more embarrassed than ever. Luke helped her to a chair, and she practically pushed away from him, eager to forget the entire humiliating incident. Collapsing into the seat, she wanted to die, to forget that this night had ever transpired, to dissolve into eternal sleep which had nothing to do with the seductions of ruthless gunmen.

"Please, just go," she whispered brokenly, resisting as he tried to make her more comfortable. Ignoring her protest, Luke covered her with a linen tablecloth that he found in a drawer.

"Look, I just want to be sure you're okay." He lifted her face, growing annoyed as she rejected his help once more.

"I'm fine. Really. Now will you please just leave me alone?" She picked up her glasses and replaced them on her face, glaring at him with that oddly piercing stare he'd seen too often earlier.

"Sure." Luke nodded, growing justifiably angry. "You know, I don't expect gratitude or anything. But you're the damnest woman I've ever met. What are you mad at me for?"

"I'm sorry if I ruined your evening," Amanda said, hiding behind her well-honed defenses. "I suppose most women just fall into your arms."

"They don't usually throw up," Luke agreed, growing more furious by the moment.

"Then it's just as well we'll be parting come morning. As Homer says—"

"Amanda." Luke's voice was deadly. He reached across the table, picked up the whiskey bottle, then settled himself into a chair while she watched in horrified fascination. He cocked his gun, then placed it within reach. "Don't you dare."

Amanda closed her mouth, then drew the linen up more snugly around her shoulders. If there was one thing she didn't need to learn in school, it was when to back down.

This was obviously the time.

Gunfire woke them just before dawn. Luke was awake in a second, snatching up his gun in one fluid motion, then he posed at the window in shocked disbelief.

"Jesus, what is this?" He fired in return, amazed to discover that the shots were indeed directed at the deserted restaurant. Pausing only to reload, he saw Amanda scramble for her clothes, then for the bird cage. Shaking his head in disbelief, he watched her place the owl safely beneath the table. Only then did she see to her own comfort. Struggling into her dress, she ducked as a window broke and glass danced across the floor in a thousand tiny prisms.

"Get down! This isn't one of your damned novels, they're shooting!"

"Who is it?" Amanda peered out from beneath the table where the owl rustled furiously.

"How do I know? I didn't ask for a calling card. You're not wanted or anything, are you?"

"No!" Amanda said indignantly. "I—"

The pot crashed to the floor, spinning from the force of a lead bullet. Conversation ceased as Luke struggled desperately to fight off their invisible attackers. Amanda took one stunned look at the pot, then crept across the floor to join him at the window.

"I can help you load." She withdrew the bullets, placing them in a convenient location near his left hand. He was about to correct her when he saw that it was easier this way, that it eliminated a movement and a fraction of a second that could mean a life. Scooping up the bullets, he then shoved them into the gun, talking almost to himself.

"It's not Indians. Thank God for that. Though who the hell would be shooting at us now . . ." Picking off a gunman that appeared into view, Luke's voice deepened and he whistled. "Damn if that doesn't look like Butch Winters. Part of the Haskwell gang."

"Why would they come back?"

"Doesn't make sense to me. They got the money and the jewelry. It's damned foolishness on their part." Squeezing the trigger, he neatly shot another outlaw, this one within twenty feet of the building.

Amanda paled, then rose to her knees and peered out the window. She could barely see the gunmen, but something about them did seem familiar. No sooner did they spot her when the gunfire erupted into a blaze of fury, and Luke flung her to the floor like a sack of oatmeal.

"You trying to get killed?" The gunfire roared, and in desperation, he fired back, wondering what it all meant. Amanda lay on the floor, breathless, more frightened than even the day before. Then there had been a train full of people to help fight the outlaws off. Now, for some ungodly reason, they were back, and she was alone with no one to help her but the southern gunman who had every reason to despise her.

Forcing down her emotions and the renewed queasiness in her stomach, she made herself think. Outlaws. The train. Rising to her knees, she took care to stay well away from the window and she spoke excitedly, her strange eyes gleaming.

"The train! The nine-fifteen should be here shortly."

"Great." Luke replied, still firing into the woods. "Maybe we could all take a nice trip to Denver."

"You don't understand," Amanda said in frustration. "The abandoned car is still on the track. When the train collides with it, we'll have a chance to escape."

The escape part caught his attention. As Luke reloaded, he had to admit her plan had merit. It seemed even more plausible when the train whistle blew a few minutes later. The iron horse plunged between them and the outlaws, acting as an effective metallic screen from the gunfire. Normally, the delay would have only lasted a few moments, but the loud crash that followed gave them the perfect opportunity, and neither one of them had any desire to waste it.

"Let's go." Luke grabbed her hand, quelling his frustration when she stopped for the carpetbag and the owl, then scrambled out the door with him. A supply trail led directly behind the restaurant and into the woods. Luke drove her mercilessly down the path, knowing full well that the outlaws would be upon them within a few minutes. Amanda struggled breathlessly, still trying to carry the carpetbag and the cage and run at the same time. Luke saw her effort and snatched up the cage with an oath, then dragged her deeper into the woods. He didn't stop until they came to a rusted and abandoned train track, and on it was, unbelievably, a deserted handcar.

"Great." Luke helped Amanda up, onto the rusted cart, then placed Aesop safely in the center. Amanda put her carpetbag aside, then stared at the apparatus.

"Grab the other end." Luke shook his head in disbelief. The woman was worse than a cloistered nun. Amanda nodded, then awkwardly snatched at the iron railing that rose in front of her face. Pushing downward with all of her one hundred and eighteen pounds behind her, she managed to lower the bar enough to allow him the leverage he needed. Luke thrust forcefully down on the opposing bar. The gears screeched in protest, but the cart creaked along the track and moved a few feet. Encouraged by their success, Amanda pushed again and Luke followed, forcing the ancient car to resume an old journey down the tracks, even as they heard gunfire in the distance.

"Looks like we did it." He shouted to be heard above the racket of the handcar and the distant gunfire. Amanda nodded, her hands white against the iron bar, her heart pounding in terror and exertion. The car picked up speed, barreling around a curve. The cage slid across the floor of the car and Luke stopped it with his booted leg. Gradually, the din of the gunfire died as the woods and the Harvey house faded behind them. Luke glanced at Amanda. Her face was covered with sweat, her hair straggled, her glasses crooked. She shoved a lock of damp hair out of her eyes and glanced up at him, catching his triumphant smile. She started to return it, when she looked behind him and a scream died in her throat.

The track ended as abruptly as it began.

Butch Winters slowed his horse down to a brisk walk as the woods closed in around them. They were gone. The path from the abandoned Harvey house led straight into the forest, and except for an old supply hut, there was nothing. A pheasant whirred from the brush as another man reined up his mount, then spat at the dusty ground beneath him.

"Damn, Butch. We had her. Christ, I saw that thin-necked spinster at the window, jest as clear as that day in town when Sam shot that fool Haines. Who would have thought she'd have the guts to write about it in that book? Least she had the sense to change her name."

"She ain't got that much sense. We tracked her, didn't we?"

"Yeah. All the way from Boston." Damien spat once more and glanced at the woods. The silence made him nervous. "Good thing that fancy woman Sam kept knew how to read. Little thing—just about fifteen, I would say. Remember her? How she used to sit in that room, scared to death of Sam, and pass the time reading penny novels? It was her that tipped Sam off, and her that helped him write to that New York publishing house." Damien chuckled at the thought. "Must've thought it was a fan letter. That publisher told Sam everything. Who Fess Tyson was. Where she lived—"

"Shut up, Damien. You talk too much." Butch wiped the sweat from his face, wrinkling a thin, twisted red scar on his cheek. "She can't have just disappeared."

Both men stared into the woods. Trees were stacked like poles in an endless infinity before them, while lime-colored ferns warned of cover—Indian cover.

"I don't like it," Damien said. "It's too damned quiet."

"For once, you're right," Butch agreed, tightening the leather reins in his fist. "I ain't gonna find her here. Somehow, she must have gotten help. Did you see that gunman with her?"

"A good shot, no matter who he is," Damien said. "Looks like a hire to me."

"Huh," Butch grunted thoughtfully. "I thought he looked familiar, too. Doesn't matter, though." Butch cocked the gun, then fired it senselessly into the bush where the pheasant had disappeared. The bird tumbled out, riddled with shot, useless for any purpose other than a killing.

"Amanda Edison is a dead woman. Gun or no gun."

Amanda fell abruptly onto her bottom, but Luke tumbled out of the car to the hard, rocky ground. He swore, slammed his hat down upon his leg in disgust, then got painfully to his feet and turned back.

"That's it? A track that goes nowhere? You know something, lady, you're some kind of a jinx!"

"It has to go parallel to the main run." Amanda reasoned.

"This was obviously a supply car for the restaurant. If we keep walking, we're bound to come to the town, and help."

Luke stared at her, even as she reached for her bag and the owl. Damned if she wasn't right. It was unnerving and annoying at the same time, but he couldn't help admiring her a little. Even now, as she trudged along the cut trail, looking more like a school marm than a writer of penny dreadfuls, she didn't complain. Instead, he could almost hear her thinking, calculating their next move, and assessing their chances for success. She glanced back, gave him an impervious look that would have frozen the heart of a meeker man, then looked directly ahead.

Silently cursing, Luke joined her. If she was right, they could be in town within the hour. It definitely wouldn't be soon enough for him.

Abilene was everything Amanda had ever heard about it, and then some. Short, squat buildings sprang up from the ground as if rooted, while the dusty roads were well-packed from the herds of Longhorn cattle that had been driven over them. Amanda followed Luke down Texas Street, blinking steadily at the influx of sight, sound and textures. Cowboys brawled outside the Applejack saloon, oblivious to the passersby who ignored the scene and went about their daily business. Women carried baskets beneath their arms and hurried about their shopping, pausing only to brush the dust from their hot, high-necked Victorian gowns. Businessmen speculated on everything from cattle to gold, rushing from the McCoy Hotel to the bar, where the real deals were consummated. Whores stood boldly on the steps outside the saloon, their white-tasseled boots a startling contrast to the dismal brown dirt that covered everything.

Amanda choked, then rubbed at her glasses with her sleeve. She felt like a newborn baby just entering the world and absorbing everything that she could in the short time she'd been there. Breathing deeply of the acrid stench of the cow town, she reminded herself to put that in her journal;

that peculiar aroma that was reminiscent of Aesop's cage when she'd forgotten to clean it. And the sounds! She'd never written of the noise that nearly drowned her senses. The shouts of the cowboys. The lewd whistles of the street women. The soft clatter of the horses. And the enthusiastic screech of the train as it pulled into the station, followed by the harsh scrape of the gears against the track.

"You coming?"

Amanda glanced up, coloring when she realized Luke had been talking to her. She felt drunk on sensation and she quickly nodded, uncertain of what she was agreeing to.

"There's a ticket station across the street. You can book passage without any trouble if you still have your old stub. There's a good restaurant if you're hungry, and a bath house if you want to get cleaned up." Luke gestured to an old frame building nestled beside a boardinghouse. "Well, I guess this is it."

She stood in the street, looking at him with that strange, intense stare that made him even more uneasy than it did earlier. He wondered if she realized how exotically pretty she was, even with her disheveled hair that she made no attempt to straighten, or her frumpy dress. Something about her aroused pity in him, an emotion that was foreign and not altogether welcome. He shrugged, and extended a hand to take her carpetbag.

"Won't hurt to have a bite to eat. Why don't you straighten out your ticket and I'll go get us some seats," he said.

Amanda exhaled in relief. She smiled and nodded shakily, unable to explain her own reaction. It really made no sense. She should be glad to be rid of him, to be back to civilization and away from outlaws and deserted restaurants. But she was grateful for the reprieve, for however long it lasted.

The ticketman scrutinized her ink-splotched ticket, scraped away the bird droppings, then reluctantly stamped the wrinkled receipt and handed it back to Amanda with a curious glance. Giving the man an absent smile, she tucked the ticket back inside Aesop's cage, and ignored the owl's rustling. Returning to the restaurant across the street, she entered the establishment, completely unaware of the ticketman's gaping stare.

She saw Luke immediately and joined him at a sturdy wooden table. A surly waitress sauntered toward them, her gaze taking in the dangerous looking southerner and his odd companion. Amanda took a seat across from Luke, acutely aware of him as a man in this civilized setting. The night before came vividly back to her in detail. This man had touched her where no man had before, had undressed her, attempted to make love to her . . . and she had thrown up. Once again mortified by the memory, Amanda immediately delved into her carpetbag. Anything to take her mind off last night. She retrieved a pencil and a notebook, and began to furiously record her observations of Abilene.

"Can I take your order, suh?" The woman shifted from one shoe to the other, her eyes never leaving Amanda.

Luke nodded. "I'll have the beefsteak, rare, potatoes, gravy, green beans, apple pie and coffee. Amanda?"

She said nothing, but continued to write, oblivious to everything. Her pencil scratched across the paper and she made little sighs and squeaks as a particularly valuable note was duly recognized and recorded. Luke was reminded of a bloodhound, irresistably taken by a scent.

"Amanda?" He asked again, louder this time.

Amanda glanced up, then blushed as she became aware of the impatient waitress. "I'm sorry, did you want me?"

"Your order," Luke said, gritting his teeth. She was beginning to embarrass him. "You did want something to eat?"

"Yes. I mean, I think so. Whatever you're having." Happy that she settled that dilemma, she went back to her work. Her hair tumbled down around her, effectively shielding her from the waitress' disdainful glance, which unreasonably irritated Luke. "Oh, I am sorry." Amanda glanced back up, shoving her glasses and pushing her hair out of her face.

"Yes?" The waitress asked, rolling her eyes.

"I also need a mouse. For Aesop. If you have one."

"A mouse." The waitress repeated incredulously.

Amanda nodded, then returned to her scribbling. The waitress glanced at Luke. He gave her a beatific smile.

"Just add it to the bill. I'm sure you have more than one rodent around this place."

The waitress backed away, her eyes wide, while Luke chuckled. For the first time since he'd met her, he appreciated Amanda's eccentricities.

It was just too bad she'd never know it.

The waitress returned with the food, unable to resist a glance at Amanda as she placed a brown parcel that was neatly wrapped with twine on the table. Unflinchingly, Amanda opened the bag, peered inside, then smiled, satisfied. She retied the wrappings, and placed the package inside the tin in her carpetbag.

"A nice fat one. Aesop will be so happy," she beamed.

Luke choked, then indicated the food. He waited until the waitress left before softly chiding her. "Stop worrying about that damned owl and your work. Eat." He indicated the steaming food.

"I'm not worried," Amanda said defensively, though she took his advice and put her papers aside. "I just wanted to make some notes. Did you know this town is called the wickedest town in the United States? It's fascinating."

Luke swallowed his coffee and replaced the cup, staring at her in disbelief. "What's so fascinating?"

"All of it," Amanda said dreamily. "It's so different from the east, and yet the same. On the surface, it seems so chaotic, but there is a marked civility. As Socrates said—"

"Civil?" Luke laughed abruptly. "Abilene? Don't kid yourself. This town has a reputation that it's earned."

"I think it's exaggerated," Amanda insisted.

"It's a good thing you aren't going to be here long." Luke shook his head. "You'd be in for a rude awakening. Excuse me for a minute." He stood up, reluctant to leave her, but she was already rereading her papers and scarcely heard him. He picked up his cup and went to the counter for a refill, leaving Amanda happily buried in her notes.

Amanda finished everything on her plate. She was about to order seconds when she noticed a man at the next table staring. He wore a rich coat and a gaudy, embroidered vest beneath. His hair was black, brushed with some kind of grease, and his moustache was obviously waxed. He smiled, and Amanda, uncertain of what to do, returned his smile. Satisfied that he had caught her attention, he indicated the seat across from her.

Amanda nodded, puzzled. Westerners were friendly, she'd read that. Perhaps the man was lonely. She slid over, making room for him, immediately repulsed by something in his manner and the way he stared at her. Yet, he aroused her curiosity. He was like no man she'd ever met before, and she wasn't about to pass up the experience.

The man took a seat beside her, his quick dark eyes skimming her dress, aware of the lovely figure it concealed. Dressed in a bright silk gown with a few ostrich feathers in her hair, she would bring him a hefty procurement fee from Jennie Rogers. The local madame had elegant and discriminating tastes, and this young woman would just suit the bill.

"Glad to make your acquaintance, Miss. My name's Shiler. Henry Shiler, to be precise." He grinned, resembling a hissing copperhead, and extended a hand.

"Please do. Be precise, that is," Amanda said, accepting his hand, her eyes shining. The man would make a great villain for her next book. She took out her notebook and made detailed descriptions of his hair, clothes, and manner.

"I didn't catch your name." He stared at her, his smile fading as she continued to write.

"I didn't tell you. This is wonderful." Amanda looked up and gave him a brilliant smile. "I'm so glad you joined me."

"So am I." He frowned when she finally put the notebook away and gave him a penetrating stare. Her eyes were unbelievable. Blue-green, swirling with golden flecks, like the ocean at dawn. Without those glasses, and with her hair done up, she would be the most requested girl in town. "I'd like to make you a business proposition."

"Oh, I don't need any more money," Amanda said quickly. "I have more than enough."

"You do?" The gambler took in her threadbare dress and tattered lace sleeves. He could swear her gown was splattered with ink. Deciding she was just being modest, he leaned closer with an understanding smile. "Honey, you can talk to me. I know what it's like. You've obviously had some schooling, so you haven't been poor for very long. But I can help you."

"The lady doesn't need your help."

The gambler glanced up and saw Luke standing beside the table, his gun hand resting lightly outside the holster. Henry Shiler moved away from the table, showing that he had no intention of drawing. He didn't like the look of the gunman, and even a deal for the woman wasn't worth his life.

"I was just making the lady's acquaintance. I meant no harm, mister."

Amanda nodded in agreement. "He just wanted to offer me a job. Isn't that kind?"

"Really?" Luke glanced back at the gambler, who had turned a shade paler. "What kind of job would a gambler offer a lady? And an educated one at that?"

"A gambler?" Amanda's eyes lit up and she leaned across the table. "Are you really? What kind of game do you play? Do you cheat? What does a gambler make in a year? Do you count cards?"

"What is this?" Henry got to his feet. "What are you, the law or something?"

Luke clenched his teeth. "No, it's just Amanda. I think you'd better get going. Unless you want your life duly recorded in the next penny novel."

The gambler stared at Amanda, who was glaring at Luke

with barely concealed frustration. He took the gunman's advice and removed himself, muttering under his breath.

He was scarcely gone when Luke attacked. "What the hell's the matter with you? You don't invite a man like that to your table unless you're willing to go along with what he has in mind. Didn't you learn anything in that damned college you went to, other than quoting dead philosophers?"

"I certainly did!" Amanda snapped, her eyes glittering with anger. "What right did you have to ask him to leave? I was just getting started. He was providing valuable research material."

"I'll bet," Luke snorted incredulously. "What kind of research? The kind you do on your back?"

Amanda paled, looking stricken for a moment, and Luke immediately felt bad that he had hurt her. "Look, I didn't mean—"

"I know what you meant," Amanda snapped, gathering up her bags. "And I think it just as well that we end this acquaintance. 'Friends are as dangerous as enemies.' Thomas De Quincy." Amanda started for the door, her shoulders squared, even as she hefted her bag and the cage. Luke started after her, then on second thought, let her go.

It would be just as well for both of them.

The thought was barely formed when gunfire shattered the normal sounds of the cowtown and people screamed, scrambling for cover. Amanda stood frozen in the doorway that was now riddled with bullets, her numb fingers slowly opening, and Aesop's cage tumbled to the ground.

"Get down!" Luke dove at her, grabbing for his gun, even as another fusillade of shot poured from the street. Stunned, Amanda scrambled back inside the restaurant. Luke aimed his gun, but it was already too late. Whoever had fired was gone, the street deserted. Reholstering his weapon, he turned back to Amanda, helping her to her feet, then he cupped her chin and forced her to look up at him.

"It's you," he said in wonder, rudely examining her lovely face for some kind of clue to this mystery. She tried to pull away from him, but he wouldn't let her. "Jesus Christ, it's you they're after!"

Chapter

4

"No!" Amanda gasped, horrified at the thought. Yet even as she denied it, reality pushed its way into her consciousness. It was too much of a coincidence. The logical side of her mind overrode her emotions, telling her that, for some reason, someone wanted her dead. Her knees grew weak, and she swallowed hard, fighting to quell the dizziness that threatened to overcome her. She heard Luke shout for water, even as he helped her into a chair. Amanda was scarcely aware of the stunned murmurs of the restaurant's customers, or knew that some of the men rose from their positions on the floor to stare out into the vacant street. Someone called for the sheriff, while the waitress brought the water.

"Drink this."

Amanda tried to refuse, but Luke forced the glass to her lips, spilling the chilled liquid down her throat until she choked. She glared at him, then closed her eyes until the weakness passed.

They were shooting to kill her. If it wasn't for Luke, she would already be dead. Insulated for all of her life in a safe scholastic shell, Amanda felt like a newly hatched chick facing a world that was dangerous, even deadly.

"Feel better?" Luke asked, ignoring her scowl.

Amanda nodded her head and pulled the owl's cage closer to her feet, as if accepting comfort from the close proximity of the barnyard bird. "Why?" Her voice was sharp, demanding an answer.

"Damned if I know," Luke said dryly. "But think about it. The Haskwells came back after successfully looting the train, risking capture. For them to show up here, and open fire as soon as they saw you . . . For some reason, Sam Haskwell wants you dead."

Amanda nodded, her shoulders sagging. Suddenly, the idea of taking a trip was not nearly as appealing as it once was.

"Well, little lady, looks like you're lucky to be alive." The portly sheriff left the crowd of people gathering at the entrance and made his way to Amanda. He barely glanced at the floor peppered with lead. "Sam Haskwell is nobody's baby. You clearing out of here soon? I don't need that kind of trouble."

"I . . . had planned to leave today. I was going to take the train."

"Forget that," Luke interrupted. "It'll be too easy for them to trace you, let alone kill you. We've seen that already. Your best bet at this point is to join up with a wagon train. You could take the Chisholm trail to Texas from here. Cost you about the same, too."

"Would be mighty surprised if they would want you," the sheriff continued as he spat into a brass spittoon. "No one needs the attention of the Haskwells, and on a wagon train, it could be deadly. You'd be looking behind you for days."

Amanda glanced outside. The railroad platform looked conspicuously empty. The frontier families, who were so obvious an hour ago as they assembled and loaded up with supplies, were now gone.

"My advice to you would be to head back east," the sheriff said. "Whatever's waiting for you in Texas will still be there a few months from now. Maybe by then the heat will die down."

"You mean she'll take the trouble with her and you won't have to deal with it." Luke said. "The Haskwells would have no problem locating her there. She'd be a sitting duck."

The sheriff shrugged. "I've got two deputies; one can't shoot and the other's sick from licker. I have enough trouble trying to keep this town under control. And you want me to fight them?"

"I think the lady gets your meaning," Luke said in disgust.

The sheriff nodded. "I wish I could be of more help, but I can't. You'll be out of town today?" Amanda nodded, her eyes stricken. "Good. I'll consider this matter finished, then." Pulling his hat down over his face, the sheriff walked out of the restaurant without looking back.

Amanda got to her feet. Luke was right; to go home might make things worse. She shuddered at the thought of the gunmen, terrorizing her home town and frightening Mrs. Pincus into a panic. Forcing herself to think clearly, she weighed her alternatives.

She didn't have a choice. There was no sense to go backward; she would have to continue forward. Yet, she couldn't do it alone. . . . Amanda's eyes returned to Luke.

He was talking quietly with the townspeople, assuaging their fears, assuring them that Amanda was indeed leaving. There was a cold authority about him that made the people listen, coupled with their memory of how quickly he had drawn when the gunfire started. Leaning against the wall, his black Stetson removed, his dark hair curling crisply in the heat, he looked devilishly handsome and completely in control. Amanda was amazed at the contrast between the gunman and the townspeople. All of them were afraid of the Haskwells—except him.

She needed him. It was as simple as that. She'd think of a way to convince him to help her, to escort her to Texas and protect her from the Haskwells. A guilty flush stained her face as she recalled that night in the Harvey house, then she immediately dismissed the thought. No, she wanted Luke to perform a job for her, just like any other hire. Anything more than that was impossible.

As if hearing her thoughts, he glanced over at her, their eyes meeting. Excusing himself from the townspeople, he returned to her side. "We'd best get you out of here. A mob isn't a pretty sight at any time. They seem calm enough now, but if the shooting starts again, who knows?" Luke picked up her bag and bird cage, and eased Amanda through the door.

Outside, he stopped short of the train platform. Shading his eyes against the sun, he noticed how damned vulnerable she looked, with those odd glasses and her tangled hair. She seemed lost in a world where she didn't belong, for all of her startling intelligence. Luke shrugged. It wasn't his business—and complications like Amanda, he didn't need.

"You should head to Wichita and hook up with a wagon train there. One that hasn't come this far north, and didn't hear about the ruckus. Don't ride off by yourself. Try to act like you belong with one of them." Luke's eyes ran over her odd dress, her owl, her bag bulging with books and notes. Amanda would draw attention no matter where she went.

She stared up at him, and he could almost hear her mind ticking. "Luke, I want to make you an offer. A proposition, to be more exact."

"A proposition." He couldn't help but smile. With any other woman, he would think she had more in mind than business. With Amanda, he knew better.

"I've been given a ranch, three hundred acres in all, in the richest part of cattle country. The land itself is worth a good deal, but the business opportunities are endless. I need your help."

"What kind of help?" Luke wasn't about to make it any easier for her.

Amanda blushed, hating to ask him for anything. Forcing aside her emotions, she continued, with a voice that was like ice. "I have no experience with a gun, as you know. I don't have the physical capability to fight these outlaws until I can discover why they want to kill me. I need someone who is good with a gun. Unafraid of outlaws. Someone without scruples, or morals, who can be bought for a price . . . "

"And you think I fit the bill."

"Yes." Amanda nodded. She'd gotten it out—the worst had to be over.

"How much?"

"I beg your pardon?"

"How much money are you willing to pay?"

"Twenty dollars."

Luke's eyes widened in disbelief. "Twenty dollars? To take on the Haskwells? Are you out of your mind?"

"Fifty?" Amanda interrupted. "Seventy?"

"A hundred," Luke said decisively. "If you want to hire me as a gun, you'll have to pay the going rate. Haskwell's worth three hundred. I assume you don't have a lot of loose cash. What else have you got?"

Frantic, Amanda's mind spun. "Only the ranch . . . "

"I'll take half." Before Amanda could do more than gasp, he continued ruthlessly. "That's it or nothing, lady. I'm taking you to Texas, down that goddamned cattle trail, through Indian country, with one of the worst western outlaws wanting a piece of your hide and you don't even know why. One hundred and half the ranch is my price, and that is provided you agree to the rest of my terms."

"Such as?" Amanda choked in anger. She had to have his help—he knew it, and was taking full advantage.

"I am the boss on this trip. You do as I say, no matter how many goddamned books you've read. I'm not going to argue over every decision. You got it?"

Amanda's mouth went dry. "But what if I know better?"

"I mean it. The first time you disobey me, I'm leaving. There's too much at stake here. And once we get to Texas, you go your way and I'll go mine, even though we share the same property. I want no strings." He tilted her face towards himself, looking behind her glasses to see if she really did understand his meaning. "And I think after last night, we'll both agree that it's best to keep our relationship strictly business."

Mortified, Amanda couldn't stop the hot rush of color that stained her cheeks a bright red. He was making sure that she didn't misconstrue his help, that he wanted nothing more than the terms he was offering. Embarrassed beyond words, Amanda wanted to hit him, to hurt him as much as he'd just hurt her. Instead, she gave him an icy nod.

"Certainly. 'Friendship is constant in all other things, Save in the office and affairs of love.' Shakespeare." She almost grinned in satisfaction as he snarled, then he stalked off toward the wagon train to make their arrangements.

She won, and he had agreed. But she wondered why she felt so much like crying.

"Blasted spinster!" Damien spat a wad of tobacco onto the ground and reined up his horse. Dust kicked up from the churning hooves on the plain, enveloping them in a cloud of red clay. "Thought I had her that time. Clean shot and everything. The woman must be blessed."

"Will you shut your mouth?" Butch stared down the lonely road to the cow town. No one had followed them; the noise had seen to that. Yet he knew that their boss would not be pleased with their failure to gun down the prissy authoress. Haskwell accepted excuses from no one. He wanted results, and settled for nothing less.

"We'll have to trail her. Christ, I'd hoped to have this thing done by now. We'll have to find out what she's doing, where she's going. You still got that barber friend in town, the one who cut my ear?"

"Yeah. He didn't take too kindly to your decorating his chair with lead," Damien said sullenly.

"Ain't that a shame. Tell him unless he wants me to come back and do the rest, we want to know where that girl's heading. And who she's going with."

"Right." Damien grinned, his sallow face wolfish. "Don't worry, Butch. She'll be on Boot Hill with the best of them."

"She'd better. Or I'd hate to be the one to tell Haskwell we've failed."

Damien's smile disappeared. He jerked on the reins, and started back toward town.

The Drovers Cottage hotel stood beside the railroad. Cowboys sat on the shaded veranda, whittling long chunks of cottonwood while watching the trains unload. Rows of single windows stared out into the street, echoing the vacant gazes of the cowhands below. Spruce green shutters framed the windows, offering the only touch of color on the beige clapboard hotel.

Amanda followed Luke inside, dragging her bird cage and carpetbag behind her, oblivious to the disbelieving stares that her appearance warranted. Inside, she could see past the register desk to the bar and restaurant, and what appeared to be a billiard room. A stout, matronly woman glanced up from behind the desk and gave Luke a broad smile.

"I'm Lou Gore. Can I help you with something?" The woman's face wrinkled with worry when her eyes fell upon Amanda. "Does your lady need assistance with those . . . things?"

"We're not in any hurry," Luke said smoothly, shooting Amanda a warning look. "We just need a room for the night."

"You're in luck, I've one left. Cattle train arrived yesterday, you know. Got the stockyards filled. There's two things you boys all want when you get to town." Lou beamed as she scribbled out the names. "You've got the one, and I'll help you with the other."

"Whatever do you mean?" Amanda put down the owl and scrutinized the hotel matron. "What are the two things?"

"Amanda." Luke's hand tightened on hers, then he sent Lou an apologetic smile. "It's been a long ride."

Amanda gasped in outrage, but the woman gave her a sympathetic glance and nodded.

"I know, it's hardest on the ladies. Hauled across country on some godforsaken trail, and for what? Gold, cattle or homesteading. Expecting too, some of them are." She smiled at Amanda, taking in her rumpled dress and stained sleeves. "I'll take good care of you, honey. A nice bath and bed, and you'll feel like a new woman in the morning."

"But I feel fine . . . " Amanda protested, earning another approving glance for her bravery.

"You two just come with me and I'll take care of everything." Ignoring her protests, the woman hefted Amanda's bag, then escorted them up the staircase to the long, narrow corridor lined with doors. Selecting room number twenty-one, Lou fitted a key into the lock and opened the door.

"There you are, bag and baggage. I'll send a girl up with a bath. The dining room's downstairs, with a place for male refreshments. And if you need anything else, you just holler."

Amanda waited until they were alone, then stared at Luke quizzically. "Why did you only get one room? Did she forget the key?"

"No," Luke said patiently. "She thought we . . . wanted a single room."

"Why?" Amanda asked innocently.

As a reply, Luke's eyes caught hers and he smiled, a warm, sensual grin that reminded her instantly of that horribly embarrassing incident that happened between them. Her eyes dropped and she heard his chuckle, hating him more than ever.

"I see you've caught on. Believe me, that is what most people would think. But don't worry, I have no intention of taking advantage of the situation. I want you in the same room, until I can find out what became of Haskwell's gang. We have no idea of where they are—they could even be holed up in this hotel. And until then, it will reduce the need for explanation." He waited until she nodded in reluctant agreement, still blushing hotly, then he continued. "I'll be across the street at the store. I'll get us some supplies, and tickets for the stage to Wichita. That'll give you plenty of time to do whatever you have to do and send for some supper. Think you can manage?"

"I can manage just fine," Amanda snapped. " 'For solitude is sometimes the best society.' Milton."

Luke's eyes blazed and he opened his mouth to reply. On second thought, he didn't trust himself. Picking up his hat, he stalked out of the room.

The road to Texas never seemed quite so long. Suddenly, he wondered if it was worth it.

Amanda stood alone in the center of the room, gazing at the sturdy oaken bedtable, the chest of drawers, and the bed which dominated the room. Aesop squawked, and she sighed, then removed the black felt cover and opened the cage door. The sleepy baby barn owl spilled into her hand like a soft ball of down. Amanda cuddled the owl to her breast, reassured by his muffled heartbeat and his sharp, clawed feet that scratched her palm.

"Aesop, we make a fine pair, we do." The owl ruffled his feathers, but settled comfortably against her dress, his eyes blinking sleepily. Amanda smiled, running her fingers along one disjointed wing. She remembered the day she'd rescued him just a few months ago—a small, battered fledgling hopping around on the ground with a broken wing. The biology professor's cat had stalked the tiny bird, and it was only by distracting the feline with her hair ribbon that Amanda managed to save the little owl. In spite of the titters of her classmates, she'd kept the little bird with her at all times, feeding him with an eyedropper when he was small, until he grew to the size where he accepted tiny field mice. It hadn't escaped her notice that Aesop lived much the way she did, nor that they had a lot in common. The loneliness she'd known all of her life overwhelmed her, and her throat tightened. Placing the slumbering bird back inside the cage, she softly shut the door.

Aesop would have to stay in his prison.

But tonight, she was escaping hers.

•　　•　　•

The bar down the street was exactly as she'd pictured. Gaslights gleamed from the ceiling, the light scarcely penetrating the smoke-filled interior of the Applejack saloon. Women dressed in bright shades of scarlet, gold, and sapphire, with black plumes in their hair and gay white boots on their feet, sat boldly on the laps of the cowboys. Amanda gaped as more than one woman giggled appreciatively as a randy cowboy slipped his hands inside her low cut dress, greedily caressing her ripe round breasts framed in black lace. Gamblers sat at the felt-covered tables, studying cards and the faces of the other players with a surprising intensity. Businessmen gathered in the corner, sipping whiskey and tucking important papers inside their eastern styled suits, while the barkeep struggled to keep their glasses filled and their spittoons empty. It was raunchy, dirty, sweaty, and smoky. It was also full of life, passion, risk, and excitement.

Amanda was mesmerized.

Taking a seat at one of the small round tables, she scrambled for her bag and retrieved a thick notebook. Her hand didn't seem to move fast enough as she scribbled her impression of everything. God, this was so great. Taking a deep breath, she recorded the musty, smoky scent of the room, the smell of sweat, the odor of cattle, the excitement that was almost tangible. She had written so many bar scenes just like this one, and to actually be in one was like walking inside one of her novels. The point broke on her pencil and she frowned in frustration. Amanda tossed it back inside the open carpetbag beside her and fished around for another. When her head popped up from beneath the table, she was surprised to see she was not alone.

"Excuse me, ma'am. But are you lost or something?"

Amanda glanced up, surprised to see the bartender staring at her oddly. She shook her head. "No, I'm in the saloon. I'm not lost in the least." She returned to her scribbling, ignoring him.

The barkeep scratched his head. "Ma'am, we're not accustomed to ladies coming in here, if you know what I mean. There's a restaurant next door, if you want something to drink."

"Oh, I'm not thirsty. And I'm very sorry, but you're wrong. There are ladies here." She gestured to a buxom blonde saloon girl, who giggled from a cowboy's lap.

The barkeep coughed, then continued delicately. "Ma'am, that's real generous of you, but they ain't ladies. You'd best leave. There could be trouble." He glanced at the nearby tables where the interested cowboys and businessmen listened to the exchange in amusement.

"What sort of trouble?" Amanda leaned on her elbows, fascinated with the prospect.

"Well, um. Men can't let loose and have fun with real ladies around. It puts a damper on things. And some of these cowboys haven't had a woman in a long time. They get pretty rough when they're full of whiskey. I'm sure you'll be much more comfortable next door."

"Thank you, you are so kind, but I am perfectly comfortable here," Amanda continued. "And I find your argument very faulty. With all the saloon women around, why would my presence incite a cowboy when there is a ready receptacle for his passion at hand? And I fail to see how my presence can have any effect on their activity, since I do not wish to prevent it, partake of it, or comment on it. I only wish to observe."

"Out!" The barkeep fought to keep his temper under control as the men nearby chuckled. "Madame, I must ask you to leave."

"I'll have to refuse," Amanda said bluntly. "This is a public place, and I wish to remain."

"Damn you!" The barkeep's eyes hardened, as if trying to decide whether to physically toss her out or to drag her across the floor. "Who's here with you? You got a husband or a brother?"

Before Amanda could respond, a cowhand interrupted. "She showed up in town this morning with a hired gun. Luke's his name, as I recall."

"Luke?" The cowhand spoke up. "There's a fellow

named Luke playing poker in the back. Big, with dark hair. Looks like a gun."

"Fetch him." The sheriff waited until the cowhand left, then leaned closer to Amanda. "Now you'd better come peaceably ma'am. This ain't no place for a lady . . . "

"I'm sorry, but I can't yet. I've not finished my work."

"This him?" The cowhand indicated a tall man behind him, and Amanda's eyes widened as Luke strode forth, looking anything but pleased to see her.

"It's me. I'll handle this. Amanda, come with me."

Amanda's smile vanished as Luke glared at her. He was angry. She could see the set of his jaw, the glittering tension in his eyes, and his gritted teeth. Shrugging, Amanda shook her head in calm rebuttal.

"As I've already explained, I see no reason why I cannot remain. I'm a writer. I need to see this, to experience life. As Emerson said—"

"Amanda." Luke cut her off before he killed her. He stared at her thoughtfully, while the cowboys and the barkeep waited to see this lean, dangerous man put the woman in her place. Amanda stared up at him innocently, completely unaware of the position she'd put him into. Her hair tumbled from its knot, her eyes were wide and unblinking like that damned owl, and a bird feather clung to her breast. There was something incredibly naive about her, like a child wanting desperately to overindulge in sweets, and who cannot understand why a parent forbids it.

Luke turned to the barkeep. "If I'm responsible for her, can she remain?"

The cowboys murmured in surprise, but no one protested. The bartender eyed Luke's gun, the worn grip just clearing his holster. His gaze went back to Amanda, who was smiling in excitement.

"I don't like it." The bartender wiped his nose with his sleeve. "A woman means nothing but trouble."

"Why that's the most ridiculous—"

"Amanda." Luke shot her a cold look that effectively silenced her, then continued. "As I said, I'll take responsibility. Anything happens, I'll handle it. Any objections?" He stared at the cowboys, who had already observed his gun and had drawn their own conclusions.

There were a few disgruntled mutterings, but no one openly challenged him.

The bartender shrugged. "All right then. But if there's any trouble . . . "

"She goes." Luke agreed.

The bartender shook his head and returned to the counter, while the cowboys resumed talking and drinking the full mugs of beer. Amanda's eyes lifted and she sent Luke a grateful smile which he promptly ignored.

"I'll deal with you later. Don't move from that spot. If you want to experience life, I'm the last one to stop you. I'll just give you one word of warning: 'Be careful of what you pray for. You may get it.' "

Puzzled, Amanda sank back in her chair. "Who said that?"

"Me." Luke slammed on his hat and went to the bar and ordered a whiskey.

Chapter

5

Amanda stared across the room at Luke's back. He was enveloped in a crowd of cowboys and trailhands, drinking his whiskey, effectively ignoring her existence. The men around him did likewise, refusing to allow her presence to interfere with their fun. Leafing through her notebook, Amanda's eyes kept returning to her handsome partner. He fit in perfectly, his dark, good looks accentuated by his rough attire and the bawdy atmosphere. He laughed at something a saloon girl said, and Amanda forced herself back to her book, amazed to feel a surge of annoyance. If he was trying to get a rise out of her, he was doing a damned good job.

Determined not to let Luke distract her, Amanda wrote furiously, absorbing herself in everything around her. Unobtrusively, she eavesdropped on nearby conversations. The cowboys, having successfully driven a herd of Longhorns to the stockyards, were flush with money and excitement. They enjoyed whatever benefits they could wring from their pay, while the town businessmen encouraged their presence.

Not so the ranchers.

Amanda glanced up as a trailman entered the saloon, wrapped his arm around the shoulders of a young, peach-fuzzed cowboy, and called for whiskey.

"Must have six hundred cattle out there," the trail driver said enthusiastically. "Bring us all a pretty penny. McCoy's paying fifteen dollars a head for a Longhorn. You'll be a rich boy, Jake, if you stick with me."

The youthful cowboy grinned, and downed the proffered whiskey. He choked on the contents, then spewed it out on the floor. The trailman guffawed, pounding his back helpfully while the other cowhands roared.

A rancher sitting quietly beside Amanda rose, his chair scraping ominously on the floor. His hat was not felt like the businessmen's, but was made of a cheap sacking material, and his sleeves were worn through, exposing work-toughened hands. His trousers were stained from prairie grass and rough clay, but it was his face that caught Amanda's attention. Creviced like a mountain pass and beaten from the weather, it was a face that told more about his life than any novel could attempt. He approached the trailman, and at once the laughter died.

"Fifteen dollars a head is good money," the ranchman agreed. "Except that you're killing our cattle. I've lost two more just this week."

A murmur went through the crowd as the Texans protested, and the local ranchers nodded in approval.

The trailman tossed back his whiskey and placed the shot glass aside. "There's no proof that the Longhorns are responsible for your cattle dying." He stared at the rancher, his eyes an open challenge.

"The fever started within a month of the first drive," the ranchman continued. "Spanish fever, they call it. Been raising cattle all my life. Never had trouble before. Same thing's been happening to other ranches. Herb Wessel lost three so far this season. Bob Rutherford, five."

"That's a pretty grim charge." A cowboy stood up, his hand brushing past his gun, the holster jutting forth. "You can't just blame the Longhorns. Anything could've started the trouble. Cattle die every day."

"Actually, there is proof," Amanda interjected, fascinated by the discussion and excited that she knew something on the subject. "A veterinarian in England has discovered that splenic fever, also called Spanish fever, is carried by a tick on the Texas Longhorn. His research is well documented."

The cowboys were silent, stunned by Amanda's little speech. Luke cursed softly, then got up from the bar, not at all surprised to see the ranchmen getting to their feet and the Texans fumbling for their guns.

"That so?" The trailman, feeling the tension, tried to avoid the coming battle. "Then why aren't the Longhorns killed?" He grinned, sensing a victory.

Amanda piped up confidently. "It's obvious, of course. The Texas cattle, having been exposed to the virus for decades, are now immune. What is an annoyance to a Longhorn is deadly to the domestic breed. Just read Professor Gamgee's treatise on the subject. It's fascinating—".

"Southern scum." A ranchman spat. "Go the hell back to Texas and take them filthy things with you."

Any pretense of civility shattered as the ranchman threw the first punch. Amanda's mouth dropped in shock as a cowboy fell across her table, scattering her notes. The gaslights shattered as guns blasted, and glass tinkled to the floor. The bargirls screamed, holding onto their plumed fans as if for protection, while the Texans fought back with obvious relish.

"Come on, dammit!" Luke grabbed Amanda, even as she bent down to scoop up her papers. She barely had time to snatch up her bag when Luke hauled her toward the door. Glancing back, Amanda gasped as another fusillade of fire shattered the whiskey bottles behind the bar, and the floor was doused with an amber rush of liquor.

"Jesus." Luke shoved her through the door as the cattlemen scooped up the whiskey with their hands, gulping down the liquor between punches. Fascinated, Amanda tried to sneak another glance, but Luke pushed her resolutely through the door and out to the dusty boardwalk.

"Where are we going?" Amanda struggled to break free, but Luke held tightly onto her wrist.

"Out of town. Thanks to you, we no longer have a place to stay. When word gets around as to what started that fight, we won't exactly be welcome. And I have no intention of paying for the damage."

Amanda grimaced. She hadn't thought of that. She hadn't thought of anything except her own interest in the conversation. Clutching her carpetbag, she suddenly realized that she was missing something.

"Wait!" Stopping in the middle of the street, she saw Luke glance back in disgust as she indicated the hotel. "Aesop! I can't leave without him!"

"Amanda! Forget that stupid owl!" Luke shouted, but she had turned and was heading toward the hotel. Gritting his teeth, he was momentarily tempted to let her go, to take the advantage and head out of town. But as she stood outside the hotel, gunfire blasted through the saloon window. Amanda gasped, then flattened herself against the wall as a cowboy tumbled out of the saloon doors.

"Let's go! Jesus . . . " Luke swore, then grabbed her hand and took the stairs two at a time. Amanda struggled to keep up with him while the noise below gave her an added incentive to try. Luke stopped at the door, gave it a swift kick, then reached inside and snatched up the bird cage.

"Here!" He thrust the owl at her, as if not trusting himself to carry the bird. Footsteps sounded below, and even over the noise from the bar, Amanda could make out the sheriff's voice.

"Great. Now how do we get out of here?" Luke shot her a sarcastic look.

Amanda thought for a moment. "Lou said they did laundry. I should think there would be a laundry chute, or some kind of entrance for the wash women to gain access to these rooms, other than the lobby below."

Luke shrugged. He had to admit the idea had merit—and anything was better than spending the night in the county jail. "All right, lady, you got us into this. Let's give it a try." Snatching up her carpetbag, he indicated the hall. "After you."

Encouraged, Amanda crept down the hallway, not at all surprised to see a narrow door at the end of the corridor. Pushing the panel open, she was even less amazed at the sight of a long wooden ramp that descended down into what looked like a basement. Taking a link of Aesop's cage between her fingers, Amanda fastened the owl's cage to her dress, using the rumpled sash tied around her waist as an anchor. She then took a seat at the top of the chute.

"See? There is nothing to it," Amanda said confidently, then gasped as she lost her balance and slid into the darkness below.

"Luukke!" Amanda screamed. Blackness enveloped her, and she hurtled down through the musty stillness, her bottom thumped on the wooden slates beneath her, her arms and legs banged by the force of the ride.

"Amanda!" Luke pushed on the back of the door, then followed, his large body shooting downward at even a faster rate than Amanda.

The laundry chute seemed to go on forever, down into a pitch black basement that Amanda could smell long before she landed in a pile of dirty laundry. Coughing on the mildewy odor, she stood up, amazed to find that no bones were broken and that her legs still worked. Dirty clothes and tablecloths clung to her, and as she wrestled with the laundry and the squawking owl, Luke tumbled down the chute and landed directly behind her.

"Luke! Are you all right?"

The look he gave her was murderous. Even in the dim light, she could see his expression and had enough sense to back up several feet.

"Oh, I'm just fine. Couldn't be better. You?" Luke responded.

Amanda sensed the sarcasm in his voice, but didn't know how to respond to it. "Well, I feel all right, nothing's broken. Aesop seems to be fine, too. I appreciate you asking—"

"Amanda," he snapped. "Find a damned light."

Uncertain of why he was so angry, she found a candle

on a table and lit the slender taper, throwing the room into a painful illumination.

"Great," Luke grumbled, throwing a stained tablecloth across the floor. Wading through the wash, he tried to find an exit, some kind of small entranceway for the maids, but found nothing. "What an idea! Lost in a goddamned wash bin. The next time you get a brainstorm, do us both a favor. Stop thinking."

"It wasn't my fault," Amanda said defensively. "You agreed. Besides, there has to be a way out of here. How else would the laundry women get in?" She kicked at the laundry, trying to clear a path. Light fell on the wall, revealing a door that was locked on the outside. Amanda tugged on the round metal ring that hung from the center, but it was firmly secured. Turning to Luke, she shrugged helplessly.

Without a word, he flipped open his holster and shot at the latch. Amanda dove for cover as the wood shattered and flew across the room. Aesop squawked and rustled in his cage as Luke kicked the door, rewarded by a glimmer of the night sky outside.

Amanda peeked out from beneath a pair of trousers. "Do you always go shooting your gun off like that? No doubt that will bring the sheriff, if nothing else." She brushed the soiled clothing off with an injured expression.

Luke shrugged. Used to responding with action, he hadn't given the consequences a thought. It was annoying sometimes, the way this woman was always right. "It got us out, didn't it?" he said defensively. "Get the damned owl and let's go. We've got to make time now, before the fight's over."

Amanda stepped through the clothes, and out into the star-studded night. Grimly, she stared at the open fields where the sky seemed to meet the land in one continuous line of crushed black velvet.

"Wichita is about eighty miles from here, isn't it?" Amanda asked.

Luke nodded.

"How are we going to get there?" She dreaded his response.

This time, he didn't even smile. "We walk."

Howard Fisher froze as he felt the sharp, keen edge of a razor pressed against his soft, round throat. It was long past business hours when he had come down from his comfortable home on top of his barber shop to clean up for the next day. He was proud of his establishment, with its sparkling clean windows, soft accomodating chairs, and rows of lime-scented lotion and cologne lining the counter. He had been in the process of sweeping the dark wads of hair from the floor when he'd heard the door softly close behind him.

"Shop's closed." Before he could even turn and acknowledge the stranger, his arm was wrenched behind his back and the cool metal blade touched his neck.

"Closed, is it?" the man chuckled, his sour breath hot against the barber's face. "I guess I'm in luck, then. I ain't looking for a shave or a haircut. I'm looking for you."

"Who . . . " The barber sputtered in fear as the man released him abruptly, then took a seat in one of the chairs.

"Remember me, hairdresser?" Damien grinned as the barber stared at him, recognition slowly dawning. "That's right, we were here last summer. My friend hasn't forgotten your haircut. His ear still bleeds every once in a while."

"What do you want?" Dread filled the barber's eyes as the blade twitched in the lamplight. He watched it in horrified fascination as Damien tested the sharp edge, drawing a bright bead of blood.

"Just thought since you did my friend such a disservice, you might be eager to help us out now. We're looking for someone."

Howard relaxed. So he hadn't come to kill him after all. A wavery smile came to his face and he nodded. "Who?"

"A man and a woman. He's a gun—Luke somebody, I hear. Good looking, big . . . a gun. Southern, they say." Damien shrugged, wiping the blood on his pants. "You

wouldn't forget the woman. Looks like a spinster, or a
school marm. Back's as straight as if a ramrod's been stuck
down it. Carries a carpetbag and a caged bird."

"I've seen them." Howard spoke quickly as Damien fingered the razor. "They came into town this morning. The
shooting started right after they arrived—seems someone's
gunning for the lady." The barber's eyes widened as he realized what he'd just said. "You?"

"Where they headed?"

"I don't know. I heard they tried to hook up with a wagon
train, but no one wanted to take them on. You riding with
Haskwell now?"

"You don't know where I can find them?" Damien ignored his question and continued ruthlessly.

"Try the hotel." The barber wet his mouth nervously.
"Maybe they plan to take the stage in the morning. There's
a ruckus at the saloon, so I don't think they'd be there.
They're in enough trouble without barroom fights. Going?"
The barber couldn't hide his relief as the outlaw started for
the door.

The outlaw turned slowly. "Sure. Say, you've been a real
help, friend. I'll tell old Butch you ain't as bad as we thought
you were. One thing's only fair, though. Since you made old
Butch bleed, I don't think he'd like it if I left you in one
piece." Damien grinned, his dark eyes empty and lifeless,
like an idiot's.

"But . . . " Howard gasped as the razor slashed across
his throat. Crashing into the counter, he was hardly aware
of the lotion spilling, cementing the hair to the floor in a
sticky wash of lime scented liquid. Warm blood flowed over
his white shirt, and the barber slowly sank to the floor as
the lime cologne dripped steadily from the counter.

Damien strode from the barbership with a grin. Butch
would love this one—and he couldn't wait to tell him.

Morning dawned as softly and smoothly as the opening
of a red rose. A thin flush of light sparkled the prairie grass,
then crept over the endless, undulating field like a sheer gold

covering on a green silk dress. Dew glittered like casually tossed diamonds, and the brilliant purple of the larkspur, the scathing pink of the geranium, and the bright yellow bloom of the sunflowers dotted the plain like well-chosen ornaments. The sky seemed to touch the land, blending at once with the softly waving grass, then continuing upward to dance with the clouds. It was beautiful, restless and wild, much like the horse Luke had been watching for the past half hour.

He had spotted the animal upon waking, amazed to see the sinewy dark creature gamboling through the open field as if at home in a grassy meadow. The horse was obviously young, not even three years if he could estimate, and was having a grand time rushing up to the small prairie dogs and frightening the tiny animals back into their burrows. Racing along the horizon, the horse embodied the freedom of the plains and the spirit of the open land.

Amanda woke, blinking at the sudden rush of sunlight and the sweet scent of the warm, waving grass. Aesop rustled in his cage, and with regret, she remembered she hadn't fed him last night. In their rush to put as much distance between themselves and Abilene, they had traveled through much of the night, stopping only when Amanda needed a rest. Luke wouldn't permit her more than a few minutes before he had her back on her feet, heading always south.

Yawning, she struggled to reach for the carpetbag, oblivious to everything else. Raising the cover on the bird cage, she winced as Aesop shot her an injured expression, then proceeded to turn his head around backwards in total rejection. Amanda sighed, then opened the tin which was punctured with small air holes and removed the best of the mice. There were only 3 left. They'd have to catch more mice soon, or perhaps a tiny lizard. Idly, Amanda wondered if Kansas had lizards. She opened the cage and offered Aesop the fat mouse.

The owl hooted, his head appearing suddenly as hunger overtook pride and he snapped at the rodent. Crunching and squawking, he rustled in his cage, letting Amanda know he wasn't too happy with her, even though he would eat.

"Will you shut that damned bird up?" Luke snapped.

Amanda glanced over at him, surprised at the vehemence in his tone. "But . . . "

The bird rustled and Luke gave her a disgusted look. "Can't you see it?"

"See what?" Amanda slid down to her belly, the way he was doing, and looked toward the horizon. "Oh, it's a horse. Isn't he pretty?"

Luke groaned, then turned to her, his expression filled with restrained patience. "Yes, it's a horse. And if we catch him, it means we don't walk for the next five days. Do you think you can keep that bird's beak shut until I try?"

"But how are you going to do that?" Amanda stared at him, her eyes wide and innocent, brimming with intelligence.

Luke shrugged. He'd been wrestling with the same thought since he'd awakened and had seen the horse galloping along the field. He hadn't time to bring supplies, any of the things he knew they'd normally need. When the barroom brawl broke out, he knew enough to run. He'd seen one lynching by a vigilante mob, and it was enough to convince him not to hang around when you're the unwelcome stranger in town.

"He's probably broken from a herd. He's too close to us to be completely wild. If only I had some sugar, a carrot or an apple—"

"Oh, I've got that." Amanda fished inside her carpetbag, and to Luke's disbelief, brought out a fat red apple.

"Where the hell—?"

"At the hotel last night. There was fruit on our table. I thought we might like it later."

Luke stared at her incredulously, then his eyes went to the bulging bag beside her. "You don't happen to have a rope in there, do you?"

"No, but I have this." Amanda unwrapped her sash, then

handed the frayed length of grey silk to the gunman. "I'd be pleased if you didn't tear it. It holds Aesop nicely."

Luke took the apple and the belt and got to his feet. There were times when eccentricity paid off.

And this looked like one of them.

Approaching the horse, Luke whickered softly, then held out the apple so that the animal could see the round fruit in all of its glorious seduction. It was a mare, and obviously very young and spirited. The horse hesitated, then threw back her polished black head and raced playfully around Luke, stopping just at the edge of the field. Talking softly, Luke continued to approach the animal, making no sudden moves, nothing that would scare the creature.

"Come on now, girl. I won't hurt you. It's just an apple. I'm sure you're hungry."

The horse watched him walk closer, and to Luke's relief, displayed no signs of agitation. The animal's eyes were quiet, her ears up, her steps playful rather than frightened.

Luke knew all about horses. On his plantation in South Carolina, they were a way of life. He was riding Tennessee Walkers before he could talk, his father believing that fear came with age—and in a way, he was right. Luke learned to raise the gentle, domestic breed, to ride and jump fences, and to race them over the long dirt roads that led to the next homestead.

This one, a mustang, he thought, was obviously well bred and worth money. As the horse skittered past once more, Luke saw the imprint of a brand on the animal's flank, and the remnants of a halter around her beautiful head. Shrugging, he approached slowly, holding the sash loosely in one hand, the apple in the other. It wouldn't be the first time he'd had to borrow something without asking.

Amanda stared as Luke stood in the center of the field, watching the horse with an intensity she could feel, gauging his movements and reacting accordingly. Dressed in his rough buckskins and white shirt, his dark hair glinting blue-black in the sunlight, he looked a part of the scene, as wild and as rough as the animal he sought to outwit. There was something virile about the way he stood his ground, the confidence yet lack of arrogance in his manner, and the challenge of man against a liberated beast that was immensely compelling. Amanda's stomach tightened and she rose slowly, unable to take her eyes from him.

The animal neighed softly, then stopped, apparently tired of the game. Luke smiled, then held out the apple and stood absolutely still, letting the horse approach on its own time. He was rewarded for his patience when, after a few moments of hesitation, the horse stepped closer, then reached for the apple and allowed Luke to stroke the silken flesh of her neck and shoulders.

"There, girl. You're a nice horse, aren't you?" Slipping the sash around the horse's head, he tightened the loop to the old halter, then led the animal forward.

The horse's acceptance of the situation indicated even more strongly that she was not only part of a herd, but probably someone's riding mount. They'd have to be cautious when they approached town. It wasn't uncommon to be hung for a lesser infraction, excluding such damning evidence as this, but Luke didn't care. Taking chances had become a way of life for him.

"You've got him, he's beautiful! He's so . . . big." Amanda's throat went dry as Luke led the horse closer. To Amanda, horses were something that pulled carriages in the streets of Boston. She'd seen the huge animals in their stables at school, and had even offered one a carrot when the stableboy, taking pity on the odd bookworm who had no friends, allowed her the privilege. But that was the extent of her firsthand knowledge.

"Of course she's big. And she'll get us to Wichita in two days instead of four or five. Won't you girl?" Luke ran a fond hand down the neck of the handsome mare, completely comfortable with the large animal.

Amanda stared at him doubtfully. She hadn't thought of this while watching Luke capture the horse, so entranced was she with the scene. Luke slid onto the horse's back with an effortless ease that intimidated her even more. Reaching

for Aesop's cage and her bag, she clutched her baggage
tightly and gazed at the hand Luke offered.

"No," she said obstinately. Amanda saw his mouth drop,
but she ignored him, and took a seat on the ground. She
wasn't going anywhere near that horse, whether Luke liked
it or not.

Chapter

6

"What do you mean, no?" Luke thought she was joking, but when he looked at her, he saw something he hadn't seen in all the time he'd known her. Her sea-colored eyes were filled with fear.

"I just can't." Amanda shrugged, refusing to elaborate.

Luke stared at her thoughtfully, fighting the desire to physically haul her onto the horse and be done with it. But something about the way her shoulders trembled, betraying her fear, and the way she stared at the horizon as if afraid to meet his eyes, gentled his resolve.

"Amanda, there's nothing to be afraid of. The horse won't hurt you. I'll hold onto you; you won't fall."

He talked to her in the same, soft tones he'd used to trap the horse, the same tones he'd used the night he'd seduced her. That thought made Amanda more obstinate, and she shook her head, drawing her baggage more closely around her as if for support.

"You go on ahead. I'll find some way to get to Texas. As Hugo said, 'Danger for danger's sake is senseless'."

"Amanda," Luke snapped, all pretense of patience gone. "Get up on the goddamned horse."

Amanda looked up at him, wincing at the blaze of anger

that shone in his stark, blue eyes. Mentally, she weighed her alternatives. If he rode off and left her, she could go back to Abilene. The thought of what she'd face there was worse. Her only other option was to walk alone to Wichita. Luke said it would take five days, five days alone in an endless prairie, with nothing but wild animals, renegades, cowboys and Indians . . .

She rose to her feet, hating everything about this man, his supreme confidence, the easy acceptance he had of the situation. She saw him relax slightly, as if he'd been toying with his own options. Extending a hand, he indicated the bags.

"Hand me that stuff first."

Amanda obliged, watching as he threaded the carpetbag through his gunbelt, then tied Aesop's cage to the sash. Before Amanda could protest, he swung her up, onto the horse's back and astride between his legs. Gasping, she struggled as her skirts billowed up, exposing her legs and a generous portion of her thighs to his amused gaze.

"You . . . swine!" She fought with the voluminous material, embarrassed to the core, uncomfortable in this unladylike position. She could feel his body shake with laughter as he helpfully tugged at the dress, assisting her as she tried to pull it down to a more modest degree.

"Come on, Amanda. Swine? With all your education, you can think of something better than that."

She would have loved to hit him, but he untied the cage and thrust it into her hands. Wrapping the silk cord around his wrist, his other arm tightened about her waist, just below her breasts. Amanda squirmed, a hot flush coming to her face, but Luke only restrained her more firmly.

"If you don't stop wiggling, we'll both fall off. It's just a horse, for God's sake."

Amanda squeezed her eyes tightly shut as the horse snapped at her ankle, anxious from the odd motion the mare felt on her back. Freezing, Amanda ignored Luke's light laughter as he kicked the animal's flank, urging her on. The horse, still playful and full of energy, cantered across the plain while Amanda screamed. Thankfully, the wind took her cries and she opened her eyes just once, to see the grass rushing by. They seemed to be outracing the clouds.

Clutching onto Luke's arm, Amanda shut her eyes tightly. She had wanted to experience life, but this time, she got more than she bargained for.

"Damn you, Damien! What the hell do you mean they're gone?" Butch spat on the ground, then wiped the traces of wet tobacco from his cheek. His scar curled in disgust as his partner shrugged, seemingly unconcerned.

"They can't last long, Butch. The woman caused a ruckus in town last night. She started a brawl, taking the side of the ranchmen over the Texans. Ain't that rich? The boys nearly busted up the bar. Sheriff's looking for 'em, the barkeep . . . in fact, the whole damned town's looking for 'em. They disappeared."

"They can't just disappear," Butch said, though he rubbed his chin thoughtfully. "They're not at the hotel?"

"No, and that's the funny thing. Their stuff's cleared out, so they must 'ave gone back. But no one saw them leave."

"Huh," Butch grumbled. "They probably sneaked out during the fight. Only place they could be is the trail. And they didn't have no horse, no nothing?"

"Not that I can make out." Damien grinned. "I went down to the saloon after meeting with old Howard Fisher. Finished up your work, Butch. Had the man pissing his pants. He told me what I wanted to know. I left him bleeding all over his fancy barber bottles."

"Teach him for cutting me."

"Right. Anyway, by the time I got to the saloon, the girl was gone. No one's spoken up about a horse thief, so I 'spec they're walking to Wichita. Never make it on foot, no food, no water. They're as good as dead."

Butch scratched his head thoughtfully. "I don't know about you, but I ain't too eager to ride that damned trail. Maybe this is good enough for Haskwell."

"Right." Damien agreed. "After all, does he gotta see

their damned bones? If the trail don't get 'em, the sheriff will. Either way, Fess Tyson is a dead woman. And her gun is too."

Riding a horse was not only damned uncomfortable, it was actually painful. Amanda suffered for the first hour or so, fidgeting and squirming—each time the mare reached back and snapped at her bare legs. Luke tightened his grip on her, until finally she was sitting right up against his thighs, his arm just below her breasts, practically cutting off her breath. She was about to protest, but she heard his voice right next to her ear.

"If you keep that up, we're falling off. And if we lose the horse so help me . . . "

She didn't want to hear any more and, thank God, the wind took his voice away and she got her wish. Squeezing her eyes shut, she tried to ignore the prairie grass that was whizzing by at a ridiculous speed, the spirited tension of the unpredictable animal beneath her, and the humiliation of sitting with her legs spread in Luke Parker's lap. Worse, the combination of the heat from the sun and the scent of the man behind her, the muscular feel of his body touching hers, and the embarrassing sensation of her bottom bouncing against him reminded her of things she fought not to think about. That night with him in the Harvey House. How it felt to have him kiss her, touch her, love her . . .

I want no strings, she thought.

Amanda couldn't help the rush of pain. God, she wished she could forget all that. And now she was alone with him, on the way to Wichita. On the way to Texas.

Stop it, she told herself. It was a mistake, it was over and done with. Still, as she squirmed in his lap, trying in vain to pry her body away from his, she was overwhelmingly relieved when the noonday sun was high and he slowed the horse.

"There's a stream up ahead. Figure we can water the horse and you can tend to whatever," Luke said.

Amanda blushed to the roots of her hair, but she was

grateful beyond words. She had needed to make a stop for the last hour, but didn't have the faintest idea of how to bring that up with a man, especially a man like Luke. When the horse stopped before a stream, she nearly tumbled off the animal in an effort to be free of them both.

"Easy there," Luke chuckled, then stopped when he saw the murderous look she threw him. "What's the matter now?"

"Where am I supposed to . . . " Helplessly, she indicated the wide open prairie, with little more cover than the shrubs growing along the stream bank.

"Oh, that's right. You've never been on a trail, have you?" Swinging down from the mustang, he tied the sash to a young cottonwood, then dug a hole in the ground with his boot. "That's it."

Amanda stared at him in astonishment. "I couldn't possibly . . . "

"What do you think you do? There aren't any damned chamberpots out here."

"You don't have to swear."

"Amanda." Luke tried to be patient as she ignored him and scooped up the water to offer Aesop a drink, refusing to look at him. "I'm going to walk away now. When I come back, you'd best be ready because I'm riding. Get it?"

"I get it," she snapped, furious with his cavalier attitude. Waiting until he was well out of earshot, she did as he suggested, wishing that she was back in school, at home in her boardinghouse, anywhere but here. She had more than a few unkindly thoughts about her editor, and for the first time, wondered if it was all worth it. Finishing with a splash of cool water and an icy drink, she glanced toward the horizon.

It couldn't be, but it was.

The small cloud of dust grew larger as the group of riders approached, and Amanda screamed, running toward the clump of brush where Luke stood with his back to her. She had no idea of what he was doing, but he looked anything but pleased to see her when she ran up behind him.

"Luke! Someone's coming! You don't think—"

"Jesus Christ," Luke swore, then gestured toward the horse. "Go untie her, dammit! Of all the luck . . . " He kicked furiously at the ground, still refusing to turn around. "Now!"

Amanda ran toward the mare, her fingers shaking as she fought with the sash, trying to undo Luke's knot. He joined her a moment later, just as she freed the horse. He grabbed the sash, commanded the animal to lie down, then gestured toward Amanda.

"Get that damned bird and take cover behind those shrubs. Don't come out no matter what. Damn, I can't believe they followed us out here."

Amanda's mouth went dry, and she scurried to do as she was told. Taking refuge just beyond the stream, she saw Luke snatch up his gun, using the mustang as a shield. The dust cloud grew larger, then the first shots rang out, the sound softer out here in the open air, but somehow more deadly.

"Luke—" Amanda cried out, hating the helpless feeling of watching as the men approached, their guns firing.

"Stay the hell down and shut up!" Luke snapped.

Amanda didn't even think to get insulted. Gunfire ruffled the grass beside her and she flattened down, terrified. Luke rose just a fraction of an inch, aimed his gun at the first rider, then fired. At once the man tumbled to the earth, his body rolling while his mount came to a halt just a few feet away. The two others reined up their horses and found themselves staring down at the heavy Colt .44, and the deadly eyes of the man who held it.

"Go ahead and fire," Luke said softly. "I guarantee I'll take one of you with me. Whether it's you," he indicated the gangly deputy, "or you," he gestured to his bewhiskered companion. "One of you will not wake up tomorrow. Now, who wants to die?"

No one spoke for a moment, and all eyes fell to the ground. Luke's boot was planted firmly on the sheriff's chest. A small trickle of blood issued down the lawman's sleeve, from a wound that looked more painful than dangerous. The two men exchanged glances, then the sheriff spoke in a resigned voice.

"Drop 'em, boys. Ain't worth a killing, just to fix Jack Haley's mirrors. That bar's been needing work, anyway."

The deputies tossed their weapons to the ground, the older man first, then the younger. Luke glanced back at Amanda, his gun still trained on the two men.

"Grab their guns and stay down."

Frightened more than a spooked doe, Amanda crawled forth and did as he said, her hands shaking as they touched the hot metal of the Colts. She scooped them up into her skirt, then scuttled back to the brush, aware of the men's eyes on her as they glanced from her to the gunman.

"Now you boys take off on those horses and don't look back. I'll just keep your boss here with me for a spell, to make sure you aren't tempted."

The two men started to object, but the sheriff, responsible for their lives, indicated that they should ride. Reluctantly, the two men tugged on their reins, then slowly started back toward Abilene. Luke waited until they were gone from sight before he removed his boot and helped the sheriff to his feet.

"You lettin' me go?" The sheriff rubbed his wrist, massaging the flesh wound, half-expecting a bullet as a reply.

Luke shrugged. "I'm not going to kill you. But I'm keeping your horse."

"What?" The sheriff's head snapped up and he stared at Luke, realizing that he was lucky to be alive, but unwilling to part with his mount.

Luke gestured to the horizon. "If I know your boys, they'll come gunning back here, hell for leather, once you're with them. I can't risk that. Now, it's well past noon, and Abilene is more than a stone's throw. I suggest you start walking."

The lawman scooped up his hat, glanced at the horse, then turned back to the trail. He was beaten, and he knew it. Luke waited until the sheriff had walked far enough away

that he was beginning to fade from sight before he turned
back to Amanda.

"All right, let's get out of here. They'll be after us in less
than an hour, I'd say."

"But—"

"Hold onto the horse while I get the other. We don't have
time to discuss this in committee."

"I'm not a committee!" Amanda protested, snatching up
the sash and gripping the slender silk cord in both hands.
Luke rode up a few minutes later, accepted Aesop, then attached the metal cage to the leather reins of his new mount.
He slid down, and helped Amanda onto the sheriff's horse
before taking the mustang bareback.

"Let's get going. I have no desire to be hung as a horse
thief, do you?"

Amanda had nothing to say to that, especially when she
noticed a tiny cloud way off in the distance once more.
Whether it was the men returning or reinforcements, she
didn't bother to calculate.

Sometimes, it just wasn't worth it.

Nightfall came to the prairie in a blazing splash of color.
Amanda had seen sunsets before, but when she gazed at the
western sky, washed with crimson, scarlet, flaming trails of
fuchsia, deep purple, and magenta, she felt utterly awed and
humble. Without the obstruction of houses and trees, the
sky seemed to reach right down to the earth, to wrap her
in its hot seductive embrace, to include her in one final moment of glory before the curtain of darkness descended.

They had been riding hard all day, and although sitting
on top of her own mount with a real saddle and bridle was
an improvement, Amanda decided she would never love
horses. She'd fallen several times, and her muscles refused
to relax or adjust to the strain of riding. The sheriff's mount
had none of the exuberance of the spirited creature they'd
found on the plains, and was a little easier to manage. Surprisingly, she discovered that there was one aspect of sharing a horse with Luke that she missed. She had enjoyed him

holding her, the security she felt in his arms, for all of the other embarrassing aspects. Briskly, she reminded herself that she wasn't supposed to feel any of that, yet as she stared at the back of the man before her, she couldn't help thinking it.

Amanda would have been surprised to learn that Luke was having much the same problem. For all Amanda's fussing and fidgeting earlier, he missed having her that close to him. Reminding himself that such thoughts were not only foolish but dangerous, he forced himself to concentrate on the situation at hand and to find some sort of cover to pass the night. They seemed to have lost the sheriff's men, but Luke knew better than that. Come morning, the Abilene lawmen would be hot on their trail again, and a good night's rest would only increase their odds of escape.

They were approaching the outskirts of Newton. Luke could see a tiny shimmer of light in the distance, and the dark silhouette of the cattle town's small hotel and bank illuminated by the moon and starlight. Slowing up the mustang, he gestured to Amanda.

"Let's set up camp here. There's some cover by that clump of trees, and fresh water near that stream bed."

Amanda glanced in confusion at the building in the far distance. "But that looks like a town—"

"The last thing we need is to show up in Newton tonight. It's too close. We're on the run, remember? Hotels have register desks, and people who can report to the sheriff."

Amanda flushed, aware of the sarcasm in his voice. Following his lead, she dismounted. Every muscle in her body screamed in pain.

Luke lit a small fire of brush from his tinderbox. "Look for dry wood, buffalo chips . . . what's the matter?" Luke didn't miss the scorching glance she sent him, nor the sparkling mist that clouded her blue-green eyes. He could almost feel her discomfort as she hobbled across the field to tether her horse next to his, beside the bank where fresh green grass and ample water was available. Painfully, she lowered herself to the grass, but that didn't help much either. The part of her that hurt the most came into abrupt contact with the ground, and she squealed in agony as she came quickly back to her feet.

And he looked like he wanted to laugh. Amanda had never wanted to hurt anybody before in her life, not even the children who had laughed at her growing up. Yet, she wanted to kill this cowboy who stood before her, looking so damned handsome and appealing, with that smug look on his face. Furious, she lunged at him, unable to stop herself from striking him. Bruised arms came into contact with his own strong ones as Luke forcibly held her wrists in a tight grip.

"What the hell—" Luke started.

"Go ahead and laugh at me! Just because I don't know anything about your stupid horses, or your dirty old trails, or that we have to hide from sheriffs, you, you . . . wretched old gunslinger!" Amanda kicked him, gratified to see his expression change from amusement to chagrin.

Chapter

7

Luke's features gentled as she fought with him, losing all appearance of a straightlaced bookworm. Her hair, never properly restrained to begin with, fell around her face like the untamed mane of a wild horse. She hadn't worn her glasses since they'd taken the trail, and the sun had tanned her face, highlighting her cheekbones and making her eyes look incredibly bright. In that second, she reminded him of his little sister, who'd never had any of Amanda's difficulties, and who was as open and free with her emotions as Amanda was closed.

"Stop it, come on, calm down. You'll only make it worse." Somehow, he was comforting her, holding her in his arms, stifling her movements with his body.

Amanda sobbed like a little girl. She was hot, tired, dirty, and disgusted. Everything hurt, from her hair down to her feet, which were rubbed raw from walking and riding. Her corset dug into her, her muscles screamed, and her legs stung from the brush and the nips of the mustang. Worse, she had let down her guard in front of this man, this southern gunman who'd let her know every step of the way that he could barely tolerate her.

And now he was holding her, caressing her back in the

way one comforted a child, his hand rubbing the tense muscles in her neck as no one had ever done for her before. She
couldn't stop crying, even though she realized in the logical
part of her mind that it was ridiculous. Mortified, she cried
harder, no longer fighting him, letting all of her pent up feelings spill forth.

"It's all right, Amanda, don't cry. You did just fine, it
will be all right."

She could hardly hear him, but his voice sounded good,
quiet, and reassuring. He smelled good, too, like horses,
sweat, and leather, a scent that was foreign to her but intriguing at the same time. Gradually, her sobs died to hic-
coughs, and only then did he release her, his one hand still
holding her back while the other fished in his pocket and
pulled out a calico handkerchief.

"Blow." He held the rag to her nose and Amanda obeyed,
no longer capable of resistance. Looking up at him through
star-spiked lashes, she wiped away the tears that glistened
from her cheeks.

"I'm sorry. I didn't mean that. I feel so foolish," she murmured.

"Why?" The expression in his eyes was kind, without a
hint of condescension.

"I . . . I got your shirt all wet." Forlornly, Amanda stared
at the once-white shirt, clearly able to discern damp streaks
amid the grey dust that clung to him.

Luke laughed, a sound so infectious she was forced to
smile. "I don't mind. That's the first hot water to hit my
body in days."

Amanda smiled, then looked down, puzzled by the
warmth in his eyes, those incredible orbs of deep blue that
could take her breath away. His hand reached up to her face
and tipped her chin toward him, making her look at him
once more. The shadows danced from the fire as the night
deepened around them, but they didn't diminish the intensity of those eyes, and when he bent down to kiss her, she
couldn't stop that either.

He teased her at first, gently brushing her lips with his

own, then darting his tongue between her teeth and with-drawing just when she wanted him to proceed. Forgetting everything else, she leaned closer, pulling him to her, want-ing to feel his hard body next to hers—wanting him. He seemed to be holding back, but when she leaned into him like that, she felt his shudder and heard his hoarse whisper.

"My God, Amanda, we shouldn't be doing this."

The kiss deepened, and his tongue took possession of the hot sweetness of her mouth, in direct contrast to what he was saying. Amanda pressed closer, amazed at the flow of feelings that set her body on fire. He had yet to touch her, but she was beginning to crave his hands on her body. Some-how, with the way his mouth took hers, and his tongue teased her, penetrating and withdrawing, he was making her desire him with a passion she didn't know she possessed.

She made a soft noise in the back of her throat and he leaned down, pressing feverish kisses along her neck. His hands caressed her, soothing the aching muscles, making her as weak as spooned jelly. His hips pressed against hers, and Amanda became aware of the hardness of him, of a jut-ting male part of him that seemed to be seeking entrance to the softness of her that was on fire for him. Amanda un-abashedly gripped him closer, loving the feel of it all, becom-ing dizzy with sensation and need.

"Do you like that?" His hand traced down from her throat to cup her breast, his thumb brushing the erect nip-ple, making her squirm against him. Amanda nodded, then her eyes closed as he bared a breast and began to knead it with his fingers.

Hot excitement surged through her, excitment so intense that she didn't bother to hide it even if she could have. He fumbled with the buttons of her dress and she helped him, wanting more of the feelings he was artfully arousing in her. Hot blood surged to meet him as he stripped the dress and underclothes to her waist, then cupped both breasts in his rough hands.

The sandpaper quality of his fingers aroused her, as did the mind-numbing kiss he gave her at the same time.

Amanda sighed, reaching for him, letting her hands explore him the same way he explored her. She touched him innocently inside his shirt, gasping at the firm hard muscles beneath, then her hand slid lower, to where his chest hair traced down. She had scarcely reached his belly when he grabbed her hand roughly, his grip almost painful.

"We've got to stop this," he panted, though his eyes burned a hot blue, like the flame of a candle. "If we don't stop now I won't be able to."

Amanda wanted to object, but he forced himself away from her and retrieved a flask from the saddlebag. He took a long drink, then he glanced back toward her. When he saw her standing beneath the cottonwoods, her dress around her waist, her body exposed to his gaze, he shuddered in suppressed desire and annoyance at himself.

"Get dressed," he said harshly, then gentled his voice. "I'll heat some cloths for your legs. It will help the pain."

Mortified, Amanda slid the dress and chemise back over her arms and buttoned it with shaking hands. He didn't want her. The first time between them had been so horrible that he didn't want to go any further. She sank down to the grass, unaware that night had stolen over the land, or that Luke was building up the fire. Pain overwhelmed her, emotional pain, and when he approached her with his shirt soaked in hot water, she nearly threw it at him.

"I can take care of myself," she reminded him. "As Homer says—"

"Amanda." Luke cut her off, still fighting the desire that surged through him. "Put this on your legs. We have to ride tomorrow, and you won't get very far in the condition you're in." *And I won't get anywhere in the condition I'm in,* he amended to himself.

She snatched at the shirt, turning so he couldn't see her tear-streaked face, revealing to him what the darkness would have hidden. Night sounds, katydids, and the rustling of nocturnal animals mingled with the crackling from the fire. Amanda put the cloth on her legs, feeling the warmth soak through to her battered skin, then she curled up in the grass, her stomach lurching, her throat tight.

What in God's name was happening to her? Amanda didn't understand any of this. She didn't know why her body wanted him, nor why her emotions made her feel wretched inside. For the first time since they'd set out, she regretted her decision to have him accompany her. She'd made a bargain with a man she hardly knew, set off with him on a journey where there was no one to advise or protect her. She was at his mercy, yet that wasn't what frightened her.

It was herself. Amanda Edison had always been in control. Her brilliant mind had done that for her; made her able to take any situation in hand and triumph. And now this man barely had to kiss her and she was like any other simpering schoolgirl, as weak in the knees as in the mind.

She should be glad he'd stopped. It was the agreement they'd made, yet as she watched him drink his whiskey, she wanted to hurt him the way she was hurting. Luke Parker was definitely a distraction.

And one she couldn't wait to do without.

Luke waited until he was sure she was asleep, then he softly covered her and returned to his bedroll. That same refuge eluded him, however, and when he was tired of trying, he sat up and helped himself to more of the whiskey-laced coffee and a rolled cigarette. Drawing on the carefully wrapped cylinder of tobacco, he leaned against a small boulder and contemplated the sleeping woman beside him.

God, how he wanted her. He could still feel the powerful urge to take her in his arms, to hold her, kiss her, and love her as he'd tried to once before. Yet, it was impossible. More than impossible, it was downright dangerous.

Enveloped in darkness, Luke opened his jacket, reached inside his shirt and withdrew a tiny silver locket embossed with gold leaf. The raised filigreed heart outside was worn completely smooth, and the gold decoration now blended perfectly with the silver, metal melting into metal. Snapping the tiny clasp, he held the open locket toward the fire and gazed at the faces of the two women inside.

His mother and sister. Luke studied the faces, so alike except for the passage of time. Lillian, his mother, possessed the high cheekbones, delicate nose, and soft blue eyes that betrayed her French ancestry. It was a proud face, showing little of the hardship she'd borne, raising two children alone after her husband died of tuberculosis. Thankfully, John Parker had left a plantation that was self sustaining, so while the family didn't advance financially, they were able to maintain the gracious lifestyle he'd created for them.

Luke's eyes sought out the younger woman's and even now, after all this time, the pain assaulted him. Suzette was fourteen when he'd last seen her, fourteen and full of life. No raving beauty, the features that were so refined on her mother were devilish on her, and the grin which she flashed so often was full of mischief. Coddled but not spoiled, she was sure of herself and she enjoyed every precious minute of her life. She had a wonderful future ahead of her, as the only daughter of one of the most respected families in Charleston. Yet, now she was gone, murdered along with her mother by a band of renegades during the war, her lively body hushed by the only real enemy she'd ever known—death.

Luke blinked as the pain rose up inside of him. God, it was so unfair. When he'd heard about the tragedy, he left the fourteenth division of the Confederate Army, and was branded a deserter. But he had to get home, to see for himself, for surely it was all a horrible mistake and Suzette would come running down the ivy-covered lane giggling and out of breath, and she would fold him in her arms and take him to the house where his mother waited. And there was nothing. The house had been burned, and behind the blackened foundation lay two hastily dug graves. The horses, the lovely furnishings . . . everything was gone.

Softly closing the locket, Luke let the metal warm in his hand as if he could somehow bring the two people inside back to life. He couldn't, he knew that. But he was determined to achieve a few things. He'd had it all once, and he would get it back, no matter what it took. He'd regain the lifestyle his father had attained, and this time he'd never leave. He'd protect what was his, with his life, if necessary. He'd become respected once more, live where the name Parker meant something other than deserter.

And he'd get his revenge. Anger welled up within him as he was told, over and over again, the name of the cutthroat who'd cost him so much.

Haskwell.

He'd been tracking the gang for months, finding them always one step ahead, hearing of their horrible deeds in every town they'd entered. They left men dying in their wake, providing an easy way to track them. By the time he'd reached Kansas, Haskwell was the most hated name in the West.

Luke glanced toward Amanda, who tossed and turned on the prairie grass, her dreams troubled. Somehow, this bright and eccentric young author had attracted the attention of Haskwell. For that reason, among others, he had to avoid complications. Since he'd discovered the truth, that the gang was gunning for Amanda, he was more than determined to avoid intimacy with her at any cost. Emotions made one vulnerable, and if he admitted the truth, he felt guilty about the way he was using her, even if it was necessary. Amanda was like a magnet, drawing the outlaws wherever she went. He wouldn't need to track them now, not with her at his side. Sooner or later, Sam Haskwell would reveal himself.

And Luke would be waiting.

Later that night, Amanda woke, and pulling out her journal, quickly recorded her thoughts.

It is late, and the earth is asleep. Even the stars seem dimmer, as if aware of the coming of dawn and the inevitable extinquishment of their tiny lights. The night sounds, katydids and crickets, the rustlings of raccoons and field mice, have long since died, leaving a silence that seems thunderous in my ears.

I can hear Luke's gentle breathing, and the occasional movement of his body in slumber. I can't see him, for the fire has become nothing more than a greyish ash, a dismal memory of its former brilliance. I like having him nearby. Isn't that strange? A few weeks ago, I wouldn't have known him from any of the hundreds of strangers I might pass in the street. Tonight, he is a comfort to me in this wilderness.

I can't stop thinking about when he held me, and I felt wonderfully alive. He seemed to want me, but then he pulled away. I know he regrets that first intimacy between us, but something inside of me broke when he left me standing alone, my arms empty of his warmth. It must have been the whiskey. But for that, he would not have kissed me, and I would not have felt this wretched pain. I must dispose of it before it happens again, for I fear the result should he touch me like that once more.

Chapter

8

She was reading when Luke awoke. He glanced across the smoldering campfire, almost half-expecting to see that she'd gone. Instead, she sat fully dressed beneath the one shade tree their camp had to offer, a notebook spread across her lap and a thick volume in her left hand. She read quickly, turning pages with her thumb, pausing occasionally to mark something in her notes. There was an intensity about her that was fascinating to watch, even as her cold aloofness irritated him. Rising to his feet, Luke stretched, trying to gain her attention.

Nothing. She barely glanced up, then her eyes dropped back to her book and she was once more immersed in the words of some poet or philosopher. Luke found himself growing angry. Her coolness only increased his guilt, and made him overwhelmingly aware of the way he'd treated her.

"Good morning," he said, clearing his throat.

"Hello."

She dipped down into the book again, answering him only absently, as a clerk would when engaged with a column of figures.

"Any coffee left?"

Amanda shrugged. "I suppose there's some in the pot. That is, if you didn't use it all up last night."

There was no sarcasm in her voice, but Luke knew what she meant. Snatching up the coffeepot, he poured out a cup of the thick, black brew, then glanced around for the whiskey.

The canteen lay just a few feet away. Lifting the metal container, he immediately noticed it was lighter. Damn. He hadn't realized he'd drunk so much. And today, he could tell he would need a whiskey, just to deal with Amanda.

Luke opened the lid and turned the container over. A single drop spilled out. Shaking it, he stared as another drop sprinkled his coffee, but that was it. The canteen was empty.

"What the hell happened to the whiskey?" he bellowed at Amanda. He had drunk a lot, but not that much.

She looked up, her expression as serene as if she was attending a morning tea. "I dumped it out."

"You what?"

"You heard me." She continued in that same, dry, intellectual voice. "I decided that your ill-mannered behavior last night had to be due to some outside influence, particularly since you had made it abundantly clear that our relationship was to be strictly business. You violated the terms last night. My only recourse was to eliminate the source of the problem, if we are to complete this trip successfully." She indicated the sodden ground beside her.

Luke froze, unable to decide if he should kill her now or later. "Amanda—"

"I think we should be riding." She placed her books neatly inside her carpetbag, then stood up and faced him. "The sheriff will no doubt catch up to us if we wait much longer. Is there something else you wished to discuss?"

Everything. He hated the pain he saw in her face, pain from what she must have misconstrued as his rejection of her once more. But what could he say? "I didn't sleep with you, Amanda, not because I don't want to, but because I'm using you"?

She squared her shoulders and started bravely toward the horse and his heart went out to her.

"Let me help—" Luke took a step toward the horse, then stopped as she threw him a murderous look.

"No, thank you. As Emerson once said, 'Every man alone is sincere; at the entrance of a second person hypocrisy begins.' "

"Fine." Luke gathered up his belongings, then swung up on his own mount. He was furious, with himself more than Amanda. Snapping on his makeshift reins—a pair of his own suspenders—he started for the trail, barely glancing back to see that she followed. She was there, perched on the horse, her body poker straight and unforgiving.

Thank God they'd be in Wichita that day. And then, the trail.

Sam Haskwell sat at the poker table, idly dropping the gold coins before him into a neat stack. Cold, handsome and ruthless, he'd made a fortune out of doing what occupied him right now—judging other people. "Find out what makes them afraid, what they are hiding, and who they are hiding it from," a gambler had once told him. Sam thanked the man before he shot him, but never forgot the lesson.

"Hit?" the dealer asked. The other men, cowhands looking to increase their newly acquired pay and businessmen looking for diversion, glanced up expectantly at the dark-haired, moustached Irishman who sat beside them.

"Sure, Jack. Give me three." Ignoring their smiles, Haskwell leaned forward, tossing the cards and scraping up the replacements. Born Sean Kelly on an Irish trade ship that New York refused to let dock for fear of tuberculosis, he'd entered Philadelphia as a boy and quickly learned the value of a pseudonymn. Philadelphia had taught him something else. As he watched his family struggle to make a living, hauling brick for the Main Line mansions, Sean had decided that he'd use his one talent to his best advantage.

It was a policeman who'd taught him to shoot, a cocky young Welshman who'd finagled his way onto the force and arrested Sean during the Philadelphia riots. The Welshman, taking pity on a fellow Celt, showed him the intricacies of the western Colt guns. Sean found that he had a good eye, and by the time he was eighteen, had killed his first man and was forced to head west. There, the same talent that would see him hanged in the city made him rich. He was careful not to get caught, to kill anyone who'd seen him shooting. So far, it had worked. Except for that woman who'd written that book . . . but even she didn't concern him much. If Winters and Damien had done their job, the girl would be dead even now.

A blonde saloon girl giggled, then placed a full shot of whiskey before him. "You gonna play, handsome?"

Sam grinned, then turned to the men at the table. Three had folded, and the hand had gotten down to himself and a young sapling of a cowboy. The cowboy worked to look confident, though his pale, lashless eyes kept returning to the hand that Haskwell held. Grinning more broadly, Sam tossed in another chip, then displayed his hand.

"Damn." The cowboy swore, his brogue as thick as Jameson's whiskey. Haskwell chuckled, then added the young Irishman's money to his own ample pile. Angry as the other men laughed, and flush full of whiskey, the cowboy got to his feet and drew his gun.

"All right, mister. You've been cheatin'. I'll be wantin' me money back, nothing else."

Sam's smile faded as the bar grew quiet. The boy's gun trembled and he struggled to keep the barrel trained on Haskwell. The poker dealer stood up, and spoke to the young cowhand.

"Look, son. We don't want this kind of trouble. No money's worth it. Do you know who you're threatening?"

"He's cheatin'. Look at his face! I just want—"

The shot rang out before the boy finished the sentence. The boy jumped, his own gun discharging harmlessly. His Stetson fell to the floor, circled the boards, then stopped. It had a hole shot right through the middle.

"Next time, laddie, that'll be your head." Haskwell spoke

quietly, though his tone carried a message that was unmistakable. "Jack, get him out of here."

The dealer hauled the protesting cowboy out of the saloon, while the piano player resumed his music. The dealer threw the boy out into the street, then returned a moment later and wiped his hands on his pants.

"Sorry, boys. Ready?"

The players nodded, and Sam tossed in a coin. He felt the other men's eyes on him, and the silent question that followed. He hadn't killed the boy, and he could have. Why? Because the spaulpeen reminded him of himself at that age, or worse yet, the others he'd left behind?

You're getting soft, Sean, you are, he berated himself. *It comes with age, this weakening of the heart.* Angry, he turned over his cards. He'd need to reestablish himself quickly. Before he lost his edge.

Luke was getting out. No question about it—as soon as they got to Wichita and Amanda hooked up with a family on a wagon train, he was going.

The thought comforted him even as the outskirts of the cattle town appeared in the distance, followed by the outlines of buildings silhouetted against the endless horizon. Glancing back, he saw the same disapproving expression on Amanda's face that he'd seen all morning. Anger razed him, followed by the inevitable guilt. Damned spinster! There she sat, as straight as a child in the first row before a preacher, her hair pulled back and escaping in polished brown curls from her bun. If she wasn't shaming him with a glance, she was spouting philosopher's quotes, or spilling out his precious whiskey on the ground. As much as he wanted her land and the chance to start over, he was sick of it.

He'd get Haskwell on his own time and the rest be damned.

Feeling better now that he'd decided, Luke rode into town and dismounted his horse outside of the three-story brick saloon. He waited for her to join him, and as she slid from the horse, sending the animal a disdainful glance, he cleared his voice and broke the silence between them.

"Amanda, why don't you go on and get a room? I'll ask around about the wagon train."

She stared at him, knowing what he wasn't saying. He was leaving her. He refused to look her in the eye as he glanced back toward the saloon, as if already calculating the result of his freedom. None of it meant anything to him; not the night they had once shared, nor the bargain they had made. It wasn't the first time she'd been shuffled off somewhere, an oddity to be exploited rather than loved. She'd forgotten how much it hurt.

"Where is the hotel?" she asked coldly.

"There's a couple, but there's a good boardinghouse at the end of the walk. Just tell Mrs. Mathers I sent you. I'll make my own arrangements later." Luke hated the way she stared at him. The sun glinted from her soft brown hair, and that damned curl that escaped from its knot, framing her face. She never looked lovelier—why did he have to pick this time to notice that?

"I see," Amanda replied. "Goodbye, Luke." She picked up Aesop and her carpetbag, then started across the street, her head held high and her shoulders squared. The cage started to fall and she scooped it up, trying to balance the rusty metal enclosure along with the bag. People stopped to watch the strange young girl, who was oblivious to everything except her owl.

"Amanda!" Luke started to go to her aid, but the look in her eyes stopped him.

"Please don't bother on my account," she said briskly. "I understand how you must feel. Not every man can keep a contract, even if it is what they call a gentleman's agreement."

"What?" Luke stared at her incredulously. "Who said—"

"And after you assaulted me last night, and forcibly removed my clothes, I have to assume you're incapable of keeping your word."

"Amanda." Luke forced a smile, his teeth gritted. The

crowd grew thicker as Amanda dipped into her bag and replaced her glasses. She looked at him the way a mad scientist examined a specimen about to be tortured. "Will you let me explain?" Luke continued.

"I trusted you," Amanda said accusingly. Her eyes blazed. "Now I find that I am forced to agree with John Lyly. 'Children and fools speak true.' " She turned, picked up her things, and marched toward the boardinghouse.

Luke heard the titters of the crowd, then felt their accusing glances as he stalked away to the saloon. Furious, his face flushed with anger, he entered the bar and ordered a whiskey.

He'd made the right decision. And the sooner he was out of this, the better.

Amanda collapsed as soon as she entered the boardinghouse bedroom, for once neglecting Aesop and flopping the birdcage onto the floor. *My God,* she thought, *what have I done?* She had no doubt that Luke wouldn't return—she'd seen that look before. It was the same withdrawal she saw on her parents' faces when they finally decided to send her off to school.

She should have known better than to trust him. Her mind returned to the previous night, and she shivered with regret. She should not have let it happen. They'd had an agreement. Yet, he seemed to want it as much as she did until . . . Amanda couldn't bear to think of the rest—it was much too humiliating.

Confused and upset, she did what she always did when life became unbearable. Reaching over the cage, she dipped into her bag and pulled out her notes. There, alone with nothing more than the paper as her witness, she spilled out everything she felt inside. What she thought about Luke, about the trip she would most likely now take alone, and what life was showing her now that she was free. Tears spilled out along with her feelings and she let them, wanting nothing more than to purge all of the roiling sensations she had felt for some time now. She wrote it all down—how she felt when Luke touched her, laughed with her, loved her. Finishing, she fell back against a worn rocking chair, mindless of the scratchy horsehair seat, and slept.

She awoke a short time later. The papers lay around her on the floor, a hurricane of splotched ink and pale white parchment. Picking up a sheet, she cringed at what she'd written, amazed that she had penned so much of her innermost thoughts. Embarrassed, she stuffed the work into the grate and quickly ignited the pile. Slowly, the flames took hold and the paper burned, the notes returning to a safe grey ash. When the fire began to die, she got to her feet. She needed time to think, and the room was beginning to close in on her. She would take a walk, wander around the town, and try to make sense of what she'd written.

And worse, what she was beginning to feel.

Butch and Damien entered the saloon and exchanged a grin. It was always a good night when Sam was winning, and the thick pile of chips stacked in front of the outlaw could mean little else. Chomping on a cigar, Damien nudged Butch, then sauntered toward the table.

"So life's not treatin' you too bad." Damien gestured to the cards, then grinned at Sam, his yellowed teeth clamped to the cigar like a blunt holder.

Sam glanced up, gave Damien a sharp look, then quietly folded his hand. "I don't suppose you lads will object if I call it a night, now would you?"

The dealer glanced at the other players, who shook their heads. None of them wanted to tangle with Sam, in spite of the fact that he had most of their money.

"That's very friendly of you all. I'll be down later if any of you want to get even. Until then, the whiskey's on me."

The tight-lipped smiles loosened, then a cowboy shrugged and slapped Sam on the back. Haskwell gestured to Butch and Damien, then made his way through the crowd to a thick red curtain covering the entrance to the back room.

Inside, he waited for the two men to enter. Instantly, his

Irish smile vanished, replaced by a cold sneer that couldn't be mistaken for anything other than displeasure.

"What the hell are you two doing here? Didn't I tell you not to meet me in public?"

"It was his idea," Damien sputtered, indicating Butch. "We have news."

"It had better be good news. I've had too many things go wrong the last few weeks. Did you take care of that little matter you were working on?"

Butch and Damien exchanged a glance. "No," Damien replied. "We lost her."

"What?" Sam rose from the chair he'd taken, his dark eyes blazing. He struggled to get his anger under control. "I hope this is a joke," he said softly. "You'll see I'm not in a funny mood."

"Calm down," Butch interjected. "She's apt to die anyway. The girl's got a gun with her. Luke something, they call him."

"Now you listen to me." Sam's brogue thickened as he stared the two men down. "I don't give a damn about a gun. I don't care if the girl has fifty men helping her. I want her dead."

"They're on the trail," Butch continued quietly. "They have no food, no supplies. They've been run out of town by the sheriff. Not only do they have the law on their backs, but they've scarce a horse or water." Butch grinned. "They won't make it to Newton at this rate."

"Fools!" Sam spat, slamming his fist down on a table. "I could make it, and so could you! I'm not paying you to leave her death up to chance! That Fess Tyson woman witnessed me shooting Haines, then wrote about it for chrissakes. All she has to do is show up, and the prosecution would have a field day. I should have shot her in Boston when I had the opportunity, but that landlady stuck to her like glue. Now she's been warned." Sam's eyes narrowed as he glared at Butch and Damien. "Get out of here and don't come back until you can tell me she's dead! I want proof that Amanda Edison no longer lives! Do you understand me?"

Damien's head bobbed quickly. "Yes, boss. We'll get her, don't worry."

"Good. I'm warning you both." Sam looked from one man's face to the next. "You return with another story like this one, and it'll be your last."

She was gone when he returned. Luke strode into her room, alarmed at the silence that greeted him. Everything else had gone smoothly. The bartender at the saloon assured him that a wagon train would be leaving in the morning, and that they were looking for additional passengers to share the cost. The timing couldn't be better. Amanda would be out of town before the sheriff or Haskwell could catch up with her. If she was lucky, Haskwell would not be able to trace her—in which case, Amanda would be free. But where was she?

His breathing slowed as he saw her carpetbag and the bird cage. She must have decided to take a walk or go into town for supplies. Amanda would never leave Aesop for any length of time.

Sinking down into a padded rocking chair, Luke waited for her to return. The picture of her walking across that street earlier wouldn't leave him. He wondered what she was thinking now—if she was crying, or perhaps, even relieved. Glancing impatiently around the room for some other clue as to her whereabouts, he noticed a crumbled paper in the fireplace.

Amanda was always writing something. Perhaps she'd left a note, then decided she was too angry to extend even this courtesy and threw it out. Luke reached toward the grate and removed the half-burned sheet, then spread the paper out on the table.

I don't know what's happening to me. He's leaving—I see it in his eyes. Why does that tear at me, make my life seem meaningless? He's a gunslinger, a cowboy without a name, a drifter. Yet when he holds me, touches me, his hands so rough and gentle at the same time, I lose myself in a hot vor-

tex of desire I never knew existed. Am I better for this knowledge? When the feeling goes on, I think that I am, for everything around me takes on a new brilliance. I see the flowers of the plains—the red geranium, the crimson lupine, the rippling blue green grass—and I see beauty. I look past the undulating field to an endless horizon—blue sky meeting land. I cannot tell where one leaves off and the other begins. I feel as if I could fall into the heavens, become weightless, a creature of spirit instead of flesh. He has given that to me, in the moments when he is gentle and kind.

He held me last night and I could feel his anger. I do not know what I said to inflame him, but his hands burned where they touched me, more than the heated cloths he used to ease my suffering. It doesn't matter. I want him. My head is filled with the sound of my blood rushing through my veins, my skin is as sensitive as a newborn's, my mouth is alive, wetly anticipating his kiss. I want to draw him inside me, let him ease the ache he's created, yet I know I cannot. I

He couldn't read the rest. Stunned, Luke let the paper crumble between his fingers, the charred ashes returning to what they were meant to be. He felt as if he had peered into the recesses of Amanda's innermost thoughts, and found them astounding.

That she could write like that . . .

Passion inflamed every word. And not the rose-colored feeling most Victorian women described, if they did at all. No, Amanda wrote of sexual desire—of physical love between a man and a woman.

He's leaving. Why does that tear at me?

He closed his eyes. It was all so easy until Amanda came along. Amanda with her owl, her wall of quotations, her strange ocean eyes that would tear the soul out of a gentler man. If he had half a brain, he'd get on the first train and ride out of here. He'd pursue Haskwell on his own, then maybe settle down in the South somewhere, with a sweet belle who was as complex as rice pudding. . . .

It doesn't matter. I want him.

He could still feel the smooth paper clinging to his fingers, and the soft sensation of ash rubbing against his callouses.

You're right, Amanda, he thought. *It really doesn't matter. Not now.*

Chapter

9

"Oh, it's you." Amanda entered the hotel room and closed the door. She gave Luke an icy stare. "I thought you'd be gone by now."

Luke shook his head. "Not at all. I have no intention of going anywhere. Where have you been? I was beginning to get worried."

"You were concerned about me?" Amanda gaped at him incredulously. "Why?"

Luke fought the rising irritation he felt. "I was worried because you were gone so long. I believe that's why you hired me, isn't it? To protect you?"

"I thought that was over." Amanda's nose wrinkled and her eyes widened behind her glasses, revealing her concentration. "You broke our agreement, and you intended to leave. As Carlyle once said—"

"Amanda." Luke gritted his teeth. "I brought you something. Don't you want to open it?"

Amanda's eyes went from the gunslinger to the bed. She noticed for the first time a package wrapped in brown paper and tied with twine. Fingering the parcel, she glanced back at Luke.

"You bought me a present?" When he nodded his head

in affirmation, she continued thoughtfully. "I'd like to know why you did this." She indicated the package. "And why you are here. And why you are looking at me like that."

The smile Luke returned was one she hadn't seen in days. It was warm and wonderful, as if he could see right inside of her, to all those secrets she kept hidden. Feeling like a trapped hare, Amanda toyed with the string. She had to fight the impulse to run.

"Amanda, Amanda. When are you going to stop this? Open it," Luke said.

Unable to figure it all out, Amanda decided to think later, without his distracting presence. She turned her attention to the gift, and had to admit that she was dying of curiosity. Slowly unwrapping the twine, she couldn't hide her delight. No one ever bought her a present. Her parents contributed to her school, saw that she had enough pocket money for books and supplies, but they never thought to give her a gift. Now, with the crude brown paper crackling in her hands, she couldn't stop herself from shaking or the silly grin from spreading over her face.

It vanished a moment later, replaced by awe as she pulled out a beautiful indigo-blue gown. Beneath the gown was a new corset and chemise. Made of first quality plush, the dress boasted a French-lace collar and cuffs, and pearl buttons that marched down the back like a troop of Yankee soldiers. A bustle gathered in the rear to emphasize a woman's hips. Amanda touched the material, rubbing the rough lace between her fingers, overwhelmed by the dress and by the man who had given it to her.

"Do you like it?" Luke chuckled. "I looked all over this damned town before I could find what I wanted. Thank God one of the matrons took pity on me and helped me explain to the dressmaker what size you are."

"But . . ." Amanda couldn't take her eyes off the gown. "Don't such garments take weeks to make?"

"Usually." Luke agreed, pleased by her reaction. "But in this case, I was lucky. The gown was made for a girl from back east. By the time she actually arrived here, she had gained thirteen pounds and the dress no longer fit."

"I'm sorry." Amanda looked up, then smiled foolishly. "I mean, I'm sorry for her. She must have been heartbroken to lose such a pretty dress." She reverently folded the sleeve, then tucked the garment back inside the wrapping. "Too bad I can't accept this."

"What do you mean?" Luke asked, exasperated.

" 'A lady can only accept candy and flowers. And those, preferably, from her affianced.' "

"Don't tell me who said that—"

"Elizabeth Hall, my etiquette instructor." Amanda smiled. She looked at Luke, and her expression was unguarded—full of warmth and girlish laughter. "Although I often thought some of those rules unfair and pretentious, I suppose it has served some good, putting strict requirements on our mating practices. In this case it serves more as a hindrance."

"Then you think of presents as foreplay?" Luke couldn't believe his ears.

"Certainly," Amanda said, the crispness back in her voice. "I mean, think about it. All other species have mating practices, and they're not so different than ours. Male birds preen and puff their feathers, then engage in a sexual dance designed to arouse the female of the species. Male cichlids actually enfold the female fish into an embrace, then together they fertilize the eggs. And a male gambusino, a livebearing fish, splays his fins to get the female's attention then he inserts his anal fin into the female—"

"I get the idea," Luke groaned. He tried another approach. "Amanda, the gown is paid for. I'm sure the dressmaker won't take it back at this point, especially since the original owner had to have another wardrobe constructed. If you really feel that badly about it, we'll work it out when we get to Texas. Maybe come up with another agreement."

Amanda's head lifted slowly, then she stared at him, her eyes unnaturally wide. Luke felt as if he was being dismembered. When she finally spoke, it was as if everything was weighted on his next response.

"Then you've decided not to leave." It was a statement rather than a question.

Swallowing hard, Luke nodded. "I'm sorry for the way I acted last night. You were right. I'll try not to violate the terms again. However, I didn't think that meant I couldn't give you something if I wanted to."

"No," Amanda said quickly, overwhelmingly relieved by his words and the truth she saw in his face. "But I think we should work it out when we get to Texas. And I did need another dress." She played with the material again, as if suddenly realizing it was hers.

"Fine. And I hope that I can have dinner with you tonight. I mean, this will be our last civilized meal for some time, and I hate to eat alone. Do you mind?"

"No, that's all right." It was more than all right. For someone who'd spent a lifetime eating alone, his offer meant more than he'd ever know.

"Good. Then why don't you send for a bath and put that on? I've made arrangements with a wagon train and ordered supplies. When you're ready, you can meet with some of the families we'll be traveling with, and then we'll get a bite to eat."

She nodded, barely aware of his presence. Luke hid a grin as she swept the dress out of the paper wrappings, then held it before the mirror. Stunned, she couldn't hide her excitement as she saw the woman she could be, with the indigo-blue bringing out all the strange colors in her eyes, and the polished depths of her chestnut hair.

Luke closed the door, then stood in the hallway, more than satisfied with the results of his gift. Amanda needed a little romance in her life.

And he was just the man to provide it.

Amanda pulled on the gown, heedless of the damp moisture that still clung to her body from her bath. Freshly scrubbed, she felt indecently excited as she smoothed the gown over her hips, then tried to close the back. Her corset and chemise had been ruined from riding and the night she'd struggled with Luke, and she was very grateful he'd included new undergarments. Rows of buttons paraded down, from her neck to below her bustle, all of them tiny and hard to fasten. When she finally managed to secure a few of the buttons, she peered into the mirror and saw that they were fastened wrong, and that the material had buckled open.

Darn! Amanda undid the buttons, then, holding the dress together, wondered what to do next. She had no maid, knew no one in this boardinghouse other than Luke, and she really didn't want to ask him. For tonight, just one night, she wanted to be the lady she'd always read about, written about—genteel, sophisticated, and sure of herself. And an unbuttoned gown was a bad way to start.

A shrill giggle interrupted her thoughts, then she heard a woman's laughter clearly through the wall. The laughter died to a soft murmur, then Amanda heard the odd sounds of bed ropes squeaking. The noise died as quickly as it started, followed by silence. Shrugging, Amanda walked out into the hallway, hoping to find a chambermaid, or anyone who could help with the dress.

A woman stepped from the room next door. Amanda stared at her curiously as the gaslights enveloped her in a yellow glow, making her reddish hair take on a shimmery effect and igniting her dressy satin gown into a brilliant saffron. The woman paused, seeming as surprised to see Amanda as Amanda was to see her. She ventured a shy smile, then relaxed as Amanda quickly returned it.

"Is something wrong?" The girl spoke in a soft, musical brogue. Her perfume floated around her like a sweet cloud. "It isn't a fire?" She stared hopefully at Amanda, who shook her head.

"No, nothing like that. I . . . I just needed help with this dress." Amanda indicated her open gown, then blushed as the young girl's smile deepened.

"Well, hell honey, I can do that. Aileen O'Connell was

the finest ladies' maid ever, before Sherman took Atlanta.
That's when I got into this business." Following Amanda
into her room, she began to secure the dress.

"What business?" Amanda stared at the young woman
reflected in the glass. Originally, she thought her to be
around twenty five years old, but now she appeared much
younger—hardly eighteen. The brighter lighting in the
room also revealed a sprinkling of freckles across her nose,
and the hint of a dimple around her mouth. Rouge made
her rather plain face seem prettier, and her low cut gown
emphasized a generous figure for a young girl.

"The business." Aileen giggled. "You know. I don't
mind. The money's damned good. And some of the men are
nice. Why Jake Fontaine in there reckons to be governor
of Texas. Says he'll take me there, too. Just think—one man,
one bed, every other night off. It'll be heaven." Aileen
sighed as she finished the gown and gave the bow a final
pat. "There! What a nice waist you have."

"Then you're a prostitute!" Amanda faced the woman,
her mouth dropping in surprise.

"A saloon girl, I prefer to call it," Aileen said slowly. "I
know the way you gentlewomen think, so if you don't mind,
I'll be going now—"

"Oh, but you can't." Amanda reached for her bag and
quickly got out her notes. "You have to tell me all about
it. How did you start? How much do you make? Do the men
really pay you just to have sex with them? Are they nice
to you, did any of them hurt you . . . "

"If you ain't the oddest creature I'd ever met." Aileen
grinned, noticing the strange way Amanda's eyes looked
when she put on her glasses, and the way her hair seemed
to have a life all its own, tumbling wildly over her face and
shoulders. "Why in the good Lord's name would you want
to know all that?"

"I'm a writer," Amanda said, as if that explained everything. "And I'd really like to know. I haven't hurt your feelings or anything, have I?" Anxious now, she placed her
papers aside and searched the girl's face for signs of with-

drawal. Finding none, she continued happily. "Seems I always do that, and I don't mean to. I just really want to know. 'Knowledge is power.' Francis Bacon."

"I don't take it back, you are an odd bird." Aileen flounced down on the bed, then eyed Amanda critically. "I'll tell it to you, if you really mean it. But why are you getting all gussied up? Ain't nothing for a gentlewoman to do in this town but to embroider and take tea with the ladies."

"There's a man. I mean, Luke." Amanda blushed to the ears. "We're going to dinner, and just for once I wanted to look as nice as the ladies he's used to. He's from the South, too."

"Oh." Aileen nodded wisely. "Southern belles, their voices like melting sugar. About as interesting as a stale teacake, but I can understand what you're saying. Mind if I offer a suggestion?"

"Not at all."

"Your hair's all wrong—it shouldn't be falling in your eyes like that. And those glasses have to go. Tell you what. I'll fix your hair for a price of a whiskey, and answer whatever you want to know. Deal?"

"Deal," Amanda agreed, scooping up her notes in absolute bliss. By the time they were finished, she'd decided it was well worth the two bits. Her notebook was ten pages full, and as she gazed into the mirror, she stared in astonishment at the woman who looked back.

"Aileen, how can I ever thank you—" Amanda shook the young girl's hand, more amazed when Aileen laughed loudly.

"Honey, I've been needing this whiskey more than I can say. And to tell you the truth," she plucked shyly at her dress, then glanced up from beneath rusty lashes, "I miss talking to a real lady. You ain't like the other women, pulling their skirts aside when they see me. No ma'am, you're a real lady, no matter how many books you've read. I've been around enough to know." She gave Amanda's hair a critical touch, then nodded in approval. "When you go out with your beau tonight, he won't be able to take his eyes off you. And you remember what I said. No spoiled southern brat can hold a candle to this."

Amanda felt emotion filling her. No one had ever so openly befriended her before. She had always been the teacher's pet. Everyone had wanted to copy her work, to sit beside her and benefit from her knowledge, but no one wanted to be friends with her. Instead, they'd made fun of her, put ink in her hair and pine cones on her chair. She returned the young woman's smile.

"Thank you, Aileen. You know, I used to be afraid of the world. This is the first time I've taken a chance, and it's turning out to be wonderful. I keep pinching myself, wondering how I can be so lucky." Amanda gave Aesop a reassuring tap on his cage, then started out the door.

Aileen watched her go, then picked up her lace shawl and followed. It was strange, but she felt protective of the woman she'd just met, and instinctively knew how vulnerable Amanda really was. The world was hardly wonderful.

And no one knew that better than Aileen.

Luke was waiting for Amanda when she descended the stairs. Clad in charcoal-grey trousers, a crisp white shirt and dinner jacket, a stark contrast to his blue-black hair, he looked devastingly handsome. He lounged against the mantle, smiling at something a cowboy said, holding a glassful of smoke-colored liquor. His eyes lifted as Amanda descended the stairs and he froze.

She was absolutely beautiful.

The indigo dress he'd bought her had looked nice in the store, but looked incredible on her. The material fit her slender figure perfectly, accentuating her softly rounded breasts and her womanly hips. The french lace at her throat brought his attention to her face, made his eyes linger there. With her hair pulled back in a charming nest of curls and her dowdy glasses gone, the sharp angles of her cheekbones traced down to a finely shaped nose and a seductive mouth that looked faintly moist. As she approached, he could see that the dark color emphasized her eyes. They seemed like enormous pools of blue and green.

Amanda stood before him, puzzled by his reaction and the way he stared at her. Self-consciously, she smoothed the dress and examined it for Aesop's feathers. Finding none, she anxiously patted her hair, thinking that it was in disarray, but Aileen had secured each curl with a pin. More confused than ever, she faced up to him and frowned.

"Why are you looking at me like that? Don't you like the dress? I can go back to the room and change, if you're not sure. Or maybe it's the hair—"

"Amanda." Luke chuckled, drawing her two hands into his own. "You look lovely. Gorgeous. I had no idea that a simple gown or a hairstyle could make such a change. Shall we?" He offered her his arm, and after staring at it for a puzzled moment, she accepted his gesture and allowed him to escort her outside.

The restaurant was across the street, a few doors down. Luke smiled as she glanced around her, drinking in the warm seduction of the night. When she looked upward at a sky made of crushed velvet, he indicated a star pattern.

"Sagittarius. See those three stars right in a row?" He pointed out the constellation, his hand resting casually around her shoulders. "That's the archer's bow. It indicates the coming winter. The Indians recognize it as the time to start preparing for the cold months ahead."

Amanda looked at him, amazed. Although she was familiar with the science of astronomy, she never thought of it in practical terms. Luke was obviously knowledgeable on the subject. He continued to surprise her, and she felt inexplicably safe and secure with his arm around her and the open admiration she felt in his eyes.

As they proceeded to the restaurant, Amanda became aware of the eyes that followed her. Two cowboys, whittling on the boardwalk steps, stopped carving at the sight of her and actually stood to better watch her pass by. A primly dressed farmwife gave her an icy glance, then held more tightly to her gaping husband. Businessmen headed for the bar gave her warm smiles, while their feminine companions looked her up and down appraisingly, as if sizing her up as a threat.

Amanda was enthralled.

She had written about such women, watched and envied them, never dreaming that she would one day be among their ranks. For however long it lasted, this night—this magical, star-spun night—was hers. And she intended to enjoy it to the fullest.

The Full Moon restaurant was about as elegant as a cow town could boast. Amanda followed Luke's lead and entered, dazzled by the candlelight and the soft glow of the gaslamps. A handsome man dressed in a dark suit indicated a table, and Luke ushered her forward, walking behind her.

Every man's eye followed her. Luke saw the cowboys, men long on the trail and appreciative of a glance of a beautiful woman, stop their meal and glance longingly at the stunning brunette making her way to her table. The jaded businessmen paused from their drinks to watch her, their eyes following even after she passed. It was only the expression on Luke's face that made them turn back to their meal, and then only reluctantly.

Luke held her chair, fighting his desire to take her out of here, to a place where he could have her all to himself. One of the men, a young cowhand, obviously taken with Amanda's radiant beauty, tried to get her attention. Luke stood between them as he offered her a chair, annoyed to find himself in the role of protecting her from other men's advances. He felt duped by his own hand. The duckling had turned into a swan, and he'd been stupid enough to provide the feathers.

"Thank you." Amanda smiled, then accepted the seat.

Her voice was sweet and musical and Luke felt his warring emotions intensify. Taking the seat across from her, he smiled, trying to hide his gritted teeth. The wine steward approached, thankfully distracting him.

"Your order, sir?" The waiter smiled at Amanda, who innocently smiled back.

"Do you have something decent in a burgundy?" Luke struggled to hide his irritation. Was everyone taken with her? When the steward nodded, he looked toward Amanda. "Is that suitable?"

She nodded. "Burgundy is my favorite." Actually, she'd never tasted any wine, never tasted spirits in fact, except for that night in the Harvey House.

"Fine." Luke nodded acceptance to the waiter, who departed with a nod. It was then that he noticed the table beside them. Three elegantly dressed men, gamblers and cattle traders, he suspected, were watching Amanda with unabashed appreciation. She was returning their smiles, basking in the attention. Luke scowled.

Amanda looked him straight in the eye. "Is something wrong?"

"Yes," he said bluntly. "Don't return a man's stare like that. Unless you're prepared to accept what follows."

"What do you mean?" she asked, but Luke didn't respond. The wine steward returned, the glasses neatly balanced on a tray. Amanda reached up for hers and without her glasses, misjudged the distance. The wine toppled over, staining the white shirt front of the blonde gentleman seated beside her.

"I'm so sorry!" Mortified, Amanda's hands clasped over her mouth.

The man shook his head, then snatched up his napkin and proceeded to sop up the purple liquid. "Not at all, don't give it a second thought. I was trying to think of an excuse to meet you, and you've given me the perfect one." He stood up and extended a hand. "My name's Mr. Ashton Richards."

"Miss Amanda Edison." She shook his hand heartily, grateful that for some reason this man accepted her in spite of the wine dousing.

"Charmed." His smile seemed sincere and he indicated the empty chairs beside her. "I've just returned from Colorado, to do some cattle trading, and I have to admit that you are the prettiest woman I've seen in days. Would you mind if we joined you? I would understand if you are occupied." He glanced sideways at Luke.

"Not at all," Amanda said quickly, overcome by the man's generosity. "I'm sure Luke won't mind, we've plenty of extra chairs." She suddenly turned to Luke, as if in afterthought. "Do you mind?"

Luke didn't trust himself to speak. He was furious.

Chapter

✑ *10* ✑

Luke had planned for a romantic evening, just the two of them. There was nothing he could do about it now, nothing that wouldn't create a scene or show his raw anger. Nodding coldly, he stood up and allowed the three men to join them. Amanda, he decided, he'd deal with later.

"Mighty appreciated." Ashton took the seat next to Amanda, while the other two men sat across from her. They seemed equally delighted with the arrangement, and as Amanda sipped a new glass of wine, they introduced themselves.

Gilbert McMahon, a dark Irishman, discovered that Amanda shared his interest in horse breeding, though she seemed to abhor the animals themselves. However, when he debated the merits of the Indian paint horse with the English-bred, he found her opinions were startlingly intelligent and full of insight. Andre Deville was astounded to discover that she had an appreciation of American painters—Remington, especially. And Ashton couldn't take his eyes off her.

Her laughter tinkling like fresh champagne, Amanda charmed them through the sumptuous prime rib, the ripe fruits, and the wonderful rich chocolate cake for dessert.

Luke watched her in growing fury, unable to decide whether she was enjoying herself at his expense, or if she really didn't know what she was doing to him. She was in the midst of a lively discussion with Ashton regarding the present generation, and with a sigh, the American businessman laid down his fork and grinned.

"Miss, all I can say is that you are a woman among women. May the future hold many more like you," he toasted her with his glass.

"Oh, but it will," Amanda said earnestly. Forgetting everything other than her own mental stimulation, she leaned across the table, her eyes sparkling with intensity. "It is a certainty. As the species evolves, it will become necessary for women to enter the work force, to regard education with the same importance as men. Physical strength will no longer be the final determinant of power, for once women hold equal positions with equal pay, in jobs where mental brilliance bears more significance than mere anatomy, there will be more—"

She was surrounded by stony faces. Luke forced a smile, his hand tightening around his glass. Amanda could have cried. She'd done it again. Somehow, she always managed to start trouble, even when she didn't mean to. Frantically, she went over her last words, but she couldn't decide what had taken the merriment out of the evening.

"Miss." Ashton cleared his throat. "You don't honestly subscribe to the theory of evolution?"

"Oh, that," Amanda said innocently, relieved. "How could one not? How could you look to the flower and fauna of South America, see how it's adapted to the environment, and not believe? How could you see the desert cactus with the ability to store water, the polar bears of the north with their thick winter fur, the Appalachian mountain goat—"

"It is a godless theory!" Gilbert said, flushing with outrage. "Man is made in the image of the Lord!"

"I'm not arguing that," Amanda said, puzzled. "But when? To me, it is not a contradiction. God may have started all life, but is it wrong to assume that it would change? Nothing in life is static." She glanced earnestly from one man to the next. "Have I said something that has upset you all?"

Andre started to grin, then chuckle, then finally, burst out laughing. The other men felt their own outrage fading, then they too began to laugh. When the Frenchman finally wiped his eyes, he gazed at Amanda in open admiration.

"My dear, what a rage you would be in Paris! A woman who thinks! May we all be damned." Observing her flush, he continued in a charming voice. "Don't let these rustics fool you, miss. There is no more intoxicating combination, even if it is frightening. But what would man really prefer? A glass of ice water, clear, simple and pretty, or a glass of ruby wine, rich and deep with untasted pleasures?" He raised his goblet, letting the wine dance in the candlelight, the purple gems dancing over the snowy tablecloth.

The other men grinned in agreement. Amanda sank back in her chair, more puzzled than ever. Everything she'd done tonight—spilled the wine, talked to the men, argued and showed her mind—had always resulted in censure and disapproval. Now, for some reason, the very same actions were applauded. Why? What was different?

"Amanda." Luke interrupted her thoughts. "They're beginning to play music. Would you care to dance?"

"I thought I'd claim that honor—" Ashton began, then backed off when Luke gave him a furious stare. "Perhaps the next one, miss."

Amanda nodded, dizzyingly aware that the gods had bestowed on her the one perfect night she'd wished for. Rising to her feet, she allowed Luke to lead her to the floor, while musicians scraped their violins. Sweet, sweet strains of music flooded the room, reminding her of the sophisticated East, somehow transported to the rough and ready West.

She was so delighted with her success that she didn't notice Luke's anger until they were spinning on the floor. His hand tightened around her waist and she glanced up, surprised to see no twinkling laughter in his eyes, only a dark rage. Amanda couldn't figure out why. She had made some

mistakes, dreadful ones, but then she always did. Why was
he looking at her as if fighting to control his anger?

"Is something wrong?" She bit her lip as his eyes blazed.
She could feel the tension in his body, the tightness in his
steps. He looked down at her and Amanda cringed.

"No, why would anything be wrong? Are you enjoying
yourself tonight?" Luke asked tightly.

Confused, Amanda nodded. "Yes, I am. I thought that's
what you wanted when you bought the dress—"

"I bought the dress for my own appreciation, not for
every other man in the room," Luke spat out. "It seems it
doesn't take much to turn you into an ordinary tart. Just
a hairstyle, a new dress, and a lack of common sense."

Stunned, Amanda stopped, heedless of the other dancers
who paused to glance at the handsome couple. "I never—"

"I thought I knew you, Amanda," Luke continued in the
same cold voice. "I thought at last, there was a woman who
was pure, who was intelligent, who faced the world with an
innocence that was at once as charming as it was frustrating.
I also thought you needed me, but tonight you've proven
me wrong. Evidently, all you need is the proper accoutre-
ments, and you can do battle all by yourself."

"I don't understand—"

"Don't you?" Luke smiled, though no mirth showed in
his eyes. "Here comes your ardent companion, to claim a
dance, no doubt. Enjoy yourself, Amanda. I think it's time
I said goodnight."

He dropped her hand and actually walked away, stopping
only to nod coldly to Ashton. Amanda had no choice but
to accept the other man's hand, and allow him to continue
the waltz. Suddenly, everything was different. Ashton was
handsome, charming, and kind, but the light seemed to have
gone out of the night.

"I hope your companion didn't leave because of us," Ashton said smoothly. "He didn't seem too happy."

"No." Amanda shook her head. "He looked angry. I
don't understand . . . "

"He's jealous, my dear." Ashton's hand rubbed her waist

in a gentle caress. "As I would be, also. He is your be-
trothed, perhaps?"

"Luke?" Amanda laughed shortly. "He's a gunslinger.
I hired him to take me to Texas."

"I see. It's interesting that he seems so attached to you,
since he's little more than a hire. Southern, I suppose?"
Amanda nodded, and Ashton chuckled. "I thought I de-
tected an accent. Probably lost everything in the war. Lots
like him. Gentlemen once, scavengers now."

Amanda stopped dancing and stared up at her companion, her eyes narrowing in thought. "I'd hardly call him a
scavenger. Luke has worked hard since the war. He per-
forms a valuable service for me, and has saved my life more
than once."

"You are too kind, miss." Ashton smiled, undaunted.
"And I suppose he misinterprets that kindness. It's obvious
he means nothing to you."

"What are you talking about?" Amanda asked, her voice
like ice.

Ashton shrugged. "The way you invited us to your table,
spent the evening conversing with us. You must have been
trying to tell him something. Then, this dance . . . I am sure,
had your attentions been occupied, you would not have encouraged this acquaintance. However, I am extremely glad
you did." He squeezed her hand.

Amanda paled. Surely, Luke didn't think the same
thing—then she cringed inwardly. He had to. Why else
would he have been so angry?

"I've got to go," Amanda said abruptly.

"Surely you don't—"

"I have to leave right now." Amanda pulled away from
Ashton, hardly aware that she'd left the man standing in
the center of the dance floor, wondering what had happened. Amanda couldn't have cared less. All she wanted
was to find Luke and explain to him.

If it wasn't too late.

Amanda ran up the street, oblivious to everything except
Luke. She had never deliberately hurt anyone before in her

life, and so this doubly stung. Not only had she hurt him, but she made him look like a fool in public. Even though they were leaving Wichita and would probably never see any of those people again, she had no doubt that Luke's pride had been injured.

Amanda hurried faster, her feet skipping on the dusty boardwalk. She hadn't done it intentionally, but how could she make him understand that? She knew etiquette, knew all of the book rules by heart, but she hadn't understood the subtleties. She was having too good a time to even think about it.

His room was empty. The innkeeper provided her with the number, and although she pounded on the door, there was no answer. Her shoulders dropping, Amanda leaned against the wall, forcing herself to think. Luke was tired and angry. He'd eaten a full dinner, but drank very little. Her mind went back to that night on the prairie, when he'd finished half the tin of whiskey. . . .

The saloon. Where else could he have gone? Relieved, she turned quickly, then started down the stairs, remembering the tinny sounds of the piano and the bawdy laughter that she'd heard ringing out in the street.

Thankfully, it was just three doors down. Breathless, Amanda stood outside for a second, forcing herself to relax. Trying to summon as much dignity as possible, she walked through the swinging doors and into the smoke-filled tavern.

The room was full to the brim with cowboys and ranch-hands, trail drivers and cattle hawkers. Ignoring the whistles and encouraging hoots directed her way, she stepped through the throng, her eyes scanning the crowd. Normally, she would have been entranced by the spectacle of the western bar, but tonight, her mind was on one man. When she glanced toward the bar, she smiled in relief. It had to be him. It was Luke's broad back, his sparkling white shirt, his raven black hair. Even from across the room, she recognized him. He was laughing, then he turned toward her, obviously losing some of his anger in this congenial setting.

Amanda started to wave to him, then her smile froze as a saloon girl wrapped her arm protectively through his, then whispered something in his ear.

Amanda felt the heat rushing to her face and her legs weakened. She hardly heard the calls from the cowboys, and the heated shouts from the men, too full of whiskey. The piano continued to play, but Amanda didn't hear that, either. Slowly, she turned and left the saloon, returned to the boardinghouse and to her room. Perhaps it was just as well that she couldn't explain herself to Luke. He wouldn't have understood.

No one ever did.

Luke drank down the shot glass of whiskey neat, grateful that the raw liquor seemed to numb his shattered male ego and temper his burning anger. Amanda. She'd looked so damned beautiful tonight—did she have any idea of the way she'd treated him? From the time she put on the new dress—his dress—she seemed like a different woman. Gone was the naive bookworm who innocently quoted everyone from Shakespeare to Twain. In her stead was a seductress, who boldly invited men to her table and managed to charm everyone with a tinkling laugh or a dissertation on Darwin. Luke could have throttled her.

"What's the matter, cowboy? You don't look too happy to see me," Susie whispered, wiggling against him, her body soft and full like a ripe golden pear.

Luke smiled. It was good to feel the unabashed admiration of a real woman. He glanced down at the saloon girl. Blonde and pretty, with ash-colored hair and sherry eyes, she gave him a flirtatious grin as she wrapped her hands around his waist.

"It's not you," Luke replied, allowing the girl to caress him. "I was thinking of someone else."

"Well, whoever she is doesn't make you happy. More the fool she. I think you're right handsome, and I plan to spend the whole night making you real pleased." She giggled, then rustled her scarlet skirts deliciously.

Luke stared at her, assessing her virtues. The girl really was attractive, and an obvious expert at her craft. There was no burning intelligence in her eyes, no cold dissection of his faults as if he meant no more than a professor's frog, no casual dismissal of him as soon as another man arrived. In fact, she was looking at him with open admiration. Normally, he wouldn't have given a saloon girl a second glance, but tonight, she was proving to be a balm to his wounded self image. He took another drink from the bar, downed the potent whiskey, then offered her a glass.

"Do you know Shakespeare?" he asked suddenly.

"Who's she?" Susie's nose wrinkled, perplexed. "Is that the new saloon girl? If she's been trying to muscle in on my territory . . ."

Luke chuckled, throwing back his head in delighted, masculine laughter. "Perfect." He picked up the whiskey bottle, then started for the stairs. "Are you coming?"

Susie nodded, then scampered from the bar toward the private rooms at the top of the staircase. Pausing to retrieve a key from inside her bodice, she carefully unlocked the door, then stepped inside and turned up the gas.

It was better than Luke had thought. Wichita had benefitted from the cattle trade in more ways than one, he mused, as he took off his jacket and placed it on the back of a rosewood chair. A fire crackled cheerfully in the grate, throwing ghosts against the walls and floor, while a bottle of good wine cooled in a silver bucket beside the nighttable. The bed was ample, a good sized mattress with a brass headboard, and the sheets were turned down invitingly.

"Now you just make yourself comfortable, honey." Susie cooed. "And Susie will be right back." She disappeared into the dressing room with a giggle, carrying a garment so flimsy it could scarcely be given the name.

Luke grinned, pouring another whiskey and then slowly began unbuttoning his shirt. The night unfolded outside like a beggar's blanket and the wind howled, but here it was warm and secure. He had scarcely finished the third button when Susie reappeared, clad in the diaphanous nightgown, looking incredibly lovely. It was then he noticed that the garment was blue. Christ, why did it have to be blue?

"Here, let me do that." Brushing his hands aside, she fumbled with the buttons, undoing them one at a time, and pressing sweet kisses to each bare inch of flesh she exposed. Luke's fingers sank into her hair.

God, it felt good to be with a real woman again.

Very good.

Alone in her room, Amanda let Aesop out of his cage, grateful for his silence and wide, unblinking attention. Slowly, she struggled to loosen the beautiful gown, wanting nothing more than to strip away all vestiges of this evening. When she finally managed to undo all the buttons, she let the dress slip from her body, gently folded the garment, then placed it away inside her carpetbag.

Aesop watched her quizzically as Amanda straightened. Clad only in a light shift, she took a seat before the mirror, and began to pull out her hair pins. Tears began, and by the time she'd finished and her chestnut-colored hair was tumbling about her like a sable fall, she was crying, unable to stop the flow of emotions fighting inside of her.

She had done it again, and this time she hadn't even realized it or meant to. Luke would probably never forgive her. Even if he did, there would always be this embarrassing memory between them. Why was she always so awkward, always saying and doing the wrong thing? Why was everything so effortless for other women, yet not for her. She could do calculus with little more effort than adding up a shopping list; she could remember everything she'd read, not just for days but years. She had a brilliant mind, yet when it came to the man she loved—

She froze. Aesop instinctively knew something was wrong, and hopped onto the dressing table to affectionately gnaw on her finger. Amanda scarcely noticed. A white-faced woman stared back from the mirror, numb with realization.

She was falling in love with Luke Parker.

And she didn't have the faintest idea of what to do about
it. Unable to think clearly without writing, she picked up
her journal.

*He is with another woman. I saw the way he looked at her,
the way he slipped his arm around her, holding her, just the
way he's held me. Why does that make me miserable?*

*I have no claim on him, just as he doesn't on me. We are
traveling companions; he is a hired gun. He can take any
woman he wants at any time. I have no right to say anything,
no right to complain.*

*But when I think of him, of them, of him smoothing her
hair and telling her she's pretty, of her sharing the feeling
of belonging to him, even for those few short moments, I am
overwhelmed with pain.*

*Tonight I had one magical night with him. He thought I
was pretty; I saw that in his eyes. He bought me a dress,
wanted to dine with me, dance with me. It was all going so
well until I met those other men. I didn't know he would get
so angry. The truth is, it all went to my head, though I blush
to think of it.*

*But now I feel terrible. Inside, I am empty and aching,
hollow like the dried up trees we passed on the trail. If I never
felt so happy before tonight, then I also never hurt so badly.*

This is what it is to love.

Damned women! Luke turned up the gas, throwing the
room into an unromantic light, then began to search around
for his clothes.

"Come on, honey, you don't really mean to leave." Susie
sat up in bed, her pretty red lips pursed into a pout. "We
have all night."

"No thanks, I'd better be going." Luke pulled on his
pants, wanting nothing more than to be far away from this
warm and elegant room. Frustration ate at him. In spite of
Susie's experience, her encouragement, her erotic ideas and
clever hands, all he could think of was Amanda. Amanda

looking lovely in the indigo dress. Amanda laughing with
the men at the table. Amanda, who even now could be—

Clutching the sheet to her full breasts, Susie protested.
"Just because you couldn't . . . I mean, it happens all the
time. You aren't the first cowboy who couldn't, didn't—"

"I'd rather not discuss it, if you don't mind." Luke could
feel his face getting hot. Christ, he was blushing like a
schoolboy.

"But it's not uncommon. I mean, if you got a little sleep,
wore off some of that whiskey, I'm sure you could—"

"Susie, I appreciate it. Really. But you're right—I am
tired, and I've had too much to drink. I just want to go back
to my room. Here." He tossed her a roll of bills. "Keep the
change."

Susie tucked the money inside her top dresser drawer,
then watched him as he tugged on his boots and pulled on
a shirt. He seemed to attack the buttons, as if taking out
his anger on them. She made one last attempt.

"Honey, you've already paid. Even if you just want to
sleep here, I won't hold it against you."

Luke flinched. "That's nice of you, but really, I've got
to go." He placed a chaste kiss on her forehead, then started
toward the door. The last thing that caught his attention
was the thin nightgown that Susie had tossed onto the floor.

Damn! Why did it have to be blue?

Chapter

11

Amanda felt the contrast between the rough muslin of the gown that she slipped over her head, compared with the luxuriant dress she'd worn the previous night. Gazing into the mirror, she was relieved and disappointed to see that the woman she had been was gone, and the old Amanda stared back from the looking glass. Her hair fell wildly about her face, tamed only when she pulled it back into a schoolmarmish bun, and her dowdy dress hid most of her slender figure, emphasizing only her face, her hollow cheeks with their high, square bones, and her swollen, blue-green eyes.

Pressing a cold cloth to her eyelids to relieve the redness, she thought of Luke last night with the saloon girl. It was an image she couldn't wipe out, no matter how hard she tried. Pain welled up in her again, and she forced it down. She couldn't accept what she thought she had felt last night. It was all wrong. It was the dress, the magic of the night, and her loneliness that made her think there was something more to this relationship. After all, Luke had spent the night with another woman. . . .

Amanda removed the towel. The cold cloth had helped a little, so she repeated the process. By the time she had finished, there was no evidence that she'd spent the evening doing anything other than sleeping.

Satisfied, Amanda picked up Aesop and her carpetbag, the new dress carefully folded and placed inside, then she strode determinedly to the front desk and got the number for Luke's room. Marching up the steps, she turned the corner, then rapped sharply on door sixteen.

"I'm coming, Jesus, stop that yammering." Luke stumbled to the door, flung it open, and stared in disbelief at the fully dressed and proper Miss Edison.

"Are you ready? We are scheduled to leave early this morning, if you remember correctly," Amanda said, her voice as crisp as autumn leaves. "We still have to purchase supplies, sign on with the wagon train, pack our belongings, and make the arrangements—"

"All right, all right, I get it," Luke said, rubbing his forehead. "Give me a minute. You can wait in here."

Amanda entered, taking deep satisfaction in the way Luke looked. His hair was disheveled, and his clothes were a mess, as if he'd slept in them. Black circles enveloped his eyes, and a dark stubble clung to his chin.

"I am surprised to see that you aren't ready," Amanda continued in the same icy voice. "For someone who is normally so punctual—"

"Amanda." Luke's words held a threatening note. "Don't push me. I have one hell of a hangover, and I'm in no mood to fence with you."

"My, that is a pity," Amanda continued, unable to resist. "Especially since we are going to be going all the way to Texas together. That is, if you haven't changed your mind again." Her eyes cut right through him.

Luke stared her back down, his beautiful blue eyes penetrating, then he slowly began to unbutton his shirt. Inch by inch he exposed his wrists, then his shoulders, then his torso from the waist up. Well-muscled and bronzed, attesting to an out-of-doors life, his body was magnificent. He leaned over the washstand, liberally dousing himself with water, then scrubbing with the cake of strong soap that the housekeeper provided. Droplets of moisture ran down his chin, glistening from his tanned flesh, while his muscles flexed and twisted with his movements.

"I think I shall be going," Amanda gulped. Faced with the sight of his obvious masculinity, unclothed and wildly seductive, she felt herself quickly losing ground.

Luke glared at her. "Stay where you are. I have no desire to go scouting around this damned town, looking for you."

Amanda nodded, turning her attention to the window, her eyes fighting to look back at him. When he finished washing, he slipped on a clean shirt, then dipped his comb into the water and slicked back his hair. When he finally approached, he looked even more handsome than he had the night before. Amanda could have hit him.

"Look at me." His voice was gentle and Amanda glanced up, her own eyes shielded and suspicious. "Amanda, I want to apologise for what happened last night. It occurred to me that I might have over-reacted—"

"Might have?"

"Did." Luke amended. "I was going to come down to your room last night and talk to you about it, but it seems I drank too much damned whiskey. Guess you were right about that, too."

Amanda stared at him in amazement. He looked so charming, so ingratiating, that she had to fight to keep her own anger alive.

"You see, I never dreamed you'd look as beautiful as you did in that gown, with your hair done up. Seems I got used to thinking of you as my own Amanda. I suppose it happened while we were alone on the trail together. You were lovely last night, and you didn't deserve the kind of treatment I gave you."

"Why did you?" Amanda looked at him speculatively. "Was it because I invited those men to our table? Ashton thought so."

"Did he?" Luke smiled thinly. "In a way, I suppose."

"I don't see why," Amanda continued in the same, analytical tone. "I just thought they seemed lonely and interested in our conversation. Ashton said—"

"Amanda." Luke cut her off. "If you say his name one more time, I swear I won't be responsible for what happens." Luke took a deep breath, obviously fighting his temper and the headache. "I'm trying to say I'm sorry."

Amanda fought the rising swell of tenderness she felt inside of her. He looked so honest, so vulnerable, and so damned appealing, that she had to restrain the impulse to reach out and caress his hard muscled arms that she'd seen naked just a few moments ago. In spite of everything, he seemed to care for her. Her spirits soared.

"I accept your apology," she said softly. "And I feel I owe you one. I didn't realize that inviting Ash—I mean, those men, to our table would upset you. . . . " Amanda's voice trailed off as she noticed something black and lacy laying on the bed, just behind Luke. It was, unmistakably, a woman's garter.

"I know," Luke said quickly. He gave her a warm wonderful smile, then took up her hands. "Now can we start over? We have a long trip ahead of us."

Amanda tore her eyes away from the lace undergarment and gazed at him. For a second, he saw open pain, then the tough mask fell and she was the old Amanda again. Luke had seen a warmer expression on the face of a bluecoat.

"There is no need to start anything," Amanda said coldly. "We are merely traveling acquaintances. And as for last night, it is best forgotten. I mean, I suppose it's natural for you to be jealous."

"Jealous!" Luke stared at her incredulously, his smile fading. "What are you talking about?"

"It's nothing to be defensive about," Amanda continued casually. "It happens with all primates. Particularly males. If you've ever watched a male dog marking his territory, you know what I mean. But it usually is a mating signal, and I just wish to clarify our relationship."

"And what is that?" Luke asked, furious.

"We have none," Amanda said abruptly. "Now you've

kept me waiting long enough. Unless we wish to miss the wagon train all together, I suggest we proceed. Is there something you wish to add?"

Luke's fist clenched, and he snatched up his coat, unaware that he'd picked up the garter at the same time. Not trusting himself to speak, he followed her out of the room, Amanda with the cage in one hand, the bag in the other. He kicked shut the door.

Amanda Edison had ice water in her veins. And he'd had the dousing to prove it.

"There ain't no room on the wagon train." The man Luke had been introduced to as Pop Finnegan spat a wad of tobacco juice into the brass receptacle at the end of the bar, then continued speaking as if there had been no interruption. "Been filled for days. Don't need no more tag-alongs."

Luke glanced outside. There were only six wagons waiting to leave. Luke could see a few men lashing supplies onto the back of the covered wagons, and a small number of women and children preparing the provisions for the long journey ahead.

"There seems to be plenty of room," Luke remarked. "Take a look."

Pop shoved aside his beer and got to his feet. "I told you there ain't room, and if I said there ain't, there ain't. We've got six good, hard-working Christian families, the Reverend Jacob Weaver and his followers. Don't need no one else."

"I'm sure there must be a misunderstanding," Luke continued reasonably. "We do intend to pay."

"I don't need no damned money. This happens to be a religious group. What we don't need is this kind of trouble." The stout little man's eyes flickered from Luke to Amanda.

"That is rather short-sighted of you." Amanda stopped from scribbling her notes and glanced up at the two men. "We are, after all, entering Indian territory."

"I know that!" Pop bellowed. Luke glared at Amanda. The eccentric woman was sitting properly at the next table, barely pausing from her endless writing, her hair already coming loose and tumbling down. Aesop rustled in his cage. Amanda petted him with her pencil, then resumed scratching across the paper in a barely legible scrawl.

"Then you should be aware that you'll need all the men you can find," she continued. "The Longhorns won't be coming through again until the good weather, which indicates that the Indians are more likely to attack. I believe you know that the Commanches have developed quite a hunger for meat, a desire which currently isn't being appeased by the stray cattle. Therefore, it stands to reason that you will need all the help you can get."

"Yeah, but—" Pop started.

"And Luke is a gun." Amanda indicated the gunslinger with the point of her pencil. "I've hired him myself. If I understand correctly, the danger from Haskwell is based on supposition, while the danger from the Indians is much more than hypothesis. In which case—"

"What the hell is she talking about?" Pop glanced back at Luke, who was glaring at the woman before them.

"Amanda—" Luke began.

"Luke can help," Amanda finished, ignoring his interruption. " 'Half our misery from our foibles springs.' More."

Pop glanced from the man to the odd-looking woman. Amanda smiled at him, gave him a searching look through her glasses, then turned back to her work. Pop scratched his head.

"Who is she?" Pop said reluctantly. He stared appraisingly at Amanda, really looking at her for the first time. The woman had come in with the gunman, carrying a bird cage and a frayed bag that seemed about to pop its seams. She had quietly taken a seat, produced endless sheets of paper from the bag, and proceeded to write, ignoring everything around her. Pop was left with the impression that she was a little "touched." But as he examined her closely, he saw that her slender figure was apparent in spite of the ink-stained dress, and the Victorian lace did nothing to detract from her soft curves. With those glasses gone and her hair pulled back, she might even be pretty.

"Amanda?" Luke forced a smile. He stared at the writer, a cool smile coming to his face as she rustled inside the bag. "Amanda happens to be my wife."

"That so?" Pop asked in disbelief.

"I am not!" Amanda's head popped out of the bag and she glared at Luke, furious. "I wouldn't be married to you if you were the last procreative opportunity . . . " She began, but Luke shot her a look so stern that she stuttered into silence.

"She's a long way from home, and a little confused," Luke said. Amanda didn't miss the threatening note in his voice. She gazed haughtily out the door, crossing her arms and tapping her pencil in annoyance. As soon as her attention was elsewhere, Luke gestured to his head with a circling motion.

"Ah." Pop nodded. "Had an aunt like that myself. Used to tell everyone she was from France when her blood was as green as an Irish shamrock. Never understood the woman. Died just a few years ago. Played 'Take me Home Again' at the wake. I'll wager she turned over in her grave."

Amanda choked and Luke silenced her with a forceful glare. "We can be ready within the hour. Is that good enough?"

"Fine, fine." Pop agreed. "Now you take care of the missus, and I'll see that we all get to Texas. Just like Aunt Mathilda."

Amanda was furious. Not trusting herself to remain, she waited outside while Luke completed the business arrangements with the man called Pop. She was so angry that her knuckles whitened as her hands tightened on the bird cage and her bag. When Luke finally strode outside, she had to restrain herself from physical action.

"How dare you!" she spat, her turquoise eyes dark and flaming with emotion. "How could you tell that man those lies? Pretend we were married! And act as if I didn't have all my senses—"

"Amanda." Luke grinned, though he wisely stepped back

a few paces. "If you're honest, you'll understand why I did what I did. And you have to admit, you deserved it."

"What?" She no longer cared that they were in the middle of a public street, or that her voice rose to a high pitch. "You have some nerve!"

"We couldn't go on this trip together without being married. Didn't you hear him say there was a reverend on board?" Luke continued quietly. "I've explained this before."

"That's still no reason—"

"It's more than enough reason," Luke said sternly. "Pull yourself together, Amanda. The last thing we need is to get thrown off this train because we're unwed. And with Haskwell after you, I didn't think you'd want to be packed off somewhere, with some other family, maybe one without a gun among them."

This part made sense, though she still glared at him, leveling the carpetbag as if debating whether or not to hit him with it.

"And you had to contradict me in front of the man. If I hadn't acted as if you were crazy, he might not have believed us." Luke grinned, pushing his Stetson back from his face, revealing a warm, white smile. "Now calm down. You might even come to enjoy it. In any case, you'd best find a way to live with it. Like it or not, Amanda, you're about to become Mrs. Luke Parker. At least for the duration of our trip."

Amanda stared at him indignantly, aware that he was enjoying himself. But she wasn't too worried about the marriage part.

How bad could it be?

"What do you mean, they just left?"

Butch Winters leaned against the register desk at the boardinghouse, staring at the innocuous scrawl across the pages in disbelief.

"I'm sorry." The short, thin man at the desk shrugged, then gestured to the book with the tip of his pencil. "It seems that they both checked out this morning. I show a Mr. Luke Parker had registered for the both of them, but I remember the woman as well. Strange, with a birdcage and a carpetbag."

"That's her." Damien shoved himself from the wall, then jostled Butch. "Just our luck, ain't it? This girl's as slippery as a fresh-greased pig."

"You don't remember anything else?" Butch questioned slowly.

The man glanced from one of the outlaws to the other. Butch stared back at him, his scar curling as his expression changed from annoyance to suspicion. The counterman shrugged, and his face turned a shade whiter even as he kept his businesslike demeanor.

"All I can tell you is what's written here. You'll have to check with the sheriff if you want more information." He closed the book abruptly, then turned to the shelves behind the counter, as if intending to go back to work.

Butch and Damien exchanged a glance, then Butch softly pulled his gun. When the counterman turned around, he found himself looking into the barrel of a Colt .45.

"Look, friend. I have no desire to play games. I want to know where they are, and I want to know now. Do you understand?"

The man nodded quickly, sweat beading on his forehead as Butch cocked the gun. "I think I remember something. They did mention meeting a wagon train this morning."

"That's more like it." Butch nodded in satisfaction. "Let's see what else I can help you remember." Without warning, the gun exploded. The counterman snatched at his arm, gasping in shock as a bright red stream of blood ran warm and wet down the sleeve of his white shirt.

"Please don't kill me." He choked in pain as Butch recocked the gun.

"I'm getting awfully tired of this, and I've got better things to do than to waste time jawing with you. Where are they headed?"

"Texas." The man answered immediately, ignoring Damien's chuckle. Fresh blood flowed from his wound, but the gun did not waver. A dizziness rang in his ears and he braced himself against the counter. "I heard they were taking the Chisholm trail, straight through to Texas. Hooked up with a Reverend Weaver and his followers."

"Ain't that fittin'." Damien laughed. "Just think, Butch, they'll have their own little minister there. They can even have a Christian burial."

"Please . . . " The counterman gasped as Butch leveled the gun. Panic set in, coupled with pain and weakness, and the room began to spin. Slowly, everything went dark, and the man slid to the floor in a crumpled heap.

"Will you look at that." Damien grinned, leaning over the counter and peering inquisitively at the unconscious figure on the other side. "Looks like he up and fainted."

"Save me the trouble of killing him." Butch shrugged. He started to replace his gun, then noticed that the cock had already been pulled back. "I hate to waste good lead. I think our friend here has told us everything he knows anyway."

Butch pointed the gun at the bloody man passed out on the floor and pulled the trigger.

Damien laughed, put on his hat, and followed Butch out the door. He hated to waste good lead, too.

Chapter

12

He was trying to make her life miserable.

Amanda Edison stared at the heap of clothing lying at her feet, waiting to be sewn. As Luke's wife, she was expected to perform all the tasks for him that the other wives did for their husbands. She had to do his wash, serve his meals, prepare his bedding. For someone like Amanda who'd been fiercely independent, playing this role was unbearable.

At least he didn't sleep with her. Yet. Since the beginning of the journey, he'd kept night watch, sleeping early, then rising when the moon was high and very full, to watch for any signs of Indians, desperadoes or cattle thieves. At such times, Amanda could see him from the interior of the wagon, his face thoughtful and oranged by the firelight, his muscular body tense and still. She wondered what went through his mind as he sat there, staring into the flames, drinking the bitter black brew that passed for coffee, and quietly smoking hand-rolled cigarettes.

It was at these times she wanted him. The feeling nearly overpowered her, and she fought to keep from rising, putting her arms around him as a real wife would, and sharing the warmth of her body and the comfort of her company.

But Amanda didn't dare. She couldn't forget what had happened between them, nor that he sought refuge with the first available female when they had disagreed. He was a southerner, a killer, an educated man who had spurned everything for the life of a drifter.

She picked up an article of clothing, and saw it was his buckskins. The knee was torn out, probably from the previous day when he'd lassoed a bolting cow and had fallen from his horse. He'd hurt himself, she realized, observing the blood stain on his pants. Yet he had grinned, handed her the clothes, then chucked her under the chin and reminded her that a good wife would have them ready as quickly as possible.

Her cheeks burned. He was taunting her all right, trying to evoke some kind of emotional outburst. Angrily, she had bitten her lip, staring at the trousers, longing to fling them into his face and tell him the deal was off. She couldn't, though, and he knew it. She needed him until they got to Texas, much as she hated to admit it.

Aesop rustled in his cage and stared back at her with blinking amber eyes. Amanda smiled, suddenly remembering who and what she was. She was not one of these religious women, quiet and placid and obedient. She had a mind—a good mind—and if it couldn't be used now, then shame on her.

"Amanda?" Aileen stared across the fire at her as Amanda picked up the buckskins and began to shred them. "For the love of God, what are you doing?"

Amanda smiled, her strange eyes lighting with intensity. She had been surprisingly pleased when she discovered that the woman who'd helped her in the hotel room with her hair and dress was traveling with them, as the new Mrs. Jake Fontaine. They had married that very morning, with only the justice of the peace as a witness. Jake had insisted, especially when he realized that the wagon train would separate them permanently, and Aileen—he decided after one incredible night—would make a perfect wife.

"I'm seeing to Luke's trousers," Amanda replied seriously. "Logically, this is my only alternative."

"I don't get it." Aileen's nose wrinkled as Amanda displayed the buckskins, now torn from ankles to crotch.

"Think about it," Amanda continued. "Luke's forced me into this ridiculous position, masquerading as his—"

"Don't say it!" Aileen glanced toward the group of religious women, sitting a short distance away.

"He's punishing me because he's angry," Amanda continued in the same cool, detached voice. "Therefore, he is getting pleasure out of forcing his will on me and making me perform domestic acts for him. The only thing I can do is either accept the situation, or convince Luke that he doesn't want me as a wife."

"And you've decided—"

Amanda came as close to giggling as she ever thought possible. "By the time I'm through, Luke Parker will wish we were wed, only so he could get a divorce."

Aileen shivered, then went back to her own sewing. Luke Parker didn't look like a man to trifle with.

She only hoped Amanda's wonderful mind had taken that into account.

"I'm not believing this crap." Sam Haskwell threw down the telegram onto the glossy cherrywood table, then ran his hand angrily through his pitch-dark hair. The hotel room above the gambling hall was richly appointed, but Sam didn't notice the plush imported carpets, the tinkling chandeliers, or the warm blazing fire that threw shadows on the softly painted cream walls. "One girl! One damned girl! How in the hell can she do it?"

"I guess I'll go now. . . . "

"Sit there!" Haskwell paced the floor, barely glancing at the beautiful young showgirl named Honey. He had found her downstairs, singing in a voice that was pure heaven, wearing a sparkling beige gown that looked like little more than a veil over her naked body. Sam had taken one look at the singer, with her jet-black hair and startlingly rich brown eyes, and had ordered her sent up to his room. No one questioned Sam Haskwell. He heard that she had protested, but the sight of his weapon convinced her otherwise.

Now, as she sat on the very edge of the bed, looking like a startled doe about to dart off, Sam forced a smile.

"It's nothing. Just another example of incompetence. It is so hard to find good men to do a job. Would you like to know more about it?"

The young girl shook her head in the negative, her eyes enormous as the killer approached her. She bit her red painted lips, then drew her legs up beneath her, nearly passing out in fright.

Sam grinned. "Ah, but I think I will tell you, nonetheless. The telegram is about a woman who crossed me. She witnessed a gunfight between myself and another man, then had the audacity to write about it." The memory still enraged Haskwell, and his black Irish eyes glittered. "Do you know what I did then?"

"No." Her voice came as light as a graveyard whisper.

"I ordered her killed." Sam's anger dissipated as he saw the genuine terror in the singer's eyes. Slowly his hand went to the back of her dress, and he toyed with the hooks, his movements tantalizingly slow and filled with menace. "I sent two men after her, but up until now, they haven't been able to succeed." He slipped the gown to the girl's waist, even more gratified to hear her indrawn breath of terror. Long, satiny hair spilled out over the girl's shoulders, and he brushed it back, baring her round breasts to his gaze. He had been right. She was wearing nothing beneath the gown, nothing except the lovely naked charms that nature gave her.

With slow, determined movements, he ignored the terror-filled tears that slipped down the girl's cheeks as he reached out and fondled a breast, playing with a nipple that hardened beneath his touch. The sparkling gown now lay in a puddle around her hips and he grinned, lifting her up, letting it fall even farther to the floor.

Honey blushed, standing on the edge of the bed, wearing

nothing more than her stockings held up by black lace garters. Sam's hot eyes went to the dark curly V between her white thighs, entranced by the contrast between her pale flesh and the sheer blackness of her hair and remaining undergarments.

"So, I'll be thinking there's one thing left for me to do," Sam continued, brushing his knuckles down that thatch of enticing curls, watching as the girl choked and hiccoughed with fear. "I'll have to take care of it myself."

Honey tried to talk, but the words caught in her throat. Sam smiled, removed his own clothes, then picked her up and lowered her down onto his lap. He thrust his finally hard erection into her tight, feminine warmth.

He wasn't losing his edge after all.

"What the hell!" Luke heard the buckskins rip as he tried to put them on, his muscular legs tearing through the tough cowhide. Furious, he stared at the torn material, then the comic appearance of his legs displayed as if in a dress. His eyes went to the tear.

It was neatly cut, from one leg to the other, as if someone had taken shears to the trousers.

Suddenly, he had a vision of Amanda that morning, sitting away from the others, her head bent over a pile of sewing. She was the picture of domestic tranquility, with Aesop at her side and a biology book in front of her. He had assumed that she'd finally accepted his presence, and maybe was beginning to admit that it wasn't so bad being tied to a man. He had hoped that, in time, she would even admit to what he knew she felt for him, even if he had to goad her into it. He hadn't been able to forget that slip of paper he'd found in her room, and the passion she exhibited in the privacy of her journal. He'd watched her by the campfire, scribbling in the book, longing to read what else she'd recorded, and waiting for the night she'd give in to desire and come to him. . . .

Apparently, his little scholar had other ideas.

Tearing off the trousers, he quickly rifled through the rest

of his clothes. It was just as he thought. Shirt sleeves were
still torn and buttons were missing, collars were unfastened,
and socks were undarned. She hadn't done anything to his
clothes at all except the trousers, and those she had made
worse. Outrage flooded through him, and as he gritted his
teeth, he thought of how immensely satisfying it would be
to turn the lovely genius over his knee and teach her a lesson
she never learned in college. As he stared at the clothes, the
absurdity of the situation struck him and unwillingly, he
burst out laughing.

He had to admire her. The woman had a brain, and apparently was determined to use it.

He stuffed the clothes into a bundle, then slipped into the
one intact pair of trousers he still had, forcing down his
laughter.

So Amanda Edison wanted to play rough.

She had no idea just how rough it could get.

"Did you wish to see me?" Amanda stood before him,
looking incredibly lovely as the moonlight made her hair
appear like polished wood and brightened the stark blue-
green of her eyes. The scent of bacon and beef drifted from
the chuckwagon, complimented by the aromatic smell of the
bitter coffee. The religious folk had finished their meal and
were starting to pray, so that Luke and Amanda were quite
alone when he'd called her. Now she stared at him through
thick black lashes, and Luke was genuinely glad to see apprehension there.

He was beginning to think the woman felt nothing at all.

"Yes, Amanda, please sit down," he said evenly.

Amanda glanced around the interior of the covered
wagon. It was far too intimate, this rough hewn cart with
its thick, canvas covering. The floor was made up of crude
seats and a warm bed, and it was here that her eyes wandered. Blushing hotly, she looked back up, then carefully
schooled her features.

"I am comfortable standing, and I would prefer to remain
so."

"Ah." He smiled, his grin filled with warmth. Amanda was instantly wary. "Suit yourself. As a devoted husband, I wouldn't dream of discomforting you." Slowly, he began to unbutton his shirt, his eyes never leaving her face.

"What are you doing?" Although their wagon was a short distance from the fire, Amanda could see him all too clearly, and the gorgeous body that emerged as he tossed his shirt aside. He seemed to consider her words for a moment, then he sat down and began to remove his boots.

"I'm undressing," he said, as if announcing the weather. "You see, I've done more than my share of the night watch, so the Reverend decided to appoint some of the other men. It's just as well. These are my last pair of trousers."

"I see." Amanda swallowed hard. She was beginning to see exactly. "I think I'll go get some coffee—"

"Don't even think about it," Luke continued, a light threat in his voice. "As I was saying, when I went to get dressed this morning, something had happened to my clothes. It seems someone hasn't sewn them at all. It also seems that the tear in my buckskins now extends to both legs, from one end to the other. Naturally, that will cause me some inconvenience, but none that I haven't experienced before. In the war, you are often without a change of clothes, so do you know what you do to keep your wardrobe intact?"

Aesop squawked. Amanda stared at Luke, her eyes as wide as cornflowers. "No."

"You try not to sleep in them." He stood up, less than three feet away from her, and began to unbuckle his belt. "Otherwise, your shirts become sweaty too fast, they wrinkle and tear. Even your trousers should be removed. When you're down to one pair, you don't have much of a choice, do you?" He raised her chin, forcing her to look at him.

"I wouldn't know." Amanda choked, the color staining her cheeks a bright pink. She was aware of him shucking his trousers and then his drawers, of him standing so close to her that she could feel the warmth of his body, even through her own clothes. It was erotic and strangely com-

pelling, to be standing in the confinement of the wagon, with
Luke buck-naked just a few feet away. She almost swayed
toward him, her fingers aching to touch the bronze chest
that faced her, or the masculine heat just below his waist
that she knew without looking was hard and ready for her.

She wanted him. God, how she wanted him. Yet, she was
afraid. Luke had the power to hurt her, and she didn't want
anyone to have that kind of power. Closing her eyes, she
let a single tear drop as his fingers gently caressed her face,
then softly, enticingly, her lips. She gave a little gasp as he
pulled her into his arms, his body, naked and arousing,
pressed against her own. Any doubt she had about his own
arousal was swiftly destroyed as she felt the heat of him rubbing against her, throbbing and unforgiving.

"Feel that and tell me you don't want me."

It was as if he could read her mind. Amanda's lips parted
to flatly deny him, but his mouth took hers in a kiss, her
words with it. It was just like the night in the Harvey House,
just like the night when he seduced her with such expert
tenderness. Amanda could do little more than push against
him half-heartedly as his tongue played with hers, then
slipped inside her mouth in a wildly exciting rhythm that
made her forget everything except the man who held her.
A moist heat spread through her body like hot honey, flooding her veins, culminating there, where his hardness teased
her with a searing promise.

"Amanda. Mandy, sweet Mandy." He groaned, cupping
her round bottom, pulling her impossibly closer. Logic
swept from her mind, reason deserted her. No book ever
taught her how to deal with this, and now, although every
instinct was against it, her body cried out for what he was
giving her.

"Please." She whispered when his mouth left hers,
though her body still leaned toward him. She gasped when
he cupped a breast, his thumb brushing the taut nipple
through the fabric, arousing her in spite of herself.

Yet, he felt her resistance, knew she was still fighting both
herself and him. Gently, he released her, staring at her with

a frown, angry at himself for the desire she aroused with little more than an innocent kiss. He had meant only to teach her a lesson, and now found himself tortured as well.

She gazed at him with passion-drugged eyes, and he saw those eyes cloud with confusion, then mortification as she realized what had happened.

He had taken pity on her and released her. Embarrassment flooded her, and she covered her mouth with the back of her hand, fighting the sobs that threatened.

"Here." He handed her the clothes. "Fix them by morning. Or else you'll be sleeping with me naked every night. And I'm not sure either one of us could take it."

She nodded, horribly grateful when he eased away from her, then slipped into the bed, covering his dark, masculine body with a quilt silvered by moonlight.

Amanda may not have known everything. But she knew when to quit.

"He ain't gonna be too happy about that telegram."

Damien spat onto the ground, then settled more comfortably against the pine bluff. They were already deep in Indian territory, the last legal refuge for the Five Civilized Tribes. But there were others about, others that didn't conform to any government edicts, who saw a white man as nothing more than a potential scalp. Damien didn't like to think about that, and he pulled down his Stetson and glanced about uneasily.

"Haskwell don't like much," Butch agreed. "And he was pretty pissed about us losing that girl. How long we been tracking her now?"

"Too long." Damien shaded his eyes and stared at the endless horizon. "We should have been able to catch up to her easily. If it wasn't for your horse going lame, we'd have had her."

"What the hell did you want me to do? When you steal a horse, it sometimes happens. I should kill that sheep rancher. Trust a sheepman to have a lame horse."

"You know, if Miss Amanda Edison had turned to school

marming like any normal woman, this wouldn't have happened. No, she had to write a book and finger Haskwell," Damien said.

"And if she should take it into her head to testify, he'd be dangling neck first from a cottonwood," Butch sneered. "She's startin' to piss me off, too. I ain't had to work this hard since we went after Clyde Barnes."

"I remember old Clyde." Damien grinned, his soulless eyes showing dim emotion. "Chased him from Nevada straight east to Texas. Caught him in the panhandle and staked him out for the Indians."

"Right." Butch grinned, his scar whitening. "By the time them Commanches were through with him, old Clyde had nothing left but his—"

"Butch, lookey there." Damien cut off this pleasant discourse and pointed to a puff of dust in the distance.

Butch rose, then joined his companion on the bluff. There, just below them, was the outline of a small wagon train keeping faithfully to the Chisholm trail.

Butch and Damien exchanged a grin. Seems like luck was turning their way.

"I have to admit, I don't understand." Aileen gazed at Amanda, her freckled face wrinkled in a frown. She bent over the swiftly rushing Canadian River, beating a shirt against the rocks, forcing the crystalline water to cleanse the garment. "I wouldn't mind being married to Luke Parker. He's quite a handsome man."

"I am aware of his physical qualities," Amanda replied, dipping her feet into the pool—anything to keep from thinking about that night. Luke had her completely in his power, and he knew it. She, Amanda Edison—who'd won prize after prize at college for her treatise on "Natural Selection and the Earth Today," on her calculus papers, on her editorials—was putty in the hands of the southern gunslinger. She could almost hear his smug laughter. It wasn't to be borne.

"And he's nice enough. Just yesterday he helped Jake

when that bear cornered his calf. Scared the living heck out of Jake. But Luke has good aim and a cool head. He killed the bear and helped Jake out of a jam, without anyone getting hurt. Even Pop said it was quite a feat."

"I know," Amanda said.

"Then what is it? I remember that night you were going out. Didn't it go well? Does he have problems in bed? Can't go the whole trail? I can help you with that. Sex happened to be my former occupation, you know."

Amanda felt her color rise straight up to her hair. "I don't think that's his problem." She choked, pulling her feet from the water.

"What then? What is really bothering you?"

Amanda shrugged. "Luke just isn't . . . right for me. And I have no intention of calling any man my master! And it's other things. I don't know how to describe it." Amanda glanced down at her journal.

He called me Mandy. He held me and I wanted him so badly I could think of nothing else. This desperate longing never ceases, but grows by day like the endless fields of bluebonnets. I'm afraid I shall be consumed by it, lost like Tantalus, stooping to drink from the water which is always receding and must always recede. . . .

"Then what are you going to do?" Aileen laid out a shirt, then reached for a pair of trousers, holding them in the water once more. The water swirled through the legs, washing away the dust and grime from the trail, taking the sweat and smell of cattle from the rough material. The current was so strong that Aileen had to grasp the material with both hands to keep it from washing downstream. "I think it's a mistake to keep defying him. It didn't work the last time."

"Perhaps," Amanda replied coolly. But her emotions were neatly capped. Pride and intelligence dictated that she win this one, and not just the battle, but the war. Her lack of self-control frightened her, along with the thought of what would happen if they were alone again. "But then again, perhaps I haven't tried hard enough. As John Dryden said, 'Beware the fury of a patient man.'"

Picking up Luke's laundry, Amanda sent it over the river's edge, and watched it float downstream, ignoring Aileen's gasp of horror.

Chapter

13

"I think we should cross here."

The Reverend and his followers looked at Luke doubt-fully, then their eyes turned back in unison to Pop Finnegan. The trail driver spat a wad of tobacco juice onto the ground, then turned his attention back to the river.

"Why here, laddie? Looks rougher than the rest."

"It is," Luke agreed. They were standing on the bank of the Canadian River. Luke was actually waist-deep in the muddy water, using a stick to test the depth and the current. Tossing the stick aside, he stepped closer to the bank, ignoring the freezing brown liquid that swirled around his legs.

"I think we're better off here in spite of the rocks," Luke said finally. "That still pool down farther indicates depth. I know these damned rivers. From the last rains, they're liable to be much deeper than even a month ago. That little puddle could drop off fifteen feet."

Pop scratched his chin thoughtfully while the Reverend nodded. "I think he speaks the truth." The preacher looked at Luke with renewed respect. In the past few weeks, Luke Parker had proved invaluable to them. Not only could he shoot with a deadly accuracy, but he seemed to know this land like the back of his hand. Even the flank and drag riders, cowboys hired by the religious men to get their Herefords to Texas, seemed to consider Luke the main authority.

Pop shrugged. "Well, if that's what you all want to do, I ain't going to argue. But those rocks look dangerous to me. We'd best be right careful how we go about getting them wagons across. . . . Why, will you look at that." Pop's words cut off quickly and he gestured to the river.

Luke glanced at the water, started to turn, then his head swung quickly back. There, in the midst of the churning river, floating placidly downstream, was a pile of clothing. Pants, shirts, socks—all came drifting downstream, splashing over the rocks, then continuing down past the group of men.

Pop cleared his throat. "Looks like your buckskins, Parker."

Luke stared, fury building up inside of him. It couldn't be, she couldn't have . . . but the parade of clothing continued to float by. Cursing, he tried to reach one of his shirts, but the current took it swiftly past him and it disappeared downriver, along with the rest of his wardrobe.

"I don't believe her. Jesus Christ, I don't believe that woman!" The words tumbled out before Luke could stop them and he trudged from the water, shaking like a wet wolf, his anger palpable.

"I'll be damned." Pop spat amid the incredulous stares of the religious men. "You think your wife did this? She sure is crazy. Pretty thing, too. What a shame."

"I'll be back." Luke leaped onto his horse, jerking the reins and kicking the animal into a gallop. When the dust settled, Pop turned to the Reverend and shrugged.

"Just like my old aunt Mathilda."

Luke caught up with her at the wagons, where she sat in the dust as the other women packed up their belongings for the river crossing. Amanda was surrounded by books, and was making notations in her journal. She glanced up when she saw him, ignoring the thunderous expression on his face.

"Cumulonimbus." She indicated the puffy cloudscape. "That is an indicator of rain within the next twenty-four hours. I would suggest we put off our crossing until then."

Luke stared at her in disbelief, barely aware that Aileen scampered off, eager to get far away from his wrath. Fury sent the blood pounding through his head and his hand tightened so hard on the reins that the horse reared.

"Is something wrong?" Amanda got calmly to her feet. She had forgotten the clothes, forgotten everything in her latest scientific interest. But the look on his face reminded her, and the color drained as she suddenly realized she was in trouble. Big trouble.

"I think I'll go help Aileen now." Amanda picked up her journal and Aesop's cage, as if nothing unusual was happening. As if his entire wardrobe, newly sewn, was not floating downriver along with a collection of prairie grass and twigs.

She started to walk past him, but Luke's hand shot out, capturing her wrist. Amanda struggled, dropping the cage.

"Let me go—"

"Get up on the horse." He didn't recognize his own voice, it was so laced with anger. Amanda shook her head and tried to pull away.

"I'll ride with the wagon," she replied cooly.

"Get on the horse. I'm not telling you again." His teeth were gritted, and his beautiful blue eyes blazed. When she hesitated another moment, he simply reached down and effortlessly hauled her onto the saddle, knowing full well she'd rather die than ride like this. Forcing her into the seat before him, he tucked her skirts beneath her, then tightened his arm possessively around her waist and pulled her up against him. Amanda cried out as he kicked his mount, and headed west.

"What are you trying to prove?—" she began, hoping to maintain a cool distance between them. He glared down at her with such open anger that she instinctively shuddered.

"How dare you? Especially after the other night, how dare you do such a thing? I'm beginning to believe you are crazy," Luke thundered.

"I am not!" Amanda twisted in his lap, then gasped as he tightened his grip. "Take your hands off me! As Carlyle said—"

"Amanda." His voice was cold and even, far more frightening than his open rage. "Listen to me carefully. If you're trying to discover my breaking point, you're almost there."

She believed him. She could sense the barely leashed tension in his body. His rippling muscles were so close to her own skin that she could feel the hardness of his flesh, as if it took everything in his power to check his temper. Amanda swallowed hard, wondering if perhaps she hadn't miscalculated. It had only happened once before, but the mistake had cost her a grade.

This time it could cost her far more.

"Where are we going?" Though she knew she was treading on dangerous ground, the anticipation was undeniably worse.

"We are going downriver," he replied in the same icy tones. "There's a bend a few feet below where the Canadian forms a pool."

"And?" Amanda didn't want to be spared any details.

"You are going to retrieve my clothes. Every last one of them."

"What if they aren't there?" Ever the working mind, Amanda couldn't help but ask.

Luke glared at her. "Pray."

"Why looky here, Butch. We got us a band of religious folk."

Damien grinned as the Reverend came to the forefront of the group, his Bible lifted in his hand. Women sobbed quietly as the two gunmen rode into camp, firing sporadically, sending the children scurrying beneath the wagons. Now they stood in the semicircle, sheltering their little ones from the outlaws, while the scarred man called Butch kept his gun trained on the minister.

"What is it you want? If you are looking for money, we

have very little. We only wish to travel to Texas, there to live in peace," the Reverend Weaver said quietly.

"Ain't that real nice, Butch?" Damien chuckled, his soulless eyes looking out onto the cluster of holy men and women. "They want to go in peace! That's right brave of you, Reverend, but not real smart. We're looking for the girl."

Aileen glanced at her husband, while Jake stood a few feet back and watched the flat prairie. Luke and Amanda had been gone for less than an hour. They could come back at any time with the rest of the men, without realizing that they were riding into an ambush. Bravely, she walked up to the men, holding her shawl tightly around her, as if for protection.

"There is no one else," Aileen said quickly. "Just us. The Reverend Weaver and his followers. You must have the wrong—" She gasped as Butch grabbed her, his smile evil.

"You don't look like no Reverend Weaver's nothing." He chuckled as she struggled to get free. "And we think you're lying. Search the place, Damien."

"Let go of my wife," Jake demanded, his lined face white with anger.

Butch cocked his gun and held it to the girl's head. "Make me, cowboy. Now you just be real quiet and cooperate, and the little missus won't get hurt. It's not her we want. We want the other one. The writer. Amanda Edison."

Jake's fists tightened. Aileen stood completely still, warning him with her eyes not to do anything foolish. Helpless and furious, he watched as Damien rifled through the wagons, searching for a sign of Amanda. The other women huddled near the chuck wagon, glancing toward the river, some of them sobbing. Damien's head popped out of the canvas, a huge grin spreading across his face.

Aesop's cage dangled from his finger.

"It's her all right." He grinned as Butch's hand tightened on Aileen's shoulder. "It could only be Miss Edison."

Butch nodded, releasing Aileen. He watched the girl stumble across the prairie, and into her husband's arms. He gestured at them with the gun, indicating the group of women.

"Now all of you just mosey on down here." He pointed to the closest wagon. "Damien will make sure you're real comfortable before tying you up. Looks like we got some more riding to do, to find them." Actually, that suited Butch just fine. The less witnesses and trouble-making church folk around, the better.

"And you," he glanced at Aileen. "You're lucky I don't kill you for lying to me. But I ain't got a lot of lead, and I don't want to waste shots. You just join the others and don't start no more trouble." Butch grinned evilly. "We plan to do that all by ourselves."

"Put me down!" Amanda struggled furiously as they reached the river's edge and Luke hauled her—like a sack of old flour, she would remember later—into the cold rushing water's edge. Gasping furiously, her dress plastered to her like a wet sack, she glared at him.

"Go get them back." Luke ignored her diatribe and gestured to the pile of clothes that had fortunately collected at the river's bend. "Now."

"You can't mean—" Amanda glanced back to the river and shuddered. There was at least twenty feet between herself and the opposite bank where the clothes were laying in a sodden pile, twenty feet of rapidly rushing water and indeterminable depths.

"Yes, I do. Don't push me, Amanda. Get the damned clothes!"

The barely restrained fury in his voice startled her and she stared at him, realizing the effort he was making to control his temper. She glanced at the river again. Twenty feet. It might as well have been a hundred.

"I can't," she said simply.

"What do you mean, you can't?" Luke took a step closer, his face tightening with outrage.

Amanda instinctively backed up. She hadn't quite thought this all through, she realized belatedly. And she also hadn't understood the implications of being within his power. Back east, she always had the protection of school and of her books against any unpleasantness. But here, there was no one to shield her from him, and from his raw anger. The idea unnerved her.

"I just can't," she said, choking on the words. His eyes blazed and she understood that he thought she was defying him once more and pushing his patience to the limit. There was no sense in this. As embarrassing as it was, she was going to have to tell him. She lifted her head and faced him bravely, her hair wet and clinging to her neck, her dress soaked and muddy. "I can't . . . swim."

"You what?" Luke stared at her, his anger draining as she turned away from him, tears springing to her eyes. The ridiculousness of the situation struck him, and he started to laugh, softly at first, then more deeply as Amanda glared at him.

"Go ahead and laugh at me!" she spat, color rushing to her cheeks. But as he continued to chuckle, her anger overwhelmed her and she rushed at him, tripping over an exposed rock. Her body hit his and the two of them tumbled into the river, falling from the edge into the pool. Amanda sputtered, then Luke pulled her to her feet, ignoring her panicked struggles. She clung to him in fear like a frightened kitten as the water rushed past her, threatening to take them both downstream in a silent, deadly wash.

"Amanda, stop it." His voice penetrated her panic and she quieted, even more embarrassed as he slipped his hands beneath her and carried her to the bank. He plopped her down on the ground, then stood before her and shook his head incredulously.

"Can't swim. Jesus, lady, is there anything you do right? For somebody with so much brains, you don't know a damned thing."

Furious, Amanda glared up at him, but Luke looked so in control, his legs planted far apart, his muscular arms crossed as he gazed at her in amusement, that she was speechless.

"Now you sit there. I'm going to the other side and I'll toss you the clothes. Move and you'll live to regret it, I promise you. Understand?"

She nodded miserably. Once again, she didn't have a choice. She was beaten. At least he was giving her a reprieve. As he turned and dove gracefully into the still water, she had to admit it could have been a whole lot worse.

Luke emerged on the opposite side of the river, gathered up an armful of clothing, then swam back to the bank. When he could stand, he threw the soaked garments to Amanda, waited until she had successfully gathered them into a pile, then he returned to the bend. Two trips later, all of his clothes were assembled on the river bank, and Amanda, looking completely contrite and amazingly pretty with her hair soaked and her gown clinging to her, waited for him as he climbed out of the water.

"Bring them to me," he ordered, slicking back his hair with his fingers.

Burning, Amanda did as she was told. She hiked up the bundle of muddy clothes, then stood before him like a recalcitrant child determined to test her parent's limits. Luke grinned, then his smile vanished as her face lifted and her eyes met his.

"I want you to rinse them and get the mud off. When they're clean, we'll put them on the back of the horse and then return."

"But—" Amanda glanced up at the startlingly blue sky. "The cumulonimbus! It's going to rain—"

"Amanda," Luke gritted, his patience snapping. "Wash the damned clothes."

Swallowing hard, she nodded, then sat down at the river bank. Sometimes, it just didn't pay to have a mind.

Even a very good one.

"You see 'em, Butch?"

The outlaw shook his head, then scanned the open prairie. Damn, normally he could see for miles, but a wind had kicked up and with it, the dust. His vision was cut off from almost everything, except for the dirt directly around him and the silver ribbon of a river snaking through the soft green grass.

"Let's try down by the water. Least we can keep our course if this damned wind keeps up."

Damien nodded, unable to see much himself. It was as if that damned girl had some kind of power. Then he grinned as he reined up his horse. Even if she did, it wouldn't be enough to help her.

Nothing would.

It not only rained, it poured. Amanda felt a single plop on her nose, then stared in disbelief as the sky seemed to open and buckets of hail and rain splattered the dry prairie.

"Get up here!" Luke's voice cut through the deluge, and Amanda had a fleeting vision of him rushing for the horse in the sheeting rain, then hoisting her up into the saddle where she'd placed his clean clothes. He kicked the horse into a gallop, then started across the plain, keeping one arm wrapped tightly around Amanda.

She was freezing. Pop Finnegan had warned them that the weather on the trail could be treacherous, and she had to agree he was right. Unwillingly, she snuggled closer into Luke's arms, seeking protection from an unbelievable rainfall, and from the hail that was the size of crabapples. Chill seeped through her clothes and she sneezed, wondering why she had ever left Boston, why she had thought it necessary to take her editor's advice and head out on this horrible journey. She was experiencing life all right, and it was far more real than she ever thought possible.

"Jesus." She heard Luke's indrawn breath as the horse stumbled in a prairie hole, then slowed to a painful walk. Amanda could feel the uneven gait of the animal as it tried desperately not to fall. Mud oozed from the newly soaked ground, making terrible sucking noises, and the horse tottered.

"We've got to stop before this horse goes lame," Luke called to her. "Christ! A goddamned hail storm."

Amanda hardly noticed his language, or that fact that his fury had returned two-fold. All she cared about was getting dry and warm again. Visions of Mrs. Pincus' boardinghouse floated before her and she thought of her thick down quilts, the warm fires that made even a New England house comfortable, good lights, lots of books . . .

Amanda could have cried. She tried to reason her feelings out philosophically, but she discovered that logic was related to comfort. She couldn't recall a single quote that would have helped at a time like this, and she was certain that even Milton never spent a day out on the prairie scrubbing clothes or being doused by hail and rain.

"There! I see a house!" Amanda cried. In the distance, she could make out the dim outline of a roof, and the grey column of a chimney. She turned to Luke, then froze as a familiar sound echoed in her ear, much like corn popping in a grate.

"Oh no, not again—" Amanda gasped as Luke whipped out his Colt, then quickly reined up the horse. The animal reared, throwing its sleek head back in the rain as the gunfire rang out—from nowhere, it seemed.

"Jesus!" Luke urged the horse forward, toward the house that Amanda had spotted. He fired behind him, but the rain effectively hid anyone from his sight.

"We're almost there!" Amanda cried, losing her breath as the shots rang out. Luke lurched forward as if pushed.

"Luke?" She paled as he nearly fell from the horse, just as they reached the house.

He didn't respond.

"Git 'em, Butch?"

Butch grunted, crawling from behind a clump of laurel, hail pounding the ground around him. Wiping his face with his neck cloth, he grinned, his scar curling.

"That wasn't no bobcat. I hit him all right."

"Old Haskwell'll be damned happy to hear this." Damien smirked. "Might even pay extra."

Butch grunted. "Let's finish them off and get the hell out of here. I don't like the looks of this damned rain."

"You ain't gettin' like them Indians, afraid of a little bad weather? This hail don't mean a thing."

"Maybe not. But just the same, I'll be glad to be back in Abilene, with a whiskey and a woman," Butch said.

Damien cocked his gun and grinned. "With this reward money, you'll get more than that, Butch. Much more."

Amanda barely slid from the soaking wet saddle as Luke tumbled forward, his body heavy and clumsy. Thankfully, he was still conscious enough to respond to her anxious motions as she helped him to the hut. His legs dragged across the prairie grass, and Amanda thought he would fall when she struggled with the door and he had to stand unaided. She pried the rustic panel open a minute later, just in time to see him collapse to the floor.

"Luke!" She ran toward him, but the fall seemed to have jarred his senses and he got painfully to his feet, then managed to walk the distance to a beat-up chair that waited beside an empty grate. Blood streaked across his forehead in a nasty looking wound, which he absently wiped with his sleeve. He sank into the seat, then opened his eyes and stared at Amanda as if suddenly recollecting what had happened.

"Are you all right?" she whispered.

"No," Luke answered, then quietly passed out.

Chapter

14

Amanda didn't know what was more terrifying: the sound of the hail pounding on the roof, the unconscious groan that Luke made, or the absence of gunfire outside. Somewhere, somehow, they had found her. Instinctively she knew that, and like a hunted animal at bay, found herself very close to freezing in sheer terror.

Her eyes went back to Luke. He still lay slumped in the chair, taking a bullet that was meant for her. Pain welled up inside of her and a hot mist stung her eyes. She had lied to herself that day, about her feelings for him. This man, for whatever reason, meant something to her. And now . . .

Stop it, she told herself furiously. *You won't do either yourself or him any good.* Bringing a chilled fist to her mouth, she forced herself to think.

Luke needed her. This was not the time for emotionalism, but for action. She tried to recall what her books said to do at a time like this, but school had never taken gunmen and outlaws into account. Remembering the basics, she pulled at his coat. The saturated buckskin came off with a few rough tugs, and she laid the coat on the floor. Next, she eased him down, making his head level with his feet, hoping that his blood circulation would improve. She then wiped away the blood and examined his wound.

It didn't look great. Amanda choked when she saw the red gash on his forehead. Fighting back nausea, she ripped off part of his shirt sleeve and tied a makeshift bandage around his head, hoping to stem the blood flow until help could arrive. Surely, the Reverend and his men would look for them—

Gunfire blasted through the open window and Amanda sobbed, her throat aching with terror and suppressed tears. She fumbled for Luke's gun, her fingers cold and numb from the rain. Stumbling to the window, she tried to keep her nerve. Dear God, instead of learning Socrates, why hadn't she learned how to survive?

The renewed barrage of fire made her shake uncontrollably. Balancing her hands on the sill, she closed her eyes and squeezed the trigger. The heavy Colt blasted, shooting out at the faceless enemy through the grey curtain of rain. Amanda couldn't help the tears that fell, nor the fear that overwhelmed her. She hadn't counted on experiencing this much life, nor had she counted on losing it so quickly. Amazingly, the only thing that she regretted was Luke. As she fumbled with the bullets, grateful that she'd watched him and knew how to reload, she found herself wishing that things had been different. That before she died, she had fought with him less, told him the things she'd told her journal, told him that she—

That she loved him. Tears stung, but she wiped at her eyes, then repositioned herself at the window. Dear God, why, out of all of life's lessons, did she have to learn this one so late? She fired again, wishing for a miracle, knowing the odds against escape were very low. She was a woman alone, inexperienced with a gun, fighting off vicious outlaws. She couldn't do it forever. Even now she could hear their gunfire returning, the ground rumbling . . .

Amanda sat straight up, the smoking gun in her hand. The rumbling continued, louder this time, echoing over the pounding rattle of the hail. Panic built in her heart, threatening to explode as she recognized the noise.

Stampede.

If there was one word that would strike terror in the heart of any cowboy, that was it. Amanda had written about the phenomenon many times, had even heard stories about it, but had never witnessed it first hand.

Until today.

The thunder grew louder and Amanda sank to the floor in desperation. There was nothing for her to do, nowhere to go. The hopelessness of the situation was appalling, but there was no escaping facts. A strange calm came to her as she realized that her fate was out of her hands. Closing her eyes, she forgot science, forgot physics, forgot everything except a primitive need to make contact with another person. With Luke.

Amanda rose to her feet, and returned to his side. His color looked better, and when she checked the head bandage, she was grateful that the bleeding seemed to have stopped. Her fingers touched his face, marveling at the rough texture and the visible veins like the roots of a tough oak tree.

"Luke," she whispered as the stampede grew louder. She needed to be with him, to feel the warmth of his hands as she closed them within her own. She had been such a fool. She thought of the night in the Harvey house when he'd wanted to make love to her, and now she wished that they had. She wanted the memory, wanted to close her eyes and keep it—the way she'd kept a smooth black stone in her pocket as a child, a charm to take out and reappreciate.

"Luke, I—"

His eyelids flickered and Amanda's breath caught. The cattle grew closer; she could hear their hooves pounding the ground, tearing everything that got in their way. The hail rattled and the rain tore at the shack. The wind made a ghastly echo through the room and Amanda crossed her arms, hugging herself, drained of all emotion. Something snapped, and she thought she heard a cry, but then the cattle were all around her. She brought her hands to her ears, unable to bear the earsplitting noise. The earth rumbled beneath her and the cabin shook as if from an earthquake. Amanda fully expected it to come down around her at any moment. The door, battered by the rushing Herefords, crashed in and she screamed. . . .

The cattle passed by, black rushing shapes that came out of her worst nightmare. They ran past the door and around the shack walls, bolting toward nowhere in sheer, uncontrollable terror. Amanda couldn't look at them—an apocalyptic vision come to life. Hundreds of cattle ran by, the dreams of the religious families destroyed as the beasts rushed blindly over the prairie. Their numbers gradually lessened, until they trickled down to a few remaining Herefords. Slowly, the noise died and the ground stopped trembling. The rain fell, but lighter, and the hail eased until all that remained were tiny balls of ice rolling like marbles across the battered prairie.

They'd made it. Somehow, impossibly, they'd survived. Amanda's hands slowly dropped away from her ears and she was filled with the blessed sounds of soft rainfall. Tears tumbled down her cheeks. She wiped her face with her sleeve, then her eyes fell to the floor and her heart stopped.

Luke was staring back at her with a familiar grin.

"Well, author. Looks like you wrote us out of this one."

Butch climbed out from beneath a conclave of rocks, grateful that he'd managed to find shelter at all. Damien hadn't been as lucky.

He'd heard his partner's screams during the stampede, but couldn't do anything to help him. The beasts had run roughshod over everything that stood in their way. Even now as Butch picked his way among the rubble, he could see the ruts and holes where the prairie grass had been torn up.

Damien's body lay fifteen feet away, fifteen feet from shelter and safety. Butch stood over the bloodied and mottled form, now barely recognizable. He reached down and felt for a pulse, uncertain whether he really wanted to know.

Damien was alive. The pulse was thready, but there. Butch grunted, letting the battered arm fall back to the equally battered earth. He'd have to find a horse, and then make a pallet to get Damien back to town where a doctor could stitch him back up. As if hearing his thoughts, Damien moaned. Butch counted three breaks in the man's leg alone.

Swearing under his breath, he set off for the horse. This was Amanda Edison's fault, he thought. And once he got help, she'd answer to him.

For Damien.

"Luke, I'm so sorry!"

Amanda rushed to his side, unabashedly hugging him, thrilled that he was alive. Luke rose up on one arm, wincing as Amanda stumbled into him.

"Easy, Mandy. I'm okay, really. You did a good job with the bandage." The gash on his forehead was little more than a flesh wound, Luke discovered as he adjusted the cloth, and obviously looked worse than it felt. He glanced around, saw the rainfall, and grimaced. "Looks like we're stuck here until they find us. I guess the horse is gone."

"Does it hurt badly? This was all my fault, I should never have sent your clothes downriver. I thought you were gone, I thought I could never tell you—"

"Tell me what?" Luke eased himself back down, deciding he didn't want to look too healthy. For whatever reason, Amanda had let her guard down. She even looked different. Emotion colored her face and sparkled her eyes with a passion he'd only guessed at before. It was like seeing a book with its cover torn off, and the pages whipping enticingly in the wind.

"Well . . . things." She blushed, her cheeks taking on a rosy hue that made her even more attractive. "I was so scared that you were hurt, when I thought you were . . . "

The rain softly pattered above them, and the wind blew,

bringing a scent of dank, carnal earth and crushed grass through the window. Amanda turned away, unwilling to face him, and even more unwilling to confront her own emotional turmoil.

Luke stared at her for a long time, then gently took her hand, pulling her closer to him. "Did you hate it that much, pretending to be married to me? Is that why you tried to drive me away?"

"No!" Her eyes widened, startled, then her face searched his, as if to seek out the truth of his question. "How could you think that?"

"Amanda." Luke groaned, chuckling deep within his hard, lean body. "You tore my clothes apart. Sent them downstream. Defied me at every turn. Threw quotations in my face when I tried to reach you, and invited men to my table when I tried to seduce you. I have owl feathers in everything I own, and no whiskey when right now I'd kill for it." He grinned at her embarrassed expression. "Yes, I'd say you haven't made it easy."

"I never meant for you to think that," Amanda said, blushing to the roots of her hair. "It's just when I saw you with that saloon girl, I thought—"

"Nothing happened," Luke said, wincing as he recalled that night. "I thought about it, I even attempted it, but I couldn't get you out of my head. Believe me, Amanda, a man doesn't lie about a thing like that."

She believed him. He looked too chagrined not to be telling the truth. Plucking shyly at a fold of her skirt, she shrugged. "It's so illogical! I mean, why should I mind? I don't understand the things I feel. . . . "

That was dangerously close to the truth and they both knew it. Luke picked up the hand that held his, his eyes never leaving hers, and kissed the back of her knuckles. Amanda shivered, amazed that such a slight touch could be so unnerving and so arousing at the same time. She was getting in too deep and she knew it, and didn't know how to stop. This was more frightening than when Luke asked her to swim the river, and her eyes reflected her panic.

"Luke, I think—"

"Don't think." He pulled her into his arms, then smoothed the hair away from her face. "That's your problem, you think too much."

"But it doesn't calculate—"

"Amanda." He groaned, fighting the urge to silence her in an age-old way, developed—he was certain—before the theory of calculus. " 'Reason and love keep little company.' "

"Shakespeare," Amanda sighed, offering no resistance when his mouth took hers.

For the first time in her life, Amanda abandoned knowledge, for her mind told her this was folly, but her heart urged her on. She giggled like a child when his stubbled chin tickled her face, then she stopped giggling when his lips brushed hers, gently at first, then deepening as passion took them both to a new level of existence. And because it was unhurried—they were trapped alone in the nester's hut until at least the rainfall ended and the Reverend's group set out to find them—they savored the moment, each of them wanting everything the other could possibly give.

Amanda began to relax in his arms. Shyly, her hand clasped the back of his neck, amazed at the strength she could feel in his broad shoulders and the enticing crispness of his curls beneath her fingers. His mouth seemed to mold her lips to his and she sighed, amazed at the gentle warmth she saw in his beautiful blue eyes, and the way her body was beginning to respond to his long, sweet kisses. She parted her lips, meeting his tongue with her own, and a rush of pure liquid sexuality coursed through her, making her arch her back to be closer to him.

Luke groaned, then his hands slid down to below her waist, pressing her body against his in a dizzying statement of how much he wanted her. She gasped, and he deepened the kiss, his tongue plunging into her mouth in a frank imitation of the sexual act he was beginning to crave.

He was making her crave it too.

Amanda felt as if she was drowning in pleasure. She was

lost in a hot, endless kiss that made her behave in ways that she never dreamed desirable, never dreamed of at all. Somehow, they had turned and he was on top of her, his legs tangled in her skirts, his weight leaning on his arms as his hands cupped her head. Passion flared hotter as his body made intimate contact with hers, promising more, and then delivering with the next heated kiss. His hands slid sensuously down her body, cupping her breasts, his thumb brushing the nipples until they hardened, outlined against the damp material of her dress.

His hands moved lower, seeking out the arched curve of her legs, her slender waist, her rounded bottom. Amanda rolled on top of him, her explorations just as eager. She marveled at the contrast of his work-roughed hands against her own bare skin. Her chestnut hair fell loosely around her, tickling him, making him chuckle even as he kissed her again. He reached up, his fingers working the buttons of her dress, and she sighed, lifting her hair out of the way, making the task easier for him.

It was wonderful to let a man undress her. Amanda felt like an explorer, on the verge of a new discovery with every moment. The dress and chemise slipped sensuously down her body, aided by his hands, which felt even better as they cupped her waist. Then he brought her back down on top of him, startling her as his mouth made hot wet contact with a bare, aching breast.

Amanda never imagined it could be this good. Her fingers locked in his hair and she urged him on, reveling in the powerfully erotic feel of his tongue encircling, then sucking on her nipple. She leaned on her arms, wanting it to go on, wanting everything he had to offer.

Then his hands were beneath her skirts and his playful manner gone. She gasped as he roughly pushed her damp dress aside, then purposefully sought out the dark curls between her legs. His fingers raked through them, then slid lower, caressing her intimately, making her writhe against him.

"Luke, I want—" she breathed, panic setting in. She had

meant to say that she wanted to stop, but his mouth took hers—and with it, the last vestige of logic.

"Me too," he whispered, mistaking her meaning. "God, Mandy, I want you so badly. I want to be gentle, but I don't know if I can. . . . "

He pushed her onto her back and Amanda felt him, hot and probing between her thighs. But he kissed her again and she was lost, forgetting everything except that Luke wanted her. She never felt more beautiful—or more a woman—than now, in his arms. She parted her legs at his urging, aware that something wonderful was about to happen. Her body felt like an overripe peach, bursting with juice. Blood pounded in her head and her pelvis burned, aching, wanting something she couldn't explain.

He entered her a little bit at first, then, unable to restrain himself, he plunged deeply into her. Amanda gasped. Passion fled as he drove into her and pain became a reality. She struggled against him, but he mastered her as easily as he had the captured horse, and Amanda quieted, following his urgings. She bit her lip and her eyes flew open, amazed at the excitement in his face and the driving force of his body. Her discomfort increased as her initial pleasure fled, and she was aware of a scraping dryness between her legs and the damp ground beneath her. She began to count strokes, grateful when something seemed to especially please him and he groaned, shutting his eyes tightly, and drove even more deeply into her. The ache became a raw pain, and Amanda was thoroughly relieved when he finally withdrew, taking the burning lance with him.

Luke collapsed, drained of all energy. She was so exquisitely tight and so responsive that he wanted to stay like this forever, plunging into her warm wet body, making her forget everything except this. She'd given him an earth-shattering orgasm that was the sweetest he'd ever recalled. He smiled as he remembered his initial impression of her, as a cold, withdrawn school marm. She had proven to be anything but.

Drenched in sweat, aching from his wound, Luke rose

on one elbow and gazed down into the face of the woman who'd just given him unbelievable pleasure.

"My God, Amanda," he breathed, brushing the long hair away from her face, wishing he could have seen her at that special moment. "Wasn't that just incredible?"

She stared at him, her eyes bright and clear of passion, her nose wrinkled in confusion.

"No, it wasn't." She shrugged, as if discarding a puzzle that wasn't worth dissecting, then moved away from him. She snatched up her dress and chemise and pulled them roughly over her body, then she fished out her tortoiseshell glasses and put them on. Gazing at him through the spectacles, she frowned. "In fact, I think the whole thing's been much too exaggerated, though from a scientific standpoint, it makes sense."

"What does?" Incredulous, his mouth dropped as he rose on one arm, then he saw that she was serious. She was looking at him like a mad scientist peering into a glass jar at a particularly undesirable specimen.

"That it shouldn't be pleasurable for a woman." Her freckled nose wrinkled and she tapped her cheek with her forefinger, giving him a speculative glance. "For most other species it isn't. Hence the mating dances and the brilliant coloring of the male peacock designed to attract a female's attention. Surely if the female derived as much enjoyment from the act of fertilization as the male—"

"Amanda!" Fury made his jaw tighten, and the lazy aftermath of passion disappeared, replaced by raw anger. This woman was unbelievable! His male pride stung, Luke glared at her while Amanda delivered her next line like a female archer, taking deadly aim.

"—there would be a population explosion. So even though I've devalued myself in a marital marketplace, I am glad we did this." She smiled sweetly, not realizing that the brilliant red that stained his face was from a blush, and not passion. "For I've learned something valuable. I don't ever want to do this again, and therefore, have no reason or desire to marry. I will also take full responsibility for any progeny that may result from this act of intercourse, so you need not worry. I can take care of myself."

Chapter

15

Luke thought he was losing his mind with anger. This couldn't be happening. Yet even as the Reverend arrived with Pop Finnegan, bringing help in the form of a wagon and a horse, he couldn't take his eyes from Amanda.

She didn't seem to notice that anything was wrong. In her simple, matter of fact manner, she informed the trail boss of Luke's injury and what she had done to treat it, then she climbed out of the rain and into the back of the wagon, and reached for her carpetbag. By the time Luke had joined her, after Pop had checked the bandage and the wound, she was scribbling happily into her journal, barely aware that he existed.

No woman had ever treated him this badly. Raised in South Carolina in the genteel life of a wealthy plantation owner, he had been accustomed to women who were gentle and sweet, who looked up to their men and let them know how much they appreciated them. And Luke, who had been told he was handsome since the age of thirteen, warranted a great deal of feminine attention—all of it positive. Even the Hamilton twins, with their ripe red lips and rich dark hair, followed him around from the time they could walk. He was used to them hanging on his every word, blushing when he so much as touched their hands or ruffled their hair. Later, when he returned from the war and was branded a deserter, the women still made a place for him in their parlor, despite the fact that he was socially ostracized and shouldn't have been received. Their fathers and husbands didn't acknowledge him, but his warmth and his charm had won him a place in the hearts of the women that was not easily destroyed.

Yet Amanda had cut him to the quick. He sent a glare in her direction, but she was oblivious of him, her pencil scrawling across a sheet of paper, filling it with her blunt observations of life. She was a cold woman, Luke thought, prim and without the slightest consideration of his feelings. His face reddened as he thought of her appraisal of his lovemaking. Christ, he was actually blushing. He should leave as soon as they returned to camp. No one more deserved such ungallant treatment, and it would make him feel great to see her surprised expression when he rode out of camp, this time for good. Nothing was worth this, not the ranch or even his desire for revenge. Haskwell he could get on his own. He really didn't need Amanda.

But even as he decided to do just that, his mind rebelled. He couldn't let her get away with this. Leaving would be too easy. For the sake of all mankind, he couldn't unleash Amanda on the rest of the world. He had to triumph over her, had to prove to her and to himself that she was wrong. He would make her take everything back that she'd said to him—not just for tonight, but for all the rest of the times she'd slighted him. His male ego demanded it.

As if reading his mind she glanced up at him, and at least had the decency to look away when she saw him glaring at her. She returned to her books, but her hand trembled as she wrote. Luke gritted his teeth.

Amanda Edison had challenged the very heart of him. And he had to win, no matter how dirty the methods he used or how unethical his tactics. It had become a matter of pride.

•   •   •

"Pull up your skirts, let's see your legs. We paid our money—let's see your legs," Honey sang to the group of men, her voice warbling with fear. The men came to their feet in thunderous applause as the showgirl stepped out onto the stage, her scarlet plume dipping over one eye enticingly, her matching dress hiked up to expose an indecent length of black stockinged thigh.

The dress had been Haskwell's idea, as had been the stockings. Honey lifted her dark head and sang, her soft brown eyes searching out the crowd for one man, praying that he wouldn't be there, that something had intervened and taken this man out of her life. . . .

She saw him a dead second later, seated at a poker table, his white shirt sleeves rolled up and his face thoughtful. He scanned the cards in his hand, then threw several chips onto the table and sat back with a smirk. A few minutes later, he was scooping up the chips, laughing in an Irish brogue that was filled with sinister menace. Then his eyes met hers.

Honey choked. She felt impaled as Sam smiled, his eyes fixing her like a pin through a specimen. Continuing to sing, she removed one long white glove, then laid it over the hat of a lounging cowboy. His companions barked their laughter, even as she scanned the room, looking for an escape.

The front door. Honey's eyes turned toward it hopefully, knowing that her dressing room door was watched at all times—for her protection, Sam had told her. There was no other way out through the rear of the building, but here she had a chance. Perhaps, when Haskwell was distracted enough, she could enlist the help of one of these cowboys. She could then walk right out of here, with no one the wiser.

Relief flooded through her and she belted out the lyrics to the racy song, gratified to find all the men's eyes on her. God, why hadn't she thought of it before? It would all be so easy, and she'd be rid of this man who held her captive in such terror; who showered her with gifts, then made love to her in the crudest possible ways. Her fear was an aphrodisiac to him, and she shuddered to think of what he would resort to next, just to see the terror in her eyes. She had to get out of here, and tonight she would do just that.

A young, gangly cowboy grinned up at her, his soft blue eyes telling her that he thought she was pretty, and that he wanted her. Sending a seductive smile through the room, Honey paused by the man, then dropped her other glove onto the floor beside him. The men roared as the cowboy blushed, then dipped down to retrieve her offering. As he lifted his head, he found his face close to hers as she whispered quietly.

"Follow me out of here in about five minutes, sweetie."

Honey pressed a kiss to the tip of his nose, leaving a red smear of lipstick. The cowboys guffawed, then slapped the young man's back, congratulating him on winning the lady's favor. The cowboy's face was beet red, but he nodded and smiled, good naturedly wiping away the lipstick even as Honey sashayed away from him toward the door.

The poker dealer nudged Haskwell. Sam glanced up from behind the cards and saw Honey remove a glass bracelet, then drop it teasingly into a cowboy's lap. She wiggled and cooed, breathlessly whispering her song while making her way through the crowd. Every man watched her; every man wanted her.

"I'm in for five, Tommy." Haskwell tossed in a chip, his black eyes never leaving the young girl. Honey leaned over another man, her breasts nearly brushing his face, her little bottom thrust out in a suggestive pose. Haskwell grinned. She was doing what he had taught her, and working the crowd well. The little strumpet had turned into a virtual gold mine, in more ways than one. He watched her ruffle another man's hair, then slip a proffered gold piece down the bodice of her scarlet gown.

"Looks like Honey's got herself an ardent admirer," the dealer remarked, indicating the young cowboy who got to his feet. "He's been watching her for the last half hour."

Sam's smile vanished even as Honey turned and gestured quickly to the cowboy, all the while keeping an innocent smile on her face. She glanced at Haskwell, saw that he was involved with his cards, then nodded quickly toward the swinging doors at the front of the saloon. The cowboy, unable to believe his good luck, followed the beautiful woman with the flashing dark hair and the sparkling red dress.

"Put him out, Tommy." Haskwell never lifted his eyes from his cards, though his voice was filled with rage. "And then bring her to me." He indicated the seat beside him. "A beautiful woman always brings luck, don't you agree?"

The other men chuckled and nodded. Honey barely reached the door when a man grabbed her, then another brought his gun crashing down on the cowboy's head. Thinking it all part of the act, the cowboys slammed down their beers and roared. Tommy slung Honey over his shoulder, her lacey legs kicking in outrage, her little bottom in the air, then carried her to the poker table. He deposited the showgirl into the seat beside Haskwell, then brushed off his hands and grinned.

"She was heading for the door all right, boss. Was gonna meet her little boyfriend later. But we took care of him." Tommy indicated the cowboy, who was still lying in the center of the floor.

Terrified, Honey turned to Haskwell, her breasts heaving inside the low cut dress, her feathers drooping. Haskwell smiled coldly.

"That was not a nice thing you did, me darlin'. Were you thinking of leaving me now?"

"No!" Honey gasped, fighting for breath. "I was just—"

"Flirting with the boys," Haskwell finished for her. "Isn't one man enough for you?"

"Please," she pleaded with him. Her dark eyes looked like brown glass, shimmering with panic. "Just let me go. I won't . . ."

"Take her upstairs, Tommy." Haskwell returned to his cards, dismissing her as he threw away a deuce. As the dealer rose and took the young woman's arm, Haskwell glanced up once more. "And when I return tonight, I'll see that you never want another man again. Do you understand me?"

Honey gasped, tears spilling down her cheeks. "Please, Sam, I didn't mean it, don't do this—"

"Get her out of here, Tommy." Haskwell waited until the dealer had forcibly escorted the sobbing young woman away, then he turned back to his cards, surveying his hand with a huge grin.

This time, he held all the aces.

" . . . and then they tied us up and left us here. Thank God the Reverend didn't come right back but set out to look for you, or you still might be there. I can't believe those men were after you! And you don't even know why?"

Amanda shook her head in the negative.

Aileen sighed, then continued chattering. "Jake found a penknife in his pocket and managed to get us untied, though it will be lucky if none of us get pneumonia, after being out in the rain and hail all that time. Amanda, are you all right?"

Amanda glanced up, her strange ocean eyes distant and deep in thought. Aileen shivered, then swallowed a mouthful of whiskey from Jake's flask. The rain had thankfully stopped and the campfire burned cheerfully, but all of them were in a melancholy mood. The cattle were gone. None of them looked forward to the round-up job that awaited them come morning, when the frenzied Herefords lost their terror and would be wandering the prairie in confusion.

"Aileen." Amanda tapped her notebook with her pencil, allowing Aesop to perch on her arm. She nuzzled the little owl affectionately, then turned the full force of her curious stare back to the woman before her. "When you were a saloon girl, and you were with a lot of men . . ."

"Yes?"

"Well," Amanda glanced at the religious men who were gathering into a prayer group, then continued bluntly. "Did you ever get pleasure out of the act?"

"What?" Aileen wiped her mouth and stared at Amanda in disbelief.

"Well did you?"

"Sure." Aileen chuckled, then her smile faded as she noticed Amanda's disturbed look. "Why else do you think we'd do it? It's not for the babes, I can tell you that. Why are you asking?"

"It's nothing." Amanda sighed, returning to her books. "I was just formulating a theory."

Aileen watched her closely, observing the way Amanda bit her lip and the tremor of her fingers. There was more to this than a scientific theory. Aileen would have bet her life on it.

"I have to admit though, I used to think only the men got something out of it," Aileen continued, noticing Amanda's interest perk up. "The first few times for me were terrible, but that was when I lived in Philadelphia. He was a handsome man, Johnny was, and a carpenter at that. But he could do more for a woman with his hands—"

"But you said it was terrible," Amanda interrupted.

Aileen nodded. "At first. When a woman's never been to bed with a man, the first time isn't always great. For the woman, that is. The man thinks he's the cock of the walk."

"Why?" Amanda's brow wrinkled.

"Well, it's a conquest." Aileen shrugged. "Men like to be the first. It makes them feel special."

"Hmm." Amanda chewed on her pencil, then absently brushed her hair out of her eyes. "That really is appalling. You mean it is always pleasurable for a man? And that they put a value on something that can only please them? Interesting."

"I don't know if I explained it right." Aileen didn't like the look on Amanda's face. "I mean, a man doesn't like to think that his woman has been with a lot of other men."

"Yet he is praised by his peers for doing just that," Amanda mused. "This sounds like a double standard to me. You know, I have a feeling this is related to the unfortunate connection between mating and procreation."

"What?"

"Man's insecurity is due to his doubts about his own prowess, and the legitimacy of his heir," Amanda explained.

"The first one I can understand, if not applaud. The second is more complex. In ancient Celtic times, a woman could take as many lovers as she desired—once she produced an heir. This satisfied the man's fear of paternity, yet did not preclude the relationship to a monogamous state."

Aileen's nose wrinkled. "Then you are saying . . ."

"Perhaps the ancient Celtic men were more sexually secure," Amanda concluded. "Either that, or the same value wasn't placed on sexuality. I'll have to ask Luke."

Aileen glanced toward the man seated across from them at the campfire. Something had happened between them, of that Aileen was sure. Luke had been glowering at Amanda all evening, and the eccentric woman beside her hadn't even noticed the displeasure directed her way. And Amanda had been even more preoccupied than normal. Judging from their conversation, Aileen had a very good idea of what had happened, and what hadn't.

"I'm not sure that's a good idea," Aileen said, dragging Amanda to her feet as the women assembled to clean the tin dishes. "He seems like he's in a bad mood. Maybe it's his injury."

Amanda frowned, but she joined the others as the women scrubbed the plates, using precious little water and the abundant sand from the prairie. Amanda automatically helped them, even though none of them spoke to her. Word had gotten around that Amanda was "touched," so the women avoided her. Amanda didn't mind. Loneliness was something she was used to, and at least she had Aileen. From their position beside the chuck wagon, she could see the Reverend rise to his feet, and then call to one of the women beside her.

The plate the young blond girl held slipped from her fingers and fell to the ground, rolling in an oblique disk before spinning to a crash. Slowly, she walked across the five feet of firelight that separated them, then stood before the preacher, her legs shaking beneath her.

"Sinner!" the preacher chanted. "You have sinned before God! Is what I understand true? That you took up with a shopkeeper's son during our stay in that God-forsaken town?"

"I did nothing wrong!" the young girl sobbed, then fell to her knees. "I only walked with him!"

"Sinner! Harlot! The Bible speaks of such women! Listen and be cleansed!" The preacher opened his book and began to read of Mary Magdalene, and in Genesis of the curse upon women. His eyes took on a strange gleam, like that of a spooked horse. When he finished, he cast a scornful glance at the sobbing girl at his feet.

"Rise up and return to your work. Rethink your sin, child, and you will be saved. It is only by prayer that you will be redeemed. Repent now, or there will be no hope for you later," he intoned.

"What exactly is her sin?"

The Reverend stared across the fire, the Bible still in his hand, holding it as a shield against the woman placidly cleaning a plate. "Did someone say something?"

"I did." Ignoring the indrawn breaths around her, Amanda put her plate aside and stepped forward. "What has she done wrong?"

"Amanda." Luke interrupted, speaking to her for the first time all night. He looked incredibly handsome, lounging by the fire, the cut on his forehead giving him a devilish appearance that was very appealing. He forced a smile. "These people aren't the least bit interested in your religious opinions. Drop it." The threat in his voice was clear.

"On the contrary." The Reverend stared at Amanda, his eyes like bits of chipped glass. "I am very interested. We don't believe in having wolves among the sheep. This woman has sinned. She has walked with a shopkeeper's son, not of our faith. For that she must be punished."

For the first time Amanda could remember, she was more angry at what she had witnessed than interested in debate. "Does this law also apply to the men of your fold? Jacob Green dallied in the arms of a saloon girl the night before we left. I heard the men talk about it. And Horace Whitney has a son in Abilene that he pays a goodly sum for."

The wives stared at Amanda in horrified disbelief. Her self-assurance died as the men glanced at her with the same expression they'd use when faced with a rabid dog. It was true—they did talk freely around her, assuming she was too crazy to understand them. But she sounded lucid enough now. Then they looked at Luke, who was staring at Amanda in silent fury.

"Sir." The Reverend slammed the book down, his eyes blazing at Luke. "I have never heard such blasphemy! I understand that this woman is ill, but I will not tolerate such talk. Are you going to discipline your wife, or shall we?"

"She's not my wife!" Luke barked.

The gasp that went through the people was almost tangible. Luke regretted his words as soon as they left his mouth, but there was nothing he could do to take them back. The Reverend glared at Luke, then Amanda, his eyes reflecting his outrage.

"Jacob, get my gun. Martha, fetch my other Bible, the one with the wedding prayers. We shall rectify this matter immediately."

"No!" Amanda gasped, understanding at last. "I will not marry him! I'm not of your faith, and you can't force me!"

Luke glared at her, his eyes burning with anger, but the Reverend seemed little swayed by her words. Luke started to walk away, but he was stopped by the older man called Jacob, who held the rifle across his chest like a shield.

"Silence, harlot!" the Reverend shouted. "You have lived with this man, as his wife, without the blessing of the Lord! You returned even this night, after spending the day alone with this man in a secluded cabin! We shall mend this sin in the eyes of God. Otherwise, we shall leave you both here on the prairie. Which shall you choose?"

One of the men grabbed Luke and held his arms behind him, while one of the women pushed Amanda forward. Aileen sobbed quietly. Jake held her, his arm around her shoulders. There was nothing any of them could do. They were alone, in the middle of Indian country, dependent on this wagon train for their existence. None of them could risk angering these people, no matter how they felt.

Amanda stood beside Luke, unable to accept what she knew was happening. Luke stood across from her, and she cringed from the open fury she saw in his eyes. His expression, never particularly gentle to begin with, now blazed with anger, and the hot blue flame in his eyes rivaled the campfire. Belatedly, she realized how ignominious this must seem to him. Luke, who no doubt pictured himself wed to some soft southern belle, was now being shackled to her, a woman he could barely tolerate.

Amanda could have cried. She had never thought her life would take this kind of a turn. She had never planned to marry, to call any man her lord and master, let alone Luke. She shivered as she thought of the feelings she had for him, and now he would be tied to her for life. Luke, of all men, meant something to her and therefore had the power to hurt her.

And now, as the Reverend opened his Bible and began to pray, Amanda was seized with the desire to run. Her eyes flickered to the perimeter of the campfire and she reached for a fold of her skirt, intending to bolt. Perhaps she could find some lonely nester, who would help her until she could find a way to Texas. . . .

Luke's hand closed around her wrist and she found herself forced to his side. Her head flew up and she saw that he was now even more furious, having ascertained what she meant to do.

"Don't even try it," he murmured, holding her tightly. The Reverend's voice droned on. Amanda searched Luke's face for the slightest understanding and found none. He obviously blamed her for what had happened, and was now determined to see this through. After all, he had only to gain. He didn't want her, never did. But he would now legally own half her ranch, half of her income, half of her. . . .

"No!" Amanda struggled.

The Reverend closed his Bible and gazed at the two furious people before him.

"I now pronounce you man and wife."

Chapter

❧ *16* ❧

The words seemed to settle around them like the earth around a tomb. Amanda glanced at Luke and saw the gleam of fury flash in his eyes, then a cold, stark anger set in. She swallowed hard, inadvertently thinking of that day when he tossed her into the river. The expression on his face was very similar now and she shuddered, imagining what it would be like to see that expression harden into permanence.

He didn't want her. The hypocrisy of the whole situation made her want to scream. They were now wed, husband and wife, living in a state that was supposed to be sanctioned by God and man, and was condemned by both. Amanda glanced down at her dress, her plain blue cotton muslin that was ruined by rain and mud. Somehow, she never pictured herself married, but even when she entertained an occasional daydream of the sort, usually for the purpose of writing a wedding scene, the bride wore a white dress and carried flowers. She looked at her ringless finger, suddenly noticing the ink-stained sleeves of her gown and her broken fingernails.

She wasn't the same as other women, and she knew it. No wonder Luke fought so hard when they forced him to marry her. She thought of all the times she was an embar-

rassment to him and she cringed. No man had ever loved
her. And now Luke, who was obviously the kind of man
that every woman would want, was shackled to her by a
lynch mob wedding.

"I'll get you a ring."

She glanced up, startled by his cold voice and the way
he seemed to break into her thoughts. She released the fold
of her dress which she'd been grasping, and shook her head.

"It isn't necessary."

Luke gritted his teeth, took her arm and led her past the
preacher and the religious men who stared at him in a mixture of triumph and pity. The women were silent, exchang-
ing frightened glances, obviously identifying themselves
with both the strange young woman and the furious man
who was now her husband. Amanda scarcely noticed, but
Luke saw it all and slowed his pace, trying not to betray
his justified rage. When they reached the wagon, he ignored
Amanda's attempts to climb inside herself and he helped
her up, earning a glare for his efforts.

"Amanda, we need to talk." Luke entered the wagon, his
voice as stern as her physics teacher on a Monday morning.

"There is nothing else to say," she tried to say evenly.

"Amanda." Luke placed both hands on her shoulders,
holding her firmly without hurting her, yet forcing her to
stay within his reach. "If you have half the brain you were
born with, you'll listen to me and listen closely. If you think
I intend to abide by this farce of a wedding, you are wrong.
As soon as we get to town, I plan to seek out a solicitor.
In the meantime, if you wish to survive, don't keep testing
me. You stay out of my way and I'll stay out of yours."

Amanda flushed hotly, pink staining her cheeks—thankfully hidden in the darkness. She had known that he was
angry, and that he would not easily accede to being forced
into a marriage, but to calmly insist that she accept the situation was more than Amanda could take.

"I am very glad you plan to seek out a solicitor, although
I could tell you now that you are wasting your time and save
you the fee. The marriage is legal and will stand up in court,

in spite of what either of us say. You may, however, seek out a divorce if you can find grounds."

"Grounds?" Luke's blue eyes blazed and his fingers tightened on her shoulders.

"Adultery, abandonment, something like that," Amanda said thoughtfully, her voice without emotion. "Although you may have some difficulties. I do not have the means to abandon you, which is why you are here at all. And I have no desire to partake of sexual intercourse with any man. So therefore, you might want to put your mind to coming up with something else. I have a book called *Mankind and the Law,* which may be of some use. I'll be happy to lend it to you." She tried to pull away from him, ignoring the increasing fury on Luke's face and the vise-like grip he had on her arms.

"Amanda." Luke couldn't believe this woman. How he kept from strangling her was a restraint he would be forever proud of. "You don't seem to understand. As your husband, I have legal rights over you, in every way you can imagine. You cannot own property, you cannot live separately from me unless I agree. You cannot refuse me marital rights, which I will be more than happy to enumerate if your wonderful mind ignores the implication. And if you disobey me, legally I can beat you. Do you understand what I am saying?"

Amanda stared at him, appalled. "You can't mean . . ."

"Ah, I see reality is finally penetrating." Luke tried to get some satisfaction from her stunned expression, but found none. "In other words, more so than at any previous time, you are completely within my control. The law recognizes that fact, and now, so does the church."

Amanda gasped, stunned at his reasoning, but she had to admit he was right. He smiled, though his eyes held no mirth, and he shucked his pants and climbed into bed. "Goodnight, Amanda. I hope you sleep well." He turned his back to her and immediately fell asleep.

Amanda watched him relax, and instantly knew the moment sleep overcame him by the change in his breathing and the slight alteration in his position. Strange, she thought, slipping her dress over her head and climbing beneath the rough woolen blanket. It was the first time in her life she'd ever shared a bed with a man and never had she felt so alone.

He felt warm to the touch, his body heat radiating to her in spite of the space she was careful to maintain between them. It felt good to have his male warmth near her, and she wondered if people had always felt this way. They must have, she reasoned, thinking of the studies that had been done of animals that went crazy when separated from their own kind when too young. And yet, it was apparent that Luke didn't want her, that he hated the idea of really being married to her.

That cut her, but rejection was something she had become accustomed to. It hurt doubly from him, though, and Amanda wasn't sure why. Maybe it had something to do with this mating business, but her mind kept returning to their lovemaking, and the odd, unsatisfied way it had made her feel. Yet now, with him in her bed, she felt a surge of something—of a desire that didn't make sense—coupled with a keen disappointment that her marriage was a farce that didn't even belong in a Shakespeare play.

She really had but one choice to salvage her pride. Tomorrow, she would confront him.

And she would try to forget that this was her wedding night.

Luke was dreaming of his home in Charleston, where the grass grew so rich that it seemed to contain every hue of the color green, from the pale sweet lime of the new grasses, to the dark green-black of the shaded lawns. His mother was in the house, overseeing the evening meal, and his sister was running outside, her laughter like a spring brook, fresh and clear.

He was up in the hayloft with Georgina Hamilton, experiencing his first kiss. Georgina giggled, her gown a delicious rustle in the fragrant hay, and she opened her mouth eagerly, letting him explore the soft, honeyed interior. His hand rose to her dress and he cupped the fullness of her small breast. It felt like a warm, ripe apple. Georgina chuckled, giving him a wide-eyed look, and his hand slid to the laces. . . .

Luke awoke slowly, reluctant to leave the dregs of such a dream. He could still feel his hand cupping a breast, only this one was larger, more womanly. . . . His eyes flew open. It was Amanda's breast he held, Amanda's warm and luscious body beside him. He snatched his hand away, dimly aware that she was watching him almost as if studying him. It was then he realized that she was fully dressed, and that her carpetbag, bulging with books, was placed in the center of the wagon, with Aesop sleeping beside it. None of her things were about, no papers or inkwells, pencils or books. Everything had been packed, and only the skeletal walls of the wagon stared back at him. She rose from the position she was in and put on her shawl.

"What are you doing?"

"I'm leaving," Amanda stated, her voice crisp. "And don't try to stop me."

"I see." He tried not to sound amused. "Where are you going?"

"Home," Amanda said decisively.

"Back east?" Luke asked calmly, as if trying to get all the facts straight.

"No," Amanda shook her head. "To Texas. There is nothing for me in Boston. I have the ranch in Waco."

"And no one to run it for you, or help you with it," Luke reminded her.

"I'm sure I can hire someone."

"And how are you going to travel?" Rising up on one arm, his expression amused, Luke gestured outside. "You can't ride a horse, we're in the middle of Indian territory, we have limited food, and once we cross the river, limited water. There are outlaws following you, and the wilderness is full of trappers, hunters, squatters, and animals. You wouldn't last two days."

"Nevertheless, I intend to try." Amanda picked up her carpetbag and her bird cage. "Goodbye, Luke Parker."

"Put that stuff down," Luke barked, losing all patience. "You're not going anywhere. If you find it so repulsive, being wed to me even for one night, then I can assure you that I will leave you alone. I have no intention of forcing my presence on any woman, especially you." He rose, ignoring her presence as he slipped on his pants. His naked body glowed in the morning sunlight, hard and tanned, like a bronze image. Amanda had to fight the memory of that body beside her during the night, and her desire to touch him. Any thoughts like that were dashed as he continued, his voice stern and forbidding.

"Don't let me find out you've tried to run away, or so help me, I'll give orders that you be confined to the wagon. Like it or not, as I explained last night, you are under my protection, and I intend to see that you make it safely to Waco. What happens after that, we'll both decide. But now I've got to help the men find the cattle, and I have no intention of chasing after you. Got it?"

She stared at him furiously, her hand clenching her belongings until one at a time, she dropped both parcels to the wagon floor. "I speak several languages," she said haughtily. "I believe I understand."

He stared at her, thunderstruck that she would bait him. He was married to her, forced into a legal and binding entanglement with a woman who defied him every chance she got, let him know how little she thought of his lovemaking, and even debated with a preacher—which resulted in this mess. When he spoke, it was with barely restrained passion.

"Amanda, if you're testing me for some God unholy reason, be warned. You reached my limit a long time ago, and I won't be responsible if you continue. Do you understand that, or should I repeat it in another, more pleasing language?"

She was interested to know which one, but wisely decided that this was not the time to ask. She was even more convinced of the wisdom of this decision when he reached for his shirt, threw it on as if it was made of lead, then stormed out of the wagon.

Butch rode into Caldwell, his horse nearly at a walk. Damien lay on the crude pallet he had assembled, his face pale, his clothes spattered with blood. Yet he was still alive. Butch had stopped and checked his pulse every few hours, and although it was thready, he could still feel the faint throb of life beneath a bloody sleeve.

"Yo, Doc." Butch spat, then wiped his lips with his sleeve as he opened the wooden door. A single lamp threw a small circle of light around a table where a rancher sat, his arm in a sling. The doctor glanced up, then returned to the man's wound and continued wrapping the injury in cotton.

Butch gave the man a cold glance. "Get out."

The rancher got to his feet, observing the way Butch fingered his gun, and headed for the door. The doctor frowned, then drank a slug of whiskey before turning to the outlaw.

"What is it? Gunshot?"

"No, it's my partner." Butch stepped through the door, then returned a moment later, carrying Damien in his arms. He laid the body down gingerly on a crude wooden table, then stood back.

"My God, what happened to him?" the doctor gasped, then helped himself to another drink. The man that lay before him was unrecognizable, so badly was he injured. Open lacerations bled from his face, his exposed arms, and his legs, while bone fragments gleamed through his torn pants.

"You gotta fix 'im, Doc," Butch said, picking up the whiskey and taking a swig himself. "Cattle stampeded all over him. Damien's been with me since he was six, Doc. He can't die now. Not yet."

The doctor nodded, understanding immediately. Picking up a wad of cotton, he began to swab the man's wounds, aware that Butch had taken a seat directly beside him and had cocked his gun. The doctor began to sweat and the alcohol-induced euphoria fled, replaced by a cold, wet dread.

If Damien died, he had a feeling he wouldn't live long either.

He was right. Emotional, yes—and obvious—but also, right. She wouldn't last one day, let alone two. She couldn't manage alone in a wild country where wolves roamed along with cattle-hungry Indians, as well as snakes and God only knew what else. It was one thing to write about battling the elements; it was another to actually live it.

Frowning, Amanda stared outside the wagon to the campfire where the men gathered. Luke stood inside the center of the circle, obviously respected, his opinion important. She winced as she thought of his anger, and decided it was best to keep some distance. She had spent the first part of the trip deliberately defying him, and had only gotten more attention as a result. Yes, distance was the answer, until she thought of something better.

She departed from the wagon. The cowhands, unwilling to postpone the roundup, had awakened at dawn and were packing up their horses, while the women worked steadily to secure their belongings inside the wagons. A nervous tension ran through the group, and all of them were aware that their economic fate was closely linked to the results of the next twenty-four hours.

" . . . Shorty spotted a few cattle near the bluff this morning. I reckon if we head out in the same direction they did, and span the area, we should round up most of 'em."

Luke nodded, barely glancing up as Pop Finnegan drew the directions on the dirt with a stick. Amanda walked slowly across the plain, intending to get some coffee and stay far away from the men. Luke shot her a preoccupied glance, then returned to their discussion, ignoring her presence as if she didn't exist—as if he didn't notice how the sun washed her hair, or how she looked barely sixteen, dressed in a loose gown, with her braid swinging freely down her back.

"What we should do is split up. Send groups out. We can meet back here in about an hour and report. If anyone has sighted the cattle, then we can join in a roundup," Pop concluded.

The men gruffly agreed, all of them tense at the prospect of failure. They started for their gear, pausing in disbelief as Amanda's clear voice stopped them.

"You know you're all wrong. The cattle aren't at the bluff."

Luke stared at her as if she'd lost her mind for real, while the others gaped at the audacity of this woman. She'd been caught in an indecent relationship with a gunslinger, forced into marriage just last night, and instead of appearing embarrassed or bewildered, she returned their stares with a strange, eerie intelligence.

Satisfied that she had gotten their attention, Amanda withdrew a notebook and a pencil, then indicated a sketch of the plains that put their crude drawing to shame. "You cannot assume that the cattle are gathering near the bluff, simply because they ran blindly in that direction last night. By now, the frenzy should have worn off, and the cattle would be looking for water. I think if you search the river banks, you would meet with more success."

Pop Finnegan spat a wad of tobacco onto the ground, then sauntered over to where Luke and Amanda were talking. "You're wasting your time if you listen to that," the trail boss said, giving Amanda a cold look. "And we haven't got all morning. Are you riding with us to the bluff?"

Anger tightened Luke's expression, but Amanda stared at him thoughtfully, her logical mind ticking. She extended the book.

"You can check my reasoning, if you would like."

Jake turned to Luke. "I think she may have something there. It's at least worth a try."

"Fine," Luke nodded coldly, his eyes locking with hers. "You can come with me and we'll test your theory. I'll check out the river and meet you all back here."

"But you don't need me to—" Amanda started.

"You're coming with me." His tone warned her not to cross him.

So much for keeping her distance. Amanda followed him, aware of the resentful eyes on her. Luke obviously thought she'd intended this as a ploy, to give herself a chance to escape. She would have liked to explain to him that such wasn't the case, but she could tell he was in no mood to listen. She mounted her horse, still hating everything about the animal.

The morning air had a pristine quality to it that made her glad to feel the wind brush against her face, and the sky overhead was like a pale blue bowl rimmed in gold. The Canadian River snaked past, throbbing like a vein of life for the prairie, bringing with it secrets of distant lands: of Indians and nomads, of eastern oceans and far off plains. Hackberry and Indian paintbrush dotted the landscape, and the startling brilliance of a field poppy dotted the waving grass like a drop of blood on a green velvet dress. It was hard to believe that the the storm's devastation had occurred the previous night, because with the exception of the cattle ruts, the land had already recovered and had made its peace with nature once more.

Luke rode ahead of her, his back still stiff with anger, his body language telling her everything that he wouldn't. He was obviously furious with her, and angry that she'd challenged him in front of the men. She bit her lip when he finally paused, waiting for her mount to catch up.

"Amanda," he said, his temper barely restrained. "We've been riding for over a half hour now, and I don't see a goddamned cow anywhere."

"I would appreciate it if you would refrain from—"

"Don't." Luke warned. "Especially today."

She shrugged, gazing at the flowing river, aware of his eyes on her. She rustled for her notebook, found it amid several of Aesop's feathers in her bag, and rechecked her maps. "I still believe my conclusion is valid," she began. "I think there must be another factor . . ." her voice trailed off and her eyes widened as she stared at something behind him.

"What is it? A cow?" Luke started to turn, when Amanda's words stopped him cold.

"No," she whispered. "An Indian."

Chapter

17

Moving cautiously, Luke reached for his gun and turned, finding himself face to face with a redman.

It was an Indian all right, but not the warlike, grinning savage he expected. The man that stared back at him had the bronze skin of the Plains Indians that so resembled buttered leather. His face was so old and creased that Luke could almost read the man's life there—the hardship and change from a world of security to one that promised annihilation. His nose was long and straight, his lips cracked, but it was his eyes that held Luke's attention. Black and shining like broken pieces of coal, his eyes were mirrors into his soul, reflecting hopelessness.

The Indian made a guttural sound, then gestured with his hand. It was then that Luke noticed the man's clothing was patched and torn, held together with strips of leather that strained to break free with every movement, and that he wore no feathers. Whatever coups this Indian could claim, he obviously no longer found the need to publicize them.

"I think he wants us to follow him," Amanda said, nodding to the Indian.

"Like hell." Luke's hand closed around his gun, the metal

cold and reassuring against his fingers. "If it's just himself then he won't take us alive."

"I doubt if he's alone," Amanda said thoughtfully. "The Plains Indians, although nomadic in nature, tend to travel in a group. The rest of his tribe could be around us even now, waiting for a show of resistance."

It made sense. Furious, Luke pocketed the gun, then dismounted with Amanda. "Great, this is just great! Captured by a redskin who looks older than my father. Do me one favor. Next time you get a great idea to help us all out, don't."

The Indian gestured again, more impatiently this time. Luke and Amanda obeyed the cryptic command and followed him into a grove of cottonwoods near the river, leaving the horses tied to a branch. It was just as Amanda had predicted. The tribe, a paltry group of old, sick men, women, and children, were huddled in teepees. The children played—like children everywhere, oblivious to their surroundings—while the men, once fearless warriors, stared bleakly at the endless plain that used to be their domain. The women moved slowly about their tasks, making baskets of rushes and preparing scant food over a meager fire, but even they seemed drained of life. Two of the Indian women, obviously pregnant, looked anxiously at Luke and Amanda, then their eyes fell to their sides as they saw the visitors brought no food or clothing.

"I have a feeling they aren't part of the Five Civilized Tribes," Luke said quietly.

"Actually, they might be," Amanda said. "The tribes were sequestered within this territory as punishment for supporting the Confederates during the war. You can see the result of that decision. With their hunting lands cut off and the buffalo disappearing, they are reduced to this."

Luke glanced around at the camp, appalled at the abject misery and poverty he saw. The children appeared half-starved, while their parents had the look of people who were perpetually hungry and had ceased caring. The Indian who had found them gestured again, and spoke in a demanding voice.

"He said he wants meat," Amanda translated. "I studied the basic dialects of the tribes for my fifth book, *Texas Brave.* He heard that we would come this morning. The spirits told him last night, when the earth thundered and the ground split in anger."

"When our cattle stampeded," Luke supplied.

"Exactly. He says the spirits told him help would come to him this morning, in the shape of the enemy."

"Wonderful." Luke shrugged. "Seeing as we have no cattle, that would be a bit difficult. What if we can't deliver?"

Amanda looked up at him as if afraid to reveal the answer. "Then, he says, they plan to kill us."

"I'm sorry, son."

The doctor picked up his flask and drank heavily, then wiped his lips and stared at the body lying on the table. He had worked straight through the night, but nothing could stop Damien's bleeding. Worse, he suspected, were the internal injuries. Even as he sewed and patched each of the outlaw's visible wounds, Damien's skin grew whiter as the precious blood seeped away inside. At two in the morning, he thought the outlaw would be able to pull through. By four, he was doubtful, and by nine, he was certain they would bury the man this day.

And now, as Damien drew his last breath, the doctor knew he would soon join him. Butch had been sitting across from him all night, with a gun on the table as a deadly reminder of his reward should he fail. The doctor collapsed into a chair, knowing he had tried his best, and that it wasn't good enough.

Butch rose and stood beside the table, looking at the crushed and battered body of his partner. "You know, Doc, I ain't never rode without him," Butch said. "He's been with me since we were kids, robbing coaches and stealing payrolls."

"I know." The doctor held out the whiskey, and after a moment's hesitation, Butch took it.

"I can't imagine him dead. It's like losing your favorite gun, or a good saddle, all broken in and fitted to your ass." Butch drank freely, letting the whiskey burn down his throat and numb the little feeling he had left inside. "You know, Doc, this was all because of a woman. Amanda Edison."

"You both loved her?" the doctor asked, encouraging the outlaw to drink.

"Nope. We both wanted to kill her." Butch shrugged. "Crazy dame, Miss Amanda is. Everybody in every town we been in remembers her. She carries this old carpetbag and a pet owl." Butch sneered at the thought. "Easiest woman in the world to track, but she was cursed with one thing."

"What's that?"

"A brain." Butch drank again, then played slowly and menacingly with his gun. "It ain't fittin' for a woman to think too much. Makes them nothing but trouble, and they're trouble enough as it is."

"What did she do that you want to kill her?"

Butch looked up at the doctor, then began to smile, a cold, chilling grin. "You think to get me all lickered up, then you can run and tell the sheriff my plans. That's okay, Doc. Ain't no sheriff in hell gonna stop me now. You know, Doc? He don't even look peaceable." Butch indicated the body lying on the table, then he rose and holstered his gun.

"You did a good job, Doc, so I'm gonna let you live. I want him buried, though, and in a Christian graveyard. Any problem with that?"

The doctor nearly passed out in relief. He shook his head, then took back the bottle and drank the rest. Butch nodded approvingly.

"Yeah, drink up, you deserve it. Now I've gotta find the telegraph office. Haskwell ain't gonna like this, but you know something, Doc?"

Butch grinned as the doctor glanced up. "I don't give a blessed damn."

"You should have let me shoot them while we had the chance." Luke muttered as the Indians trussed him up, took his gun, and sat him before the fire. Amanda, they let alone, apparently having decided that this odd white woman was not much of a threat. They continually sent her questioning glances, however, even as the old man who'd captured them produced a pouch full of coffee, beans, and a single rabbit. The food, Amanda surmised, was probably pilfered from the wagon train's store, and the game was the pitiful result of the day's hunting.

"You couldn't shoot them," Amanda said skeptically. "They're pathetic. This is probably all the food they've had today, and if the wagon train hadn't come along, they wouldn't have the beans either. They're old and sick, all of them."

"We're still captured—by a group of hungry, old sick Indians," Luke said in disgust. "Got any ideas to write us out of this one, author?"

"I should just leave you, after the way you treated me—"

"Amanda!" He stared at her, horrified, as if he thought she might do more than entertain the idea.

"Don't worry, I'll think of something," Amanda replied, feeling far from sure herself. The Indian women gave her a hollow-eyed look, then went back to preparing a meal from the old man's offerings and the food they had scrounged earlier. Amanda thought of the countless times she'd written Indian scenes, the stories she'd penned about the noble savage capturing a poor white woman and taking advantage of her. Somehow, she hadn't pictured this as a result of her books, but faced with the grim reality of the situation, she couldn't help but feel guilty. Any of the men in Washington who decided this fate might have read one of her stories. Amanda winced at the thought.

The men gathered around the fire, and their eyes brightened at the scent of the food and the sight of the plates cov-

ered with one stingy chunk of rabbit and a large quantity
of beans. They ate avidly, a rapt expression coming over
their faces as they indulged in the food. When they finished,
they sat on their heels with earthen cups of the whiskey that
Pop Finnegan would sorely miss the next morning.

"Maybe I can reason with them," Amanda suggested.
"Perhaps I can convince them that we aren't the salvation
they predicted coming."

"Try it." Luke shrugged. "But if it doesn't work, I suggest you get my gun back."

Amanda's eyes flickered to the teepee where the Indian
had taken his gun. A woman sat cross-legged before it on
a buffalo hide, patching garments with strips of leather. She
had a dour expression on her face and Amanda had serious
doubts about her ability to get past her, even if she wanted
to. Instead, she approached the Indian who'd captured them
and began to speak in short guttural tones, accentuated with
gestures.

Luke struggled with his bindings, ignored by the Indians.
The old man listened to Amanda, then, with an expression
that needed no translation, abruptly rejected what she had
to say. He repeated the same words he'd used earlier, obviously still convinced that they were sent to bring them food.

"What did he say?" Luke asked.

Amanda shrugged. "He won't listen. He says his name
is Lonesome Bear, and that we are his last hope. He will
wait until the moon is high before killing us, though. That
gives us a little time."

"For what?" Luke glared. "Great, this is just great! None
of this would have happened if I hadn't listened to you."

"It wasn't my fault I didn't have all the data—"

"Amanda, get the gun."

She looked back at the teepee. The woman still sat there,
but even as Amanda watched, she rose from her position
and went to the river for water. There was more than ample
time. She glanced at the Indians once more, the few remaining who looked at her with those strange, black eyes, and
she just couldn't do it. There had to be another way.

As if in answer to her thoughts, there was a rustling over-head in the sunwashed cottonwoods. The leaves had fallen, leaving the branches painfully bare and bleached white, thrust against the sky like skeletal fingers. There, on the closest bough, was a familiar little owl, flapping his wings awkwardly in the chill wind.

"Aesop." Amanda smiled as the bird squawked, obvi-ously considering her departure akin to abandonment. When he decided she'd suffered enough, he left the unwel-coming perch and fluttered down to her shoulder, leaving a few stray feathers behind.

"Amanda, get the damned gun!—Jesus, what the hell's going on?"

Amanda was wondering the same thing, for the instant the Indians saw the bird, they stopped what they were doing to stare in awe. Women dropped their work, while the men gaped at the sight of the owl. The oldest Indian crept for-ward, his finger stabbing in the air toward the bird. He ap-proached Amanda, then fell to his knees in mute respect.

"What is it?" Luke asked in disbelief.

Amanda glanced at the bird, then at the Indians. "I think it's Aesop. A lot of the tribes believe owls are sacred, that they represent a good spirit. At least, it appears that way." She turned to Luke and smiled. "I think we may have found a way out of here."

"It'll take more than that owl to get out of this," Luke said, but his dubious expression changed as the Indians seemed afraid of Amanda and backed away as she ap-proached. She walked boldly toward Luke and proceeded to untie his hands, and none of them made a move to stop her. Free at last, Luke got to his feet and rubbed his wrists, waiting for an attack, but the tribe kept a respectful distance and muttered to themselves, pointing repeatedly at the owl. Amanda walked easily into the teepee, secured Luke's gun, then joined him outside the perimeter of the fire.

"Start walking away, and I'll follow. If something goes wrong, I'll shout," she said quietly.

"No," Luke said firmly. "I'm not going to leave you here."

Amanda looked at him with a penetrating glance. "I don't have time to debate this, nor can I afford to take your natural protective male instincts into account. Do as I say, Luke Parker. Otherwise, violence will be our only alternative."

Luke's face flushed. She was impossible! He should leave her to these wretched Indians. He turned on his heel and strode past the cottonwoods, got fifteen yards beyond, then stopped. No matter how infuriating Amanda was, he couldn't leave her alone. The Indians seemed compliant enough, it was true, but half-starved and angry, they could take the offensive at any time. Besides, she had saved his life.

The Indians did nothing. Amanda stepped into the clearing a few moments later, looking as unconcerned as if she was a schoolgirl walking thoughtfully home from a familiar route. Luke was so relieved when she approached that he didn't know if he wanted to kiss her or strangle her.

He did neither.

"Let's get out of here before our friends decide Aesop isn't a god." Luke took her hand, intending to lead her quickly away from the Indian camp, when Amanda stubbornly shook her head.

"We have to find them a cow," she said simply. "After all, it was foretold. It is not our place to question destiny."

Luke's mouth dropped, and he stared at her as if she'd really lost her sanity this time. "Are you crazy? If we don't get out of here they might take it into their heads to make us their sacrifice! What are you trying to prove, anyway?"

Amanda gave him the full force of her stare, the one that she used to intimidate professors before dashing their theories to shreds. "I am going to look for a cow. If you don't care to join me, then I will see you back at the camp. I knew I wouldn't take to this marriage idea, and this is why. I can make my own decisions, Luke. And I will do so now."

With that she turned and strode briskly toward the open

prairie, looking painfully ridiculous with an owl perched on one shoulder, her hair tied back in a childish braid, and her chin as high as any military man's. Luke wondered what the sentence was for spouse murder, and decided that no jury would convict him when they heard his side of this story. Thrusting his gun back into the holster, he went after her, reminding himself of one thing.

This is why *he* didn't take to the marriage idea. And it didn't look like it was going to get any better.

They found their mounts a short distance away, still sequestered in the trees. The Indians obviously hadn't gotten to them yet, and they mounted without interference and rode away from the grove. Amanda led the way and kept to her word. Instead of heading back to the wagon train and safety, she rode straight toward the river to continue the course they started that morning. Furious, Luke caught up with her and was about to give her a much needed dressing down, when he reined up his horse in astonishment.

All of the cattle, or almost the entire herd, had gathered at the river, exactly as Amanda had predicted. Hundreds of the handsome Herefords, exhausted from their frenzied run, now drank quietly of the rushing waters or lay at the riverbank in dazed confusion.

Luke turned to Amanda in frank admiration. "I've got to hand it to you, woman. You've got one hell of a brain."

She blushed, as pleased—he realized—as most women would have been had he complimented their beauty. "It was nothing, just a bit of deductive reasoning," she said.

"Whatever it was, I'm impressed," Luke admitted. "We'll take one of them to the Indians, then we'll get some help to ride the herd back. Looks like you saved us days of work."

Amanda said nothing, but smiled and nodded. They exchanged a long glance, devoid of the tension that usually sparked their discussions. Amanda turned away first, feeling shy and awkward at his approval. She jerked on her reins and indicated the camp.

"I think we should go now, so we can get through before nightfall."

Luke nodded and joined her. For all the times he'd cursed her unusual gifts, today almost made up for them. Maybe it wouldn't be so bad, being married to a genius. Especially once he had made her his.

Chapter

18

Haskwell read and reread the telegram, unable to believe its contents. Amanda Edison was still alive! Not only had she continued to elude his men, but Butch had given up the chase for the time, because of his partner's death.

Bitch! Haskwell crumbled the paper in his fingers, ignoring the startled looks of the poker players around him. Amanda had come to represent everything that was wrong. His investments weren't panning out; he'd seen that in the paper. A recession, the experts were calling it, but the price of gold and silver had plummeted, making his mining shares almost worthless.

The only place he'd been doing well was at the gambling table. Sam grimaced, then tucked the telegraph inside his jacket. Even his recent winnings seemed tied to a woman. His luck ran good when Honey was with him. The men all loved her, and gold poured in after her singing. He'd bought her a new dress to wear tonight, sapphire blue this time, to set off her raven-black hair and those dark eyes. Yes, Honey was turning out to be a lucrative investment. She still occasionally tried to get away from him, but Sam was too smart for that. He had no intention of letting his good luck charm go.

And now it looked like he'd have to finish off Amanda Edison himself. Tossing down a whiskey, he rose to his feet and started toward the dressing room. He'd have to hire a coach and trace her through Indian country, but none of that overly concerned him. No, it was almost as if she was causing all of this: his losses, his lack of respect from his men. Christ, five years ago no one would have written him such a message, that they were giving up the chase simply because of a dead man. He'd left the West littered with dead men and never looked back.

And he wouldn't this time. As he approached Honey's dressing room, he stood outside and smiled as he heard her frantically trying to pick the lock. He waited until the sound of scraping metal stopped, then he slowly opened the door and held out the key.

"Looking for this?"

Honey whirled in shock, a hairpin clutched in her fingers, her dark eyes wide with terror. The hairpin tinkled to the floor. Her face paled at the sight of the outlaw and she stood in the center of the room, wearing the blue sequinned dress with glass diamonds flashing from her ears and throat. Her glossy black hair was piled up on her head, and her eyes were as wide as silver dollars. She was surrounded by roses, all of them blood red—Sam's favorite color. She looked exactly like what she was: a beautiful young whore.

Sam dangled the key in front of her, enjoying the control he exerted over this lovely creature. "You weren't thinking of running out on me again," he smiled, but his eyes were like black ice, cold and unrelenting. "Remember what happened last time."

"No, Sam, I wasn't," Honey lied, licking her lips in fright. "I just . . . wanted a drink, that's all. Usually the man comes when I knock, but no one did."

"A drink." Sam strode across the lavish dressing room and stopped at a silver champagne bucket. Lifting a white linen towel from the top, he fingered the chilled bottle. "Isn't this your year, sweet?"

"Oh, I forgot." Honey giggled nervously, the sound like a tinkling bell. "I'll have some of that."

"Let me pour." Sam filled a tulip-shaped glass, then handed it to the beautiful singer. He watched as she gulped it greedily, trying to numb herself against feeling, against him. The champagne tickled her nose, but she drank as if it was water, emptying the glass and eagerly accepting a second. Her breasts rose and fell with her shallow breathing, betraying her fear, and her skin gleamed a warm white, like the mother-of-pearl handle of his gun.

It made him feel good to see her fear, made him feel more like a man. In the beginning, she had fought him and tried to resist him. Now, except for an occasional attempt at escape, she did anything he wanted.

Anything.

Sam grinned, then slowly removed his gun, taking care not to make the motion obvious. Honey guzzled the champagne, and didn't notice anything until the gun was pointed at her throat, directly above the glittering choker. She gasped, spilling the wine on the exposed curve of her bare breast, her eyes widening with terror.

"You know, me darlin', I'm getting a little tired of you trying to run away. Are you unhappy with the way I treat you?" Sam gestured to the dressing room. Beautiful gowns lined the closet and the table was filled with an assortment of perfumes and powders. The scent of roses filled the room, cloying and thick, like the inside of a funeral parlor. "Isn't it enough for you?"

"Don't do this, please," Honey breathed, closing her eyes. The cold feel of metal pressed against her soft, white skin. "I'll do whatever you want. I promise."

"Whore." Sam grinned, lifting the strap of her dress with the nuzzle of the gun. "You'd do anything to save this precious skin, wouldn't you? It will be a shame to have to kill you after all."

"No, Sam!" Honey's eyes opened and she pleaded with him. "I won't—try to get away again. I just wanted a drink.

And I was lonely." She attempted a smile, but her red lips trembled with fear.

"You were lonely. For me?" Sam asked, enjoying this more and more. Honey nodded frantically, her earrings flashing in the dim gaslights. "Now if I could believe that, darlin', that might make a difference."

"I'll make you believe," Honey whispered, gasping as the gun slid across her chest, still wet from champagne, to the opposite shoulder strap. Sam removed that one in the same manner, and the blue silk ribbon slid down the other gleaming shoulder, leaving her shoulders bare.

"Yes, it would be a shame to let a pretty woman like you die. But I've got to go away on business. And I can't leave you here alone, you've proven that. So I either have to kill you now, or take you with me."

Honey undid the back of her dress, her fingers shaking. Taking a deep breath to steady her nerves, she let the gown slip down, nearly exposing her pale milky breasts to his heated gaze. "I'll come with you." She tried to sound enticing. "We'll have a good time, Sam. I can make you feel real good."

Sam grinned, then traced the gun around the shimmering blue material, tugging it even lower. Honey's breasts spilled out, and he traced the tip of the weapon across each throbbing nipple, then down to her waist. "Take it off," he whispered hoarsely.

Honey complied, fighting for her life. The dress slid to the floor in a liquid, sapphire puddle. She wore nothing beneath except for black silk stockings and garters, and the sparkling jewelry. She trembled as he placed the gun aside and fondled a breast, brushing his thumb across the tip and making the nipple harder. She was damp when his hand slid lower, to the silky black curls between her legs, her arousal intensified by fright the way a man on his way to the gallows would often get an erection.

"All right, Honey me girl," Sam whispered, his brogue

deepening as he pushed the singer to her hands and knees. "Make me feel good, me darlin'. Real good."

Honey did.

It was a strange thing for Amanda, after a lifetime of rejection, to feel accepted and appreciated. Pop Finnegan gruffly embraced her when the cowboys returned the herd, and Aileen was as proud as if she had raised Amanda herself. Even the Reverend heartily shook her hand and praised her courage in dealing with the Indians, and noted that her unusual intelligence was a precious gift from God—one that she should continue to to use and not be ashamed of.

Luke spared no detail in making Amanda out to be the heroine. And if Luke conveniently left out the fact that Amanda had donated one of the cows to the Indians, Amanda tactfully understood it was in her best interest to let that deed go unheralded. Few of the others had any appreciation for the redman's plight, and Amanda needed little education to understand that.

Later, after a good beef dinner, Pop brought out his best bottle of whiskey, the one that he had been saving for Texas, and decided to open it in celebration. The voices of the men grew full and rich, obliterating the normal night sounds as they sang trail songs and danced around the fire. Aileen glanced toward Jake, and at his nod of approval, accepted an invitation to dance from one of the cowboys. Taking the man's arm, she kicked up her heels. Pop played the fiddle, and the men took turns clapping and dancing, twirling the Irish woman on their arm and shouting encouragement to the others.

Slowly, the religious folk began to join the merriment. Their own livelihood saved, they forgot their stern beliefs for one night and they shyly began to dance. Amanda watched from her perch on the wagon, scribbling into her journal. Aesop sat beside her, munching grasshoppers and live beetles, gifts from the grateful people. She didn't notice Luke approach, and wasn't aware of him watching her until she heard his choked cough.

Amanda glanced up, followed his gaze, then saw he was staring at Aesop. The little owl had just regurgitated the undigestable part of the night's meal, and was gently depositing the remains on the floor of the wagon. Amanda shrugged.

"He does that whenever he's eating bugs. With mice he throws up hair and bones—"

"Amanda." Luke cut her off quickly and forced a smile. "I didn't come over here to discuss Aesop's eating habits. I came to ask you to dance."

"Me?" Amanda stared at him questioningly. She had put on her glasses again, and her eyes seemed enormous, two sea green lamps that stared at him unblinkingly.

Luke nodded. "Yes, you. Come on, they're starting a reel."

"But I don't know how to . . ." Amanda protested, but Luke was reaching toward her face and gently removing the offending glasses. Amanda stared at him, feeling suddenly as naked as if he'd removed her clothes.

"I'll teach you," he said firmly, refusing to allow her to beg off. He clasped her hand, his own rough and warm as he pulled her down from the wagon and toward the campfire. Amanda shook her head frantically. It was one thing to waltz at the restaurant with an experienced man who wouldn't mind a stubbed toe or two; it was another to dance something this raw and exciting with a man like Luke.

Aileen shouted encouragement and Amanda could do nothing but follow. Luke led her to the circle of light, then stood beside the other couples and smiled down at her. Amanda looked up with such dread that he chuckled, then slid his arm around her waist as the music began.

"You look like you're about to be slaughtered. Come on, Amanda, relax. It's fun."

"Luke, I do this about as well as I swim." Panic set in as he twirled her around, then led her expertly around the fire.

"Just follow my lead. I'll do all the work. That's right, bend your knee." Luke slipped his arm through hers and guided her through the steps as Pop played "Buffalo Gals Won't Ya Come Out Tonight." After a few moments, Amanda discovered he was right. It was fun, and easy. Luke did all the hard steps, and Amanda discovered that if she just went along with him, she could dance. The thought was so heady that she got carried away, and stepped forcibly on his foot a moment later.

"I'm so sorry!" Amanda stammered, flushing crimson. She wished that she was far away, safe back in the wagon with her books.

Luke grinned. "Amanda, I've got boots on. It would take more than your slight weight to put a dent into these. Stop looking so embarrassed and let's try again. We've got all night."

Amanda took his hand with considerable trepidation, then allowed herself to be drawn into the dance once more. She marveled at his patience. No man had ever shown her this much kindness before. She caught Aileen's smile and she grinned back, enjoying herself and finally relaxing, knowing that even if she made a mistake, it would not be fatal. Breathless, she swirled with Luke, and when she'd mastered the steps well enough and mustered up some confidence, she even allowed the other cowboys to coax her into dancing with them.

Luke reluctantly let her go, knowing that the cowboys would cherish the chance to dance with a lady, and a pretty one at that. Flushing from excitement and exertion, Amanda took on that odd natural beauty that he'd seen a few times before. She looked young, vibrant, and winning, her eyes sparkling with fun and her smile lighting up her face. Her dress clung to her slender figure, and with a grace she didn't know she possessed, she picked up one corner of it the way Aileen was doing and swirled around the camp-fire.

He was proud of what she had done that day, although it took him a while to appreciate her reasoning. The sympathy she had shown to the Indians was remarkable. He couldn't help but think of his own experience as a Confeder-

ate soldier, and feel a kinship for these men who had lost
much more than he had, for the same cause. And even
though Amanda was a Northerner, she felt for their plight.
Luke smiled at the thought. She was an intriguing mixture
of intelligence, logic, and beauty—a combination that he
was beginning to appreciate.

When the music finally stopped, the men broke into loud
applause. Amanda stood next to Aileen and Jake, her
cheeks blooming with color, her hair falling from its knot
to frame her face with soft chestnut curls. She glanced up
and saw Luke watching her across the fire with frank approval. He excused himself from the other men, then joined
her.

"You look beautiful tonight," he said honestly.

Amanda blushed hotly, her heart pounding. "Thank you.
For the dance, I mean."

He nodded, struck a sulphur-tipped match on his boot
to light a cigarette, then gestured toward the prairie. "Pop
wants to really push on once we cross the river. Since we
won't have much time alone, I thought you might want to
take a walk tonight."

"A walk?" Amanda repeated incredulously.

Luke smiled—a warm, wonderful smile that made her
knees turn to jelly. "Yeah, a walk. Got any objections to
that, lady author?"

"Well," Amanda hesitated. "I do have a lot of writing
to do. And I want to research the Hereford breed. I thought
I could learn something useful for the ranch—"

"Amanda." Luke took her hand firmly. "We got married
last night. Technically, this is still our honeymoon. Unless
you're afraid of something?"

"Absolutely not. Prairie life, unbeknownst to many, is
relatively safe at night—"

"I am very relieved to know that." Luke propelled her
away from the others.

The moon was full, a pale disk that washed the grasses
with silver and made the cottonwoods take on a ghostly
cast. An autumnal wind ruffled the leaves, sending the scent

of the oncoming winter across the plains. Canadian geese flew overhead in a perfect vee, their wings tipped with starlight. It was beautiful, wild and free. Amanda drank in the awesome beauty. They would be leaving this all behind soon, and starting a new life in a strange land. She would be Luke's wife until that time. . . .

Amanda turned awkwardly toward him, noticing for the hundredth time how handsome he was. There was a dangerous sensuality about Luke that she knew other women would appreciate, and a restless intelligence that equalled her own in ability. Everything about him intrigued her, and for that reason, she wanted to run as much as she wanted to stay.

"We'll be reaching Texas in a few days," Luke began, breaking the silence. "We're crossing the river tomorrow, now that the cattle have been rounded up. It can't be too soon for me, with that last attack."

"So you think it was Haskwell."

He nodded, confirming her fears. "Without a doubt. Once we get to town, I want you to register a complaint with the sheriff. I might not be around to protect you all the time, and once we stop moving, you'll be an easier target. This time for me it was just a flesh wound. Next time, one of us could get killed."

Amanda nodded, hating the tightening she felt in her throat. He was still planning to divorce her in Texas. For some reason, the thought ripped her apart. She held onto the cuff of his buckskin jacket, ignoring his look of surprise. Her voice was shy and hesitant, even as her fingers curled intimately within his coat.

"Luke . . . I take it you're not mad at me anymore."

He didn't say anything for a moment, then reached up to gently touch her face. "I guess I overreacted earlier. I'm sorry."

It was an apology, and a heartfelt one at that. Holding her breath, Amanda plunged in. "Would you then . . . I mean, could you kiss me? Just once, like we really were married, and you wanted to?"

He stared at her long and hard, taking in the import of what she'd just asked. For another woman, it would mean little—a flirtation, or worse, an experiment in sexuality. For Amanda, it meant much, much more. Washed in moonlight and dressed in a plain, muslin gown that showed the full effects of hard wear, she looked beautiful. Innocent. And beguiling in a way she would never understand. As Luke pulled her into his embrace, he knew that somehow she had come to mean something to him, something that Haskwell had little to do with. A thousand pictures entered his mind at once, of his clothes floating downriver, of her owl squawking at him, of Amanda peering through her glasses and composing some of the most incredible feelings she had yet to reveal to him.

His lips brushed hers, softly at first, then more persistently until she sighed and reached for him, her arms sliding about his neck, her fingers locking in his hair as he drew her even more closely against him. Then when he finally kissed her, it was unlike any kiss he'd ever given her.

Amanda felt shaken to her soul. She clung to Luke, feeling like she would stumble, that she would become one with the star-studded blackness above and fall into infinity. He was penetrating the wall she'd built around herself, a fortress of books, to the woman beneath. Sweet joy filled her, along with a sense of terror. At once she understood what it was to risk, to have no beliefs, no guarantees, nowhere to look for the safe and right answers. It was frightening and exhilarating at the same time.

When Luke released her, Amanda wanted to draw him back, to experience more. But Luke was already taking her back toward the camp. It was almost as if he wanted to avoid her, for he excused himself as soon as they reached the campfire and volunteered for the night watch. Giving him a solemn, penetrating glance, Amanda returned his goodnight wishes and went to the wagon alone, watching him walk away from her, after a kiss that seared both of them and would have ignited the wettest pine.

What was Luke up to, anyway?

• • •

Luke took a swig of whiskey from the jug the men passed around, trying to ignore the figure of his wife silhouetted against the pale white canvas of the wagon. Gritting his teeth, he fought the urges of his body as she removed her dress. He could see her ripe young form, beautifully curved, emerging from her gown. The men made ribald remarks, and Luke gave them a frozen glance that sent them choking on their liquor and leaving them apologetically silent afterward.

He couldn't go to her, not yet. She would still be apprehensive after their first attempt at lovemaking, and she still did not trust him.

Yet, as he watched her now, he could see her sitting inside the rustic wagon, her legs crossed, her pen dipping frantically into the inkwell then scribbling in her journal. When in God's name would she ever tell him what she told that damned book? It was infuriating. Luke had to fight the compulsion to go to that wagon, pull her into his arms and force her to reveal those secrets to him. But he had to use his own mind this time.

Snatching up his lantern, Luke started away from the fire, toward the black encrusted water. He heard Pop Finnegan's puzzled outcry.

"Where the hell are you going?"

"To the river," Luke replied bluntly.

The religious men and the Reverend exchanged glances, clearly wondering if Amanda's "strangeness" was catching. "What the hell are you doing that for? It's damned cold!" Pop called.

"I know," Luke shouted angrily.

The religious men broke into laughter, which they quickly hushed up as the Reverend gave them a disapproving look. But even as he opened the Bible to conduct prayers, there was more than one choked cough, though no one dared say anything.

After all, it was only the second night he was married. And a pretty poor marriage it seemed at that.

•   •   •

He kissed me tonight, when I asked him to. Somehow, at some time, he has become a part of me. I love him, yet I cannot face that, nor can I tell him. It is incredible the power that this naked emotion has—the power to cut so deeply that I fear I may not recover—and yet I feel more alive than ever before.

We are married, I am his wife. The thought of that is dizzying, yet I know it would not be so if he hadn't been forced. I don't know what to do. I want to make him happy, but I don't even know where to begin. Odd that I should be in this position! There was never a math equation that I couldn't solve, though some of them took weeks, never a treatise I couldn't conquer, and yet I know less about pleasing Luke than I do about the anatomy of an earthworm.

He was happy when I found the cattle today. For the first time since I've known him, he seemed to appreciate my mind, yet I do not think that is the way to reach him. I look at Aileen and Jake, and think it is so easy for her. Jake walks with his arm around her waist, she smiles at him while helping the women to cook. I can tell that he cannot wait to be with her each night, to leave the campfire to join her inside the privacy of their wagon. Why can't I accomplish that?

He will divorce me when we get to Texas. He has sworn that, and yet the thought appalls me. Once we are in Waco, it will be too easy to just be friends or business partners. He will have the ranch, and I will have my books. For however long he is my husband, I must try to make him want me.

And time is running out.

Chapter

❧ *19* ❧

"Come on, boys, let's get these dogies through before sundown."

Pop Finnegan urged the McLafferty family through the rushing depths of the Canadian River. The prairie schooner bucked and wavered as the waters rammed into it, and the heavy canvas quickly became saturated from the river. The McLafferty children rode with the cowboys, their bodies tied to the saddles with rope to keep them from falling during the crossing, while the elder McLafferty struggled to get the wagon through to the opposite bank. One of the children cried out as a box detached from the side of the wagon and began a rapid descent downriver.

"My little pet! Papa, he's going!" Timmy McLafferty cried as the box snagged onto a floating branch.

"I'll get it," Luke shouted, fishing out the box and tying it to his own horse. The little prairie dog inside rustled nervously as Luke's horse pranced in the river, sidestepping loose twigs and debris that swirled around them. "Come on, next!"

Amanda sat on top of her horse, her eyes as wide as when she wore her glasses, her knuckles white from clenching the reins. She was still scared to death of the horse, and the endless miles of grey, slithering water didn't help matters much. She glanced up at Luke. He was shouting orders to the wagon driving in front of her, balancing Timmy Lafferty's box, and controlling the horse with just the pressure from his legs. He made it look so easy, and yet . . .

Amanda fought back tears. Luke had been preoccupied and distant, trying to get the wagons prepared for the crossing. He had readied their wagon, intending to drive it himself so that Amanda would not have that ordeal to contend with. He had crawled into the wagon late last night, and immediately fell asleep. Amanda had the faint impression that he was wet, that his coal-black hair had been slicked back, and that moisture gleamed from his chest before he crawled beneath the blankets. She dismissed the notion as ridiculous. Winter was approaching, and Luke certainly wasn't crazy enough to go swimming in the river this time of year.

"Next!"

Amanda froze. They were calling to her. Numbly she flicked her reins, but the horse beneath her seemed to share her indecision and refused to budge. Luke glanced up, his face shadowed by the black Stetson he wore, his ankles wreathed in water. He was about to shout impatiently to her, but something in her face softened him. He seemed to remember her fears, and he urged his mount through the swirling water to the riverbank beside her.

"Come on, Amanda. You can do it. I know you can."

She blushed furiously, hating her own weakness. She gave him a doubtful look, but he smiled encouragingly and waved her on. She kicked her horse, clamping her eyelids shut and trying desperately not to look at the brown waters swishing like coffee in the bottom of a tin cup. Luke called to her horse, urging the mare to cross the murky river depths and to follow the wagon just ahead. The mare, a stout chestnut that was used to following orders, leaped into the water and began the journey to the other side.

Amanda felt like she was going to throw up. She fought the rising bile in her throat as the horse plunged in deeper and the current swirled around them like a rattlesnake. She gave Luke a pleading look, but he continued to shout encouragements.

"We're halfway there. I won't leave you. You're doing fine, Amanda!"

Terror was building inside of her. She could hear the roar of the waters, the sound of the cattle lowing in protest, the whinny of the horse beneath her as the river grew deeper. The waters crept up to her boots, threatening to pull her down into their murky depths, to keep her forever sealed beneath the earth in a mystical world of gently waving seaweed and turbulent shallows. Fighting the feeling of falling, she opened her eyes, held tightly to the reins, and refused to look at anything but Luke. He was just ahead, waiting for her, his black Stetson shading his face against the sun, making it appear shadowed and mysterious. His eyes seemed to warm her like two pale blue flames. His smile was genuine and compelling, urging her on the way no argument could.

Amanda took a deep breath, then gently tapped the horse's flanks the way she'd seen the other riders do. The mare lurched forward, then picked her way among the stones, feeling for safe ground. Once the horse misstepped, and Amanda could feel the crunch of the gravel beneath and the huge animal's wavering. For a horrified moment, she thought that the horse would lose balance and send her tumbling down into the river below. But the mare quickly regained footing, and resumed the dangerous steps once more.

"That's great! You're doing it!"

Amanda smiled back at Luke, then gasped in surprise as the horse lifted her legs and stepped gracefully out of the river and onto the soft mossy bank beyond. A breath left Amanda's body in one loud whoosh as the realization struck her: she'd made it. She'd faced two of her worst fears, horses and water, and had triumphed.

"You did it!" Luke grabbed her in a bear-like hug, wrapping his buckskin-clad arms around her shoulders while still atop of his mount. Amanda flushed a brick red, but she was unbearably proud. Nothing could have meant more to her at that moment, not even an academic scholarship. Unless it was to Radcliffe.

"I did, didn't I?" Amanda glanced back at the river, as if unable to believe that she hadn't dreamed this.

"You damned well did, and as good as anyone. When we get to Texas, I'm buying you the best beef dinner you ever had."

Amanda bit her lip, trying to suppress her enjoyment, but her eyes twinkled. She'd done it. She got the damned horse across one of the most virulent rivers in Oklahoma, and without a hitch. She wanted to giggle. Then her excitement dimmed as she thought of what he'd said.

Texas.

He'd be divorcing her soon.

Amanda forced the depressing thought aside, unable to bear the implication. For better or for worse, he was married to her now. And she would enjoy it for as long as she could.

Jake caught up with Luke after the others had crossed and the cattle were safely on the same bank. It had been a successful undertaking; they'd lost no one and had no injuries. The camp was in high hopes, with the Texas border close by and the fulfillment of dreams within arm's grasp.

"It's hard to believe we've only a few days now." Jake broke the silence as they rode comfortably along for a mile or so.

Luke nodded in agreement. "All in all, it's been a good trip. We've recovered most of the cattle, so all of the families can make a fresh start. The Herefords are in good shape, in spite of the stampede. We've only lost half a dozen head, but that's to be expected."

"We would have lost a lot more if not for Amanda," Jake said gruffly. "Hard to believe that a little slip of a woman would have so big a brain." Then, after a moment, "Aileen's become quite attached to her, you know."

"So I see." Luke glanced at the former saloon girl and

saw her riding in the wagon with Amanda. "I'm grateful for that. Amanda can use a good friend."

"She's glad to do it." Jake cleared his throat, as if unable to decide how to verbalize his next words. "I understand how Aileen feels. I've come to admire Miss Edison myself. Neither one of us felt right about the way those holy folk forced you to wed. I wouldn't blame you if you wanted to undo the thing the first chance you got."

Luke gave Jake a searching look. "We talked about something of the sort."

"I kinda thought so. Aileen said Amanda's been sort of disturbed lately. I guess it would unsettle anyone, coming to a new place, alone, with a man for a husband who doesn't want her. Is that your intention, then? To divorce her when we reach Waco?"

"I haven't decided," Luke said gruffly.

"It's none of my business, except that if you do want to leave her, she can come live with us." Ignoring Luke's glance of amazement, Jake continued, looking straight ahead as his horse picked its way along the trail. "Aileen suggested it, and I'm agreeable if that's the way things work out. A woman alone stands no chance where we're headed."

"She's not alone," Luke pointed out. "I'm sharing the ranch with her."

"So I hear." Jake gave him a second glance. "I understand you made a deal with the lady, for her protection. And that half the ranch was the bargaining price. Not that I have anything to say about that. Stranger contracts have been made along the Chisholm trail, and my relationship with Aileen wasn't written in any beggar's bible. But I just wanted you to know that there was an alternative, if you don't want to stay with her."

"I appreciate that," Luke replied, wondering why he was annoyed. "But I feel protective of her at this point. Amanda is not like other women." *Any other woman,* he amended to himself.

"I know." Jake chuckled. "I heard about your clothes. It must be hell being tethered to a woman with the brains—" Then, abruptly, "Why do you think she has a price on her head?"

It was Luke's turn to look startled. He was about to deny any such thing, but Jake shook his head.

"I was a lawman before I decided to come south. Haskwell doesn't just send his men after anybody because it's Tuesday and the newspaper wasn't printed. That black Irishman's got a good reason—a damned good reason—to want her dead."

"I honestly don't know," Luke said, his brow furrowed in thought. It was a puzzle he'd been trying to figure out for days. "Amanda doesn't know either. They started attacking her on board the train west, and haven't let up since. It doesn't make a whole lot of sense. Amanda's never been anywhere, never done anything, doesn't have any jewels, clothes, or anything an outlaw could sell. Unless she has something valuable that she doesn't know about."

"I don't think that's it," Jake said gruffly. "A man will track his victim this long only if his life is threatened. Especially Haskwell. He's a gambler and investor, and will kill when cornered, but he knows better than to go looking for trouble. Do you remember the Haines murder about five years back?"

Luke's hand tightened on the leather reins. "When that sheriff was shot in cold blood, and they couldn't find the witness?"

Jake nodded, then wiped his mouth with his buckskin jacket. He took a flask from his pocket, pulled the cork out with his teeth, then took a long drink before offering the bottle to the younger man riding beside him.

"Haskwell would have hanged for that, had we found the woman who saw him. We know the bastard did it. All we needed was for her to show up."

Luke froze as the whiskey tin touched his mouth, the metal cold against his teeth. "You don't think . . . "

"She was five foot five, chestnut colored hair, and glasses," Jake replied. "That's the description."

"Jesus," Luke swore softly. "You mean, Amanda saw him?"

"It hardly matters whether she did or didn't," Jake pointed out. "If Haskwell thinks she saw it."

Luke nodded. It made sense, all of it. And if Sam Haskwell thought Amanda could hang him, he wouldn't stop pursuing her until she was dead. Hatred rose up in him. He refused to even entertain the thought. Haskwell wouldn't wantonly kill someone who meant something to him again. When he was fighting Grant at Petersburg, there was nothing he could do.

This time, it would be different.

The hot Oklahoma sun glittered brightly on the swaying fields of the Great Plains. A wagon train snaked through the grass, plodding down a trail worn through by hundreds of wheels and thousands of hooves. Soft white daisies dotted the land, while empty sacks of burlap and discarded tins testified to the human element who had made the same trek.

In the distant hills, the starving Indians watched the procession, their bronzed red bodies blending perfectly with the dusty red clay of the earth. Lying poised against the dirt, their slender bodies perfectly controlled, they waited for the right moment to pose an attack on the unwary settlers below.

Inside the second wagon, a woman took off her bonnet and ruffled her soft blonde hair. The breeze felt wonderful against her hot scalp, and she stretched, allowing it to play over her sweat-soaked dress.

Angel Hollister was tired of the trail, tired of the ugly Longhorn cattle they'd been tasked to drive up to Abilene. But she'd begged her father to take her these past months, with a girlish desire for excitement. She hadn't known what the trail would really be like—that every bone in her body would ache incessantly, that thirst and hunger would become constant companions, or that simple tasks would take on a monumental difficulty.

She also hadn't known what a blazing sunset would look like, unfettered by buildings or saloon lights, or how pristine *and clear the air would be at dawn. She hadn't anticipated the flowers, the brush plants, the geranium and columbine that appeared in the sea of softly waving grass like casually dropped presents. No, she hadn't known of any of this, nor could she explain the way she'd been feeling lately.*

It was as if her body had come alive with nature. In the past few days, she'd become keenly aware of Chase Rutherford, her father's foreman. She could see him just outside the wagon, riding with his body bent forward and his legs pressed tightly to his mount. Tall, with crisp black hair and sky-blue eyes, he could look right into her and make her blood pulse hotter and her heart do crazy things.

He saw her in the wagon and he tipped his hat, the corners of his eyes crinkling with his smile. "Morning." His eyes wandered down the front of her dress. "Care to ride? There's a waterhole a few miles south. We could make it ahead of the wagons." He smiled knowingly. "You would be a lot cooler for a swim."

She shouldn't, Lord knows, she shouldn't. Her father would be furious. Angel Hollister had always done the right thing, and had always listened to authority. Until Chase. For some reason, the blue-eyed cowboy made it difficult to think. She wanted to refuse now, but her nerves felt as tight as a guitar string and the thought of the cooling water was just too tempting. Checking to make sure her father was still well behind them, she nodded eagerly and slipped into the saddle before him, her legs fitting expertly next to his. . . .

Amanda read through the scene from her new novel, pleased with its progress. The difference in her writing was apparent. Her trip on the prairie was obviously affecting her work.

"Go on out there and sing, Honey me girl."

Honey stared back at Sam, her eyes lifeless. Clad in scarlet silk, she looked stunning, but there was an emptiness about her that made her black ostrich feather droop and her glass diamonds lose their luster. She looked beaten, frightened half to death, and pushed past the point of caring. As she gazed at the man who was her captor, she swallowed the hatred that was beginning to eat away at her. She refused to feel anything at all.

She couldn't. For the past few days, Sam had dragged her from one cow town to another, in a relentless search for a woman named Edison. None of it meant anything to Honey. Nothing mattered now except escape, and that seemed impossible.

She had given up trying ever since the last time Sam threatened her in the dressing room. She shivered as she thought of that gun pressing against her skin, and worse, what had followed afterward. Although he had yet to physically beat her, he abused her in every other way possible. He beat her down mentally, made her feel terrified all of the time. Sexually perverted, he seemed to delight in anything that humiliated her, that added to her sense of helplessness and fear. It was a stimulant to him, an aphrodisiac to the older man who needed whatever he could get to arouse him.

And now he wanted her to sing. Numbly, Honey clutched the black lace fan Sam had given her and she stared out onto the scarred and empty stage just beyond. She couldn't do it. She couldn't even remember a song, or the days when she was free, enjoying the attention of men, and letting them shower her with gold and compliments. She used to allow only one man to take her to dinner, and she always refused to sleep with him after. It was a trick she had learned early on—not to give in. It made the men crazy for her.

It was the ultimate irony to wind up like this. She, Honey Bee, who could have any man, who rejected governors and silver kings, railroad barons and rich Yankee speculators, was now the plaything of a man so cruel and worthless that she couldn't think of a name low enough to do him justice.

"Get out there." Sam's voice turned cold. "Now."

"I can't," Honey protested, her voice taking on the first glimmer of life that it had shown in days. "Sam, please don't do this. Don't make me sing. I just can't."

Sam grabbed her roughly, bruising her alabaster shoulder. "You can and you will. This trip is costing me money, and I need to make it back. Now you'll do it for me, or I'll find another way to make you earn your keep." He smiled, his black eyes glittering with menace. "There are over fifty men out there who have paid to see you, Honey darlin'. Fifty men. Any one of them or all of them would pay a tidy fortune to spend an hour between your legs. Ah, I see you understand me now. Which way would you prefer?"

"No, Sam!" Honey cried, crystal tears spilling down her cheeks and smearing the black kohl Haskwell had insisted she use. "Please, no!"

"All right then." Sam let go of her arm and shoved her gently out to center stage. "You've made your choice then. I'll let the piano player know what songs you prefer."

He was gone a moment later, disappearing through a dusty velvet curtain. Honey could hear the silence, followed by a thunderous applause as the piano man struck a few tinny chords. The curtain slowly opened, and the spotlight fell on her with a painful illumination. The clapping ceased, and the men waited in anticipation as Honey opened her mouth to sing.

"The sun shines bright, on my old Kentucky home; 'Tis summer, the darkeys are gay; The corn top's ripe and the meadow's in bloom, While the birds make music all the day . . . "

It was the only song she could remember, the only one whose words would come. She sang softly, her voice tremulous as she fought back tears, wishing she could go home and be well away from this nightmare which had become her life.

The cheer dissipated from the room like a jolly ghost no longer welcome. The men, already rich with beer, stared at the sad and beautiful girl on stage, and felt her pain. Many of them, defeated Confederates who were struggling to rebuild a new life, thought back to the homes that once waited for them—homes that no longer existed or were forever changed. As Honey sang, the sadness permeated the saloon.

More than one man roughly wiped his eye with his sleeve, while others slipped solemnly away, wanting to escape from the painful reminders of the war.

"What the hell is this shit?" the bartender swore. Instead of clapping and cheering and buying round after round, the men were acting as if they were at a funeral. Honey's voice rang out true and clear, filled with sorrow and grief. She moved gracefully across the stage, her dress falling around a figure that was now too thin. Even her hair, that wonderful arrangement of black glossy curls, seemed to have dimmed, and her eyes looked out onto nothing.

The barkeep gestured to the piano player to change the music, but the man shrugged. Every time he attempted it, Honey returned to the sad lament of the lost South.

"A few more days to tote the weary load, No matter, it will never be light; We'll sing one song for the old Kentucky home, For our old Kentucky home far away."

A cowboy sobbed, then drowned himself in his beer, while more men slipped away. The barkeep strode up to the stage, threw a menacing glance to the piano player who immediately began a cheerful ditty, then hauled the curtain shut. He turned to Haskwell and Honey, his face beet red, his black moustache twitching in anger.

"What the hell do you call that? I hired you to bring men in, not to make them leave! This whole place is as depressed as a morgue!"

"I'm sorry," Honey stammered, suddenly realizing what she'd done. "I didn't mean—"

"You're fired." The barkeep tossed a coin onto the floor. "Take that and leave. You're lucky I don't hold you responsible for loss of income tonight. Goddamn! Saturday night, and we usually pack the house! Tonight I book Honey Bee, and she drives out half the men with one song! When word of this gets out, you won't get a booking anywhere!"

"You aren't threatening now, are you?" Sam said, his black eyes narrowing with menace. His hand rested lightly over his gun, his fingers twitching, as if aching to draw.

"No." The barkeep swallowed hard. Haskwell was no one

to tangle with. The man was ruthless, and would kill with no more compunction than he'd spit out tobacco. "I didn't mean that."

"Good." Haskwell smiled, his brogue deepening. "Miss Honey isn't herself tonight. I'll take care of that. Meanwhile, you keep your mouth shut. Understood?"

The barkeep nodded. It wasn't worth his life. He watched as Sam roughly dragged the young showgirl away, her feathers bobbing like a plucked hen's. He had seen the abject misery in her eyes, but there was nothing he could do about it. Cursing, he returned to the bar and counted out his receipts.

It was a bad night all around.

The campfire oranged the night black sky, sending ribbons of flame and cinders sparkling into infinity. They had crossed the Texas border earlier that day, and already the wagon train was breaking up. The religious families headed east for places like Dallas, while the cowhands, their pockets jingling with coins, went on to Decatur.

Amanda sighed, turning over in the wagon. Jake and Aileen had gone to bed early, to prepare for their arrival in Waco tomorrow. Luke was still up. She could see him walking, his hands thrust in his pockets against the chill, his face harsh and thoughtful. He had done the work of three men that day, getting the cattle together, organizing the gradual drop off of the families, and keeping to the trail. She knew he was tired, but like a moonstruck animal he paced, his hand-rolled cigarette a red taper in the blackness.

For some reason, she shared the feeling. Every muscle in her body was as tight as a fiddler's string, and her nerves jumped with the slightest noise. Annoyed at herself, she braided her hair and wondered why the wagon seemed so empty, why she felt so alone. Aesop watched her with wide, unblinking yellow eyes, but even his presence didn't soothe her. Picking up her pencil, she stared at the page, but it stared right back at her—white and unfilled.

They would be arriving in Waco tomorrow. There would

be a solicitor in town, of that Amanda was certain. Luke
would seek him out, put an end to this marriage, and then
the two of them would—

Would what?

They had planned to share the ranch, in an equal partnership. But how could they now, after sharing so much? Try
as she might, Amanda could not imagine Luke acting as
foreman, and herself as his ranch teammate. Every time she
tried to envision any kind of working relationship, she drew
a blank as empty as her paper. They had been intimate.
They had lived as husband and wife. True, she had fought
him every step of the way until recently, when he'd made
life more pleasant than she could have dreamed possible—
but she had always wanted him.

What did Luke Parker want from her?

It was a question that couldn't be answered. Frustrated,
Amanda went back to her work. Books had always helped
her when she was upset, but she discovered that now nothing did. She couldn't concentrate. Her mind, normally brilliant, would not even piece together a sentence.
Exasperated, she tossed the pencil aside, barely missing
Aesop, who ruffled his feathers indignantly and turned his
head around away from her.

She wanted him. Amanda knew what the ache in her
stomach meant, and also knew that tonight might be her
last chance. Something had happened between them that
day, when he had encouraged her to cross the river and conquer her fears, something that made her wonder if she could
overcome her biggest fear of all.

Her nightgown clung to her and she plucked at the thin
cotton fabric, peeling it away from her damp skin. It was
useless. She picked up her journal, wrapped a worn knitted
shawl around her shoulders, then stepped outside to the
star-studded night.

He sensed her at once, the way a wolf startles when a man
enters his space. Amanda saw him near the campfire,
framed in orange and black, his face half-hidden in the dark-

ness. Without a word, he extended a cup to her, holding it out like a child tempting a timid bird.

Amanda entered the circle of light, aware that they were alone, and that the prairie had taken on a deep stillness that spoke of the late hour. She took the cup, accepted his offering, accepted him. What was it that made him so compelling, that made her body lean toward him as if of its own accord? Was this what was meant by a mating urge? Perhaps, Amanda dimly reasoned, there was more to lovemaking than what she'd already experienced. And even if it was just for the man alone, then tonight—to hold him, kiss him, let him touch her—it was worth it.

He still said nothing, but simply picked up her heavy braid of hair and kissed it. His fingers toyed with the silken rope as if with an aching desire to undo it, to run his fingers through its chestnut length the way she'd done earlier in the evening, when she and Aileen had washed down at the river. When he lifted his face, Amanda could see that his beautiful blue eyes were filled with everything she was feeling.

And wanting.

Silently, she held out the journal, the cream-colored pages whipping enticingly in the night wind. Luke glanced down at the book, and understood immediately the significance of her offering. She was giving herself to him, telling him in the most eloquent way she knew just what he meant to her. His eyes filled, and he fingered the manuscript, knowing that he could never live from this moment unscathed. He had become a part of her, and forced her to become a part of him. Little by little she had chiseled away at him. This odd woman with her sea-colored eyes and piercing intelligence meant more to him than every soft, girlish southern belle he'd ever known.

He handed back the notebook, giving her a smile that she would remember in her dreams. "You don't have to do this," he whispered. "I understand."

Tears rolled down Amanda's cheeks as she took her precious journal, the writing a scrawling blur. She clutched the book against her breasts, her toes curling in the sand against the chill. Her lips parted when his mouth brushed hers, then she eagerly met him, her cheeks wet, her body responding joyously.

" 'Knowledge without reason is love,' " she whispered. "Amanda Edison."

Chapter

20

Luke laughed softly, the sound sensual in the warm open air. Amanda shivered when his body left hers as he climbed into the wagon, then felt the steaming warmth once more when he took her in his arms. The intensity between them deepened when their eyes met and recognized the mutual feeling between them. For a moment Luke simply held her, then kissed her softly, fully, arousing her as if they'd never been together and he was a lover newly welcomed.

It felt good to have him hold her, good to feel the strength in his arms, and the sensation of desire returned. Amanda could smell the campfire on him, the sharp, cutting scent mingling with the smell of the outdoors and the spice of the pines. His hands felt cold and rough, yet their difference against her skin was compellingly sexual. Perhaps it was meant to be this way, she thought, then he kissed her and she couldn't think at all.

No one kissed like Luke Parker, Amanda was certain of that. Demanding and forceful, yet persuasive and tender, he was capable of making a woman forget just about any-thing. When he unbuttoned the fasteners of her nightdress, Amanda sighed and helped him. Both of them were aware that Aileen and Jake slept nearby, that they couldn't make noise, but the silence and the warm darkness seemed to add to the erotic atmosphere around them. As the nightgown fell down around her waist, Amanda looked up into Luke's passion-drugged eyes and felt completely lost to the powerful sexuality of the man. She let him draw her into his embrace, the softness of her half-naked body warmed by the smoothness of his worn buckskins and the man beneath.

Luke cupped her breast, feeling her heart beat wildly beneath his calloused fingers. He wanted nothing more than to take her now, to lie her back in the wagon and bury himself deep within her hot female sweetness. Forcing himself to remember her first experience, he gentled his kisses, taking his time to arouse her thoroughly. His mouth lowered, then took the bloom of her nipple between his lips, his tongue flicking over the diamond-hard point. Amanda arched instinctively, her head supported by his encircling arm, her hair spilling backward in a glossy chestnut wave. Her eyes opened slightly, turquoise pools that were smoky and hot, framed by damp lashes as she looked at him pleadingly.

"Now, Luke. Please."

Her voice was a sultry whisper, more arousing in the stillness than he'd ever dreamed possible. Ignoring her plea, he let his hand trace enticingly up from her knee, to beneath the hem of her nightdress. His mouth took hers as she moaned—his hand, warm and gentle, encountered the silky bare skin of her thigh. Amanda's body spasmed as he lifted the material aside, and his fingers raked through the soft brown curls, and downward.

She would have cried out except for his mouth on hers, stilling her words, his fingers bringing her enormous pleasure. She squirmed, helpless with desire as he lifted the rest of the nightgown over her head, then yanked it out of the way. Free from the restraining garment, she lowered herself down onto the wagon bed with Luke, barely aware that he had shucked his own clothes. When he joined her, as naked as herself, his body outlined by the firelight and the dim lantern, she smiled joyously and ran her fingers down the firm, muscular length of him.

Amanda felt him suck in his breath, and the knowledge that she could excite him with her inexperienced hands made her brave. Ignoring the passionate warning in his eyes, she boldly stroked him the way he'd touched her, and was gratified to see his eyes close and his breathing quicken. It was a wonderful, powerful feeling to arouse a man deliberately, and when his mouth crushed hers roughly, his hand impatiently parting her thighs, Amanda knew she'd pushed him to the limit.

"Amanda." She could barely hear his whisper. "Are you ready? Do you want me?"

She nearly cried out, but answered with her body, arching her back to take him. Experiencing a moment of fear as he poised between her legs, she relaxed as he seemed to sense her hesitation and instead of burying himself within her, he slowly entered her, one small bit at a time. Now, there was no pain, only the sensation of her body expanding, her hot wetness closing around him, welcoming him within her. Amanda urged him on, fully aroused now and wanting the fulfillment that she sensed he would give her this time. Yet deliberately, he teased her, making her want him even more, allowing her body time to get used to this intrusion before giving in to what they both craved. As he thrust more deeply within her, she was so aroused and so ready that the passion began for her almost immediately. Everything was obliterated for her except wanting, and her entire world was reduced to what was happening to her in that moment. Luke thrust into her again and again, and her body responded, aching for it, wanting everything he could give her.

And then it happened. Amanda's eyes flew open as her body reached its pinnacle and climaxed with wave after wave of emotion. Clutching his shoulders, her legs wrapped around his, she pulled him tightly to her, overwhelmed with joy. Her reaction was so honest and unrestrained that any control Luke exerted was lost. Spilling his seed deeply within her, he held her in his arms, her heart beating wildly against him, echoing his own.

Then, she started to giggle. At first, Luke couldn't believe the sound that came from within her, a soft, girlish laughter that sounded as sweet as a tinkling bell. Stifling her with a kiss, he smiled in the dark wagon.

"What's so funny?" he whispered.

"Nothing," Amanda sighed, contentedly. "It's just that I'll have to reformulate my thinking that females don't derive pleasure from lovemaking."

"Are you saying that you've changed your mind?" Luke grinned.

Amanda smiled, then reached for him, deciding that, at times, it didn't pay to explain.

She showed him instead.

Jake and the others awoke the following morning, and with them came reality. Luke rose to meet them, then returned with a cup of scalding hot soup and a few doughy biscuits stuck on a stick. Alone in the dim interior of the wagon, Luke insisted upon feeding Amanda bites of the delicious bread and sips of the soup. It was like having a picnic, hidden from parental prying eyes. When she finished, he helped her dress, reluctantly pulling a soft wool gown over her slender body that was still pink and glowing from lovemaking.

Like two children, they giggled and played. Luke tried to pull on her boots, but it was difficult to slip the tightly laced leather over her finely shaped feet. Laughing, Amanda tried to help him, and ended up tumbling backward in the wagon. Luke's eyes warmed, and she would have stayed there far longer if Pop Finnegan hadn't called out.

"Waco! Got to get on the trail. Everyone ready?"

"Jesus," Luke swore, while Amanda blushed hotly. He took her hand, loving the way she looked this morning, her hair tumbling about her shoulders, her skin radiant. Even her eyes glowed, reminding him of an ocean at sunset, warm and filled with soft colors. "You'll ride with me today?" It was a question, very unlike Luke—uncertain and tinged with a fleeting shyness.

Amanda smiled. "Wouldn't be anywhere else. As Shakes— I mean, I would love it."

Waco! Amanda sat in the front of the wagon, adjusting her glasses to get a better view of the town. If anything, it was even rougher and wilder than Abilene. Cattle roamed through the streets as cowhands tried in vain to keep some semblance of order, but no one seemed to notice or mind. Well-dressed men and woman tended their shops, which appeared scarcely more than a few seasons old. The saloon and the hotel looked established, but everything else had the new look of a business that had yet to weather bad times. Ships lined the Brazos River, filled with cotton and cattle products, returning with just about everything else. Amanda saw barrels of rum, kegs of good Kentucky bourbon, bolts of cloth, and piles of finished goods. Like many of the other southern towns, Waco attracted carpetbaggers, those despised money grubbers who came from the North with their sharp accents and gaudy clothes. With them came gamblers and prostitutes, the scourge of the reconstructed South. With the formation of the trail and the newly found wealth from the Longhorns, the town wore a veneer of sophistication that already showed cracks.

Amanda was fascinated. Scribbling furiously, she recorded each impression, even the dust that covered everything, including her notebook.

"How far away is this place?" Luke asked her.

Amanda shrugged. "Maybe we should ask someone. There's a store." She gestured to a wood frame building sandwiched between the saloon and the dressmakers, with a red lettered sign advertising everything from boots to grits.

"Nice place." Luke removed his hat as they entered, taking in the neat rows of cloth, tins of flour and sugar, boxes of fruit, and bushels of potatoes. Several men nodded to Luke, then stared as Amanda explored the store, poking her head into every nook and cranny. Luke sought out one of the men and asked directions to the ranch, while Amanda stood by the scale, ignoring the curious glances she received.

The shopkeeper, a plump little man whose face beamed from behind the counter, gave her a friendly smile, then returned to weighing a mound of potatoes. "Will that be all, Elvira?" he asked the small, frail woman on the other side. When she nodded, he placed her groceries in a basket. The scale bounced back to zero, but not until the shopkeeper walked away.

"You ready, Amanda?" Luke called to her and she joined him, still watching the procedure behind her. This time another man was buying apples. The scale registered a bit more than the three pieces of fruit warranted, and Amanda frowned in annoyance.

"What's wrong?" Luke noticed her interest and her silent speculation. "I got good directions. They say it's just outside of town."

"That storekeeper was fixing the scale," Amanda commented. "I swear he was."

"What are you talking about?" Luke glanced back at the ruddy-faced man who was cheerfully balancing a sack of flour. "They say his name's Mitchell. He's been here for years."

"He puts his thumb on the scale to add to the weight," Amanda reasoned. "Think about it. Every time he walks away, the scale bounces back as if pressure is off. And those apples weighed two and a half pounds. I did a lot of work with scales in school, and there's no way that fruit could have been more than two. He must have made a fortune cheating these people."

"Amanda." Luke had a warning in his voice. "We're just moving in here. It wouldn't be the best way to start out by accusing someone of thievery. Let's go find the ranch. Do you have any introduction or a copy of the will?"

Amanda nodded, her thoughts reluctantly diverted from the store, then withdrew an elegantly penned envelope. "It's from the lawyer who settled the estate."

Luke scanned the letter, amazed at the writing and the

rich quality of the stationery. The note was from Richard
.J. Phipps, attorney at law, and simply stated that a Mr. Austin Rutherford had bequeathed his ranch to Amanda Edison, aka Fess Tyson, in deep appreciation for the many
hours of enjoyment she had given him with her books.
Frowning, Luke pocketed the missive, then turned their
wagon east.

The homes that lined the street grew less bawdy and impressive as they got farther from the heart of town. Ranches
sprawled far and wide in a country that was untainted by
man. Cattle roamed freely, branded by the cowboys, inciting
range wars as hungry ranchmen gave into the temptation
to obliterate a prior mark with their own. Longhorns ranged
the prairie, along with an occasional Angus. Mesquite
waved softly in the wind, and prickly brush grew everywhere, causing the cowboys to wear chaps in order to prevent the sticky weeds from tearing their legs. In the
blacklands, cotton studded the landscape, growing rich and
prolific.

In short, there was opportunity here. Land, water, and
cattle were in abundance for the taking. Luke surmised that
the ranch would need a good deal of work, but that was
something that never frightened him. Already he could picture his own range, thick with grass and roaming with cattle. It was a place where he could begin again, maybe even
start a family.

He glanced at Amanda, but she was staring straight
ahead, fascinated by everything she saw. He smiled as he
thought of her that morning, sated from lovemaking
through the night and giggling like a schoolgirl. There was
a softening about her that was terribly appealing, even in
the way she wore her hair. Her tight bun was gone, and instead, her thick chestnut curls tumbled loosely around her
shoulders, held back with a leather cord. Her lips parted,
dewy with excitement, and her eyes widened in astonishment. Luke's eyes followed hers, then he dropped the reins
as they spotted the sign for the Triple Bar Ranch.

"My God," he breathed. "I didn't have any idea. Did you?"

Amanda shook her head in the negative. Before them stood a great stone mansion with tall white columns, looking like a southern plantation house that had dropped out of the sky onto the range. Land surrounded it, good fertile blacklands that flourished with grass—a paradise for the roaming cattle. In the distance, Amanda could see the Mexican *vaqueros* riding the ranch, whirling their lariats as the wild calves bawled in protest. It was a ranchman's dream. Amanda dismounted in stunned surprise, unable to believe this was hers.

"Looks like Austin Rutherford did all right," Luke remarked as they walked toward the house. "This is some estate! I guess he had no heirs."

Amanda shrugged, her hand tightening around Aesop's cage. Even the little owl seemed stunned by the magnitude of the land as he stared from behind his gilded bars.

"I received many fan letters from him, but he never indicated anything of the kind. He seemed merely appreciative. I even gave him an acknowledgement once, in *Colorado Gunfight.* He sent me several books on Texas that were immensely helpful."

They reached the gothic-styled porch, and before Amanda could even turn the shiny brass knob, the door opened and a manservant stepped out. Mexican and as brown as a nut, he wore a dazzling smile, and his eyes brightened like lighted sherry as they fell on Amanda. His dark hair curled around his face like a halo, and his worn mustache prickled beneath his broad nose like a furry mouse. His skin, as leathery as an old saddle, revealed his age, but his quick step and agility belied his years. Wearing a soft pair of khaki pants and a brightly colored tunic that seemed well suited to the climate, he nearly danced in suppressed delight as if greeting an old friend.

"Amanda? Miss Amanda Edison?" His smile grew impossibly wider as Amanda hiked Aesop's cage onto her arm and stretched out a hand. "Amanda Edison! Fess Tyson! I cannot believe I meet you at last! It is really you?" He pumped the extended hand vigorously. "I wait all my life to meet you. How I wish Austin were here to see you at last! Do come in, I am Pedro." He reached for Aesop, then, with a second thought, glanced up to Luke. "Is he with you?"

"Yes." Amanda smiled. "This is my . . . husband, Luke Parker."

"Ah. Husband. That is very good." Luke's hand got the same treatment as Amanda's. "Any husband of Fess Tyson is a friend of mine. Come in, the sun is very hot. I cannot wait to show you the ranch. Amanda Edison, here at last."

Luke stared at Amanda in amazement as the author stepped inside the house with the bedazzled manservant. Pedro accidentally shut the door, and Luke faced the closed portal with a disgusted glare, then opened the door and let himself in.

The interior of the house was even lovelier than the outside. Amanda stood in the foyer, drinking in the beauty of the polished marble floors, the pale blue walls, the rose draperies and the polished mahogany furniture. Everything was in perfect condition, from the good paintings of hunting scenes adorning the walls to the Chippendale furnishings.

"It's beautiful," she breathed in appreciation.

Pedro grinned. "Not what you think, eh Fess Tyson? Senor Rutherford keep this house very well. He made much money growing cotton during the war, then in cattle. The carpetbag men tried to take this place from him, but Senor Rutherford paid the taxes and they could get nothing. It is a good place for a man to settle, but not good for a woman alone. He would be happy that you married."

"I can see that." Amanda wandered into the kitchen, then onto the patio in the rear of the house. The tiny portico was lined with stones and landscaped with prairie flowers and cacti. Benches were placed at advantageous parts of the garden where one could seek refuge from the sun, or catch the waning rays.

Pedro put Aesop on a mahogany sideboard, then gestured to the stairs. "I must show you your rooms, and I have another surprise for you upstairs. Please follow me. Oh, you can come, too, Mr. Edison."

"Parker," Luke snapped. "It's Mr. and Mrs. Parker."

"Ah, I am sorry," Pedro apologized, then nodding endlessly, led them up the lavish staircase.

Upstairs, Amanda immediately fell in love with her room. It was smaller than the other rooms and less imposing. A lemon-yellow quilt covered the pine poster bed, and a comfortable dresser and chair stood on the opposite wall. But immediately beside the bed was a writing desk, and with it, a tufted wingback chair and a good gaslight. The desk was beside a window, and when Amanda peered out of the spotless glass, she could see the entire town of Waco and miles of sprawling cattle range beyond.

"It is wonderful." Amanda turned to Pedro. "But whose room was this? Surely, Austin didn't provide all this just for me?"

Pedro's smile dimmed a bit. "He had a daughter once. She was *muy bonita,* and very bright. She would have been like you, smart in school. She read all the time. But she caught the fever and died when she was very small. Senor always thought of you in the same way he would think of her. He wanted you to have her things." He ran a finger over the desk and held it out to Amanda for inspection. "I keep it very clean."

"It's lovely, just like the rest of the house. Is this what you wanted me to see?"

"Oh no, senora, there is one other surprise. This may have been Senorita Belinda's room, but Senor Rutherford planned something especially for you. Come look." Taking Amanda's arm, he led her down the hallway, then stopped and spoke to Luke. "Oh, I almost forget. That room is yours." Pedro indicated a large bedroom decorated in golds and brown, then continued down the hallway, oblivious to Luke's sarcastic glance.

"This is it." Opening the last door, Pedro could barely suppress a grin as Amanda stepped inside and gasped in delight.

There were books everywhere. From one wall to the other, from the ceiling to the floor, they lined the room like readable wallpaper. Amanda lovingly fingered a volume on Shakespeare, then Homer, then Carlyle, Dickens, Twain. There were biographies, fiction books, mysteries, and classics. Books on geography, on history, on folklore and Indian tribes. There were romances and books of poetry, sonnets and scripture. Then, directly in the center, was a reading desk, where every one of her books, written as Fess Tyson, were separated from the rest in a special shelf, with obviously well-worn covers.

"I can't believe this." Amanda turned to the manservant, her eyes filled and misty. "He gave all this to me?"

"This was his library." Pedro beamed proudly. "Senor Rutherford loved your books, Miss Edison. He think you are the world's best novelist. I cannot read, so he would read the stories to me at night. He was a good man, and you brought him much joy. He only wanted to give some back to you."

Amanda nodded, then slowly sank to the floor where she could examine each book, one precious volume at a time. Nothing could have meant more to her, not the even the riches of a sultan's temple or the wealth of a southern plantation. She was like a child, scurrying from one treasure to another, lost in the works of her beloved philosophers and poets.

Luke stood out in the hallway, seeing her transformed from the Amanda he knew on the trail, the woman who used her unbelievable mind to thwart him, to this scholarly and obviously successful novelist. He'd never been confronted with her career before, but now it struck him with full force. Amanda Edison was not just any other woman, but she was apparently well known and something of a celebrity. It was a disturbing thought, especially to a man who'd experienced self-doubt and loss. As he closed the library door behind him, he realized Amanda didn't even

look up, she was so buried in her books. That was all she
needed before she'd met him.

Perhaps, it was all she'd need now.

It was late before she left the library, and that was only
because Pedro's timid knock brought her back to reality.
The manservant entered the room, then stood before
Amanda, as if afraid to speak.

"Senora, it is well past dinner time. I call for you earlier,
but you didn't even hear me. I thought perhaps you would
like a bath and a change of clothes, *sí?*"

"Oh my God, what time is it?"

"It is past nine. Senor Parker just came in from the range.
I did not wish to disturb you, but you should eat something."

"Yes, you're right. I'll have a bath right now. And could
you bring a tray to my room? Enough for two?" Amanda
asked.

"*Sí.*" Pedro looked very relieved. "I'll do that right
away."

When he left, Amanda walked slowly to her room, deep
in thought. This was no way to start out, instinctively she
knew that. Luke obviously hadn't gone to see a solicitor,
and hadn't made a single mention of divorce since their arrival. Perhaps he meant to make this a real marriage, to run
the ranch together in an equal partnership as husband and
wife, and to one day have children. . . .

That thought deepened her blush. Smoothing her gown,
she noticed that she was still wearing the same trail-worn
dress she'd arrived in. Her hair fell in blatant disarray down
to her waist, and her boots were covered with dust and badly
scuffed.

In her room, Amanda found a steaming tub, along with
several fragrant soaps. She undressed and slipped into the
water, sighing with bliss as the fragrant bubbles closed
around her. After days on the trail, the water felt like silk
against her bare skin. She washed her hair, and then
wrapped it in a thick fluffy towel as she reluctantly stepped

from the tub and dried before a lit fire. Pedro knocked softly, then handed her tray inside the door while Amanda waited behind the concealing portal.

It felt good to be thoroughly clean again. Slipping into the one acceptable nightgown she owned, threadbare cotton though it was, she felt comfortable for the first time in weeks. Amanda gazed into the mirror, surprised to see that she had gotten thinner, that the hollows in her cheeks were more pronounced, and that her eyes looked enormous. Her hair showed the wear of the trip, looking ragged and uneven. Thankfully, the second drawer contained a sharp pair of scissors, and within a few minutes, she had restored her coiffure to all its former glory.

She slipped down the hallway and paused at the door to Luke's room, peering down the yawning corridor that was lighted with candles, feeling suddenly shy and uncertain. Her hand tightened on the doorknob, and she almost turned back.

You want him, admit it. The voice in her head spoke clearly and simply. *You have a chance, Amanda, for the first time in your life, to have what you really want. Don't botch it.* Stiffening her resolve, she opened the door.

"Amanda—" Luke's words cut off as he saw her standing in the lamplight. Framed by the doorway, her hair brushed and glistening in the dim light like spun caramel, her mouth the color of a wood rose, and her thin nightgown wafting about her like a hazy cloud, she looked beautiful. Innocent. And adorable. "Come in."

She obeyed, balancing the tray while Luke closed the door behind her. It was then that she noticed he was wearing the rough buckskins he'd donned earlier, minus a shirt. But he had bathed, and his body glowed with all its perfect muscular symmetry, like a sculpture of Apollo. He had removed his hat, and his hair glowed so black that it seemed to contain blue highlights. His eyes fell to the tray, and Amanda held it out like an offering.

"Pedro made it. I worked through dinner, and I heard

you came back late. I thought you might like a picnic in your room."

He smiled, and it was suddenly all worth it. He reached for the tray, took it and put it on the dressing table, then reached for her. "My God," he breathed, drawing in the scent of her, mingled with soap and the sweet smell of woman. "I'm so glad you came." He brushed a light kiss across her lips, her body teasing his naked chest with the thin slip of a nightgown she wore. "Let's see what Pedro made," Luke continued huskily, "or I'll start thanking you now and we'll never get to the food."

Amanda felt the heat come to her face, but it wasn't an embarrassed blush. She curled up in a polished winged chair, her feet tucked beneath her, her eyes wide with curiosity as Luke opened the dishes and displayed the exotic meal. There were platefuls of crisp corn tortillas and bowls of freshly cut tomatoes and peppers on the tray. A separate plate held strips of beef fried with peppers and onions and wrapped with cheese in a soft tortilla that Pedro called *fajitas*. Accompanying the tray was a pitcher of fruit wine that was so sweet and light that it was almost a punch.

"It looks delicious," Amanda mused, and Luke handed her a filled plate, along with a glass of wine.

Having dinner in a bedroom with a man like Luke was a lot of fun, and certainly not the scandalous activity that some etiquette books pronounced. Giggling, she accepted an offering of fresh sweet orange slices, gasping as the fruit squirted in her mouth. But the sharp, spicy food tasted even better after that, and when Luke refilled her wine cup, she let him, enjoying every moment of the odd feast.

When they'd finished, Luke poured out two cups of thick rich coffee laced with brandy, then they moved to the sofa before the fire. Amanda decided this was definitely a good idea, especially when Luke took her cup and put it aside, and then began to massage her shoulders and neck. Warmed by the fire, the brandy, and the heat from the man beside her, Amanda began to relax, and her body felt as limp as a dish rag. Strange tinglings began in her shoulders, where his talented fingers worked out all the stress and the pain from writing, then continued along her nerve endings until her entire body felt surprisingly renewed. Turning to him slowly, she saw the same emotions reflected in his deep blue eyes and she smiled dreamily.

"Luke, is it right to have a mating urge all the time?"

She saw the amusement dance in his eyes, and a smile twitched at the corner of his mouth. "Why?"

"Because that's what's happening to me."

His smile faded, and his eyes turned hot with desire as he bent down and kissed her. His hand reached up to fondle a sweetly veiled breast, the nipple peeking enticingly through the worn lace. When his hand slid lower, down past a slender waist, through the length of silky chestnut hair that spilled down her back, to cup her rounded bottom, he whispered softly, "Not only is it right, sweetheart, but I intend to keep it that way. Now and forever."

Chapter

21

This is what it means to be totally happy. Amanda stared out of the wagon, shielding her face from the sun, and watching the throngs of people that filled the street. She and Luke had spent the morning making love, then had only climbed out of bed when Pedro called for the third time. Reluctantly, they had agreed to dine at a decent hour for his sake, and now the manservant scoured the shops for fresh produce to make the evening meal.

The wagon creaked to a halt in front of the sheriff's office. Amanda scurried in the back and withdrew reams of paper, notes, and Aesop's cage. Luke lifted her down, then reached back inside for the manuscript.

"I'll join you in a few minutes. I'd like to meet the sheriff and tell him about Haskwell, just in case we need help. You all right?"

He saw the worried look on Amanda's face, but she nodded easily. "It's just been such a long time since the last attack that I was starting to hope it was over."

"It may be," Luke agreed. "Haskwell may have given up. I know his men weren't in too good of shape after that stampede. But believe me, where Haskwell's concerned, I'd rather be overly protective."

There was something odd in his voice that gave Amanda pause. She started to question him further, when a stout woman dressed in a green silk gown flounced over to the carriage, then stared in gaping awe at Amanda. Her handkerchief fluttered in the breeze and she held it to her breast, as if unable to breathe.

"It *is* you! *The* Fess Tyson! I hope you don't mind, but I asked Pedro to tell me when you actually arrived. We're delighted to have you, my dear. I am Marge Meade, head of the Woman's Committee of Waco. You simply have to join. Wait until I tell the girls!"

She waved her broad pink hand and was quickly joined by several other women. Pedro appeared, shrugging apologetically, his arms laden with groceries. Amanda answered the women's questions politely and tried to keep a hold onto Aesop's cage as well as the book, but she was jostled on all sides. She dropped several of the papers and when she tried to retrieve them, the crowd had thickened to the point where she couldn't move. Luke started toward her, but several men who had been standing nearby and hoping for an introduction seized the opportunity and handed Amanda her manuscript like knights bestowing favor upon their lady.

"You have to autograph my copy of *Oklahoma Revenge*. I've read that book a hundred times!"

"You're exactly like Austin described! Do come for dinner. My wife and children would love to meet you!"

"I thought her last book wasn't her best, but I won't tell her."

"What about the new book. When is it due? What is it about?"

Amanda clutched her bird cage in bewilderment. Luke tried to help, but he was thrust out of the way by the crowd. Glaring at the rotund Mrs. Meade, Luke attempted to elbow his way back into the group, while one of the men gave him a disgruntled stare.

"Would you please wait your turn? We all want to meet Fess Tyson."

"I happen to be her husband!" Luke said through gritted teeth. He impolitely shoved the man aside and joined his wife. "Come on, Amanda, let's get out of here."

"But they want to ask about the new book!" Amanda replied, managing to answer the questions and keep hold of her manuscript at the same time. For a writer who'd experienced very little contact with her audience, this was like a mad dream where everything was a little out of control, but heady nevertheless. She described just enough of the book to make it sound enticing, answered queries on research and her relationship with Austin, and parried critical attacks with a gusto that Luke was forced to admire.

He faded into the rear of the crowd, unnoticed by Amanda as she played to her fans. Luke withdrew a cigarette and struck a match on the sole of his boot, his eyes never leaving his wife. It was like she was born for this. For someone without experience with an audience, she handled herself deftly—and was clearly enjoying the attention.

Luke's mouth burned with the bitter tobacco. He had wanted to live as her husband, the father of her children. He could make the business a huge financial success, that much he'd determined by riding the range and talking with the *vaqueros*. There was a new method of ranching that he'd learned about from a northerner that entailed the use of barbed wire. Already Luke could see how fencing in the property would prevent thievery and result in more mating control. He had ideas of a crossbreed that would mix the sturdiness of the Longhorn with the milk benefits of the Hereford. His plans would turn the Triple Bar into a ranchman's paradise, even more profitable than it was now. His children would go to the finest schools and meet the right people. He had all the tools to start a decent, quiet life and to regain respectability.

He frowned, then stamped out the match as a handsome young man reached for Amanda's hand, declaring his devotion. Luke started to barge in, but Amanda laughed sweetly and made the man promise to buy a book before turning her attention to the bartender from the Pecos Saloon. She didn't need him. Luke strode away, furious, but Amanda didn't even look up. His plans were secure, all right, but none of them included a wife as a celebrated novelist.

Even a very good one.

"Haskwell?" Sheriff Mendez leafed through a series of poster books on his desk, then paused as he found the name. "Here it is. He has not been to Texas for many years, senor. I would not think you had much to fear."

Jake moved away from Luke's side, the large man's frame blocking the light as he picked up the book and examined the photograph. The picture displayed a handsome man, with jet-black hair and sharp eyes that looked out onto the world with a vengeance. The picture was obviously a vanity photo, taken at a circus with the strange blatant disregard for identification that plagued many outlaws. But unlike the depiction of Sam Bass or Jesse James, this man's likeness showed no warmth, no humor, no gentleness. Sam Haskwell looked like exactly what he was—a ruthless killer without scruples or a single redeeming factor.

"Normally, I wouldn't," Luke continued, examining the picture with renewed anger. "But this man is an exception to every rule. We have reason to believe that he fears my wife could implicate him in a murder. She can't, but Haskwell doesn't know that, and hasn't gotten close enough to find out."

"*Sí*, but to cross the Indian border, just to seek out your wife who is innocent, that is not the work of a known outlaw," the sheriff argued.

"No," Luke agreed. "But his men quit the job. One of them probably got killed in a stampede, and it seems the other has given up the chase. If you know anything about Haskwell, he doesn't like to be thwarted."

"You seem to have much knowledge of this man," the sheriff remarked thoughtfully, tugging at his black moustache. "Perhaps there is more we should know?"

"Haskwell killed my mother and sister," Luke said blandly, ignoring Jake's look of surprise. "I've followed his career for many years now. He always keeps one step ahead of the law, and two steps ahead of his banker. But I've never seen him give up a fight. He once tracked a man across the desert for a gambling wrong that cost him two hundred dollars."

"I can verify that," Jake stated quietly. "As acting lawman, I ran across Haskwell's trail more than once. He's a cruel man, and kills for pleasure as well as profit. He's the worst kind of sidewinder I've ever seen. He particularly likes to abuse women. There was a prostitute he took a fancy to a few years back. Made her life hell. The girl finally killed herself, just to get away from him." Jake shook his head gruffly. "I found her body. She was just fifteen."

The sheriff nodded, then closed the book abruptly. "I have three men, two good deputies who can shoot, and one man who keeps my books. I will lend you what help I can, but I must warn you that it isn't much. A gunman like this Haskwell could ruin Waco and run roughshod over this town. We will prepare as best we can."

Jake walked outside with Luke, his face grim. "That doesn't sound too promising."

"No." Luke stared at the street. Amanda was entering the post office, still fending off questions and teasing her admirers. She was so spritely and so pretty, that the thought of her falling into Haskwell's grip was appalling.

Jake seemed to echo his thoughts. "We won't let him get her, Luke. My ranch joins yours at the northern border. You hear anything, you send for me. We'll make our own posse if we can't get help from this damned one-horse-town."

Luke nodded and shook Jake's hand. "I'm grateful for the offer, but come what may, Haskwell is mine. I'll die before he gets Amanda."

Jake stared at him, his greyish brows narrowing. "Don't turn this into a vendetta, son. We all have the same goal, to see that snake dead. Don't be too proud to ask for help."

Luke replaced his Stetson, and strode across the street to the saloon. Jake watched him go, a worried expression wrinkling his face. Luke's desire for revenge was understandable.

But this time it could cost Amanda's life.

Aileen shoved the crowd out of the post office and shut the door behind them.

"Whew!" she breathed, wiping her brow. "It seems you have a lot of admirers."

Amanda smiled gratefully. The attention was fun, but she had work to do and the crowd didn't seem to hear her pleas. She had suddenly noticed Luke was gone, and looked to her friend for help. Fortunately, Aileen had no scruples about turning everyone away. Like a mother hen protecting its young, Aileen took charge and whisked Amanda into the post office. The crowd still gathered outside, but Aileen sternly ordered them away in a thick Irish brogue that brooked no resistance. The crowd finally dispersed, and Amanda smiled at her friend.

Marriage to Jake had done Aileen a world of good. She looked radiant, her round figure set off by the gay blue dress she wore, trimmed in black velvet and jet buttons. Her face glowed with health and her eyes sparkled as she laughed with the postmaster. It was hard to envision her as the whiskey-drinking saloon girl Amanda had met at the hotel in Wichita, but she was glad that Aileen had found happiness.

As she approached the telegraph desk, she noticed Luke step out of the sheriff's office, confer with Jake, then cross the street to the saloon. *Haskwell,* Amanda shuddered. For some reason, registering a complaint made the threat seem too real. She shook off the somber thoughts and handed the telegrapher a ream of papers. The man's glasses fell off in astonishment.

"You wish to send all of this? But Madam, it will be terribly costly."

"Nevertheless, I need to send the wire. Just the first ten pages of the proposal. I can mail the rest."

The telegrapher's face twitched and with a disgruntled

sigh, he began to tap the message to her New York publishing house.

Bored, Amanda took a seat and flipped through the papers that lined the desk. There was the daily news, the religious meeting record, a notice for the Woman's Committee, and the Wanted posters. These were by far the most interesting, and Amanda thumbed through them, appalled at the sinister faces that stared up from the drawings. Reading one after another, she got through the first ten, when her fingers paused at the sight of a black-eyed Irishman and her blood ran cold as she read the notice.

"Haskwell, Sam. Notorious outlaw of the West. Irishman, son of a bricklayer in County Cork. Came to America in 1856 . . ."

"Amanda!" Aileen shouted impatiently. "Are you ready?"

"The work is done, Madam," the telegrapher said. "Madam?"

Amanda froze, unable to believe what she was reading. She retrieved her glasses from a rung on Aesop's cage, and put them on, her eyes narrowing in shock.

Alleged to have murdered over sixteen men, including John Haines, in a gunfight, no survivors, witness never found; Jesse Witherspoon of Texas, for a drink of whiskey; Lillian and Suzette Parker, of Virginia, Luke Parker surviving . . .

Amanda's eyes blurred and the pages fell from her grip. It was as if all of the pieces of the puzzle suddenly fit. She knew now why Sam Haskwell was after her, why he had followed her so relentlessly. She had picked that item out of a newspaper at random, never dreaming that the real outlaw might hear of it and think she witnessed the killing. She cursed her own stupidity in using Haines' real name, but there was nothing she could do about it now. Haskwell obviously felt threatened by that description in her book, the one that so accurately described his murder of the sheriff. Logan Benteen was Sam Haskwell, Amanda realized in horror. Her fiction had come to life, and in a terrifying way.

Then something else occurred to her, something that disturbed her far more than learning Haskwell's motivation. Luke Parker surviving . . . a sinking feeling passed through her as she realized the implication of that sentence. Luke had his own reasons for wanting Haskwell. She now knew why Luke was with her and why he had been on that train. Why he had immediately known Haskwell's gang, enough so that he could recognize them on sight. Why he had agreed to come to Waco with her, a man who could have made a fresh start anywhere.

He was after revenge, and she was suddenly afraid she was nothing more than the bait to get it.

She said nothing on the way home. Luke seemed preoccupied and didn't address her much more than to ask if she'd sent her work. She nodded, grateful that she didn't have to speak, afraid that she would shout out everything and rail at him, let him know what a bitter disappointment he was to her.

She climbed the stairs woodenly, past the chandeliers that yesterday looked enchantingly beautiful, and locked herself in the library. Anguish poured through her as she dismissed Pedro and refused lunch. She couldn't think about food, couldn't think about anything other than her hideous discovery about Luke.

Tears spilled down Amanda's cheeks. She, Amanda Edison—scholar, woman with an enormous amount of intelligence, who'd startled every professor at the institute with her theories on philosophy and the war—had been duped by a southern killer. She'd been used by him to get at the man who'd killed his family. Worse, the evidence had been there all along. If she hadn't been emotionally involved with the man, she would have seen through him immediately. But no, she was worse than the heroine of any penny dreadful, giving her heart to a man who wasn't fit to lace her boots.

Her glasses fogged, and Amanda scarcely noticed. Aesop perched on her leg, his sharp little claws digging into her soft skin, but she didn't feel that either. She couldn't feel anything but pain, and the overwhelming humiliation of being made a fool. Knowing that she had aided his cause only made it that much worse. Dear God, she had practically seduced him the previous night!

Aesop ruffled his feathers and Amanda ran a finger lovingly down his back. Thank God she hadn't gotten pregnant from her first encounter with Luke, and with any luck, she wouldn't be now. Wincing as Aesop tugged on her finger, she gave the little owl a fond glance.

Once, it had just been the two of them. It seemed it would be that way again.

"What do you mean, she isn't coming down?" Luke glared at the manservant, while Pedro's moustache twitched in worry. Bathed and dressed in good fawn-colored trousers and a clean white shirt, Luke had been sipping brandy and waiting for Amanda for over an hour.

"I ask her two times, senor, but she refuse. She is writing and cannot be disturbed. I am concerned. Senorita Edison has just come from a long journey and she should not work so hard right away. But she will not listen."

"She can be damned stubborn at times," Luke agreed. Fury built in him as he understood what she was doing. Amanda was rediscovering herself as an author, and apparently telling him that she didn't need him. He had too much respect for her intelligence to believe that her nonappearance could mean anything but. She had refused lunch, declined his invitation to ride, and did not answer his knock when he first came back. She was testing him, Luke realized, trying to set the parameters of their relationship, and shutting him out once more.

"Don't worry, Pedro, I'll get her," Luke reassured the manservant. "Just set out dinner and we'll be right down."

"Sí," Pedro said doubtfully. Amanda Edison didn't look like the kind of woman who would readily accede to anyone's wishes. Even her husband's.

Chapter

22

Luke climbed the stairs thoughtfully, determined to lay down the law. He sensed that the future of their relationship rested upon the next few hours, and he had no intention of letting Amanda close herself into her safe wall of books once more. Yet as he opened the door to the library, nothing could have prepared him for what he found.

She was buried in books. Volumes surrounded her, some with tiny cards marking the pages, others placed face down with paragraphs noted in red ink. Papers were strewn everywhere, from notecards that were obviously some sort of reference material to loose sheets of written script that were impatiently crumbled and rejected. Her carpetbag stood in the middle of the floor, half-opened books and old discarded notes bulging out of it. Reams of paper were strewn all over the table, and ink bottles stood half-empty, a silent testimony to the work that had passed within the last few hours.

In the midst of the mess was Amanda. Half-hidden by a volume entitled, *Mankind and the Western Experience*, she was perched on the floor with a pencil jabbing from behind one ear, and a dripping quill thrust carelessly into her dress—obligingly leaving a pool of ink just above her left breast. Her hair, never particularly tidy to begin with, tum-

bled wildly down her back, decorated with one of Aesop's
feathers and a tiny slip of parchment. She was scribbling
endlessly, making short little squeaks and contented sighs,
followed by exclamations of disgust as she rejected a full
page and tossed the paper to lie with the rest. Aesop
marched amid the mess in complete bliss, leaving bird droppings and feathers, obviously quite used to his mistress's do-
ings.

"Amanda." Luke broke her concentration, and when she
glanced up, it took her a full minute to focus and realize
that someone else had entered her sanctuary. "What in
God's name are you doing?"

She looked around at the mess in the room, then lifted
her turquoise eyes and peered directly at him. "I am writing," she said, as if that explained all. "As you may be
aware, I have a deadline to meet. Now that we have reached
our destination, I see no reason to delay."

"Does that preclude food?" Luke asked, trying to sound
reasonable. "You have to eat."

"Digestion disturbs the mental process," Amanda said
tiredly, the icy disdain in her voice apparent. "I shall eat
when I've finished, and not before. I want to complete as
much as possible tonight, so that in the morning I may start
telegraphing my editor. I've put this book off for far too
long, while dallying with meaningless research."

"Is that right?" Luke got her meaning, and his jaw tightened with anger.

"Yes. As Cowper said, 'Absence of occupation is not rest,
a mind quite vacant is a mind distressed.' "

She turned back to her work, casually dismissing him as
one would an over-zealous servant. Furious, Luke kicked
the door to the corridor shut behind him. The papers wafted
through the air with the sudden draft like a blizzard, and
Aesop squawked, then turned his head backwards, indignantly. Amanda stared at Luke through her glasses, her
eyes wide and penetrating, and she gave him a look that
would have pulverized iron.

"To what do I owe this irrational display of temper?"

"Amanda," he said in a stern voice. "If you're trying to see how far you can push me, you've just reached my limit. If you have half the brain I know you were born with, don't dare continue."

She lost a bit of her composure, but only by the quick moistening of her lips and the slight trembling of her quill would one even suspect.

Satisfied that he had chastised her, even momentarily, Luke strode through the midst of the paper snowstorm and stood directly over her, looking overwhelmingly tall and masculine. Amanda gulped. It was difficult to maintain her icy hauteur when facing his muscular thighs, and it was even harder a moment later when he reached down and effortlessly yanked her to her feet.

"That's better. I think it's time we had a talk."

He was so damned handsome, his sapphire eyes blazing, his hair a polished blue-black, and his face rigid with anger, that Amanda momentarily regretted her discovery that he was only using her. For a sentimental second, she wished it was yesterday, when she had wanted him so desperately she was willing to open her heart to him. That thought only made her feel more like a fool, and gave her the strength to look at him coldly in the eye, and imagine him as something noxious that crept into her petri dish.

Luke noticed her expression and his jaw tightened visibly. "Would you mind telling me what's going on, and right now?"

The bald threat in his words made Amanda's quill tremble harder, but she managed to maintain an arctic glare that would have done one of her heroines proud.

"Nothing has changed," Amanda replied calmly. "We discussed all this before. About how you wanted to come out here to rebuild your life. How it was better for us to remain uninvolved. And how you wanted to get a divorce as soon as we reached Texas. I believe we are here."

The words hung in the room, weighing between them for a long moment before Luke spoke, his eyes gleaming with outrage. "Is that what you want? A divorce?"

"Yes," Amanda said quickly, the word rushing out in relief.

"And what about last night? And the night on the trail?"

Bright flags of color stained her cheeks. She was so humiliated that he dared to remind her of that, when all the time he was simply using her for his own means in the coldest, cruelest manner she would have dreamed possible. It was that thought that made her look at him as if she was slicing through his heart, and sighed with regret.

" 'All things that are, are with more spirit chased than enjoyed.' Shakespeare."

"Amanda," Luke said in an awful voice. "Look at me. I dare you to tell me that you didn't enjoy last night. That it meant nothing to you."

Amanda choked, emotion flooding through her like a sickening weakness. She removed her glasses, fighting back the stinging tears that threatened. But she'd already cried too much over him, too much over a man that had meant everything to her. Now, she had nothing left but her pride, and she would fight to the end to salvage it.

"Last night . . . was a mistake." *Now,* she amended in her mind. "I am an author, and I need time alone to do my work, and write. I don't need anyone else . . . "

That worked on his most basic fears. He struggled not to show it, but Amanda had cut him to the quick. Even now she stared at him with all the warmth of a scientist ready to drop a frog into chloroform.

"Fine," he said through gritted teeth. "But we made a deal and you're not backing out. I got you here in once piece, had my hide shot at, and for what?" He laughed dryly. "Half a ranch, and a marriage to you? A woman who doesn't know the meaning of the word? This hasn't exactly been a pleasure trip for me, either. But I was stupid enough to think you'd grown beyond all that, beyond your need to mentally fence with someone in spite of how you hurt them. That somehow, I'd helped you reach out to another human being and not be afraid of the result. I've put up with more from you in the last few months than most men would in a lifetime."

"Yes, but I think my money had something to do with that," Amanda said, hurt beyond endurance. "That and the ranch."

"Ah yes, the ranch." Luke gestured to the window outside. "All three thousand acres of it. The house is beautiful, the land rich, but I didn't even know that when I made this deal, and neither did you. Is that what you think your life is worth?"

"You agreed to protect me," Amanda protested.

"And you agreed to behave as my wife," Luke pointed out. "I wouldn't say you've kept up your part."

"It's no use discussing this any further. And I would appreciate it if you acted with some civility. I've treated you fairly, and have no intention of cutting you out of your part of the ranch. However, I wish to make you a business proposition."

"What?" Luke had to fight to keep from throttling her, and his brows lifted as he reluctantly admired her courage. She was shaking like a leaf, her glorious eyes were misted with unshed tears, but she still had the guts to face up to him and dare to fence with him. "This should be good. If it's anything like the last one, forget it."

"I want to buy you out," Amanda continued earnestly. "I have the money, and can wire for the funds in the morning. I will pay whatever you think fair, to own the Triple Bar. Name the sum."

His mouth opened incredulously. If it were anyone else, he would question her sanity. But Amanda was certainly sane, if not exactly wise.

"Ah. Now that you've seen the ranch, you want it for yourself." Luke didn't try to keep the cold amusement from his voice. "Do you have any idea of what this ranch is worth now, in gold? Land values have gone up considerably since the war, and no matter how much you've made writing, I guarantee you can't afford it."

"Is it worth that much?" Amanda asked softly. "I thought to have an appraisal done . . . "

"Save your money," Luke said darkly. "You can't afford to buy me out, unless you write a national bestseller. And even at that, I won't sell. Not for any price."

Amanda flushed, furious at his calm voice. "Then you mean to stay on, just to torment me? Why won't you leave me alone? I don't want any part of this marriage, don't you understand? I don't want any part of—"

"Amanda, stop it." Luke crossed the ten feet that separated them, ten feet of carpet littered with papers and books. "I won't let you do this again. Not to you, or to me." Before she could say anything else, his mouth took hers in a kiss that was purposefully devastating and achingly delicious. Unlike his other kisses, this was not only sexually persuasive, but emotionally scorching. It was as if he purposefully meant it so—that he would not let her return to the cold formality that had reigned between them for far too long. When his mouth finally eased from hers, Amanda fought to keep from clutching his arms just for balance. It took everything she had not to respond to the kiss, for fear that she'd be swept up forever into his embrace, and the heady desire that followed.

"Kiss me, Mandy. Just once, kiss me back."

His endearment made her heart ache and she was forced to remember the times when he was kind. She cried out when his mouth took hers again, but this time she didn't even struggle, nor did she try to push him away. She wanted him to kiss her, wanted to feel his arms around her again. Slowly her arms crept up around his neck, and she melted into his embrace, wanting the warmth of his body against hers and the feel of his heart beating beneath her.

This time, when he kissed her she let him. Her lips parted under his gentle insistence, and his tongue took possession of mouth, tasting her warm sweetness while she instinctively pressed closer to him. A shudder passed through Luke as his arm tightened around her. His free hand rose to cup her breast, his thumb brushing the hardening nipple through her dress while his tongue plunged into her mouth in a wildly sexual rhythm that made her entire body tremble. Amanda made a soft gasping sound, letting him kiss her, touch her, love her.

It took every effort to break the embrace, but Amanda had no choice. She physically pushed him away, even though her body cried out in protest as his warmth was replaced by cool emptiness. Reality came shrieking back, and with it, awareness. He was so handsome, his eyes a melting blue like the flame of a candle, his mouth warm and sensual, softened now by their kiss and promising wonderful, erotic things to come. It was hard to believe that he was simply using her, that he had risked her life by dangling her in front of Haskwell like a particularly enticing worm on a hook. That he was capable of such treachery struck her heart with an ache that made her want to clasp herself to him and beg him to tell her it just wasn't true.

"Amanda, what is it? What's wrong?" He smoothed her hair out of her face like one would a child's, his hand rough and warm against her skin. "The last night we were on the trail, you brought me your notebook. You showed me that I meant something to you. I read some of it once. 'I see the flowers of the plains, the red geranium, the crimson lupine, and the rippling blue green grass, and I see beauty. He has given that to me, in the moments when he is kind.' I wasn't wrong, was I?"

She winced, humiliated beyond words that he'd read her work. She'd never meant anything to him. This was only a ploy to keep her property, and to keep her until Luke could make his fortune and get his revenge. And he obviously didn't care who got hurt in the process.

"I'm sorry that you placed so much importance on such a simple offering." Amanda turned her face away as she spoke, unable to look into his eyes. "I only wanted a second opinion on the work, before I sent it up. You see, I was writing about a man I had once loved and lost. I never thought you would interpret it as anything else."

That much was the truth. Amanda dared to steal a glance

at him, then immediately dropped her eyes. He looked like she'd struck him. His face had turned ghastly pale, and his jaw tightened perceptibly. When he spoke, his voice was like ice.

"I see. I apologize for my foolishness in thinking that you meant something deeper. I should have known better. Stay up here, alone with your books. You deserve it." He turned and walked swiftly from the room, as if he couldn't bear being in her presence another moment. He slammed the door, and the papers fluttered into the air, then slowly drifted back down to the carpet.

Tears spilled down her cheeks, then her body was wracked with sobs and she collapsed down to the rug amid her books and pencils. She suddenly understood all those things she'd read about the pain of being in love.

And she fervently hoped that it would never happen to her again.

"Get me a drink, darlin. And now."

Sam Haskwell grinned as Honey jumped to do his bidding. Slump-shouldered and thin, she looked more like an old woman than the sweet young girl he'd taken from the stage just a few short months ago. It pleased him to see the way she leaped when he spoke to her, and the way her eyes shifted when she dared to look up. Her body never seemed entirely at rest, but twitched constantly in a nervous tremor as if she was afraid he would hit her.

He hadn't done that, yet. Actually, he hadn't needed to. Sam had learned the value of intimidation a long time ago, and Honey was a prime example. Fingering his empty whiskey glass, he thought of the previous night, and grinned with satisfaction.

He'd meant to punish her for that stunt she pulled in singing "My Old Kentucky Home," but wanted to make sure his impression was lasting. So he turned up every light in her room, watching her expression as she sat on the edge of the bed, licking her lips, looking as nervous as a cat on the brink of a river. When the room was as bright as daylight, he ordered her to remove her clothes, delighting in the blush that still came to her cheeks and the hatred that arose in her face.

Yet, she was helpless to do anything but obey, she was so terrified of him. When she was suitably unclothed, her lovely, alabaster body clearly visible in the stark light, he ordered her into their bed, her nakedness a warm pale contrast to the dark sheets. Shaking and miserable, she pleaded with him, but Sam found her terror appallingly arousing. He secured her facedown to the bedpost, then slowly, teasingly, traced her feathers all over her body. The black ostrich plume looked wonderful contrasted with the pearl-like incandescence of her skin, and he tickled her back, the slender curve of her leg, then drew them slowly upward. Horribly ashamed of herself, she arched her back, letting the pleasure wash over her even as he mounted her in the most humilating way possible and brought himself to a gut wrenching climax.

She hated him even more after that. Yet even as he untied her, gratified at the look of intense despair in her eyes, he knew he had her. She was his, to do with as he wished, until he could finish what he'd set out to do. . . .

She returned with the drink, pathetically eager to please. Haskwell grinned, then downed the whiskey in one full drink. Replacing the glass, he tamped his cigar and sat back, letting his gaze wander over the beaten showgirl.

"We'll be finished this job soon, darlin'," Haskwell said, delighted to see her startle like a cornered deer. "We're close to Dallas, and I'll have my work completed."

Honey lifted tear-drenched eyes to his. "And then, Sam?" she whispered brokenly. "What will happen, then?"

"I've just been thinking about that," Sam said cruelly, his mouth widening into a smile. "You're looking old, darlin. Real old. I swear I can see a few grey hairs at your temples, and you've certainly lost your figure. You cannot make me money, except for a few miserly pence should I toss you to the cowboys. But then you would hardly pleasure me in bed, after being used by a dozen rowdy cowhands. No, darlin, I've got quite a dilemma on my hands."

She got even whiter, her skin like milk. "I'll sing, Sam. I promise. Please don't kill me."

"They don't want you anymore, pet," Sam replied thoughtfully. "Ever since that barroom job. I can't get you a booking at any respectable saloon, and those that aren't don't want some scrawny songbird parading before them with a voice that would send a sinner to church. You just don't have it any more, my dear."

"I'll find a way," Honey promised. "Please. I can cook, sew, wash dishes—"

"You'll not be a burden to me," Sam sighed, his cigar almost out. He tossed the stub to the floor, then watched as she picked it up and put it into the spittoon for him. "Yes, darlin', you might as well start to say your prayers. In death, you'll be grateful I spared you this miserable existence. And you know far too much for me to let you go." He chuckled, pleased at the abject fear in her expression. "Yes, darlin', say your prayers."

Unbeknownst to him, Honey did.

Chapter

∽ 23 ∽

"Amanda, you can't keep moping around here. Look at these cards! Everyone wants you, and it's time you started getting out." Aileen sifted through the stack of invitations and envelopes that lined Pedro's tray. She turned toward her friend with obvious concern, noting the dusty dress Amanda wore, the ink stains on her fingers, and the air of distress that clung to her like a heavy cloak. Something was wrong, Aileen knew that as sure as she knew that the sun shone in Killarney. Gone was the vibrant woman on the prairie who plotted endlessly to rid herself of the one man she cared about. In spite of their differences, Amanda had bloomed in Luke's company, and even he seemed to enjoy their mental fencing.

Until now. Something had changed. Aileen had passed Luke coming in, and he barely gave her a nod. And Amanda, who seemed as if she had disappeared from the face of the earth, was found sequestered in this library with her books, the gaslight, and her owl.

"I don't feel like getting out." Amanda pushed back a lock of chestnut hair into her prim knot and sighed tiredly. "Aileen, I know you mean well. But I do have a book to finish, and I've wasted entirely too much time as it is. 'Life gives nothing to mortals except with great labor.' Horace."

Aileen frowned. "Well then, I can't argue with that. But what of research? Is it no longer necessary for you to see what you're writing about? We've been here for over a week, and you know less about this town than you do China."

"I suppose you have a point." Without realizing it, Amanda's eyes wandered to the envelope that bulged out of her carpetbag—the letter from her editor. She had discovered it just this morning while rifling through the bag for her notes, and had reread the missive thoughtfully. She'd experienced much more of life in the last few months than she'd ever dreamed possible, and she had to admit that it gave her work a richness she'd never approached before.

"Sure I do." Aileen wasn't quite certain why, but she sensed a victory at hand. If Amanda had to think fun was work to get out and enjoy herself, so be it. "The Woman's Committee has been dying to get you out for their meeting. Why don't we go today, and then to one of the parties later tonight?" Aileen held out the ream of invitations with a grin. "You've got enough to choose from. Everyone wants Fess Tyson at their affair."

Amanda nodded, looking at the cards with the first interest she'd shown in days. Even if her life with Luke was over, she'd have to go on. And her work was the best place to start.

The afternoon sun beat down as Luke wrestled with the barbed wire, wrapping it around a wooden fence post and hammering the glinting metal into place to secure the ranch. He had removed his shirt, and his body gleamed a soft bronze, his muscles flexed with exertion. Wiping the sweat from his brow, he collapsed into the grass, taking a moment to catch his breath and survey the fruits of his efforts.

It would all be worth it. The fence work was grueling, but once it was done, he would have saved thousands of dollars in pay to the cowboys for roundup. Within months, he could control what his cattle ate, where they wandered and their mating practices, all of which would contribute to an outstanding breed. Within years he would have the best damned ranch this side of Waco, and within a decade, the best in the state. It was all happening, and yet . . .

The wind stirred the fields. The grass bent like ruffled silk, and the wildflowers swayed like graceful ballerinas. The sun bathed the grass in a sheen of gold, the dazzling mist rising up to the clouds in a froth of humidity, only to disappear like white vapor ghosts into an endless rim of blue. Insects hummed. A dragonfly paused beside a clover blossom like a living match, anticipating the sweetness behind the soft white mound, then landed delicately on a petal to drink in the nectar. It was beautiful, restless, and wild. And it reminded him of Amanda.

She hadn't spoken to him in days. When she looked at him, there was a shadow of pain in her ocean eyes—and a new disillusionment. Luke had left her alone, thinking that whatever was wrong, Amanda would come to him when she was ready, but it didn't seem to be working out that way. Daily, she became more immersed in her work, shutting out him, her friends, and her new neighbors. He understood what her work meant to her, but even to his inexperienced eyes this was unhealthy.

The wind blew once more and the bluebonnets danced. *I see the flowers of the plains, and I see beauty. He has given that to me, in the moments when he is kind . . .*

Damn! Luke pounded his fist into his palm, and only then did he notice that he had cut himself on the barbed wire. Blood oozed from several lacerations, and crept into the crevices of his fingers like tiny determined rivers. He didn't even feel the physical pain, for what was happening inside of him was so overwhelmingly terrible. It was worse than when he discovered Suzette dead and his mother gone, for he couldn't control that nor could he have prevented it.

But this, this was within his power, and it was dying, as surely as his sister and mother died. One day he would wake up and be alone again, the way he was before he met Amanda Edison, with nothing inside of him but hate.

The fury within him waned, and determination was reborn. He wouldn't let this happen, not while he had a breath in his body. Amanda meant too much to him. It was time he admitted that to her, as well as to himself.

Amanda nodded sleepily at the Woman's Committee meeting, trying hard to hide behind the rotund Mrs. Meade and not reveal her boredom. Today's meeting was being held in the town hall, and not a breeze or a breath of fresh air came through the large open windows. The women's voices were soft and gentle, addressing topics such as the new spring plantings and the upcoming Christmas party. That was the event of the year, and all of the women discussed their gowns in detail, as well as the decorations and festivities.

Covering a yawn with one hand, Amanda shifted impatiently in her chair, earning a frown from Aileen. All she could think about was Luke. Even knowing what she did, he crept back into her thoughts with a startling regularity, appearing when she was trying to write and preventing her from concentrating on anything other than him.

Fresh puzzlement surged through her as she thought of her reaction to his latest kiss. She had successfully distanced him, hurt him with her words, yet once he held her in his arms, her mind seemed to stop working and some inner drive took over. She recalled the way her arms crept around his neck, almost in an instinctive reaction, and her nose wrinkled as she tried to sort all of this out.

" . . . and red and green are the only appropriate Christmas colors," Mrs. Mitchell huffed. Her breath smelled suspiciously of gin, and as she leaned forward, a little bottle nearly tumbled out of her pocket. "I don't know what you're thinking of, Margaret! Silver and blue are much too cold for this climate. Don't you agree, Mrs. Parker?"

Amanda blinked, reacting to the name only because it was Luke's. She really didn't think of herself as Mrs. Parker, nor Fess Tyson. She was Amanda Edison, and Amanda alone.

"I'm sorry, I was thinking of something else," Amanda answered honestly.

"Perhaps you'd like to share your thoughts, my dear. You seem troubled." Grace Brockelman spoke quietly, aware of Amanda's distraction and the other women's insensitivity. The school teacher recognized the restless intelligence in Amanda's eyes and understood her lack of interest. And yet, it was not quite fair in Grace's opinion that Amanda be left out.

"Actually, I was wondering if physical mating urges superceded common sense," Amanda said bluntly, adjusting her glasses and perking up for the first time all morning. "It could be part of our instinct, you know."

"What?" Mrs. Meade asked, appalled.

"Our need to procreate would have to be more compelling than logic, otherwise men and women would never mate." Amanda simplified her argument, ignoring Aileen's rolling eyes and pale face. "For it occurs to me that the differences between men and women would make mating an impossibility, without the physical compulsion. Don't you agree?"

The women shared a stunned silence, then Grace Brockelman began to laugh softly. She started to clap, ignoring the thunderstruck faces of the women around her.

"It's about time we converted these meetings to discuss something more important than the color of our gowns," Grace said emphatically. "I think if we learned nothing else in the past decade, it's that our lives have changed and we must change with them. We have a new chance to contribute something meaningful to this town, and Amanda Edison can help us do it!"

Grace's face became impassioned and the other women broke into renewed applause. Elvira Brannigan, the mayor's wife, stood up with her handkerchief fluttering and her face as pale as a china teacup.

"I don't think this is a good idea at all. What would Frank Mitchell say, and your Tom, Margaret! I shudder to even think of it. I feel I shall faint . . . "

There was a scurrying around for her smelling salts, then Mrs. Meade gave her a stern look. "Oh, shut up, Elvira. We're all in agreement here, and it's something we've all discussed privately for some time now. We have a chance to really do something constructive, and we aren't going to let your fainting spells stop us. Now ladies, let's talk. We've been wanting to restructure our school system for some time. Perhaps we could talk about that. Or the medical field."

"Ranch wars." Margaret shuddered. "Tensions are heating up over the use of barbed wire. Perhaps we could help ease the fighting and find a solution."

"I agree." Mrs. Meade accepted a sheet of Amanda's notepaper and a pen, ignoring the ink that spattered all over her dress. She headed her paper, then drew columns. "All right, ladies, let's get started. We have a lot of work ahead of us, and we'll be counting on you, Mrs. Parker, to lead the way."

Amanda nodded, then took out a paper for everyone else. She was finally accepted, wanted, and appreciated for what she was. It was a heady feeling, yet she could only hope that perhaps now she would forget Luke Parker.

Luke was whistling when he strode into the house, feeling a damned sight better than he had when he'd left. At least he had a plan of action. Amanda was shutting him out, but he'd broken through that wall before, and he'd simply have to do it again. She wouldn't like it, but this time he was going to set new ground rules. If he didn't, he risked everything—from losing her to finding his laundry decorating the desert.

"Senor, I try to meet you at the door, but you come in too quickly," Pedro protested, rushing up into the hallway and wiping his hands on his apron. "We have a visitor here, the sheriff."

Luke nodded, recalling that he'd noticed a strange horse outside. "Where is he?"

"I put him in the study until you arrive. Would you like a drink first?"

"No, I'll see him." A strange foreboding came to him as he walked into the tiny study that was adjacent to the porch. There was but one reason the sheriff would ride out to the ranch to see him, and that reason was Haskwell.

"Mr. Parker." Sheriff Mendez rose to his feet and extended a hand, smiling cordially, but the smile did not reach his dark eyes. "I'm afraid I have news, senor. I did not mean to intrude."

"Not at all," Luke remarked, taking a seat. "I suppose you've learned something."

Mendez nodded. "I wish it wasn't so. I just received this wire. Perhaps you should take a look."

Luke accepted the telegram and opened the envelope, frowning as he read: "Haskwell arrived in Texas, stop. Destination unknown, stop. Wire for help, stop."

"It is from the sheriff of Dallas, senor. I sent him a wire and a description of this man. Unfortunately, it seems this Haskwell is following you."

"I'm not surprised." Luke crumbled the paper and tossed the telegram into the fire. "I had a feeling it wouldn't be long before we heard something. Haskwell isn't the type to let vengeance grow cold."

"I think we need to make plans, and very quickly. I have already stopped by the Running J Ranch and talked with Jake Fontaine. He will meet with us tonight, at my office. I will have my men there also. At least, now that we are warned, we can take some steps to see your wife protected. Where is she now?"

Luke's blood ran cold as he realized he hadn't seen Amanda since that morning. He rang for Pedro, his jaw tightening as he thought of the possibilities. Fortunately, the manservant responded quickly, his face twisted with concern as Luke snapped at him.

"Where is Amanda?"

"I do not know, senor. She was here this morning, then

she entertain company—Senorita Aileen. I think they went
to a meeting of some kind."

"There was a meeting of the Woman's Committee
today," Sheriff Mendez supplied helpfully. "My wife be-
longs. Perhaps your wife attended also."

"Maybe," Luke responded, distracted. Women's Com-
mittees didn't sound like Amanda's cup of tea. Cold, stark
dread filled him as he thought of Haskwell so close, and
Amanda gone. He wanted to kill her for frightening him
like this, yet at the same time, he wanted to hold her, kiss
her, and reassure himself that she was all right.

"I suggest you send a few *vaqueros* to look for her,"
Mendez continued, picking up his hat and gloves, a thoughtful expression on his face. "And I think she shouldn't travel
unaccompanied for a while. I will see you tonight."

Luke nodded, taking the sheriff to the door. Amanda
wasn't safe anywhere, until Haskwell was dead.

"Thank you, Tomas. I'll be needing the carriage again
this evening, if you don't mind." Amanda stopped to pat
the horse gently, surprised as the stableboy, Pedro's young-
est son, rushed up in a whirlwind of energy.

"It is good that you are home, Senora. Senor Luke has
been looking everywhere for you, and he is tearing up the
house like this." Juan paced back and forth, his hands behind his back, imitating Luke.

Amanda frowned, taking her carpetbag and bird cage out
of the carriage. "I don't know why. I am a grown woman.
Mr. Parker doesn't need to know every step I take. I'll go
see him, Juan, don't worry." The little boy's face knotted
in concern as Amanda glanced up at the well-lighted house.
Hefting her belongings, she started up the path and entered
the hallway, nearly dropping the cage as Pedro wrapped his
arms around her in exuberance.

"Thank God you are all right, senora. I was so worried!
Your husband has been looking all over for you—"

"Have you found her?" Luke stalked into the hall, then
stopped short at the sight of Amanda with her cage and bag.

"Where the hell have you been?" His face was dark with fury.

Stunned, Amanda answered honestly. "I went to the Woman's Committee meeting, then I visited the red light district. Some of those women work in cribs, Luke, in this day and age! We had a discussion about procreation and the effects of sexuality as barter, when I decided to visit the fair stalls and look at the cattle. I talked to some of the men there . . . " Amanda's voice trailed off as Luke's face got even darker. "Why are you looking at me like that?"

"You are the damnedest woman I've ever known! I don't want you ever to put a foot outside this door again without squaring it with me, do you understand? Woman's clubs to the whorehouse! It's a wonder you've lived as long as you have!"

He looked so formidable that Amanda's logic fled. She placed her belongings on the floor, feeling sixteen again, awkward and somehow always wrong.

"But—" she began in protest.

"No. You're going to listen to me this time. You've called the shots long enough, and this is the result. We live in the same house like strangers, and don't even talk to each other. I've had enough of doing things Amanda Edison's way." He continued more softly as Pedro bowed out of the room to leave the couple alone. "I want you to promise me that you won't leave this house again without my permission."

She stared at him unblinkingly, reminding him of Aesop. When she spoke, her voice was calm, but he could almost read her thoughts.

"I can't promise that. I am working, and the book is almost finished. If I need to see something or get information, I shall do so, with or without your permission."

There was the slightest tinge of a sneer on the last word, and she gazed at him with all the warmth of a matador examining a bull, to decide where to thrust the sword. Luke swore under his breath, then crossed the four feet that separated them. He grabbed his wife's shoulders, heedless of her look of alarm as he shook her impatiently.

"Don't you understand what I'm telling you? It's for your own good! It's Haskwell, goddammit! He's here," Luke shouted.

The color drained from her face and she peered up at him, examining him for any possibility of a lie. Finding nothing but concern in his eyes, she pulled away, then sank down to sit on her carpetbag, her chin resting on her knee.

"Amanda?" There was more here than fear of an outlaw, Luke could see that. When she turned to look at him, her expression made him wary.

"I suppose that makes things easier for you," she said simply, though her eyes blazed. "I'll draw the man here, and you get your revenge. And if I get killed, so much the better."

"What the hell are you talking about?" Some of his anger fled, replaced by confusion. He looked down at her, a small bundle of knowledge and convoluted thinking, sitting on the floor and impaling him with her eyes.

"Your reason for being here, with me," Amanda continued coldly. "Isn't that what I've been all along? The lure to draw out Haskwell? You don't have to pretend, Luke. I read about it in the post office. Haskwell is after me because I wrote that book about Haines. The poster said that he is the alleged killer. He must have thought I witnessed the crime, and that I could testify against him. But that's not all the poster said. It also supplied the names of his other victims, including your mother and sister."

He blanched as if she'd struck him, but Amanda continued in the same, unemotional voice. "So now I know where I stand. I don't know why you hadn't been honest with me. I could have taken the truth."

"Is that what you think?" he questioned hoarsely. "That I'm using you, just to get revenge?"

"It's obvious, isn't it?" Amanda stated. "And logical. Why you were on that train. How you could identify those men so quickly. I just wish you hadn't—"

"Go on," Luke said furiously.

"—seduced me into thinking I meant something to you."

She turned to him, her eyes misty. Her hair, tied back in a prim knot again, framed her face and accentuated her sharp, intelligent features. She was trying hard to maintain her school marm demeanor, but the months on the trail had changed her, softened her outlook, and made her less sure of herself. Even now she looked at him, almost pleading with him to deny her charges, yet her back was as straight as a nun's prayer book.

"Is that what you've been thinking?" Suddenly, it all became clear to Luke. What had happened to the gay and carefree Amanda he'd seen on the trail, her inexplicable withdrawal from him, and the cold way she'd been acting since they'd come to Texas. With another woman, he wouldn't believe she'd arrive at such a conclusion, but to Amanda, if $A = B$, and $B = C$, then $A = C$—all emotions aside.

"I'd prefer that we not pretend any longer," Amanda said quickly as Luke slowly drew her to her feet, and entirely too close to him. "We both know why you are here, and now Haskwell's come. I would just like to remain alive."

"Amanda," Luke said softly, his temper barely restrained. "Sheriff Mendez and I are meeting tonight to make our plans. I refuse to let your stubbornness or independence cost you your life, and if I have to lock you in this house to get you to obey, I will. Do you understand me?"

Amanda's cheeks flushed a bright pink, but she said nothing, knowing that if she gave him any indication that she might not obey, he would make good his threat and see her confined to her room like a child. Fuming at the thought of being within this man's power, she cast her eyes to the floor in meek submission, while her wonderful mind silently calculated. Although she had no intention of curtailing her work, she was equally determined not to get killed for the sake of Luke's revenge. It was very important now that she stay alive.

Especially since she now knew that she was carrying his child.

Chapter

24

"Is that the end, Mrs. Tyson?"

Simon Ledden, the postmaster, twitched his moustache at the sight of the still-wet manuscript, his fat thumb leafing through the endless ream of paper.

Amanda nodded sadly. "This is it. Do you think you can mail this to New York today?"

The man's face softened at Amanda's obvious eagerness. "I'll take care of it myself, Mrs. Tyson. A new book, eh?" He smiled secretively. "Western, same as the rest?"

"In a way." Amanda reluctantly placed the rest of the book on the post office scale. "This one's about a woman who makes a fool of herself over a man. Common enough, don't you think?"

He heard the sadness in her voice and saw the vulnerability behind the tough mask of her intellect. Cocking his head to one side in a way that Aesop would understand, Simon reached out and patted her hand.

"Now don't fret, dear. These things have a way of working themselves out, you'll see."

"Not in this case." Amanda indicated the book. "It's finished, and already ended. It's just a shame I can't rewrite the real ending, isn't it?"

Simon nodded sympathetically, then clucked his tongue
as she strode out, the carpetbag in one hand, the bird cage
dangling from the other. *Too damned much schooling for
a woman,* Simon thought. *Leads to nothing but trouble.* Eagerly, he picked up the manuscript and began to read, his
glasses fogging almost immediately. Fess Tyson's new novel
was a shocker. And he would be the first to read it.

*The water hole was nearly dried up when they reached it.
Chase slipped down from the horse first, then tethered their
mount to a slender cottonwood before helping Angel. She
could mount and dismount as easily as him and they both
knew that. Nevertheless, she allowed him to lift her from the
horse, liking the way her body felt pressed against his as her
feet made reluctant contact with the dirt.*

"Looks like there isn't much water," Chase commented
*as he held her hand and surveyed the area. The outer rim
of the pond had become solid mud, but the interior spring
still bubbled with clear liquid. Releasing her hand, the young
foreman sat on the ground and tugged at his boots. He placed
them aside and stepped into the crisp, clear spring, nearly
sighing in pleasure as he splashed fresh water on his face and
drank deeply.*

"You coming in?"

*His smile was as inviting as the water. Angel stripped off
her shoes and stockings, wincing as she thought of the public
censure this act would create, were it known. She lowered her
legs into the water, sighing as the cool liquid caressed the hot
soles of her feet.*

*It felt wonderful to be here with him, wonderful doing such
daring things as wading with a man. He had taught her to
dance beneath a star-studded sky the previous night; she'd
never dreamed how much fun that would be with a man like
Chase. Slowly, relentlessly, he was stripping away her outer
defenses, finding the woman within.*

*She saw him watching her, the way she dipped her legs in
and out of the water, the way the little droplets clung to her
skin and trickled down her dress. Something in his face*

seemed to change, and he spoke hoarsely. "We'd best be getting back. We're still in Indian country, and it isn't quite safe."

Angel lay back on the bank propped up on her elbows, her feet still dangling in the water. She didn't want to return to the hot, shadowy interior of the wagon. She didn't want to leave him. Her body was humming, as restless as the bees scouring the clover flowers, and her blood seemed to flow hotter even as the water cooled her. Her eyes were partially closed, unwilling to reveal these strange new emotions to him. He stepped closer and extended his hand.

"C'mon, sweetheart, your father will kill me if we're not back before him."

Angel rose reluctantly, pulled on her stockings, then searched for her shoes. Chase brought them to her, then stooped beside her and slid one over her slender ankle. He did the same with the other, forcing her to hold onto his shoulders for balance. His fingers lingered longer than necessary, and he rose slowly. When his eyes were level with hers, she drew in a deep breath, shocked at the hot passion she saw there.

"My God, Angel, you're enough to make a man forget his good intentions."

"Forget then," she whispered recklessly. "I want you to forget."

" . . . unfortunately, we didn't get there in time." Sheriff Mendez ignored Luke's frown and shrugged apologetically. "We did all that we could. But this man Haskwell must have been expecting to be tracked. He left Dallas as quickly as he came."

"Goddammit!" Luke swore, slamming his hand down on the sheriff's desk. He held up two fingers with less than a quarter inch between. "We were this close to catching the bastard, and he slips away like some schoolgirl at a prom!"

"That isn't fair, Luke," Jake said calmly. "The sheriff's done what he could. He sent the telegrams to Dallas as soon as we got word, and dispatched the deputy. Haskwell isn't an easy man to nail. If he was, he'd be dead by now."

Jake spoke pragmatically, but Luke was in no mood to listen to reason. "I don't want excuses! It isn't your damned wife he's trying to kill!" he shouted.

"Maybe not, but I have feelings for Amanda, too," Jake said, visibly hurt. "I don't want to see anything happen to her. And I'm more than willing to help track him down."

"Yes, I know. I'm sorry." Luke extended a hand, which the older ranchman readily took. After a moment, Luke turned back to the sheriff, forcing himself to remain calm and rational, for Amanda's sake.

"Do you have any other news? Anything that would help us?" Luke asked.

Mendez hesitated for a moment, as if uncertain of how much to trust these two men. His eyes shifted from Luke's passionate expression to Jake's calm concern. Whatever he saw there apparently reassured him, for after lighting a thin cigar, he spoke much more freely.

"We think he has a woman with him. The reports all say he's been dragging her from state to state. The girl tried to escape from him once, in a crowded saloon. Haskwell found out about her plan and put a stop to it. The man who was to help her was severely beaten."

"Who is she?" Luke asked, impressed by the results of the investigation.

"Her name is Honey Bee," Mendez reported. "She's a showgirl, once considered very beautiful. She last performed in a saloon just fifty miles north of here. They say she was so bad the bartender threw her out, yet she once won praise for her voice. I fear it is Haskwell's influence, and like the other girl you spoke of, Jake, she isn't long for this world."

"Unless we stop him," Luke said thoughtfully. He looked at the sheriff with new respect. "What plans have you made?"

"My deputy is on his way back now. I'm putting together a group of men to try and follow Haskwell's trail. The fact that he is not traveling alone is good for us. He will need to stop, and will be more easily seen with the woman."

"Do you need volunteers?" Jake asked, and Mendez shook his head.

"I would prefer if you both stay in town, just in case Haskwell slips through our net. If you need to be gone for any length of time, I would appreciate it if you let me know. And Mrs. Parker should notify you of her whereabouts at all times. It's important now that we can find both of you easily, should we hear that Haskwell is in Waco."

"I agree," Luke said evenly. "My wife and I have already discussed this. She understands the danger, and will keep me informed of where she goes and what she does. Amanda will not make a move that I am not aware of."

"Are you certain of this, dear?" Grace Brockelman stared at the mound of corsets that lay in the center of the street like the webbed bones of a slaughtered dragon. Laces lay everywhere, some of satin, some of cotton, all of them tossed gaily by the giggling and blushing women as the pile mounted higher. Steel hooped underskirts joined the mountain, collapsing under pressure like medieval torture garments. Next came bustles and tufts of cotton padding, that sank down amid the corsets and hoops like stones dropped into a pond.

"I am not at all sure this is right," Elvira Brannigan whispered, appalled at the sight of the feminine undergarments fluttering in the breeze.

"Oh, bosh Elvira. And if you're going to have another one of your fainting spells, do it inside. This is important." Mrs. Meade puffed up like an adder, her round face puckered and threatening, and her sharp eyes narrow beneath her bonnet.

"We have to make a statement," Amanda said, tossing her own corset onto the pile, then standing nearby on a platform with a box of matches. "As women, we no longer wish to be bound to the past, either by our undergarments or by tradition. It is time we were free! These clothes were designed to change our bodies, to hide our normal curves and womanly figures, to conform to an unnatural ideal that is physically unhealthy and emotionally appalling! No wonder we've suffered for years with vapors and the blues! Our underwear is a direct physical cause for distress!"

The women applauded, the sound filling the air in the town center, competing with the piano at the Pecos Saloon. Men began to drift into the square, out of curiosity at first, then horror as they saw the indecent display of bloomers, leggings, corsets, and petticoats.

Amanda stood above it all, brandishing her matches like Joan of Arc and her sword. Her hair gleamed a brilliant chestnut, worn disgustingly loose and falling around her shoulders. Her face, burned by the sun, had an attractive stain of pink across the bridge of her nose where indentations remained from her glasses. Her dress, a simple cotton affair that looked well-worn from her trail days, was loose and moved softly as she lifted a match. Although her pregnancy was not far advanced, her body had become rounder and her corset tighter, giving her the idea to banish the garment. One thing was apparent to every man there:

She wasn't wearing a damned thing beneath her dress.

The women cheered, and Amanda continued her speech. "Not only are these garments physically destructive, but think of the mental and emotional complexities they create. We are told every time we put these on that we are nothing more than chattel, toys to be dressed and displayed for a man's benefit. What is the purpose of a corset, if not to enhance the breasts and reduce the waist! Surely, it is not for our stimulation, since the very donning of these garments is uncomfortable, even painful. We wear them to please men, to make our breasts more noticeable, our waists smaller, and bustles to make our backsides more apparent! No longer shall we be slaves to fashion! From now on, we shall use our minds to think, wear what is practical and comfortable, and let corsets be damned!"

The cheers were deafening. Even little Elvira, who was normally the color of snow and as fragile as Italian crystal, clapped her hands and cried out, *Amanda!* The other women joined suit, until the streets were filled with the name *Amanda! Amanda Edison!*

"Luke, I think you'd better come out here." The deputy stepped into the shaded interior of the office, and gestured to the street. "There seems to be a ruckus going on."

Puzzled, Luke donned his Stetson, then strode outside while Jake and the sheriff exchanged a worried glance. They followed, and all three men stood on the outside of the feminine crowd, as the women shouted:

"Amanda!"

Luke stared in disbelief as his wife struck a flaming match, then dropped it into a pile of feminine undergarments. The flimsy cotton and batiste slowly caught fire, the flames encouraged by the wind and the structure of the bustles and hoops. Lace burned. Cotton ignited. Rosettes smoldered. Whalebone collapsed. A sudden gust of wind from the north set the whole pile to blazing, and the women laughed and cheered like bare-breasted natives around a campfire.

The men looked soberly on, then one by one turned to Luke, their expressions anything but friendly. Simon Ledden, the postman, clucked his tongue. Mr. Meade shook his head and glared. Jake looked embarrassed but not surprised. Jed Brannigan, Elvira's husband and the mayor, had turned an interesting shade of red. Clearing his throat, he turned to Luke and spoke for all the men.

"I believe Amanda Edison is your wife, is she not? I think you'd best straighten her out now."

Luke grimaced, then crossed the crowd of women to the podium, where Amanda was removing her hosiery. One slender cotton stocking was rolled down, revealing a shapely white calf, then the delicate structure of her foot. Gaily, she tossed the stocking onto the bonfire, watching it ignite then disappear into the hot flames. Amanda reached for the second stocking as the women clapped. The cheers suddenly died, and a strange hush fell upon the crowd. Puzzled, Amanda glanced up, her dress pulled up high, her fingers slipping beneath the pink satin garter. Her eyes widened and her mouth formed an open O as she saw Luke towering over her.

"What in the hell do you think you're doing?"

The wrath of God was in his blue eyes. Amanda had never seen him so angry, not even the time she sent his clothing downriver. He looked immeasurably tall and overwhelmingly masculine as he dwarfed her slight figure, his hands resting on his hips as if to keep himself from strangling her.

Amanda gulped, and the dress hem slipped from her fingers. She hadn't thought of this in her eagerness to pursue the rally. The emotional encouragement of the women had seduced her, and the once in a lifetime feeling of power had been heady. But now she was faced with the consequences of this act of public defiance, and from the look in Luke's eyes, he wasn't about to be very understanding.

"I was leading the rally," Amanda squeaked. "You see, I had trouble breathing in my corset, and it occurred to me that feminine clothes were simply the reflection of male dominance. We should be using our minds, and not our bodies, simply to please the male species—"

"Goddammit, Amanda! I told you explicitly that I wanted to know your whereabouts. The first time I turn my back, you're out here, burning your underwear!" He glanced at the flaming corsets, as if unable to believe his own eyes, then turned back to her, his anger barely under control. "Do you realize the danger you were in? Suppose I needed to find you, quickly?"

She gave him a disparaging look. "I believe you found me quickly enough," she pointed out logically, though her mind dimly registered the thought that he seemed more concerned for her safety than angry at her public defiance. She still couldn't totally believe that, so she continued coldly. "I think what you're really upset about is that the male species is always threatened by a feminine show of power. We women have been treated as chattel for far too long! I mean to make a change, and if our corsets represent—"

That was as far as she got. Cursing under his breath, Luke
lost the last vestige of control he possessed and hiked her
over his shoulder, her bottom in the air, one bare leg kicking
up, one stockinged leg down. The men cheered as Luke
strode past the fire, past the awestruck women, past Elvira
Brannigan and Mrs. Meade, to the wagon where Juan
waited. Luke plopped Amanda into the back amid the hay,
ignoring her protests, then joined Juan at the front.

"Take us home. Now!"

Juan didn't hesitate, but whipped up the horses. The
wagon sped away from the town hall, leaving the smoldering corsets and the slender grey column of smoke far behind
them. Amanda slid upright, plucking hay from her hair and
gazing at the back of the furious man in front of her.

Maybe, this time she had pushed him too far. It wasn't
a pleasant thought.

The wagon thundered into the stables, and Luke leaped
out almost before it stopped. The short ride had done nothing to appease his anger, Amanda realized. The thought was
reinforced a moment later when he physically removed her
from the cart, his hands holding her waist tightly. His face
darkened as her skirt pulled up to reveal her one stocking-
less leg, then he took her hand and half-dragged her toward
the house.

"Let go of me . . . " she demanded, pulling at the fingers
that held her. Whatever he intended, she couldn't let him
hurt the baby, even if she had to tell him. And that was the
last thing she wanted to do, especially now.

"Like hell," Luke muttered, heading determinedly toward the estate. He forcibly escorted her to the columned
porch, ignoring Pedro's look of astonishment as he kicked
open the front door and dragged her into the parlor. After
slamming the door shut, he turned to her, his fists clenched
as if he had to physically restrain himself from attacking
her. Amanda stepped backward until the wall met her spine
and she was forced to stop. Luke had progressed toward her

at the same rate, so she had to look straight up at him, her eyes as wide as gold dollars, and she swallowed hard.

"I take it you aren't too pleased with me," she said.

"You're lucky I don't strangle you! What in the hell were you thinking about, burning your corset? No, don't tell me your theories. I'm angry enough now that I don't think I could stand it." He glared at her, even as she stared back, meeting his eyes with open defiance. "It seems I have several interesting alternatives here, none of them pleasant." He continued in the same, cold rational voice. "You do realize that everything I've worked to build, to start a new life and live a clean, respectable existence, is in jeopardy? Have you given no thought to the possible repercussions of all this?"

"Social change is bought at the price of stability," Amanda stated defensively. "Those within the establishment are always threatened—"

"That's bullshit," Luke snapped. "What about your safety? Suppose Haskwell showed up?"

"There is no reason my activities should have any direct bearing on you—"

"You're my wife, goddammit!" Luke swore, his blue eyes blazing.

Amanda looked at him thoughtfully, her expression hiding her true feelings and in the process, betraying everything. "I am aware that we are legally married," she said quietly, "even though it is not your intention to honor that vow. I am just the bait you are using to get Haskwell. Therefore, I find your argument lacking a constructive premise."

"Amanda, if you dare to say that one more time, I will forget all my good intentions," Luke continued, satisfied to see her startled into silence. "I have come to several conclusions today, and I want you to listen to them carefully. I refuse to let you destroy everything, simply for some thesis on the battle of the sexes. And don't even try to tell me that isn't what your rally was all about."

"I don't know what you mean," she said, truly puzzled.

"You're bringing our fights out in public," he explained. "Which doesn't do a damned thing to solve our misunderstandings, and you've put a lot of other wives into a tight spot with their husbands tonight. I could forgive that, knowing the way that you think, as mixed up as it is. What I can't forgive is what you're doing to us."

She stared at him doubtfully, already coming up with a rebuttal. Luke headed it off before she could present it. "I know you think that I'm simply using you to get to Haskwell," he continued. "I admit it started out that way, but everything changed long ago. Somewhere along the way, I started to care about you, as you did me."

She shook her head, and Luke cupped her chin, forcing her to look up at him. "It's true and you know it. Don't you think it would have been far easier for me to get Haskwell alone, without a woman and a bird trailing me everywhere? Christ, I could have gone a few days ago and gotten him in Dallas, if that was my prime motivation. But I would have had to leave you, alone and unprotected, and I couldn't do that. As much as I hate Haskwell, I love you more."

Her arguments dissipated as a stark silence fell between them. Amanda stared at him, stunned by his words. Joy flowed through her, warm and overwhelming, coupled with reserve.

"That's right, I love you," Luke continued, as if startled himself. "But I have to admit, Amanda, I don't know how much more I'm willing to put up with. You defy me at every turn, test me constantly, and try to make me as miserable as possible when we both know you don't have to. I want a good normal life together, I want to have children—maybe a little girl like you, with a mind that Socrates would admire. But I don't want it at the price of my sanity. You have a decision to make. Either you want the same things I do, and commit to this relationship, or you don't. It's that simple."

That simple and that hard. Amanda said nothing as he left her alone, slamming the door behind him. Her unstockinged leg got goosebumps in the chill and she sat down on one of the elegant chairs, absently rubbing it. The ache in her limb was nothing compared to her heart.

His patience was at an end, she could sense that. All she had to do was let go of the logic, of all the compelling reasons that held her back, and give into the feelings she revealed in her book. A thousand thoughts crowded her mind, many of which she never entertained before.

He loved her. He actually loved her. He wanted them to live together as a real husband and wife, wanted children . . . she thought of the baby inside of her and the possibility seemed far more real than it ever had before. She couldn't prevent the fleeting smile that came to her face, or the delicious giggle that welled up inside of her. She felt like soaring, like the wood doves who ambled so clumsily on the ground—but once they took off! . . . Then her eye caught her reflection in the simple hall mirror, and her smile faded.

Her hair, loosened in the rally, tumbled wildly around her shoulders. Her glasses were askew, her dress, without the foundation of a corset, sagged on her slender body. She thought of all the lovely women Luke must have known, women with flaxen hair and perfect complexions, women without ink on their hands or bird droppings on their shoes. These were the kind of women Luke would love. And yet . . .

She was being ridiculous, yet a part of her, small and as yet seldom nurtured, dared to hope. Even if tomorrow it all turned out to be just a dream, it was one she would live in.

Chapter

∞ 25 ∞

"Are we almost there, Sam?" Honey peered fearfully out of the window of the Wells Fargo stagecoach, seeing the glum shapes of buildings and railroad tracks that indicated a town. They'd seen so many towns in the past few weeks that they all began to look alike to Honey: grim, lifeless, and without escape.

"Yes, just about. In fact, we'll be staying on the outskirts of town, in an old abandoned nester's hut. If my information is correct, this should be the end of the line."

"What then, Sam?" Honey asked fearfully. She dreaded the question, but like a puppydog getting his tail cropped, she wanted all the bad news quickly and cleanly.

Sam smiled, his black eyes cold. He looked her up and down, not bothering to hide his disgust as he took in her appallingly slender body, her trembling hands, her lackluster hair, and her dull eyes. From a distance, she could pass muster, but up close, her faults were readily apparent. A pang of guilt assailed him as he remembered her as she was, but it was quickly gone. It wasn't his fault that she couldn't hold her own. This was a tough world, and only the strong survived.

"I think you know the answer to that, darlin'," Sam said

softly, delighted to see the blind panic in her eyes. "You see, you're getting to be more and more a liability. Once my work is done here, I'm heading back to Colorado, where a man can make his fortune on the turn of a card. There ain't nothing keeping me here, nor with you."

Honey's liquid eyes brightened softly. "Then, you'll let me go?" The plea in her voice was pathetic, and would have moved anyone other than an outlaw.

Sam smiled. "Can't rightly do that, now can I? Not with what you know. I'd like to, Honey, don't get me wrong. But I really don't have much choice. If you went to the law with your little story, why, they'd be on me faster than a frog on a bluefly. Really, you should know better than to ask me, I can see it only upsets you."

"Please," she whispered brokenly, almost past the point of caring. "I won't tell. I promise."

"I know, darlin'. That's why I have to kill you. But don't be too hurt. You've been good to me, and I aim to pay you back." He leaned closer, noticing how she seemed to flinch without him even touching her. "This old nester's hut has a nice piece of land out back, and a pretty apple tree. When it's all over, I'll bury you there, me girl. No finer resting place will any of Sam Haskwell's whores ever claim."

Honey started to cry, and Sam chuckled, seeing the thin trickle of tears start down her face. It was true, what he'd told her.

And he wouldn't forget to put roses on her grave.

A parcel the size of a poultry crate arrived at Mitchell's General store, wrapped in burlap and tied with a thick piece of twine. The corner bore a label from G. W. Carleton of New York, and was inscribed with a flowery logo depicting a cowboy with a lariat. Simon Ledden, the postmaster, had already informed the watchful residents of Waco that IT had arrived. He personally carried the box to the store, accumulating a following like the Pied Piper of Hamelin. By the time the ruddy shopkeeper retrieved a blunt knife to cut open the wrappings, the store was filled with men, women, and children.

"Come on now, people, wait your turn. This isn't the first time we've ever gotten a Fess Tyson novel, you know."

"It is when Fess Tyson actually lived here," Mrs. Meade puffed. "And she has promised to autograph all of our copies. Just think, a signed Fess Tyson!"

"This one's real different," Simon Ledden warned. "Nothing like her others."

Elvira Brannigan turned toward him, her pale face aghast. "Simon, you didn't . . . I mean, you couldn't have—"

"Of course he did," Mrs. Meade snapped. "He's been reading our mail for years. But the manuscript has nothing to do with the final book. These editors, you know." She gave herself an air of one with great inside knowledge and the women around her nodded solemnly.

"They would have had to do a hell of a lot of editing to make that book decent," Simon muttered. "Fess Tyson or no Fess Tyson."

"Who appointed you a literary critic?" Grace Brockleman asked. "I have it on good authority that the book is getting splendid reviews in New York. And if it isn't another penny dreadful, so much the better. Amanda Edison is far too bright to write pulp fiction, anyway. I, for one, can't wait to read it."

The final strings snapped, and the package fell open, revealing ten brand new, shiny copies of *Passion's Price*. A hush fell over the crowd as the shopkeeper reverently picked up one glossy yellow-backed novel, fingered through the pages that still smelled of fresh ink, then found half a dozen fists filled with Yankee notes thrust in his face.

"Now now, we'll all have to share. This is only the first shipment, so to make it fair, whoever has the full asking price right now—$1.50—gets a copy. But for the sake of the peace of this town, please share the books. Here, Grace, this one's for you and the school."

Grace took the gleaming yellow book and hugged it to

her bosom before darting through the crowd in an effort to get to her parlor. Mrs. Meade got the next copy; Simon Ledden, the third. Within seconds, every book had disappeared from the crate, leaving a crowd of angry Waco residents clamoring for copies.

"Next week!" Mitchell shouted, ushering them out. "We'll be getting another shipment then!"

"But I've been waiting . . ."

"What in tarnation do you want me to do, give birth to it?" Mitchell asked, successfully subduing the rest. "Now would you all please vacate the premises? Fess Tyson or not, I have work to do!"

The remaining townspeople obeyed, muttering under their breath. Even the loungers who normally spent the day whittling on the porch departed, hoping to find someone they knew who would share *Passion's Price.* As soon as they all cleared out, Mitchell whipped out a copy he'd kept for himself, one that had been paid for in full by Luke Parker.

Amanda's husband would get his copy soon enough. And this was one of the perks of owning the only store south of Dallas.

" . . . and I have to admit, Amanda, this is your best work yet. The book is wonderful. It is so real, so touching, and so amazingly sensual that I couldn't believe you had written it. You are destined for greatness, Amanda. *Passion's Price* will soon be considered a classic. I eagerly look forward to the new Fess Tyson, and I congratulate you on your triumph."

Tears filled Amanda's eyes and she reread the letter, letting the words sink in. The goal she'd struggled toward for so long was finally within her reach. She'd written a book that warranted literary merit, and the taste couldn't have been sweeter. Eagerly, she whipped out the copies of reviews that her editor had included with her letter.

" . . . fantastic plotting, rich emotion, excitement flowing through every line, reminiscent of Molière. *Passion's Price* is one of the best literary offerings this spring." The New York Sun.

" . . . luridly sensual yet compelling. Fess Tyson will shock and astonish you." The Philadelphia Public Ledger.

"The excitement of the West combined with a love story in the manner of Dumas. Written by the shining star of the frontier." The Baltimore Star Herald.

It was all too good to be true. Amanda folded the letter and put it inside her bosom, then picked up a lantern and ventured outside to the convenience, the one place she knew she wouldn't be disturbed. This time was hers, and as selfish as it was, she wanted to enjoy it alone. She placed the lantern on a hook and then sat on the wooden bench, reading and rereading the letter. All by herself, she laughed, cried, smiled, and looked at the reviews all over again.

She'd done it.

She didn't see Luke until she was coming out of the outhouse. He was coming across the field, still carrying the iron brand he had been using. He saw her expression and dismissed a cowhand, then came toward her.

"You all right, Amanda?"

She heard the concern in his voice and her smile dazzled him. "Look." Shyly, she handed him the letter and reviews. She felt so vulnerable. This was a part of her life she had never shared with anyone, and now the news was so good that she wanted to spill it out like a paper cup sodden with rainwater. But she really wasn't certain how Luke would feel about all this. She'd intimidated men before with her mind, and although Luke was different, she was dimly aware that he might not care for her notoriety. Standing first on one foot, then another, she waited impatiently until he'd read everything, and then looked up with a grin that melted her heart.

"Jesus, Amanda, that's great. Goddamn, I'm so proud of you!" He swung her up into his arms, heedless of her embarrassment or her faint struggles.

"Put me down, Luke Parker!" she shouted.

"No, I won't. And I'm taking you out to the best restaurant this town can offer. This calls for a celebration. You've worked so hard, Amanda. It's time to have some fun."

"But the ranch . . . " Amanda glanced worriedly toward the stalls where Luke had been working. "I know how busy you are."

"Not that busy," Luke corrected her. "Just give me some time to get cleaned up." He put her down, swinging her like a child in her father's arms, and Amanda couldn't think of a time when she'd ever been so filled with joy. Luke draped his arm around her waist and walked with her toward the house, still looking at the letter.

"I heard some of your books came into town. I'd sent for mine, but I guess it's been delayed. I can't wait to read it."

Amanda stiffened, but she forced herself to relax. She'd have to learn to trust. She'd come to that conclusion in the last twenty-four hours, after thinking about what he'd said. What did she have to lose by giving it a try? She had everything to gain—real happiness, a father for the baby she carried, and the opportunity to love Luke Parker. Perhaps tonight she'd even get up the courage to tell him about the child. He had a right to know, but she didn't want him committing to her just because of that. If only she could forget that poster. . . .

You will, she told herself. Her only other option was a life alone. Every time she thought back to her school days, or those long, lonely days at the boardinghouse, she knew one thing for certain.

She could never go back.

Fess Tyson had learned the meaning of love, and thus was forever changed.

The Lone Star Hotel boasted bright red carpeting, gold paint on the ceiling, and flickering gas chandeliers that lent an elegant dimness to the eating establishment. Waiters clad in dark trousers and white shirts that resembled uniforms brought steaming pewter dishes and brimming glasses of wine to the table. A stage stood in the center, draped with red, white, and blue bunting, and a velvet curtain was tightly closed with a lush promise of entertainment.

Amanda sat with Luke, entranced by the setting, her neck craning from one sight to another as she tried eagerly to take it all in. Clad in a simple rose gown with nary a bustle nor a hint of a corset, she nevertheless looked radiant. Her eyes, enhanced by the color, gleamed, while her cheeks bloomed with pink. She'd swept up her hair into a careless knot that allowed charming tendrils to escape and frame her face, softening the intensity of her stare and the piercing intelligence in her eyes. Dazzled by the hotel and excited by the night out, she looked like a child, enchanting everyone who could be enchanted with her smile.

Luke was bewitched. "You look gorgeous," he commented, once again amazed at the transformation from a dusty and ink-stained genius, whose dress always bore some marking of Aesop's, to the charming woman who sat across from him.

Amanda flushed, pleased at the compliment. "Do you really think so? I wasn't at all sure about the dress. Aileen took me to Lacey's dressmakers and made me order it. It really is a contradiction, don't you think?"

"What is?" Luke was afraid to ask.

"That we garb ourselves for male attention and then act as if we don't want it," she explained, her nose wrinkling in thought. "As a species, our mating practices leave a lot to be desired. It is perhaps a good thing that women don't have to wait to come into season."

"Why is that?" Luke choked, trying not to laugh.

"Because," Amanda continued seriously, "we put so many obstacles in the path that we'd never propagate the species. Why are you laughing?" She stared in genuine puzzlement as Luke, unable to restrain himself, broke into a deep, masculine chuckle, then drank quickly of the wine to stop it.

"Amanda," he said when he could speak, "I love you. And if we weren't here with a room full of strangers right now, I'd take you in my arms and show you just what I think of our mating practices. And yes, I'm damned glad we don't have to wait for women to go into season."

The look in his eyes warmed her and Amanda felt a pleasant flush spread through her blood like hot honey. She put her hand over her belly, thinking of the wonderful secret she'd kept these past weeks, and suddenly wanted to share it. She turned to Luke, but the curtain parted and a well-dressed man stepped through the velvet and into the orb of light in the center of the stage.

"Good evening, ladies and gentlemen," he said when the clapping had died. "Welcome to the Lone Star Hotel. Tonight, we have the best damned singer this side of Indian Country. Will all of you give Honey Bee a warm welcome?"

The applause grew thunderous, then gradually dimmed as a beautiful young woman stepped into the center of the stage. Dressed in a scarlet gown decorated with pure white feathers and glittering jewels, she captivated the men without saying a word. Fascinated, Amanda sat on the edge of her seat, trying to get a better view. The singer, a glorious brunette with a too-slender body that was enhanced by padding, walked slowly and seductively to the front of the footlights. Fiery gems sparkled from her hair and throat, and as she raised her arms to sing, the men fell silent.

"The old west, the old time, the old wind singing through—the red red grass, a thousand miles. And Spanish Johnny you!"

Amanda smiled as the beautiful woman sang of the Spanish mandolin player. And although the woman's voice sounded sad and strained to her, the men almost fell out of their chairs trying to get a closer look. Honey simply had to raise a hand and they held their breath. Her dress, barely covering her breasts, seemed to hold them mesmerized, while tiny round circles of paint decorated her cheeks like a china doll's. She was too far away for Amanda to see her expression, but when the singer pulled up a chair and stepped onto it, exposing one leg clad in sheer black hose, the men went crazy.

"The gold songs, the gold stars, the word so golden then;

and the hand so tender to a child had killed so many men. He died a hard death long ago before the road came in— The night before he swung, he sang to his mandolin."

Even Luke stared, and when the music died, the applause rivaled a Texas windstorm. Fascinated, Amanda wished she could see the woman, or talk to her, but Honey slipped behind the curtain and disappeared as quickly as she had come. Amanda sat back in her chair and sipped her water, thinking of the lovely singer.

And wondering why she'd seemed more like an apparition than a woman.

Mr. Mitchell passed it to Mrs. Mitchell. Grace Brockelman placed it in the corner of her library, next to Shakespeare and the other controversial books. Mrs. Meade passed it to Mrs. Ledden with a whispered warning, and Mrs. Brannigan fainted.

Dog-eared copies of *Passion's Price* were passed through the town like a plague, and the horrified townspeople reacted with shock, indignation, then anger. The town hall buzzed like a swarm of black hornets as the townspeople gathered there, and the mayor rapped the podium loudly with a mallet, trying to gain order.

"Now now, quiet, everyone! We won't get anything accomplished like this! Who wishes to speak?" A dozen hands shot up, a dozen furious faces with them. "All right, Mrs. Meade. You speak for the Woman's Committee. What have you to say?"

Mrs. Meade stood up, looking even more imposing than normal, dressed in somber brown and waving the glossy yellow novel like a righteous banner. "Have you ever read such filth?" She turned to the women around her who nodded, their lips pursed tightly together.

"Atrocious!"

"Appalling!"

"Why, she made us sound like a bunch of hypocrites!"

"Indecent!"

This last came from Elvira Brannigan, who had to fan

herself so much afterward that the nearby women's hats tumbled off. Nodding, Mrs. Meade continued.

"Not only is it indecent and disgusting, it is full of lies. Could anyone read the last part and not recognize Waco? She insinuates that some of us drink!" She glanced at Mrs. Mitchell, who quickly hid her gin bottle. "And that some of us are thieves!" Frank Mitchell nodded, ignoring the suspicious glances of the men around him and the women who'd paid too much for too long. "And what she had to say about the sanctity of marriage!" Mrs. Meade shuddered as if the thought was too dreadful. "I am ashamed that we have taken this woman into our midst and allowed her to influence us. She should be tarred and feathered, and that disgusting book banished!"

"That's right," Elvira added. "Think of the children! What will happen if they read such trash?"

"And newcomers," Simon Ledden said. "We need to attract commerce, and with that damned book, she'll drive them away!"

"Down with Amanda!"

The chant grew louder, until Jed Brannigan could barely contain the crowd.

Jake stood up, waved his hands in the air and managed to gain some semblance of order. "All right, all right. It's just a book. The Parkers are good people, and I think we should give them the benefit of an explanation."

"That's right," Jed agreed, glad for the chance to avoid bloodshed. "You all acknowledge that Luke Parker has established himself as a responsible man. And he's put his wife in her place before. Let's give him a chance to respond to all this. We'll ask him to hand her over peaceably, and we'll bring her to trial. It will be a civil trial, and her punishment will be decided by the people of Waco. I'll pick a group of men to go out to the Rutherford Ranch and get her. Then we'll see justice done!"

The people roared, and a dozen males volunteered. Jed selected half, then assembled the men for the ride out to the ranch. Grim-faced, they started for the eastern part of town, wanting nothing more than revenge against Fess Tyson.

Amanda leaned against Luke as the carriage rolled into the stables. A full moon shone overhead, reminding her of the trail days when she and Luke had slept beneath a blanket of stars. Dimly she was aware of the carriage stopping, of Luke lifting her out, but her pregnancy made her sleepy and she enjoyed the luxury of having his arms around her as he took her toward the house.

"Looks like we have company." Luke's voice reflected his apprehension as he noticed the horses waiting by the porch, and as he recognized the local townsmen. Haskwell sprang to his mind, but the sheriff was no where to be seen.

"There she is. Slut!" Frank Mitchell said self-righteously as Amanda and Luke walked up to the porch. Amanda froze, and Luke turned in outrage to the group of men.

"What did you say?"

"I said, slut," the shopkeeper persisted. He jabbed a finger toward her. "It's her we've come for, to teach her a lesson."

"Amanda, get inside," Luke ordered. He approached Mitchell, his teeth clenched, and he grabbed the man's shirt by the collar and dragged him up to the porch. "Now what did you call my wife?"

"Let him go, Luke," Jake said seriously. "This can't be solved that easily, unfortunately."

Luke shoved the man off the porch, watching in supreme satisfaction as Frank fell to the dirt, then scrambled up again. Luke stood in the same spot, taunting the man with his eyes, but Jed Brannigan, the mayor, stepped between them.

"Luke, I'm sorry to have to do this, but she's coming with us. The townspeople are furious. I'll have a riot on my hands if she doesn't. They want her to stand trial and answer to their charges."

"What the hell are you talking about?" Luke demanded,

clenching his fist. He saw Amanda standing frozen by the door and he snapped. "Get inside!"

Amanda obeyed, frightened by the look on the men's faces—people who she'd considered friends just a day before. Peeking through the window, she trembled as she saw Luke turn toward the mayor, his face ashen with rage.

"I don't know what this is all about," he said carefully, "but you all owe my wife an apology. And without it, none of you are welcome here, ever again."

"It's that book!" Simon Ledden interrupted as Jed attempted to explain. "She made fools of us all. And it's disgusting and perverted. Your wife is a disgrace to this town, and to you, man!"

"Because of her book?" Luke demanded.

This time, the mayor answered. "Have you read it, Luke?"

Silence fell over the ranch as Luke struggled to control his temper. "I read some of it, once. But I still don't see what a harmless book that nobody has read has to do with—"

"It's not harmless, and it's not isolated," Jed explained. "Apparently, it's selling very well, and publicizing Waco as a town of thieves, drunkards, and small-minded people. But that isn't the half of it." Jed glanced toward the men, embarrassed, then continued. "Luke, with all due respect, the book is filthy. She's written things in there that . . . " his voice trailed off and he glanced once more at the men, then back to the house. "All I can say is, read it."

"Here." Frank Mitchell handed Luke his copy. "I don't want to keep books like that in my house."

"You'll probably want to beat some sense into her yourself," Jed stated. "The townspeople are damned mad, Luke, and rightly so. We'll be back."

"You're not taking her anywhere," Luke said flatly. "If Amanda's done something wrong, I'll handle her. And legally, none of you have a leg to stand on. There happen to be constitutional amendments allowing freedom of the press and freedom of speech. And if any of you don't like what she's written, all you have to do is stop reading it."

"Wait until you get to page eighty-seven, lover boy," Frank sneered. "Let's see what you think of your sweet wife then. I have a feeling we won't need to convince you."

Luke strode inside the house, clutching the yellow-backed book, furious. The men outside heard the door slam, then nodded to each other, satisfied.

Luke Parker would see to his wife. He would have to, when he'd read what Amanda had published for all the world to see.

Chapter

❧ 26 ❧

"Damn them! Self righteous idiots!" Luke swore, striding past Amanda as she stood in the hallway. "Do you believe this? They're mad about your book! Damned one-horse-town. They should be glad you mentioned them at all."

Amanda smiled, relieved, until her eyes fell to the glossy yellow novel in Luke's hand. "What's that?"

"The book," Luke snapped, waving the novel for emphasis. "That hypocrite Frank Mitchell probably read it first himself. Then he storms in here like a minister, spouting sermons. They're not getting away with it, Amanda, I promise you that."

Amanda's smile wavered, especially as Luke entered the parlor, poured himself a brandy, then sat before the fire with the book. "Why are you reading it now?"

"They said some things that just don't sit right with me," Luke explained. "But I can't very well defend you if I don't know what I'm talking about. I've wanted to read it, anyway, and now's as good a time as any."

Panicking, Amanda watched helplessly as Luke opened the book and began to read. "Luke, you really don't have to do this. I don't care what they think. This has happened to me my whole life. I'm used to it."

"I'm not," Luke said, obviously still angry. "And I care what they think. We have to live in this town, remember? The last thing we need is for some self-righteous opinionated bastard ruining your reputation. Goddamn them!"

"Luke, but still—"

"Amanda," Luke said firmly. "I'm going to read this book, and I'll talk to you about it afterwards. That's the end of it."

Biting her lip, Amanda said nothing as Luke continued to read. There was nothing she could do to stop him. Dimly, she began to realize that not everyone would see her literary triumph in the same light she did.

It was an expensive lesson, and she only hoped she could bear the cost.

He was still bleeding. Angel bit her lip as the doctor examined Chase, then rose from the bed and slowly put his stethoscope back into his black bag. He turned to her, his expression relieved.

"He'll be alright. The Indians cut him up pretty bad, but it looks like he'll live." The doctor chuckled as the young woman hugged him exuberantly, tears in her eyes. "Now, now. No need for that. Your foreman will be just fine. I hear he was very brave."

Angel nodded, choking back the joy that flowed through her. "Yes, he was. Even though some of your townspeople criticized him for not slaughtering the tribe, Chase understood that they were sick and desperate."

"Ah." The doctor glanced meaningfully at Mrs. Miller, who quickly hid her gin bottle in her pocket. Sam Smith, the butcher, gave her a sanctimonious smirk.

"Not all of us feel that way, Miss Hollister. Them Indians are a scourge and should have been wiped off the face of the earth. Chase had the chance—he should have done them in."

"Mr. Smith, Chase did what he thought was right. He has a high sense of morals, unlike some other people," Angel stated.

The townspeople tittered at her declaration. Everyone

knew that Angel's father, Ben Hollister, had pressed charges against the butcher for thievery. The man's face went scarlet.

"Why, I oughta see you walloped for that—"

"Sam, let's go. I think the lady wants to be alone with her foreman." Doc Westcott propelled the people out of the room, then closed the door softly behind himself.

Angel smiled in appreciation, then went to the unconscious man on the bed. Chase's beautiful eyes were closed, but she could see the gentle rise and fall of his chest. The doctor had done a good job of bandaging his cuts, and it seemed that most of him was covered with white sticky plaster. Tenderly, she pressed her finger to her lips, then lightly touched his forehead.

His eyes opened immediately and locked with hers. For a long moment, he didn't speak, didn't move. They communicated without words, in a timeless way. Slowly, his hand rose and reached for her own. Instead of holding it, he brought her finger back to his face and touched it with his lips.

Desire smoldered inside of her, coupled with an aching passion. Slowly, carefully, she slid beside him on the bed, balancing on her knees. His hand slid upward, through the silky blonde tangle of her hair, then he brought her lips to his. Like a hungry man, he drank deeply of her mouth, wanting to taste all of her, wanting to know she belonged to him.

And Angel gave. Leaning toward him, she returned his kiss with a passion born of fear—fear that he might have died this day, that she might never have told him what he meant to her. Instead, she showed him.

Climbing astride him, she pulled away the encumbrances of her skirts, then straddled him, watching his expression. His eyes grew darker, and he lifted her hips, guiding her to his manhood, then slowly he lowered her onto him, impaling her as her knees met the bed.

Angel gasped with pleasure, her eyes closing, her body one with his. She began to move instinctively, coupling the motions of her body to the urgent need of his. Hearing his throaty groan, she arched her back, letting him do the work, letting him take her to forgetfulness, then fulfillment. Heat coiled

*within her like a snake in her loins, suddenly bursting forth
and spreading through her like hot honey. She felt him con-
vulse at her reaction, then he thrust into her roughly, two,
three times, before slowly relaxing beneath her and sighing
with extreme pleasure.*

*He smiled when his eyes opened once more, and his hands
slid to her waist. "Angel, my sweet Angel. You almost make
it worth fighting Indians, do you know that?"*

*"It wasn't bad for me either, cowboy." She smiled, grateful
to see him so happy. Grateful to see him alive.*

*"It was once, remember? The first time I loved you, you
hated it."*

*"That was then. I was just a lonely schoolgirl, living with
my books and my dreams. You made me a woman, Chase.
I think it was when you made me love you."*

*"God, Angel." He reached for her, kissing her hard, almost
brutally. Angel sighed, content to be in his arms. It was where
she'd stay. Forever.*

He was in the same position when Amanda awoke the
next morning, only the brandy bottle was empty and the
book nearly finished. Dread filled her as she entered the parlor, carrying the coffee tray Pedro had given her as a peace
offering. She had donned her best nightgown, a soft ivory
lace that Aileen had insisted she buy along with the dresses,
and had brushed her hair into a satin sheen. But when she
placed the tray down with a cheerful bang, Luke looked
right through her.

"Good mooorrningg," Amanda stuttered. Something
was horribly wrong. His face bore the grizzle of his beard,
his blue eyes were bloodshot, and they looked out at her
with such contempt that Amanda backed toward the door.
"If you'd rather not have coffee—"

"Shut the door," Luke said softly.

Not fooled by his tone for a minute, Amanda rushed to
do his bidding, then turned toward him, fighting the fear
that threatened to engulf her.

"Good. Now come here and sit down."

His eyes impaled her. Amanda swallowed, glanced back to the door, then at him. "I prefer to stand—"

"Sit!" he barked, color rushing to his face.

Amanda sat down. Frantically, she tried to figure out just what she could say, but until he spoke, she decided it wiser to wait it out.

The clock ticked. The fire snapped. Cinders rose into the air like orange ghosts, disappearing in the black void beyond. Outside, the cowboys called to each other, and Pedro shuffled around the kitchen. Still Luke said nothing and didn't move.

Amanda started to get up, but one swift glance from Luke made her return to her seat like a scolded child. Frantic, she prepared several defenses, but without knowing precisely what part of the book he was angry about, she could do nothing except brace for an attack.

She was almost relieved when it came, and then horrified when it did. Casually, as if performing an everyday task, Luke picked up her book and tossed it into the fire. Amanda cried out, but flames engulfed the novel until only the hardback cover remained, and even that shriveled up, the yellow jacket becoming a dismal black.

Tears filled Amanda's enormous blue-green eyes, and she turned to Luke in outrage, but he rose and walked leisurely toward the fire, watching the book burn. When he turned to her, his voice was calm, betraying nothing.

"I'm leaving you."

Nothing in his demeanor matched what he was saying. Desperate, Amanda searched his face for some of the kind understanding she had come to expect from him, but there was nothing. She saw cynicism and disgust, but nothing else.

"Luke, you can't mean—"

"Yes, I mean exactly that." He continued, as if discussing the weather. "Amanda, I thought I could forgive you anything. That's how much I loved you. But I can't forgive this, nor forget. How the hell could you write all that, especially about us?"

Pale and trembling, she rose to her feet and came to stand beside him. Timidly, she placed a hand on his shoulder, then withdrew it when he looked at her as if he hated her. Taking a fortifying breath, she explained what she thought needed no explanation.

"Luke, I didn't know that you'd feel this way. I'm a writer, and I—"

"Dissect everyone's intimate life with a scalpel," Luke finished for her. Amanda fell into silence, aware that he was more than angry. Rage coupled with humiliation and pain played over his face, and he stared at her as if she was some kind of monster. "Amanda, how could you? How could you take something that was so beautiful and make it into nothing more than a piece of pulp fiction, that anyone with two bits could buy?"

"Luke, please—"

"No." He slammed his fist onto the mantle, scarlet suffusing his face. "And you even had to put that night into it, Amanda. Our first night together. Then tell the whole world that I didn't satisfy you. Every time I think of that, and see those words written on that page, unmistakably describing you, me, and our lovemaking—the private act between two people—I want to kill you with my bare hands. Do you understand?" He glared at her, his blue eyes blazing.

Amanda nodded, tears streaming down her face. "Luke, I never meant to hurt you."

"Well, you did." Picking up his hat, he strode toward the door, then stopped short. "You've got what you wanted, Amanda. I'm out of your life for good. The ranch is yours. I'll send a solicitor out to take care of the paperwork." His eyes raked over her, and Amanda wrapped her arms around herself as if for protection. "I hope you're damned happy."

Then he walked out. The wind rushed out of her lungs and Amanda fell to the floor in a sobbing heap.

"Sam, where are you going?" Honey asked as Haskwell emerged from the bath tub and began to dress. Normally, he waited until sundown to bathe and change into his good black trousers and snowy white shirt, but since he'd come to Waco, Sam had rarely left the hotel room. Now it was barely high noon, and Sam was combing back his slick black hair and applying shaving cream as if preparing for a night out on the town gambling.

"Why, I'd say that's none of your business, darlin'," Sam replied with a grin, watching her flinch at the endearment. "But seeing as you won't be around much longer anyway, I'll tell you. I'm about to finish my business here. Remember that woman I told you about—the writer who published that book about the shooting I did?" When Honey nodded, Sam rinsed his hands of the shaving cream and then took a seat, handing Honey the razor.

"Well, I've found her. Seems everyone in this town knows Fess Tyson. Had no trouble finding her at all."

Honey whisked away a dollop of shaving cream, then stared at the throat that was enticingly bared before her. Her fingers shaking, she removed the next half-inch of cream and whiskers, fighting to still the trembling in her fingers. "So are you going to kill her?"

"Yes, darlin'." Sam sighed, closing his eyes. "That's what this whole trip is about. But don't you fret none. Why, with that money you made the other night, I can buy you a damned nice funeral."

Her fingers trembled even more, and the razor slipped on Sam's slick neck. One black eye opened and bore into her, though his voice was deceptively kind.

"You aren't thinking about cutting me, now are you Honey? I could kill you nice and easy, or I can kill you slow. The Indians do that, you know. Tie a man to a stake, strip him naked, then pour honey all over him. Then they leave him to the ants. Ever see what happens to a man in that condition?" When Honey didn't reply, Haskwell finished the sentence. "He'd beg you to kill him. Now finish that shave."

Biting her lip, Honey forced down her terror and obeyed. When she completed the job, Haskwell stood up, then examined his face in the mirror. He wiped the excess cream from his chin with a towel, then tossed it over the brass rail of the bed and nodded with satisfaction.

"Good. You did a good job. And for that, I will reward you. See this gun?" He removed one of the ivory-handled pistols from his belt and handed it to her. "There's but one bullet left in it, darlin'. I'm leaving now, and the rest is up to you. You can either take your own life, or I'll do it for you when I get back. But remember this. The man with the Indians would have prayed to have this choice. Do you understand me?"

Tears fell from Honey's eyes, and she stared at the gun in her hand, felt the heavy weight of it and the gleam of ivory and tooled metal. "Please, Sam," she whispered. "I can't."

"The choice is yours, darlin'. Now I'll be back within a few hours. Think about it, and think hard."

With a grin, Haskwell closed the door and locked it behind him. Pocketing the key, he strode down the hall, whistling a tune, and wondering where he'd heard it before.

The answer occurred to him a few minutes later, when he'd reached the street. It was the song Honey had sung just the other night.

Damn, he would miss that girl.

Amanda dismounted from the wagon and pulled her bonnet more closely around her face. The morning sun blazed, but did nothing to warm her nor to lift her spirits. He was gone—as surely as the harsh cold winter followed summer, taking all of the lush green grass and crimson flowers with it. The baby moved within her, and she cradled it with her hand. She had been tempted to tell Luke the truth, but her wonderful mind stopped her. No, if Luke Parker didn't want her, then she and the baby would have to survive alone. She didn't want him out of pity or a sense of duty.

"It will be all right, senora." Pedro smiled brightly, trying to reassure her. "Senor Parker will come home. These things happen in a marriage."

He will never come back. Amanda knew that for certain.

The slight curve of her mouth faded as she recalled the expression on Luke's face. She'd never seen him so angry, not in any of the fights they'd had. Her book had hurt him in ways she'd never anticipated, and worse, she could do nothing about now.

As if somehow her mind had formed his image, Luke walked out of the Lone Star Hotel, shading his eyes from the sun. He carried his hat, and the sunlight played on his hair, making it appear as glossy and black as a raven's wing. Clad in buckskins, a rough white shirt, and a thick leather vest, he looked like the symbol of the frontier: rugged, handsome, and enduring. He felt her eyes on him, glanced in her direction, then put on his hat and crossed the street to the saloon as if he'd never seen her.

The hand Amanda had waved froze in the air. *Luke, how can I explain? I wrote about us not to hurt you or to make a fool of you. Falling in love with you was simply the most important event in my life. Why can't you see that?* But the saloon doors swung shut, leaving Amanda alone on the street with her thoughts.

"Come." Pedro saw the exchange and placed a kind hand on her arm. "We will buy the food for the evening meal. I will make you good tacos, *sí?* And some warm enchiladas. You should not stay out in the sun for too long."

Amanda obeyed, but her heart was breaking. How could Luke just walk away from her like that? Could she have meant so little to him that he could turn his back on her completely?

Mrs. Meade strode down the street toward the dress shop, her arms laden with packages. Amanda smiled in greeting, but the stout woman gave her one swift glacial glance, then hiked up her skirts and crossed to the other side of the street. Elvira followed, fanning herself as if she would faint right then and there. Mrs. Mitchell, who was congregating outside the shop with several friends, whispered something to another woman, then the two of them broke out into laughter. Hurt, Amanda stepped up to the porch of the general store, glad to be away from them and enveloped in the cool dark shade.

The whittlers stopped their activity on the porch, their knives gleaming, watching her with baleful eyes. Amanda had to step over their legs to the door. None of them moved or offered the briefest courtesy due a lady. As she closed the door behind her, she breathed a sigh of relief, but the men inside stopped talking, then one by one turned to stare at her as if she was some oddity thrown into their midst. Several looked her up and down with appraising eyes, while one of the bolder men chuckled.

"Isn't that Fess Tyson? Hey honey, you can write about me any time. What do you say we go home and create chapter thirteen?"

"Senor, I must ask you to stop that," Pedro protested. "Mrs. Parker is a lady, and should not have to listen to that kind of talk."

"Why not, she writes it? What do you say, Frank?"

The storekeeper glanced up from bagging an order, and gave Amanda an evil smirk. "I say she deserves everything that's coming to her. If it wasn't for Jake, she'd be run out of town."

The other men chuckled, then began to exchange more remarks. Mortified, Amanda whirled around and headed back outside. Her pregnancy made her feel weak and emotional, and with her heart breaking over Luke, she couldn't even respond to the townspeople's taunts.

"Where are you going, Fess Tyson?" one of the whittlers called. "Don't like your reception?"

"Watch what you say around her," his wrinkled companion said, "or you're liable to be in the next book. Anyone who prints how her old man screws would write anything."

Scarlet splashed her cheeks and Amanda got into the wagon, hearing their laughter, wanting to be a thousand miles from here. The Fess Tyson had gone from being the town heroine to the villain. And all it had taken was one little book.

•   •   •

The ride home felt like it took an eternity. Numb, Amanda sat in the wagon, her hands folded together, her skin thick with goosebumps. She had never been so openly rejected before, not even as a schoolgirl when she'd been the laughingstock of her family. She wanted Aesop, wanted her ink and her papers, wanted her books—

Wanted Luke.

The pain inside of her was so overwhelming, she could hardly hear Pedro's soft consolation.

"It will be all right, senora. The townspeople are just angry and surprised. It will die down and be forgotten. You will see."

Amanda nodded, though she had no confidence in any such prediction. "I know. I think I'll go upstairs now. You have this evening off, isn't that right?"

"*Sí*, every Thursday." Pedro smiled, then the light in his eyes dimmed. "But I think I should stay with you tonight. I do not wish for you to be alone."

"Don't be silly," Amanda reassured him. "I'll be fine. To tell you the truth, I'd rather be alone. I have a lot of thinking to do, and its always best to think in solitude. Someone said that, I just can't remember who."

Pedro watched her walk inside the house, her shoulders square, her head held high. Amanda Parker was a remarkable woman. Her just hoped her very uniqueness wouldn't cost her happiness.

The pearl-handled pistol gleamed from the table, promising relief and an end to this existence she'd been forced to endure for far too long. Honey stared at the gun, hugging her thin body, wondering if it wouldn't be better after all.

She'd done everything else she could think of to try and get away from this man. But somehow Sam always managed to be one step ahead of her. Like a spider, plotting endlessly, he seemed to delight in outwitting her, in torturing her not just sexually but emotionally. Drained of everything except the desire to escape, Honey picked up the gun and held it to her head.

The metal felt cool and quiet. It was so easy, so easy. All she had to do was pull the trigger. Her mother, a riverboat showgirl, had died from yellow fever long ago, and her father she'd never known. She wanted to be with her mother again, to feel safe and secure and sheltered from this monster of a man who'd made her life a holy hell.

Honey clamped her eyes closed and squeezed the trigger. The gun clicked emptily. Nothing happened. There was no loud explosion, no vast emptiness before the warmth, no death colored in her own red blood.

Mystified, she opened the chamber, peered inside, and saw that there was but one bullet. Apparently Sam intended for her to put the gun to her head and pull the trigger, not knowing whether or not the chamber was filled. She envisioned herself dead—the explosion, the blood she would never see—and then worse, the feeling that would result if the gun didn't go off. Horror sprang up inside of her, coupled with a new wash of hatred.

This man didn't deserve to live. He should die, not her. He was after another woman now, this Fess Tyson she'd heard him talk about. For a second, Honey experienced pleasure that it was another woman that frightened Sam so much, another woman who'd actually published something about him that could see him hanged. Fess Tyson, whoever that was, wasn't afraid. And Fess Tyson wouldn't take her own life.

Rising from the bed, Honey put the gun in her pocket and then walked toward the door. She reached for the doorknob and turned the shiny brass fixture. As she suspected, it was locked. Her strength long since gone, she contemplated the objects in the room, then her smile widened as she saw Sam's walking stick.

Using it as a knocker, she pounded on the door. At first, there was no response, then gradually, she heard foot steps in the hall.

"Yes, I am coming . . . "

"Please," Honey forced herself to call out. "I have locked

myself in the room. Isn't that silly? Could you open the door, please?"

The bellboy, young and inexperienced, did not hesitate. He took a skeleton key from his pocket, then fitted it inside the lock of room number seven. The door sprung open and an emaciated woman burst forth like a corpse released from a grave.

"Please, you've got to help me," Honey breathed, trying not to pass out. She gave the boy a quavery smile that lurched into more of a grimace. "I need to get outside."

"Aren't you the lady who sang for us?" the boy asked shyly.

Honey nodded quickly. "Yes. Will you help me?"

"Sure." The young boy took her arm, amazed at how fragile she seemed. Up close, Honey looked more like a starved fledgling than a lovely songbird. Her wrist was as thin as the spoke of a wagon wheel, but she was still beautiful. Stunned, the boy wrapped his fingers protectively over hers and took her across the street.

Honey sighed, the gun banging against her thigh. Perhaps the God she prayed to for so long was finally listening.

Luke waited until Amanda had left town before returning to the hotel. Fury engulfed him, coupled by a pain he never thought he'd ever feel because of her.

Damn her! And damn that book! Luke had drunk a full pint of whiskey just that morning, and even that couldn't drown the emotions that raged inside of him. How the hell could she do such a thing?

He winced as he thought of the other men chuckling behind his back, though none of them dared make a remark. One look at his gunman's stance and the weapon in his belt prevented that. Yet he knew what they were thinking, and to tell the truth, he didn't blame them.

It was Amanda who had done all this. Amanda, whom he'd let crawl inside of his skin, become a part of him, who then betrayed his innermost thoughts and feelings for all the world to see. It was ironic that he, who should value things like a reputation and respect, should find himself the target of scorn because of his wife.

He wanted to kill her. Yet he also missed her with an intensity that he never would have guessed. He glanced around his immaculate hotel room, and found no owl droppings, no scrawled copies of the latest scientific theories, no open books in every room, enticing the eye with thoughts and dreams that no one but Amanda could share. It was infuriating, but at the same time revealing. He still loved her, in spite of himself.

But he wasn't able to get past the rage he felt. Tossing his hat down in disgust, he turned around and headed back to the lobby, passing a young bellboy and a lovely woman who looked vaguely familiar. Pausing on the step, Luke watched them hurry outside.

Something nagged at the back of his mind, something important, but he was too preoccupied to make sense of it all.

Chapter

❧ 27 ❧

The house was quiet when Amanda finally came downstairs, carrying Aesop in his cage. The little owl became very active at night, and although sometimes his nocturnal movements were annoying, this evening they provided comfort. Amanda sat the cage beside her in the parlor and smiled at the sight of the tray Pedro had left for her.

She lifted one of the silver dish covers, her stomach revolting at the sight of food. She was too distraught to eat, but the servant's thoughtfulness warmed her. She experienced so little kindness in the last day that even this small gesture touched her.

Aesop rustled uneasily and Amanda opened the cage, allowing the little bird to step out of the gold wires. Fluttering awkwardly, he perched on the mantle nearby, returning her stare, communicating the way he always had.

"Aesop, why do I have brains for everything except what's important?"

The owl blinked, reassuring her, but even Aesop's unqualified friendship didn't help much tonight. Amanda felt drained, tired and lonely, and the ache inside of her couldn't be easily appeased.

The curtain fluttered, and the shutter banged against the

house. *That's odd,* she thought, rising to fasten it closed. *Pedro always checks the windows and doors, especially before his day off.* Shrugging, she reached outside through the light film of lace, then stifled a scream as a hand clamped over her mouth.

"That's right, we don't want any shoutin'. You are alone anyway, aren't you darlin'?"

The Irish brogue meant nothing to her, nor did the appearance of the man as he dragged her back into the parlor. Amanda saw his dark, handsome looks, his polished white shirt, his winning smile. But his eyes frightened her more than even the gun he openly displayed. They were blank, soulless, without warmth, feeling, or emotion. They were the eyes of a goat, and it was horrifying to see them in a man.

"You don't know me, darlin', but I know you. You're a writer—Fess Tyson they tell me. I remember you from a long time ago, when I shot that fool Haines. Too bad you took it in your head to write all about it and get the damned thing printed."

"I don't know what you're talking about—" Amanda started.

"I think you do," he continued, smiling pleasantly. "I sent my men after you, but you managed to stay one step ahead of them. Nearly got you on the prairie, then that damned stampede killed one of them. You didn't think I would just give up, did you?"

Haskwell. Amanda's eyes widened and she stared in helpless terror at the man who had hunted her for so long. He was exactly as she would have pictured him, and that only made the whole thing worse. Her eyes closed and she felt the baby's light movements inside of her. If only she hadn't upset Luke, if only he was there, and she wasn't alone. . . .

"There now, I can see that you do remember. You're a talented lady, Miss Tyson. Too bad I have to kill you. But I really don't have any choice, now do I? With what you know, you could see me hanged. It must have tickled you to know this all these years, and to know that I couldn't rest until we came to this. Sounds like something I would do."

"You're wrong," Amanda whispered, regaining her voice. "I never saw any gunfight. I write them from here." She pointed to her head.

Haskwell grinned. "Sure you do, darlin'. Sure you do. Now you can go ahead and scream your head off. No one will hear you. The cowhands are long since bedded down, and that Mex servant of yours left you alone. Even his kid is asleep for the night. Fact, you're about as helpless as that broken winged bird."

Haskwell lifted his gun, his one arm still tight around Amanda, and pointed it at Aesop.

Her scream died when the gun went off, and a solitary feather drifted down to the floor.

Luke stared at the door, wondering why the sight of that woman kept bothering him. He'd seen her somewhere before. His mind retraced her glossy black hair, her tremulous smile, her voice, light and pretty as she talked to the bellboy. . . .

Her voice. It was the woman who'd sung for them at the hotel just last night. Luke hadn't paid her much attention, he was so involved with Amanda, but he could recall her on that stage, dressed in a flimsy gown and singing with a voice that must have once been wonderful. She had appeared ill, her complexion ashen, and her manner nervous even on stage.

Why was this nagging at him? He went over it again and again. She was the singer and that was the end of it. He'd never seen the woman before in his life, and she didn't mean anything to him.

Why was he so haunted by her appearance?

Amanda screamed, then stifled her cry with her hands. Aesop lay in a pile of feathers on top of the mantle, his little body barely moving. Painfully, he crept to the corner of the mantle, alive but obviously hurt. Horrified, she glared at the man who held her captive. Hatred began to build inside of her, and she tried to wrench away, earning only slightly more freedom as Haskwell held her tightly.

"Why would you do such a thing? He was just a little owl, he never hurt anyone. How could you—"

"Shut up," Haskwell snapped, disturbed at her open defiance. "You're going to join him, darlin'. Don't you understand that? You made me track you from one end of the West to the other. You need to pay for that." He grinned.

Amanda suddenly understood him, that this was part of his motivation, the compelling helplessness of his victim. Frantically, she realized she had to think of something and quickly. This man would enjoy killing her. Somehow, she had to change that.

"Please don't hurt me." Amanda tried to make her voice sound pleading. "I won't say anything. I swear."

"I know you won't." Sam grinned, relaxing his hold on her. "You won't because I'm not going to let you live. I've waited a long time for this pleasure, and I'm not denying myself any of it." He caressed the gun, watching her expression with a smirk of pleasure. "You know, darlin'? There's one thing that's been bothering me all this time. Why didn't you come forth and testify? You had to know I'd be after you either way."

Amanda moistened her lips, her eyes wide. What was he talking about? She remembered his accusations when he'd first grabbed her—that she had been the woman who'd witnessed his shooting of Haines . . . suddenly, she knew she'd been right. This Haskwell must have taken it into his head that she had actually seen a murder he committed.

"I . . . didn't want to get involved." Amanda tried to sound terrorized while her mind worked. "I was afraid."

"Smart," Haskwell said. "But not smart enough. You should have kept that little secret to yourself instead of publicizin' it for all the world to see. As it is, you give me no choice." He cocked the gun.

Amanda closed her eyes. For once, she had run out of ideas. And, it seemed, time.

• • •

Showgirl. The word snapped to life in Luke's mind and it suddenly all came together. Haskwell had a showgirl with him—a woman he'd been dragging from Kansas. And this woman certainly bore all the signs of abuse, from her trembling hands to her sad, sweet voice. And if this was the case, and the woman had escaped, it could only mean one thing.

Haskwell was out alone.

Luke sprang out of the chair, horror suddenly filling him. He'd been so outraged by Amanda's book that he'd put aside the very real threat of the outlaw. And with him gone, Amanda was like a sitting duck should Haskwell go after her.

His heart pounding, Luke ran out the door, grateful that he'd just cleaned his gun that morning. He had a feeling he was going to need it.

"Now sit down on that sofa there, real quiet like." Sam grinned as Amanda obeyed, her eyes straying to Aesop. She couldn't tend to him now, couldn't let her mind be distracted. She had to think clearly, for if she didn't, it could easily mean her life.

"Good, that's good." Haskwell nodded, noticing for the first time this woman's unusual beauty. Even dressed for bed in a soft nightgown, her hair unbound, she possessed an exotic quality that was as enticing as it was disturbing. It was too bad he'd have to kill her. "You got any prayers to say, darlin', do it now. I've five bullets in this gun, and every one of them is going into your hide."

Amanda stared into the eye of the gun. She'd lost everything in the last twenty-four hours. Suddenly, her life didn't mean all that much, but when she thought of the baby—

He came closer. Three inches. Two. Then one. She could feel the cool metal pressing against her breast and she closed her eyes, thinking of Luke, of what she'd tell him if he was here. . . .

It all happened so quickly that she'd remember it later like a blur—a bad dream gone berserk. A gun exploded, but instead of feeling pain inside of her, she felt nothing but a jolt. Her eyes opened, and she saw the gun fall from Haskwell's hand, saw him grab his wrist as if in pain. Blood was everywhere. Haskwell's hand dripped with spidery red webs; it smeared the carpet and ran on the floor. Amanda looked up in shock, unable to make sense of it all, and saw Luke. Relief flooded through her. He'd come for her, like he always did.

"Luke, he's going to kill me, he—"

"Amanda, get the hell down!" Luke's face was contorted with emotion, so much so she hardly recognized him. But she recalled that note in his voice and instinctively obeyed. Dodging behind the sofa, she heard rather than saw Haskwell scramble for his gun.

"Give it up, Haskwell," Luke warned. He cocked his gun for a second shot.

Haskwell managed to grab hold of the weapon. Instead of firing, he surprised Luke and lunged forward, knocking the gunslinger off balance. Luke recovered quickly, but not soon enough. Haskwell crawled like a vermin out of his path, and within seconds, he had Amanda once more. Panting triumphantly, one arm wrapped around her waist, he pressed the gun to her head.

"You sonofabitch," Luke said in frustration. He wanted to kill the despicable outlaw, but the man held Amanda. "Let her go."

"I'll kill her now, laddie." Haskwell's brogue deepened. "Either you get out of the way or she's dead."

"Don't listen to him, Luke," Amanda sobbed. "You can't let him get away. He'll kill someone else."

Haskwell dragged Amanda to her feet. Blood ushered forth from his gun hand, but at this close a range he could shoot just as well, and they all knew it. He backed up to the window, his face pale, but his eyes were still sharp and focused.

"It's me or her, lad. Either you let me go, or I'll kill her."

Rage shot through Luke, but he couldn't let him kill Amanda. Slowly, he lowered the gun, fighting the urge to shoot. But he couldn't risk it. If he missed or if Haskwell responded quickly enough, Amanda would die.

Haskwell stepped through the window, releasing Amanda so suddenly that she tumbled forth, her nightdress stained from his blood. In that instant, he fired, trying to kill Amanda, but Luke returned the shots. The stillness was broken by a howl of pain. Hopeful, Luke scrambled to the window, but Haskwell had already mounted his horse and disappeared into the night. The outlaw was gone.

The taste of whiskey burned Honey's tongue, but it felt so good. It numbed the pain inside of her that had grown to such a constant throb that she noticed only its absence. And now, when the liquor anesthetized the ache, she found she could actually smile.

She was free. God, she was free. Lifting a fourth amber glass to her lips, she downed the whiskey, delighting in the heady, hot sensation. She put the shot glass down, then breathed in the smoke-filled air of the saloon, a smell that seemed as wonderful to her as the scent of a fragrant meadow.

"Better take it easy there, doll." The barkeeper warned. "That's ninety-proof rot gut. It'll eat a hole right through you."

"I don't care." Honey smiled. "Barkeep, did you ever wish for just one thing, and wish it for so long that it almost seems like it happened?"

"Yes." He stopped polishing a glass and placed it on the edge of the bar, giving her a speculative glance. "Now what could a pretty lady like you want that she doesn't already have?"

Honey grinned drunkenly. There was an odd look in her eyes, and the barkeep moved the whiskey bottle away from her.

"I think you've had enough. Maybe you should wander on home."

"I can't." Honey shrugged, nearly tumbling from the bar-stool. "I've got something to take care of." She slid to the

floor, then walked slowly across the room in the precise way
of the inebriated. She stopped by the seat of a randy cowboy,
teasingly ruffled his hair, then spoke in a low, exotic whisper.

"Give me a bullet and I'll sing you a song."

The cowboy obeyed, handing her a fistful of ammunition.
Honey pocketed the bullets, then crooned to him as she
sauntered out the door. The barkeep shook his head, then
resumed polishing his glasses.

She ventured out into the night, and stood in the middle
of the road, admiring the stars and the bright, full moon.
They looked so lovely up there in the sky, she thought. It
had been so long since she could admire a moon, or see the
night sky without being afraid. . . .

A horse whickered as she stepped inside the barn. It was
dark here, with no starlight. Sitting on an empty barrel just
past the entrance, she could see the stableboy sleeping above
her and the doorway framed by black velvet.

He returned just as she knew he would, leading his own
horse quietly into the stall. He would be going now, returning to his room for his clothes and other personal belongings, and to see to her. Honey had to suppress a giggle. He
wouldn't find her dead—no, not this time.

"What was that?" Haskwell's brogue rang out in the stable as he glanced up, his senses as acute as an insect's an-
tenna. His eyes widened with shock as he saw her, walking
slowly toward him. He could smell the whiskey, but saw
no intoxication in her eyes, no drunkenness, nothing but a
deadly purpose. He tried to smile.

"It's you, darlin'. I thought—"

It was as far as he got. Honey aimed the gun at his crotch
and pulled the trigger. Blood spattered his pants in a thick
red stain. Haskwell's face went dead white and he grabbed
himself in shock and pain, while a scream ripped from his
mouth. Another bullet entered his head, effectively silencing
him. He fell to the hay, those horrible black eyes forever
stilled, his gun falling impotently to the stable floor.

Honey dropped the matching gun. She didn't need it now;

she never would again. She saw the terrified stableboy rush out for the sheriff, but that didn't trouble her either.

There wasn't a judge in the world who would convict her.

Amanda collapsed to the sofa as Haskwell disappeared. Relief washed through her—overwhelming relief and gratitude. Haskwell hadn't hurt either herself or Luke. He was gone, true, but there was time now to call the sheriff. They'd had a narrow escape, but somehow had been given a second chance.

Luke's face with tight with anger. "I thought I told you not to be alone." His harsh voice startled her in the silence, and Amanda struggled to come up with the right reply.

"I know. But Pedro had the night off, and I didn't think—"

"Dammit! For someone with so much brains, why is it you never think? Where is Juan? Why didn't you ask Aileen—" He stopped short at the sight of Aesop's little body, his good wing crushed by a bullet. "Oh my God, what happened to him?"

"Haskwell," Amanda answered, accepting the little bird from him. "He shot him."

Luke's face darkened and he turned quickly toward the door, flung it open and shouted for Juan. The stableboy appeared, yawning sleepily. He stopped in surprise as he saw Luke's face and he rushed forward, nearly tripping over his feet.

"Senor? Is something wrong? I heard shots . . . "

"Go to the next ranch and ask Jake and his wife to come out here. Now."

Juan didn't wait to question further, but ran across the yard to do his bidding.

They waited in silence until the neighbors came. Amanda sat alone on the couch, binding up Aesop's wing and feeling as if everything inside of her was breaking into little bits. She'd been wrong about Luke, wrong about everything. He hadn't forgiven her for writing the book, she could tell by the way he looked at her—*right through her,* she corrected her thoughts. And now, he'd had to walk away from the quest which had taken up much of his life to save her. It must have been ignominious for him to let the outlaw walk, and he could only resent her even more.

He stood at the window, his back to her, his shoulders broad and tight. With more feeling than she'd ever experienced before, Amanda wanted to go to him, put her arms around him, and try to explain why she did what she did. Couldn't he understand that she hadn't meant to hurt him, that she thought she had been honoring him, immortalizing the most important event in her life, by writing about him? Instinctively she knew he'd never understand, and she had no words to explain. She was too torn up herself, her nerves too shaken.

Jake and Aileen arrived a few minutes later. The Irish woman rushed to Amanda's side while Luke spoke quietly with Jake, explaining what had happened. Jake agreed to stay with Amanda while Luke summoned the sheriff and assembled a posse. Without a word to her, he left, cradling his gun as if aching to shoot.

Somehow, she'd have to get him back.

Chapter

28

Word came back in less than an hour about Haskwell's death. When one of the *vaqueros* rode up and informed Jake, Amanda relaxed for the first time in weeks. Haskwell would never hurt her, not now or at any time in the future.

"It's good news, Amanda," Jake said quietly, closing the door behind the cowhand while Aileen bustled to the kitchen to brew tea. "As long as Haskwell was free, you would have never known peace. Maybe now Luke can go on with his life."

Amanda nodded, hand-feeding Aesop from an eyedropper, pleased when the injured little bird accepted her offering. "Luke is free to go on with his life, with or without me," Amanda said softly.

"He'll come back," Jake reassured her, but he had his own doubts. Luke was a private person, not given to emotional displays. Whatever had happened between him and Amanda had cut him deeply, enough to make him leave the ranch. Jake wasn't one hundred percent sure what had done it, but he had a good idea.

Apparently, so did Amanda. "No, not after *Passion's Price*. I don't think he'll ever forgive that."

"Amanda, Luke's pride is hurt. Give him time, I'm sure he'll come around," Jake reassured her.

Amanda gave Jake a look that Luke would have instantly recognized. "There is no guarantee of that, especially now. I've made a fool of him with the book, thwarted him in every way imaginable, and stopped him from killing the one man he hated. That's an awful lot to forgive."

"Maybe you should help things out a bit," Jake suggested. "I know it would be hard, but maybe he needs reassurance. It couldn't hurt to let him know how you feel."

"I couldn't. He wouldn't—"

"You don't look like the kind of woman who would just give up," Jake interrupted. "You let him know quick enough when you didn't want him. I'm sure you can think of a way to do the opposite."

Amanda nodded. It made sense. And after all, she thought, absently petting Aesop, what did she have to lose?

The whiskey bottle was already diminished by one quarter as Luke refilled his glass, pouring slowly and steadily. He could hear the flow of conversation around him about the outlaw and a dark-haired showgirl named Honey who had quietly waited for the sheriff to arrive, then giggled outrageously when they carried out the bleeding body of Sam Haskwell. Honey was with the doctor now, being treated for shock, and Haskwell was covered with a sheet on the front desk in the sheriff's office.

Damn! Luke pounded his fist on the bar, ignored by the men around him. Haskwell was dead, he was glad about that. But he hadn't gotten the satisfaction of killing the man himself. All these years he'd waited until the right opportunity, followed the slug from Virginia to Dodge City, Abilene, and now Texas, only to have to let him go.

He'd hadn't any other choice. Haskwell would have killed Amanda with no more compunction than stepping on an ant. He couldn't have let Amanda die, yet the frustration ate at him like a bitter acid. The killer of his mother and sister lay less than fifteen feet from where he sat. . . .

God, how he missed them. For the first time since their deaths, he allowed himself to grieve. He poured over the thousand memories buried in his mind like a living binder of photographs. Suzette, laughing at him when he tried to jump the gate with the old walker. Suzette teasing him when he was sixteen, slicking back his hair for a dance, shredding his adolescent conceit. Suzette as a little girl, trustingly putting her hand inside his coat pocket for warmth and obediently following him to school, knowing that her big brother would always take care of her.

He removed the locket from the chain around his neck, heating the metal within his fingers, and he opened it once more. The calm, sweet face of his mother stared out at him, framed in silver. Somehow he knew that she would have loved Amanda, would have whole-heartedly approved of his decision not to waste another human life over something as petty as revenge. Tears came to his eyes, and he viciously blinked them back as he pictured his mother meeting his wife—a scene that would never happen. But Amanda, with her theories and book learning, her skewed way of seeing the world, would have fascinated Lillian Parker and would have reassured Suzette, who always thought women came too easy for him.

And now Amanda was gone too. Luke snapped the locket shut. He'd cut his wife to the quick. She'd never forgive him for attacking her in the most personal, private way he could—through her books. Now that the initial shock had passed, he could recall some of it, and once more found it wonderful. The first love scene made him see red, but the second and the rest were beautiful—flowing with all the passion of a woman in love. Amanda wrote without Victorian sentimentality, but her work was so much more powerful as a result. Every line glimmered with longing, and if he only hadn't overreacted, he might have been able to turn that longing into reality.

". . . *and then he touched me, and every cell in my body cried out for him. Colors began in my mind, bright webs of*

*gold, scarlet, and amethyst, tangling up my thoughts, making
me aware that nothing really mattered but him . . . "*

Luke drank down the harsh whiskey. *No, nothing really
matters now, Amanda. Nothing at all.*

Saturday was the night of the Woman's Committee
Christmas Ball. Everyone was going, from the mayor to the
vaqueros. The Woman's Committee had decided on red and
green, and had spent the week in a fervor, making sure that
the Lone Star Hotel had enough wine, food, and music to
ensure the evening's success.

Amanda stood in front of the mirror, eyeing herself critically. Although she dreaded going, she knew she didn't have
a choice. With every day that passed, she and Luke grew
farther apart. She hadn't seen him since that horrible night
when Haskwell had tried to kill her, but she knew that instead of making the heart grow fonder, distance was solidi-
fying the end of their relationship. That night in the parlor
he'd shown her what she meant to him. She had to act now,
while the feeling was still strong.

"Amanda, are you sure you want to do this?" Aileen
pulled the laces tighter, while Amanda sucked in her breath.
The corset shaped her figure to a perfect hourglass, making
her body more womanly. Her legs, encased in shimmering
black silk stockings, were held up with black lace garters
trimmed in red, while a glossy red plume danced from her
head like a fiery lance.

"I don't have any other choice. Luke won't answer the
messages I've sent him, and he's conveniently absent whenever I go to the hotel. This is my last chance." Amanda
gasped for breath, but the corset was made of whalebone
and would not give. Accepting the gown that Aileen handed
to her, she slipped it over her head, tugging it into place as
it settled slickly around her body. "It's perfect. Where did
you get it?"

"Lacey's," Aileen said. "She was making it for a saloon
girl."

"Are you sure this is all there is?" Amanda tried to pull

up the gown in front, but the dress settled obstinately back into place, revealing a generous quantity of skin.

"That's it," Aileen said dryly. "You're a little more well-endowed than the saloon girl."

Amanda stared back at the mirror, unable to believe that the reflection was her own. The dress she wore was scarlet, and not a subdued shade at that. Dipping shockingly low in the front, the satin gown was gathered into a full bustle in the back, then pulled up on the side to reveal a shapely leg. Red rouge dotted her cheekbones, looking stark and out of place on Amanda's naturally pretty complexion, and black kohl rimmed her eyes. She looked seductive, enticing, and experienced—like a high-priced harlot.

"It's perfect," Amanda said happily. "When Luke sees this, he'll forget all about being angry with me."

"But do you really think he'll want to see his wife wearing this, at the party in front of everyone?" Aileen asked doubtfully. "He seems on the conservative side."

"He won't believe his eyes," Amanda sighed. "I've given it a lot of thought, and done my research." She indicated a thick pad of scrawled notes. "Every time I've gone to a new town or a saloon, I've observed the way men behave in the presence of a woman dressed like this. Men are completely visual, you know. They are aroused by what they see, unlike women who are aroused in more complex ways. Therefore, if I dress the same way and act the same way, I'll seduce him into coming back!"

She looked as pleased as a child who had handed in a brilliant science project. She tried to turn, and nearly fell as the dress wrapped its silken length around her legs. Her feet, bound in little gold slippers, tripped on the polished floor. Aileen held her breath as Amanda's full breasts nearly spilled out and her plume wobbled precariously. The dubious expression on Aileen's face increased, especially when Amanda hiked up the gown and maintained her balance with the help of a chair.

"I don't know." Aileen tried another approach. "I

thought you didn't approve of dressing up in corsets and such."

"I still don't believe in that," Amanda said confidently. "But I don't have any choice right now. I've got to get his attention and time is running out." She picked up a gold-beaded bag that matched her slippers, and stopped only long enough to smear bright red lipstick on her full little mouth with an obviously unpracticed hand. "Let's go. I can't wait to see his face."

Aileen nodded. It was true—when she worked in a saloon, the men went wild for this stuff. But somehow, Amanda would never pass for a saloon girl, Aileen thought. She followed her out the door, cringing as the author tripped over the hemline of her tight gown.

The ballroom was filled with elegantly dressed men and beautifully gowned women. They moved beneath the crystal chandeliers like animated Christmas ornaments in vivid hues of crimson, emerald, and sapphire. Mrs. Mitchell had won the argument about the colors, and the entire ballroom was bedecked with festive green and red satin ribbons and streamers. Violinists quietly warmed up in the corner, while waiters carried trays of champagne, handing tulip-shaped glasses of the golden liquid to anyone who cared to drink.

Amanda entered the room with Jake and Aileen, keeping her coat on and bracing herself for a wave of cold animosity. To her surprise, Jed Brannigan strode up, his face beaming.

"Amanda Parker! So glad you could come. I was just asking Elvira about you the other day." His expression changed to puzzlement as he saw her made-up face, but he resumed his smile.

Amanda glanced at Aileen, but the Irish woman shrugged. "I thought you were all angry with me," Amanda said.

"Oh, maybe a little at first." Jed chuckled, then was joined by several of the other townspeople. He lifted glasses of champagne from the tray and handed them to Aileen and Jake, while Amanda declined. "But we've gotten used to it.

In fact, your little book seems to be spelling quite a profit for Waco. Newcomers have been flooding in during the last few weeks, increasing business across the board, and it can only get better. Everyone's talking about how you eluded Sam Haskwell, and how he finally got his. The woman got off, you know. Yes, it looks like you've put Waco on the map."

Amanda stared in disbelief, but Simon Ledden extended his hand and pumped hers heartily. Frank Mitchell nodded to her. Mrs. Meade detached herself from a crowd of people and rushed to join them.

"There you are, Amanda. You must come and meet everyone. Several new ladies want to join the Woman's Committee, and they've heard all about you. I told them about the corset burning, and they are captivated. Eastern, you know." Mrs. Meade puffed with an air of knowledge and dragged Amanda off toward the women.

Amanda held onto the collar of her coat, keeping it firmly closed, not wanting to reveal the dress until she saw Luke. Everywhere she looked she saw smiling faces. People that wouldn't walk the same side of the street as her a week ago were now coming up and shaking her hand as if she were a long-lost friend. It was all like a dream, one that took way too long in coming.

She was standing with several of the cowhands when she saw him. Her water glass was paused halfway to her lips and she froze when she observed him handing the servant his overcoat. He looked breathtakingly handsome, his white shirt like the purest snow against the raven black of his coat. His hair glistened in the gaslight, shining blue-black, while his muscular body moved with an animal-like grace that was apparent in spite of his dress clothes. He turned to someone behind him, and Amanda's stomach lurched as she saw a woman enter, laugh lightly at something he said, and then obligingly take his arm.

He wasn't alone. He'd brought someone with him. Her heart pounding in her ear, Amanda felt a wash of overwhelming, sickening jealousy. She recognized the woman as the daughter of the dressmaker, Sally Lacey, a gorgeous blond who cared very little about science, politics, or penny dreadfuls. Sally was dressed in a gorgeous turquoise gown, and she could dance beautifully, flirt outrageously, and sing sweetly. In short, she was everything Amanda was not.

"Are you all right, senora?" one of the *vaqueros* questioned and Amanda nodded quickly, feeling the color drain from her face.

"Yes, fine. Rafael, would you mind taking my coat?" She turned a brilliant smile on him and the cowhand nodded eagerly, accepting the woolen wrap. When he saw what lay beneath it, he gave a loud wolf whistle.

"*Muy bonita,* senora! What a dress! Miguel and Tomas, did you see this?"

The cowhands began cheering and clapping, while Amanda smiled, gratified. It was working. It really *was* easy, like addition, she thought. All one had to do was know how to calculate, and one could figure out just about anything with men.

Smiling, she accepted a finger sandwich, then giggled outrageously at a joke the cowboys made. She remembered everything she'd ever written about saloon girls and showgirls, and she practised it shamelessly. It was ridiculous, but all she had to do was look wide-eyed and laugh at everything they said, and she was a success.

"Would you like some punch, senora?" Raphael offered.

Amanda glanced across the room and saw Luke talking with the mayor and several other men, with Sally draped on his arm. Jealousy ripped through her, but she managed to decline politely. "No, I'll get it if you don't mind." She wobbled across the room, fighting her dress, the corset, and the slippers.

Being a seductress wasn't as easy as she thought. Amanda noticed the sudden silence of the townsmen around her, the inappropriate stares, and the appraising looks they gave her, as if she was a horse at auction. Several grinned in frank invitation, their eyes dropping to her bustline that seemed to hold up the tiny slip of red satin as if by magic. In spite of the outlandish outfit, she looked beautiful, and every man let her know it with his eyes.

The women were less kind. They stared in disbelief as the prim and talented authoress paraded before them in garb a showgirl would blush to wear, and they whispered among themselves. The dress swished obligingly, revealing Amanda's black-stockinged leg, and Elvira dashed down a glass of champagne.

"Dear God, what is she up to now?"

Frank Mitchell heard the whispers, then nudged Luke, who was standing beside him.

"I think you'd better see to your wife."

Luke turned quickly, then stared in shock as Amanda accepted a glass of punch from the waiter, then giggled ridiculously as Simon Ledden fought to hand it to her first. Cowboys vied for her attention, each one claiming the first dance, while the townsmen, recovering from their surprise, tried to free themselves of their more proper guests to stand by her side. The feather slipped from her head as she laughed at a joke she couldn't possibly understand, and when she reached up to adjust it, a dozen male eyes went to her breasts.

"Excuse me." Luke handed his glass to Sally Lacey without explanation. The pretty blonde pouted as he made his way through the crowd, his expression murderous. The townspeople parted like the Red Sea as Luke strode quickly across the room.

He could hear her laughter long before he got to her, and saw her bat her eyes in a blatant imitation of every whore she'd ever seen. Growing more furious with each step, Luke blushed for her as she slapped a cowboy lightly with her handkerchief, then giggled once more. He could hear her talking as she approached, and if he didn't know it was Amanda, he'd never have believed it.

"Goodness, you all flatter me. Why, this little old dress is just something I picked up!" Black-rimmed eyes fluttered. "But you can explain it all to me, I'm sure you're so much smarter!"

Luke could have died at that. He heard the cowboys' laughter, and he burned furiously. One by one he plucked the *vaqueros* away from her, then strode to the center of the men. When he did, his anger increased two hundred percent.

The dress was worse than he thought. Close, he could see every part of her body clearly outlined by the accomodating red material. Her breasts jutted forth and he longed to cup them. Her waist was so small that his hands could easily fit around it. Her belly, a bit rounder than he remembered, was still slender and led enticingly down to a wash of softly draped satin. The smile died on her red-rouged cheeks when she saw his expression, and she gasped as his hand closed tightly over hers.

"You'll have to excuse my wife. She hasn't been herself lately and is suddenly quite ill."

The men protested, and Amanda struggled. Something was wrong. She'd done all this for him, dressed this way to seduce him, and now he was looking at her as if he hated her. Desperately, she tried to stop him.

"But I don't feel ill at all! Why, I'm having the best time! These sweet cowboys are telling me all about roping a steer, and I don't know the first thing about that!"

"Yeah, let her alone," one of the cowboys interrupted. "If the lady wants to stay, she stays."

"Amanda," Luke said through gritted teeth, and she knew she was in deep trouble. "Come with me."

"I don't think she wants to," another cowboy stated. "So why don't you just mosey on back to that dame you're with?"

Without hesitation, Luke's fist came up and cracked the man hard across his face. The cowboy slumped to the floor, clutching his nose, blood trickling from the punch. His companion started for Luke, but the sight of his gunbelt stopped him, especially when Luke shoved back his jacket as if to draw.

No one else openly challenged him. Amanda struggled, but Luke dragged her effortlessly across the ballroom to the lobby. He produced a folded bill and handed it to the bell-boy.

"Get her carriage. Now."

"Luke, please. Let me explain." Amanda tried to penetrate his wall of anger, but when he turned to her, his eyes blazing, she withered beneath that condemning stare.

"Why? Haven't you had enough, making a fool of both yourself and me? Why do you keep doing this?" Luke blazed.

Amanda's eyes filled, and she suddenly knew he was right. Those men weren't laughing with her, they had been laughing *at* her. She had thought she was being seductive and exotic, and all she had been was ridiculous. Her pride burned, but worse, it hadn't even accomplished what she'd intended.

Tears streamed down her face, making little rivers of black kohl. The bellboy would return any minute. She had to make Luke understand, and yet, as he stood beside her, as implacable as granite, she had no idea of how to start.

"Luke, please," she whispered brokenly. "You once said you loved me. Don't you understand why I did this?"

"All I know is that for some reason, you are trying to drive me insane." But he softened at the stricken look on her face, some of the anger leaving him. "All right, Amanda. You have about five minutes before he gets here with the coach. Make it good."

Five minutes. Amanda sighed. She could do it in one. Suddenly sure of herself, she lifted her make-up streaked face to his. "I love you."

Luke looked as if she'd struck him. A sneer played over his lips as he scanned her up and down, noting the dress, mocking her with his eyes. But doubt followed, then the briefest flash of longing. It was that Amanda appealed to, and she struggled to find the right words.

"Why else would I have done this? I only thought I could . . . seduce you into wanting me."

He stared at her, seeing the puzzle pieces fall into place. With another woman, he would never have bought it, but this was Amanda. And to Amanda's logical mind, to dress like a harlot, flirt, and act like a simpering fool, was obviously the fastest way to a man's groin.

He couldn't help it. Though he wanted desperately to be angry, the fury faded, only to be replaced by a swelling, unstoppable laughter. Amanda stamped her foot indignantly as he threw back his head and roared, his chuckle deep and masculine.

"What is so funny?" she demanded, mortified.

"Nothing." He forced himself to stop, but every time he looked at the dress, at the ostrich feather bobbing on her head, at the make-up that was now like a smeared watercolor, he resumed laughing, until finally he regained control. She started to walk away, hurt more than ever, but he stopped her, bringing her back into his embrace. Luke cupped her chin, making her look up at him. His blue eyes were filled with laughter, and something tender, akin to understanding.

"Amanda, all I can say is, if you're going to put half the effort into winning me back as you did trying to get rid of me, I'm surrendering now." He turned to the bellboy.

"Take her to the carriage and wait for me. I have some explaining to do to another young lady." Wrapping his jacket around Amanda, he ignored her indignant expression, then continued more seriously. "Amanda Edison, you are definitely an original."

His mouth sought hers, and she returned his kiss, stepping up on the tips of her gold slippers to wrap her arms around him. Embarrassment, outrage, and fear all dissipated, followed by a warm, wonderful glow.

She'd won, although her methods might be questionable. And no one could have been happier.

The sun rose up high above Waco, lending a soft rosy blush to the grasslands and bathing the ranch in a shimmery gold. Amanda awoke in Luke's bedroom, her own blush matching the dawn as she found him seated across from her in a chair with a cup of coffee at his arm, watching her with a suppressed amusement.

"You going to sleep all day? You saloon girls don't have much stamina, do you?"

Amanda covered her head with the sheets, then peeped out a moment later when she heard him chuckling. "I was awful, wasn't I?" she asked.

"Yes." Luke couldn't deny that. "But I have to admit, that's part of your charm."

"Luke, I promise I'll make you happy. I won't write again, if that's what you want, and I won't quote dead philopsophers—"

"Amanda." He sat next to her, bringing her an offering of fresh hot coffee, and put one finger to her lips. "Don't you realize that I love everything about you? I knew you were different from the first. And I wouldn't dream of asking you not to work. Just give me fair warning next time, when you decide to publicize my failures as a lover."

"That wasn't your failure!" Amanda sat up, astonished. "It was mine! I just didn't know—"

"Let's not argue the point." Luke grinned. "And don't concern yourself. I have more guts than I've displayed lately. If you want to write about me, Amanda, frankly, I'm flattered."

Her smile grew brilliant and she hugged him, oblivious to the sheet that fell from her, exposing her breasts tipped with dusky pink and her smooth white shoulders. Luke's eyes warmed and he tipped her face up to his, taking her with a kiss.

Amanda sighed, drawing him down into her embrace. God, it had all been worth it. She'd humiliated herself, but none of that meant a damn. She had him, and that was all that mattered.

"You know, Amanda?" Luke pushed the rest of the sheet out of the way and began to caress her, loving the way she responded unashamedly, unlike any other woman he'd ever known. "There's one thing I can't figure out. Why didn't you just tell me you were pregnant? I would have come right back." He traced the round fullness of her belly, then looked up at her, his blue eyes warm and tender.

Amanda stared at him in surprise. "I don't know. I figured that I drove you away, and that it was up to me to get you back. I wouldn't think of using a child like that."

Luke started to laugh, unable to help himself. To any other woman, using her pregnancy would have been her first thought. To Amanda, that was amoral—but sleazing around in a saloon dress was not.

"Why are you laughing at me?" Amanda asked softly, though a smile curved around her lips.

Luke grinned. "I was just thinking of how much I love you. I love the way you think, the way you feel, your honesty. When I realize that I had almost lost you, it scared the living hell out of me."

"You never will again." Amanda sighed, bringing his mouth to hers. "I love you, Luke Parker. And you can quote me on that."

❧ *Epilogue* ❧

He'd left her for two weeks—two weeks that seemed like years. Angel sat at her father's table and tried to smile at the cowhands, the trail bosses, the townspeople who had once again welcomed her back into their midst. But none of it mattered now. Chase was gone and she was finally a woman— a woman alone.

"Try some of the cold wine, pet. It's very good."

Her father tried to cheer her, but Angel could only shake her head. She felt empty inside. She saw the worried look on his face and forced a smile, unwilling to cause him any more pain, but she couldn't bring herself to be festive.

Why had she spoken so carelessly and shut Chase out of her life? She thought she'd been doing what was right, protecting herself from him and him from her father's wrath, but suddenly it just wasn't worth it. She wanted him back, wanted Chase in her arms once more, and wanted to know that it had been real.

"Dance, senorita?"

Angel nodded and got to her feet. The last thing she wanted to do was dance, but this way she wouldn't have to see her father's anxious eyes and the townspeople's knowing smirks. The vaquero swept her onto the floor, smiling at her graceful *movements. Chase had taught her how to dance, on that night so long ago beneath the diamond stars.*

The music played louder and Angel remembered it all. The campfire. The hot endless trail. The waterhole. Then, the Indian attack. She squeezed her eyes shut as she remembered Chase fighting for their lives, giving her a gun and telling her to shoot carefully. It was a nightmare—one she was sure would never end—but end it did, and they both lived to see dawn. She had known that night that if death was to come, she wanted to die with Chase, for without him life had no meaning.

A tear glimmered in her eye and she determinedly brushed it away. She was done with crying. Chase had to find his own way and she had to go on. Everyone assumed that he'd used her sexually, then deserted her as secondhand baggage, but Angel knew better. She'd done this to him, when she'd hidden from her own emotions. And now, he was gone.

Another man asked her to dance, and then another. She stepped to the music, letting the primitive beat take her to forgetfulness. Her eyes closed and her blonde hair rippled down her back. When her eyes re-opened, she was amazed to see a vaquero gesture quickly from the far wall, where the French doors led out onto a balcony.

Excusing herself, Angel slipped through the crowded dance floor and outside. At first, she saw no one. The air was cool and crisp, the moonlight silvering everything. She scanned the bushes, searching for the cowhand, when suddenly a man stepped from behind the curtain.

"Chase!"

"Did you think I'd leave you?" He grinned at her startled expression. "I've come to marry you this time, Angel. Lord knows you've done everything you could to chase me away, but I just can't live without you. I love you, sweetheart."

He kissed her, obliterating the pain she felt inside. Angel slipped her arms around his neck and openly gave herself to him. She wanted him. It was as simple as that.

His lips slowly left hers and his eyes searched her face. "Is that a yes? I haven't much, Angel, but someday, I will. And we can't live here—these people haven't forgiven me for not slaughtering those Indians. But I have to live my own life. Can you do that with me?"

Angel smiled. She belonged to Chase as surely as dawn followed night. And she'd never let him go again. "Yes, Chase," she whispered. "Yes."

If you enjoyed this book, take advantage of this special offer. Subscribe now and . . .

GET A *FREE*

NO OBLIGATION (a $3.95 value)

If you enjoy reading the very best historical romances, you'll want to subscribe to the True Value Historical Romance Home Subscription Service. Now that you have read one of the best historical romances around today, we're sure you'll want more of the same fiery passion, intimate romance and historical settings that set these books apart from all others.

Each month the editors of True Value will select the four very best historical romance novels from America's leading publishers of romantic fiction. Arrangements have been made for you to preview them in your home <u>Free for 10 days</u>. And with the first four books you receive, we'll send you a FREE book as our introductory gift. No obligation.

free home delivery

We will send you the four best and newest historical romances as soon as they are published to preview Free for 10 days. If for any reason you decide not to keep them, just return them and owe nothing. But if you like them as much as we think you will, you'll pay *just* $3.50 each and save at least $.45 each off the cover price. (Your savings are a minimum of $1.80 a month. There is *no* postage and handling – or other hidden charges. There are no minimum number of books to buy and you may cancel at any time.

HISTORICAL ROMANCE –

—send in the coupon below—

To get your FREE historical romance and start saving, fill out the coupon below and mail it today. As soon as we receive it we'll send you your FREE book along with your first month's selections.

Mail to: 1-55773-521-B
True Value Home Subscription Services, Inc.
P.O. Box 5235
120 Brighton Road
Clifton, New Jersey 07015-5235

YES! I want to start previewing the very best historical romances being published today. Send me my FREE book along with the first month's selections. I understand that I may look them over FREE for 10 days. If I'm not absolutely delighted I may return them and owe nothing. Otherwise I will pay the low price of just $3.50 each; a total of $14.00 (at least a $15.80 value) and save at least $1.80. Then each month I will receive four brand new novels to preview as soon as they are published for the same low price. I can always return a shipment and I may cancel this subscription at any time with no obligation to buy even a single book. In any event the FREE book is mine to keep regardless.

Name _____

Address _____ Apt. _____

City _____ State _____ Zip _____

Signature _____
         (if under 18 parent or guardian must sign)

Terms and prices subject to change.